THE MEDICI MIRROR

Melissa Bailey read English at Oxford, before studying law in London and then pursuing a career in media law. *The Medici Mirror* is her first novel. She lives in London with her partner, who is a human rights lawyer.

Archives

CUSTOMER
SERVICE
EXCELLENCE
The Go

UK

County

D1362608

C333443167

THE MEDICI MIRROR

MELISSA BAILEY

arrow books

Published by Arrow Books 2013

1 3 5 7 9 10 8 6 4 2

Copyright © Melissa Bailey 2013·

Melissa Bailey has asserted her right under the Copyright, Designs
and Patents Act, 1988, to be identified as the author of this work.

This is a work of fiction. Names and characters are the product of
the author's imagination and any resemblance to actual persons,
living or dead, is entirely coincidental.

This book is sold subject to the condition that it shall not, by way of trade or
otherwise, be lent, resold, hired out, or otherwise circulated without the
publisher's prior consent in any form of binding or cover other than that in
which it is published and without a similar condition, including this condition,
being imposed on the subsequent purchaser.

First published in Great Britain in 2013 by
Arrow
Random House, 20 Vauxhall Bridge Road,
London SW1V 2SA

www.randomhouse.co.uk

Addresses for companies within The Random House Group Limited can be found
at: www.randomhouse.co.uk/offices.htm

The Random House Group Limited Reg. No. 954009

A CIP catalogue record for this book
is available from the British Library

ISBN 9780099580720

The Random House Group Limited supports the Forest Stewardship Council®
(FSC®), the leading international forest-certification organisation. Our books
carrying the FSC label are printed on FSC®-certified paper. FSC is the only
forest-certification scheme supported by the leading environmental organisations,
including Greenpeace. Our paper procurement policy can be found at
www.randomhouse.co.uk/environment

Typeset in Baskerville MT by Palimpsest Book Production Limited,
Falkirk, Stirlingshire

Printed and bound by CPI Group (UK) Ltd, Croydon, CR0 4YY

For Mum and Dad, with love

Prologue

Chateau de Fontainebleau

November 1542

The splinters at the edge of the hole in the wooden floor scratched the corner of Catherine's eye. She squinted and tried to focus but, as she had suspected, she could see nothing but darkness. She turned her head, placing her ear against the opening. All was quiet below. So they had not yet retired to their chamber. Kneeling upright, she pulled the silk rug back into position, masking the presence of the hole. Then she checked the two additional holes that she had requested should be made in the floor a few days earlier, affording differing vantage points into the bedchamber below. As with the first, they revealed nothing but a silent darkness.

For what felt like an age, Catherine paced the floor of her own room, waiting. On more than one occasion, from somewhere close by in the palace, she heard a door open and close, allowing the brief escape of music and laughter. But nothing followed this except the diminishing sound of footsteps and then the advent of yet more silence. Finally she lay down upon her bed and contemplated her plan. Her ladies had begged her not to go through with it, not to go to such agonising lengths. But she knew that she was lacking, that she could not please her husband, that she was not alluring to him. And that the consequence of this was that she remained child-less. She could not contemplate such a barren future stretching before her. Could not face the uncertainty and peril that that brought in its wake. She had to learn, whatever the cost. And so she had decided and had steeled herself for what was to come. She would harden her heart to the pain that it would no doubt inflict upon her, but she would watch them. She would watch her husband and his mistress as they fornicated beneath her.

Catherine sat upright, suddenly breathless, and felt a sullen fury rise within her. It was not an uncommon feeling. The beautiful, older mistress, who dominated life at Court, eclipsing her in most things, also overshadowed her in the bedchamber. And she was reduced to stealing glances. She closed her eyes, feeling tears imminent, and lay back down on the bed. She tried to push the sour-tasting feeling down, reminding herself that she was the Dauphine, that she loved the Dauphin above all others and would do more than all others for him. And that she would remain his and become Queen if she simply remained pragmatic. She would bide her time and wait. And she would triumph in the end.

The sound of a door below banging loudly stirred Catherine from her reverie. Then she heard the unmistakable voice of her husband as it rose faintly through the floorboards. She almost leaped from the bed and her limbs trembled as she ran around the room, extinguishing the candles. Fumbling in the darkness, she pulled back the carpet and saw the hole she had looked through earlier, now illuminated with light from below. Her heart pounded in her chest. The moment was upon her. Henri and his mistress were almost in sight.

And so she looked. She caught a glance of Henri first. He was in a state of semi-undress. His legs were bare and he wore only a *loose-fitting undershirt. She watched as he walked around the room, admiring the contours of his body. He was a fine-looking man, with a lithe, muscular physique from hunting and the joust. And in the darkness of her chamber, looking down upon her husband, she felt a bloom of desire. The next moment she blushed with embarrassment and instinctively looked away until the burning in her cheeks had passed. By the time she returned her gaze to Henri, he was standing beside the bed upon which his mistress reclined. She wore her signature black and white gown. For a few minutes they talked and laughed together, so quietly that Catherine could not make out what they were saying. But their complicity, their delight in each other's company was so apparent that she began to feel the rise of that sick raging feeling once again. It also caught her off guard. The ease with which they touched each other: faces, eyes, lips, hair. Their intimacy was well disguised at Court. Hiding behind a mantle of feigned respectability, they were cool, aloof and distant. Now Catherine began to see the real truth of things.*

As the Dauphin leaned towards her, his mistress rose up to meet him, kneeling on the bed. He removed her jewellery, her gown, his fingers lingering teasingly on her skin, moving across her neck, her shoulders, her belly, slowly caressing her breasts. Henri's lover submitted openly, her body giving beneath his fingers, clearly aroused by his touch. And Catherine saw for the first time the porcelain nakedness of this woman who had so bewitched her husband.

The anger drained from her and tears invaded her eyes. She blinked them away and continued to look. She saw the older woman, bold and shameless, straddle her husband, and witnessed his delight, his excitement at her daring, at her abandon. Her hair fell over them in cascades as he pinned her to him. Catherine watched their bodies moving, wild and increasingly passionate, until she could no longer blink away the tears. Then she surrendered and let them overflow, running silently down her cheeks. She had seen enough. And yet she could still hear them, their loud carnal noise. Those sounds, she thought, would haunt her for ever. Along with their counterpoint: the silence that dominated when she was with her husband in such a way.

Catherine turned and lay on her back in the darkness, trying not to imagine their sated, breathless bodies lying on the sheets of the bed below. Instead she tried to feel only the darkness within her. She breathed it in and tried to clear her mind. She would have the holes filled in tomorrow. She would have no more use for them now. She wondered if she should have listened to her ladies, who had begged her not to indulge in such a venture. Perhaps she should. Perhaps she should have continued in ignorance. But then she would never have known the truth.

She sat upright in the darkness and saw the moonlight creeping in through the window. It was bright, a full moon perhaps, a hunting moon. It made her think once again of the woman with her husband in the room below her feet. Catherine's heart hardened. She would bide her time. After what she had witnessed tonight, she knew that she could bear almost anything. But in the end she would have revenge. She might have to wait a long time.

But she would have it in the end.

1

London, 2013

I heard the ambulance before I saw it. The raucous blare of the siren before the rush of air as it sped past. A flash of yellow and green stripes and blue neon light. Scattering dust and grit in its wake, it careered down Upper Street only to be arrested by a dense queue of cars and lorries at the traffic lights. It stood still, screeching into the cold winter morning, until the traffic shuffled and shunted and it was finally on its way again.

I looked at the gridlock ahead – diesel fumes spewing forth, stereos blaring. It was the same scenario day after day. I cut off the main road and after a few moments the noise and pollution all but vanished. The route was so familiar that I could have walked it in my sleep. And over the last six months it felt as if I'd been doing just that: going through the motions, barely conscious. The thing was, I'd simply needed some time. That was my standard reply whenever my business partner, Richard, pulled me up. I simply needed some time. Given my lack of attention lately it was a wonder I still had a job to turn up to. But Richard was a good guy. And I'd produced some great projects with him over the years. So I'd become a sleeping partner recently. Big deal. When it really came down to it he didn't seem to mind too much.

As I skirted classical Georgian terraces, my hand reached out for the smooth solid blackness of the railings. Behind them there were neat window boxes perched on pristine sills and perfect miniature trees on balconies. X5s and Audis cluttered the edges of the pavement. It was a catwalk of opulence, this part of my route. Further down the hill and across the main road it was a different story. This was the point at which the crossover began. The flash cars slowly disappeared, the terraces became stunted and there wasn't so much as a whiff of a window box. The smell of elegance and money vanished. If you breathed in deeply you could catch a hint of the weariness hovering in their place.

As I walked, I thought again about Richard's message from the day before. 'I have the perfect job for you, an architect's dream. Can you come and take a look?' He'd left an address and asked me to meet him there today. Then he'd hung up.

I had to admit I'd been more than a little intrigued. So instead of going straight – my ordinary journey to the Shoreditch office – I bore right at the next lights and headed towards Clerkenwell. To my left, tower blocks mushroomed, great grey smudges of pebble-dash against the sky. Row upon row of small, square windows punctured their surfaces, dully reflecting the day. Their underbellies, emblazoned with graffiti, swathes of pink, red, orange and blue, jack-knifed the greyness. At the end of the road I took a left turn and then a right moments later. Immediately I was in a different environment, surrounded by a circle of Georgian terraced houses. In their centre was a small park, a surreal blur of green after the nearby maze of concrete. As Richard had instructed me I moved towards the break in the circular symmetry of the houses. Then it was before me, the imposing Victorian Gothic shoe factory.

It was a large three-storey red-brick building, discoloured by years of smog, dirt and rain, with a multitude of windows across its façade, those of the first floor set in semicircular arches of ochre-coloured stone. I had just walked round the ground floor, a vast open space, when I heard the clangour of footsteps pounding down the stairs in the corner of the room. When Richard appeared he had a broad smile on his face and strode purposefully towards me.

'Johnny Carter.' He grabbed my hand and clapped me on the back. I caught the faint odour of his expensive aftershave. 'How are you?'

'I'm good, thanks. Just admiring the place.'

'Yeah, she's a beauty all right. And wait till you see upstairs.' Richard let out a low whistle. 'I had a quick look while I was waiting for you.'

I smiled. Richard was always dashing around. He was the lifeblood of our practice, the boss, the business mind, the guy without whom everything would grind to a halt. Yet no matter how busy he was he still managed to look unruffled and composed. I took in the designer clothes, the subtly tousled grey hair, and wondered, not for the first time, how he did it.

He made his way towards a desk at the foot of the stairwell and began leafing through some papers. 'Did you find it okay?'

'No problem.' I picked up a pair of black leather shoes from a stack in the middle of the room. They were well made, the leather, despite its age, still fine. The business had obviously been one of quality. Whether the renovation would echo that remained to be seen. 'So, give it to me. What's the brief?'

'A residential conversion, opulent and modern, but with a nod to the past. Your speciality.'

I smiled, still looking at the shoes. He knew that I was waiting for the most important part.

'And the client's a wealthy individual, not a developer. He wants the whole place as his home. So it'll be spacious.'

'No kidding.'

'We've got a great budget and pretty much free rein to do what we like.' Richard plucked a stapled wad of material from the desk and put it to one side. 'Our instructions, such as they are, are here. Have a good look later.'

'I will. It all sounds very promising.' I had to admit, this was my favourite kind of job. A renovation project, dripping with history, crammed full of memorabilia and with no scrimping or corner cutting. I turned to look down the length of the factory floor once more. Large wooden machines and workbenches crammed with tools loomed out of the dirty light fighting its way through cobwebbed windows. I listened to the noises of the factory. Creaking floorboards, groaning metal, murmuring old pipes, subdued but present nonetheless. 'So what do you know about the place?' I said, turning back to face Richard.

'Not much. It was a family business set up in the late nineteenth century. The father ran it first, then one of the sons, James. His son Thomas followed after, when he came of age. Business started out well but trade slumped in the late 1940s. Falling demand, escalating costs, things like that, drove it into the ground. Eventually, it was just closed down.'

'And they never did anything with the building?'

'No, I guess not.' For a few moments Richard flicked through some papers in front of him. 'It says here that it's only sold now because of the recent death of the last surviving Brimley – the grandson of James. He wasn't married and didn't appear to have any relatives. His Bloomsbury house – which had been passed down from his grandfather – is being cleared out but is still for sale.' He paused. 'I think that over time perhaps the factory just got forgotten.'

'Forgotten?' It was hard to imagine how someone could let this place just slide into decline, untouched. I turned and looked once again, more closely this time, along the length of the floor, into the shadowy corners at its far end, into the darkened spaces beneath the workbenches and behind the cupboards. I closed my eyes and listened to the subtle whispers of these spaces, their melancholic, dusty breath. 'How does someone just forget about this?' I said it more to myself than to Richard.

'I don't know. Maybe it's lack of interest. Or maybe it's something altogether more personal. Maybe they wanted to forget.' Richard shrugged. 'Anyway, whatever the reason, it's been unoccupied for over five decades.'

That was an age in terms of London property development. I looked at the dust-covered clutter surrounding us. 'And there's still so much stuff here. Can I use what I want?'

Richard nodded. 'The client was quite specific on that. Take what you need and discard the rest. He doesn't want to keep anything beyond what's incorporated into the renovation.'

'Okay, understood.'

'The survey's already been done and the surveyor's CAD drawings are here.' He tapped a thick pile of printouts on the table. 'There are loads of copies, all 1:100 at A1 – but shout if you want anything different.'

'Great, thanks.' My gaze moved past Richard to the staircase in the corner of the room. I was desperate to see what lay beyond it. 'So, is it time for the tour yet?'

He smiled, reaching for some papers on the desk. 'Sure. Let's start at the top and work down – I think that's the right way to do it.'

As we climbed the stairs he fed me snippets of information. The factory had three floors, with a staircase at each end, each floor containing three departments. Richard told me dimensions, referred to his notes and turned to me now and then to check that I was listening to him. I nodded, half hearing, focusing my attention more on the beauty of the old parquet flooring, the huge windows that dominated both sides of the building, the rich exposed beams in the ceilings, the vast and numerous pieces of machinery. Wheels and pulleys hung from the roof, leather, wood and metal sat alongside one another on benches and on the floor. They were all now my materials and tools.

I became aware of Richard coming to a standstill in front of me. We were at the far end of the second floor, sandwiched between lines of benches supporting metal beams.

'So, this was what was known as the clicking department,' he began. 'It's where the shoemaking process started. The leather was cut into the shapes and patterns needed for a shoe or boot, either by hand or using these presses.' He tapped one beside him and it let out a low metallic ring.

I stared at the machines, the dampening hum of metal in my ears. This place seemed somehow caught out of time. Many of the steel cutters still pressed down against leather, as if their operators had disappeared momentarily and would be back in an instant to finish the job. But the workers had never returned and everything stood exactly as it had originally. Past and present collided.

Moving into the next section, we passed row after row of sewing machines to the left and right of the central aisle. Their black bodies lay still, their wheels shrouded in dust. In many of them, pieces of leather lay trapped between the needle plates and feet of the machines. On all their sides, the white letters SINGER stood out. I tried to imagine the noise they would have generated when they were frantically working away. But the silence now was deafening. On the long benches in front of the machines were assortments of intricate tools and finished stitched uppers. The bare floor was still covered with scraps of leather which had, presumably, been cut away and discarded.

'This is the assembling department,' said Richard, 'where the pieces of leather were stitched together to form the upper part of the shoe. This was one of the few areas where women worked. The rest of the place was pretty much the domain of men.'

Richard moved into the central space on the far side of the floor where huge black machines dominated. 'I think they cut the soles out here,' he said, running his hand down a great hulk of heavy metal pressing down onto a blade. 'The leather was thicker than that used for the uppers.' He took a piece still trapped beneath the machine between his fingers.

I nodded, looking behind him where hundreds of rolls of leather, longer than six feet, lay stacked on shelves. Neat squares also lay piled in the centre of the floor. I inhaled deeply. I'd begun to notice that wherever I went in the factory the smell of leather always lingered. But here it seemed to ooze from the walls, hanging thickly on the air like invisible smoke. It crept up my nostrils and down into my chest. I felt I was breathing in a past that was almost alive.

As I looked down the length of the factory, taking it

all in, my head became filled with visions of deconstructed machine parts reassembled into modern architectural forms. Metallic table stands and lamp fittings, old machine wheels attached to the walls. The vaulted ceiling with light tunnels boring through it. Light and glass and metal inter-twined. Yes, the old industrial look with some sleek modern touches would work really well in this space.

Richard's voice broke into my thoughts. He was on the move again, heading for the staircase at this end of the floor. 'Down here is the lasting department,' he shouted as he went.

I followed him into the next section on the first floor. Before us stood a gigantic table stacked with hundreds of pairs of wooden feet. They spilled over its edges and onto the floor. I smiled. 'Cool. What are they?'

'I suppose they're lasts,' said Richard, with a grin. 'I think the uppers were stretched over them to construct the shape of the shoes.' He looked down at his piece of paper again before pointing further down the factory floor. 'The soles were attached in the next room and then right down at the end, in the bottoming department, the shoes and boots were levelled. Repairs were carried out there too.'

We walked slowly to the far end of the floor. Here shoes of all kinds, scuffed, soleless or full of holes, formed an unruly pile in a corner. Real down-and-out footwear ready for mending but left instead to rot away.

I nudged the heap with the toe of my trainer. 'Look at this. Why do you think it's all still here?'

'Maybe the owners just never came back to collect.

After the factory closed down, I mean.' Richard paused before continuing. 'Or perhaps the beneficent boss-man gave them new pairs of shoes instead.'

'Yeah, right. Fantasist.' But secretly I hoped that he was right. I looked at the pile again. There was something sad, deeply forlorn about it. Abandoned, discarded. Rather like the factory itself.

As I turned away, my gaze fell upon two rows of carefully stitched, perfectly crafted shoes and boots. All without heels.

I started to laugh. 'This place is surreal.'

Richard followed my look. 'Ah, yes. Heeling and trimming happened on the ground floor. The final stage in the process.'

Taking the stairs down out of this department, we wandered back to where we had started.

'And this is the dispatch room, where everything was inspected and passed for packing.'

I nodded, taking in again the countless boxes and racks of shoes around us. 'So basically the whole process flowed from the top to the bottom of the factory.' It was regimented, orderly and still tenuously preserved.

'Seamless, don't you think?'

'Rather like your tour.'

Richard gave an exaggerated bow. 'Thanks. But, to be honest, I haven't really managed to get my head around it all. I'll have to leave the rest to you. Is that okay?'

'Of course.' I smiled at him, feeling a sudden tightening in my chest. 'Thanks, Richard,' I said, apropos of nothing.

There was silence for a second as he looked at me. Then he shook his head. 'No need for thanks. After all, you are the creative genius, the best man for the job.' He paused. 'Which is a pain in the arse for me, because you haven't exactly been the most reliable.'

The statement was made lightly and contained no edge, no hint of malice. And, frankly, I was somewhat surprised that it didn't. No doubt about it, Richard could be ruthless when he had to be. I'd seen it in action. But he was also a good guy. He hadn't been able to rely on me during the last few months but he had carried me regardless. And now he had given me this job. My chest constricted again.

'So are things okay, Johnny?'

The question hung in the air between us for a moment. Then, 'Yeah, I'm fine,' I muttered, embarrassed. I wanted to end this conversation before it had a chance to get going. 'Just fine,' I repeated, my fingers stroking a pair of soft leather shoes from a rack.

I could feel Richard's stare on me, probing, assessing.

'Really,' I said, finally, looking directly at him.

'Good. I'm glad.' He winked at me and, sensing a shift in the conversation, I began to breathe easily once more.

For a few moments Richard talked me through some practicalities. The electricity had been reconnected on the assumption that I'd want to work on site as usual. He gave me a look as he said this as if he were humouring a small child. However, the 1940s lighting system might still prove to be a problem on occasion. There was no wi-fi for the moment but he'd organised for someone to come and get it up and running within the next day or so. So I'd be able to use a laptop and CAD on site. The water was on and there was a working toilet at the opposite end of the ground floor. If there was anything else I needed I was to call our office manager and she'd get it sorted.

Finally he looked at me as he picked up his bag to leave. 'You know, of course, that you'll need some help on a job this big.'

I nodded.

'I was thinking of Tara. Sound good?'

'Good' wasn't the word I would have chosen but in the circumstances I didn't have the heart to disagree with him. I kept my face inscrutable as I answered. 'Sure. That sounds fine.' I could, after all, think of worse people.

'Great. I thought she could start on an inventory and then, as you get going, help you draw up all your designs. But, of course, feel free to use her for whatever else comes up. Within reason, of course.'

I nodded, trying to ignore the tone I thought I heard. Something protective and territorial tinged with innuendo. But I might have been imagining it. I looked at Richard's face but he was already moving on.

'So, are you okay if I leave you to it? I have a mountain of stuff to do back at the office.'

'Of course. I'm fine.' And I was. I'd been longing for this moment since I'd arrived.

Richard grabbed his coat and on his way out clapped

me on the back again. 'Drop by the office later and we can talk through your initial thoughts.'

Then the door slammed shut and he was gone.

A couple of hours later I was standing once more in the quiet of the clicking department, looking through the large dusty windows to the road outside. When Richard had first told me the name, it had conjured up fantastical images of women's feet clicking their high-heeled way across a wooden factory floor. Shoes clicking next to the slim ankles of their owners, the sound raucous as an army of ghostly feet in stiletto shoes advanced. Click click click click. But all was quiet now. The clicking presses were silent, their metal limbs still. The only feet moving over the floorboards were my own.

I took the stairs out of that department down to the first floor. The walls of the stairwell were full, from top to bottom, with photographs. There was a sombre picture of a group of bearded gentlemen, dressed up in dark suits and ties, staring ahead unflinchingly at the camera. *Our directors, 1948* read the caption. Alongside it stood a portrait of a solitary director with dark eyes that seemed to glower at the camera. It was dated 24 May 1896. The next photograph was of four rows of Victorian women, clad in long black dresses and white aprons, each seated in front of a sewing machine, diligently stitching pieces of leather together. Their heads were bowed, eyes focused, their long hair tied back neatly at the napes of their necks. One woman, however, looking up, beautiful and distracted, had been caught out by the photographer. The date was 1898. Another showed a group of about eight women, blonde and brunette, fat and thin, grinning as they worked. *Machinists, 1936.* They stitched and sewed, caught in their black and white world. I left dust trails with my fingertips across their smiling faces. It seemed to have been a happy enough place. So why could I still feel it? A touch of sadness hanging in the air, loitering in the shadows and dark corners.

I took a breath and, as I crossed the length of the factory, exhaled slowly. Heading for the table full of lasts, I picked up one that I had noticed earlier, cut from a paler wood than the rest. I cradled it in my palm, the fingers of my other hand tracing the foot's smooth contours: the curve of the arch, the high instep, the silky smoothness from the subtle press and touch of a chisel. After all these years, it held only a faint smell: the palest residue of oak and resin. I closed my eyes and heard the vague murmurings of the factory once more. The voices of the past talking to me.

2

The following day a funny thing happened.

I'd been working in the dispatch room on the ground floor of the factory all morning. I'd now designated it mine and Tara's office. It was the perfect workspace as it already contained two big old desks and was far less cluttered than elsewhere. The only other things in the room were shoes and shoeboxes. Admittedly there were hundreds of them, but I'd stacked them neatly against the front wall. After doing this, I settled down to look over some paperwork, checking the original blueprints of the factory and looking over the surveyor's recent drawings in detail. I'd wanted to get the layout of the building and all its dimensions clear in my mind.

When lunchtime came around I was longing to get outside. The beauty of the day was distracting. Clouds like spun sugar floated across the sky and the sun possessed rare warmth for the time of year. I bought a sandwich at a nearby deli and made my way to the park, sitting down on a bench under a plane tree. I closed my eyes for a few moments, feeling the sun against my skin. Then I pulled the client's brief from my jacket pocket and began to read through it again while I ate. Absorbed in the task, I didn't surface until some time later. When I looked around, I noticed that I was not alone.

Walking along the opposite side of the park was a woman. She was about five feet, six inches tall and around thirty years old. She had pale skin and dramatic features: strong cheekbones, large deep-set eyes and a long slim nose. You couldn't have called her classically beautiful but there was something striking about her. Her hair hung dark and straight to her shoulders and was topped with a bright pink beret, which sat at an angle on her head. I couldn't help staring at her. I couldn't put my finger on what it was but there was something about her, something that appealed. She was wearing a black shirt and long black trousers and was holding what looked like a camera in her right hand.

I watched her walk from tree to tree around the park's perimeter, scanning the ground. When she eventually headed in my direction, I dropped my gaze back to my papers and feigned indifference. She passed by, her footfalls breaking the silence. She circled the bushes, then the flower beds, moving gradually inwards until she stopped at the old bandstand that stood in the middle of the park. Hands on hips, she frowned, glancing to her left, then her right. I thought I saw her lips move, as if she was muttering to herself.

She must have felt me watching because suddenly she looked right at me. I glanced away, embarrassed by my lack of subtlety. But it was too late. She advanced towards me.

'I'm sorry to bother you.' I looked up to be fixed by her green-eyed stare. 'But you haven't seen a lens cap lying around the park anywhere? One that would fit this.' She held up the camera I had spotted her carrying. A Nikon, large, expensive-looking.

'Erm, no, I haven't. I'm sorry.' Then I shrugged, trying to imbue the gesture with some semblance of sympathy.

She smiled at me. She had a nice smile. 'Oh well. Never mind. Thanks, anyway.'

She began to walk away and the movement made up my mind. 'Hey,' I called after her, 'I'm not doing anything particular right now. Do you want me to help you look for it?'

As she turned back to face me I caught the hesitation in her eyes. 'No, really, it's fine. It doesn't matter. I mean, you can only look so much, can't you?'

'Yeah, I guess so.' I felt a sudden pang of disappointment which I tried to suppress. But it must have been reflected on my face because she suddenly smiled at me again.

'Okay, sure – we can look one more time. It can't hurt, can it?'

I shook my head and stood up, slightly embarrassed that I'd made such a big deal about it all. We walked a few paces together in silence. I tried desperately to think of something to say but my mind was a white blank. She, however, was already focused on the search, indifferent to me.

'So, do you live near here?' As soon as the words were

out of my mouth I grimaced. They were almost on a par with 'Do you come here often?'

But she turned to me, seemingly unaware, and smiled. 'Clerkenwell. Not far away at all. You?'

'Just up the road in Islington.'

A slight nod. 'So what are you doing here, then?'

'I'm renovating the old shoe factory over there.' I gestured.

'Ah, nice. I'm glad something's finally happening to it. How long's it been empty?'

'Over fifty years,' I said, somewhat surprised at being able to recall Richard's summary of the place.

'So you're what, then? An architect?'

I nodded. 'I work in a small practice in Shoreditch with a friend of mine. You?'

She gestured at the camera. 'Photographer. One that constantly loses her shit.'

As I looked at her I couldn't help smiling. 'In the physical or emotional sense?'

'Hmm. Mainly the former but also the latter.' She smiled back at me, uncertainly. Then she broke the gaze and looked away, biting down on her bottom lip. In that moment I felt an almost overpowering urge to kiss her.

I coughed and tried to regain some sort of focus. 'So, what kind of photographs do you take?'

'Fashion, mostly. And usually shoes. I do a lot of adver- tising work – for campaigns, that kind of thing. It's a little dark, edgy.' She looked straight at me, her eyes twinkling.

Long eyelashes framed deep green irises. 'But perhaps that's why it sells.'

Our footsteps echoed on the tarmac walkway for a couple more seconds and then we came to a standstill. We had completed a circle of the park and found nothing. We stood by the entrance nearest to the factory. Its façade loomed over us.

'It's beautiful but kind of creepy too, you know.' She looked upwards at the smoky, discoloured bricks of the building and my gaze instinctively followed hers. With its obscured, dirty windows and dim interior, it didn't exactly look inviting.

'I suppose it is a little creepy,' I said, nodding.

'And what's it like inside?'

'A time warp.' I smiled. 'It's still full of stuff from the end of the nineteenth century. Machines, tools, that kind of thing.'

'Cool,' she said and smiled back at me.

For a moment we said nothing, simply looking at one another. 'Well, thanks for your help,' she said finally. 'But I guess my lens cap is lost.'

'Never say never. It'll probably turn up unexpectedly.'

'Yeah, maybe.' She shrugged.

Then there was silence.

I waited, expecting her to say goodbye and leave. But she just stood there in front of me.

I looked down at the brief in my hand and felt a moment's pang of guilt. I should be working. But the words leaped out of my mouth regardless. 'So can I buy you a consolatory coffee? I know a great place not far from here.'

She paused for a second. Then she smiled. 'Sure, why not? That'd be nice.'

And that was how I met Ophelia.

3

In deference to the unseasonal weather, there were four metal tables set out on the pavement below the café's long front window. Two of them were taken. A young couple sat at the first, seemingly in the aftermath of an argument, staring furiously away from one another. The woman lit a cigarette and blew smoke into the afternoon. It hung, hostile and heavy, on the air. Next to them sat a balding middle-aged man with thick-rimmed dark glasses, mostly obscured behind a vast expanse of newspaper. He had the appearance of someone desperately trying to make himself invisible. Probably from the angry couple. We took the table furthest away and sat down, me facing the other tables and Ophelia with her back to them. The waitress came over and gave us a nod. Both Ophelia and I ordered coffee from her and she turned and headed back inside.

'So is that work?' Ophelia pointed to my papers on the corner of the table.

I nodded. 'It's the client's wish-list: floating glass staircases, stone columns, refashioned metal and lots of light. The usual deal and all done in record time.' I raised my eyebrows.

She looked at me and smiled. 'But you still seem excited by the project.'

'I am. It's a great job. The space is amazing. And some of the stuff in there is incredible.'

'I can imagine. I've passed that place day after day, year after year. I always wondered what was inside, what was happening on the other side of that brick wall.'

'Well, you can come and have a look. I'll be there practically every day for the next few weeks.'

'I'd love that.' And her eyes sparkled as she looked at me. 'So you work on-site at the beginning do you?'

I nodded. 'I think people at the office think I'm a bit crazy for doing it – self-indulgent, perhaps.' I smiled. 'But I like to. I get a better feel for the space if I inhabit it for a while. How it was used, how it might be used now, that kind of thing. So in the initial stages I find it really helpful. And there are so many things still there that we might try and incorporate into the build that it makes sense to stay near them. Plus the client doesn't object. In fact, I think he quite likes the idea. So . . .' I paused, suddenly worried that I was talking too much. But if Ophelia thought so she didn't show it.

'Is the place still full of shoes?'

'Pretty much.'

'Wow. I'll have to bring my camera round sometime and take some shots. If that's not too presumptuous,' she added as an afterthought.

I smiled. Perhaps I wasn't the only one worrying about how I was coming across. 'Not at all. Any time.'

We sat in silence for a while and I shifted my gaze to the middle-aged man at the next table. He was still flicking through his paper. The couple beyond him still weren't talking. When I turned my attention back to Ophelia I saw that she was looking at me.

'So, I know you're an architect, with a thing for old spaces. Tell me some other things about you.'

I felt my brain seize up, as it always does when I'm put on the spot. 'Hmm, let me see.' I coughed and tried to think, feeling the beat of my heart suddenly against my temples. The only thing that came to mind, inappropriately enough, was my wife, Maya. And I really didn't want to talk about her.

'Well, I'm thirty-nine, I was born in north London and have lived in the city all my life. I went to school and university here. My parents still live in Islington in the house where I was born. We get on pretty well but haven't seen one another so much lately.' I paused, thinking about my brother. I had tried deliberately to put him – and my wife – out of my mind for a long time now. But it seemed, strangely enough, that they wanted to make their presence felt in this conversation. I looked up to see Ophelia watching me intently. Something, I wasn't sure what, made me continue the thought out loud. 'I have one brother, Joshua, three years older than me, who's more successful and more handsome. More everything, basically. And now he's living with my wife. So we don't speak all that much.' I laughed at that and then stopped. What was wrong with me? I was coming out with too much weirdness way too soon. I looked at Ophelia but couldn't read her expression. Still, I could imagine myself unfolding before her eyes, a man with a colossal amount of baggage.

My embarrassment was interrupted by the waitress, returning with the coffee. She placed the cups down on the table in front of us. Ophelia thanked her and then stirred her coffee slowly, still looking at me. 'Don't worry,' she said at last. 'I think I know what you're trying to get at.'

I stirred some sugar into my espresso and took a sip, hoping that the thick, sweet liquid wouldn't make me even more edgy. That was the last thing I needed. I watched the traffic move lethargically along the road in the distance. The cars shunted along, bumper to bumper, going nowhere fast. 'Sorry,' I said at last, putting my cup down. 'I didn't mean to go on about my dysfunctional home life. I was trying to save that up until a little later.' I laughed hollowly and spread my palms out nervously on the table top.

'It's okay. Really. Like I said, don't worry.' We sat in silence for a moment while Ophelia's hands played with the packets of sweetener in the sugar bowl. Her long, slim fingers were slow and methodical, stroking the paper up and down. There was something soothing about the movement. Something reassuring. 'So you don't really do the whole family thing?'

I shook my head.

'Your brother I can understand. But your parents?'

I thought about the way my father had seemed to side

with Joshua and then shook my head again. No, for the moment at least I simply wanted to stay away.

'That's so sad,' Ophelia said at last. 'So sad.' She looked down, a sombre expression on her face, shaking her head slowly. She stayed like that for a while. Just as I was beginning to wonder what she could be thinking, she raised her head and looked at me. 'You must have felt very angry when it happened.'

I nodded. 'But it was a while ago now . . .'

'Sure, but it's a big deal, a huge betrayal. It must have been hard for you.'

I nodded again, trying to avoid her gaze.

But she was scrutinising me. 'Do you still feel able, do you even want to, connect with people?'

I laughed uncomfortably, startled by her directness. It was a pretty probing question coming from someone I'd only just met. I looked beyond Ophelia at the couple sitting in silence. Their anger seemed to have subsided but they still weren't talking. They were each contemplating the middle distance, locked in their own little world. The last thing they wanted to do was connect. I understood it. There was some comfort to be derived from that. There was safety in solitude. You couldn't be betrayed or hurt if you were alone. 'I guess wanting to connect with someone in the first place is hard enough. Then actually connecting with them, really connecting, finding intimacy is almost impossible. But have I lost the capacity to try?' I smiled wanly. 'For a while I thought I had. But time has passed. Now I'm not so sure.'

Ophelia smiled back at me. 'Yeah. Intimacy's a tricky thing. I'm pretty hopeless at it. It's just too easy, I think, for me to be alone.' She paused. 'Or maybe that's just an excuse. Perhaps I'm just scared of the risk. I don't know.' There was a moment's silence. 'Was the problem with you and your wife one of intimacy?'

This was the second question to take me by surprise and I hesitated again before I answered. I was pretty sure it hadn't started out like that. But somewhere along the way Maya and I had drifted seriously apart. She was demanding, I'd always known that, but in the beginning I hadn't minded so much. It was as time went on that I had started to. No matter what I gave, it was never enough. She just needed too much of me. When I withdrew the fighting started. Great tides of anger flowed between us and, over time, left a gulf of silent rage in their stead. The distance between us intensified and little by little the whole thing unravelled. Now we were like strangers. I hadn't seen her since we'd split up six months ago. I sighed. 'Well, intimacy wasn't all of it, for sure. But you're probably right that it was a part. Whatever, we didn't talk very much towards the end.'

Come to think of it, we hadn't talked much at all. I cleared my throat. I hadn't really spoken to anyone about my wife. But, strangely, it didn't feel that awkward with Ophelia. I looked at her. She was staring at me.

'It happens a lot, you know. Perhaps you just weren't meant to be together.'

The way she came out with that statement made me

smile. So matter-of-fact, so clear and unequivocal. Six months ago I'd probably have become angry. Asked her what the hell she knew about it anyway. But maybe she was right. I'd spent a lot of time thinking about it and I still didn't know. Maybe, after all, it was as simple as that. 'Well, it certainly felt that way by the end.' I paused. 'But I thought that perhaps loving her might be enough. Naive, huh?'

She stared at me for a second and then smiled. 'No. Maybe sometimes love is enough,' she said simply.

I wondered whether she was right. I'd certainly thought so at one point. We sat in silence for a few minutes, drinking our coffee.

'So why don't you tell me something about you?'

The statement seemed to take Ophelia by surprise. 'Me? Oh, God. I don't think you're ready for my story just yet.'

The look on my face showed her that I wouldn't be put off so easily.

'Okay – how about the abridged version, then?'

'I can go with that.'

'Well, like you I've lived in London all my adult life . . .' She stopped abruptly to take a sip of her coffee. I watched her lips touch the cup and then observed her bare neck as she swallowed, the subtle movement of the muscles, up and down. She bit down on her bottom lip again. She seemed to do that when she was unsure of herself. I wanted to reach out and touch her mouth. Instead I folded my arms so that I couldn't. I watched Ophelia as she talked and noticed a small scar to the right above her top lip. It moved in time with the rhythm of her words. I tried to focus but her voice seemed to recede as I watched her fingers dancing, pushing her smooth dark hair behind her ears. My gaze moved down over her face, to her shoulders and then to the dark folds of her blouse stroking the edges of her breasts. I coughed and forced myself to look her once more in the eye. 'My parents died when I was a kid,' I heard her say.

'I'm sorry.'

'It's okay. It was a long time ago. After that I was brought up by my grandparents.' Ophelia raised her cup to her lips and drank the last of her coffee. Then she smiled at me. I felt a sudden inexplicable rush of contentment, as if I was sitting here with someone I'd known for a long time.

Looking upwards to the sky I saw that the afternoon light was changing, fading slowly towards darkness. People were leaving the café. The quarrelling lovers were gone. The middle-aged man was rising from his table, pocketing his paper. One car, then another, skidded past in their haste to jump the rush-hour queue. Suddenly we were alone.

'I should be getting back. I have an appointment this evening.'

I felt a flicker in my stomach. Fear and nausea somersaulting. I couldn't bear the idea of Ophelia leaving and not seeing her again. 'Yeah, I'd better be heading off, too.' I bit my lip and practised the words in my head. Then I said them out loud. 'Perhaps we could meet up tomorrow, if you're not busy then?'

She smiled. 'No, I'm not too busy.'

'Perhaps you'd like to come over to my place for dinner?' Before she could answer I back-pedalled, worrying that I might have overdone it. 'Is dinner too much?' I said, frowning.

'No, that would be nice.' And she laughed. The sound had a wonderfully sonorous quality.

'Great,' I said, rifling through my pockets to find a pen and paper. 'Here's my address and mobile number. Around eight?' I handed the paper to her and our fingertips touched for a second.

'Around eight,' she said, standing up.

'Great,' I said again. 'Do you eat fish?'

Ophelia nodded, smiling. 'So I'll see you tomorrow.' Then she turned and began to walk back towards the park. I watched her, in the fading light, until she disappeared.

4

The following day I was distracted.

I went to the factory and tried to settle down to some work. Sitting at my desk, I read and reread the brief and looked at the drawings. Then I read some information on the shoemaking process. I tried to concentrate, to focus on the task in hand, to turn the vague ideas I had in my head into concrete images on paper. But I simply couldn't do it. I was somewhere else. Or my mind was, at any rate. I was thinking about Ophelia. Her red lips. Her pale hands. The intensity of her look. I was thinking about what I was going to cook that evening. What I was going to talk about.

Unable to concentrate, I got up and walked to the front of the dispatch room, peering out of the dusty window that ran along the front of the building. But there was nothing going on. The road was quiet, deserted, as was the park beyond. I sighed and took a peek inside one of the shoeboxes at the top of the stack. A pair of large men's shoes – black – lay within. I replaced the lid and opened another box. This time it was men's brown shoes. I started to rifle through the contents of all the boxes.

While their exteriors were yellowed and coated in dust, the shoes inside were in surprisingly good condition. There were men and women's, lots of different styles, some old-fashioned and outdated, some now back in vogue. After hunting for a while, I eventually came across a pair of black stilettos. Size six. They had a very thin high heel, about five inches, and toes almost as slender and elongated as the heels. The leather had now lost its lustre but there was something beautiful about them nonetheless. They were flawlessly made. I ran my fingers across the surface of the shoes and something about the gesture calmed my mind. I went back to my desk, stood the shoes at the far left-hand side, toes facing me, and began finally to focus on my designs.

I surfaced a couple of hours later with some decent provisional ideas. Leaning back in my chair, I stretched and yawned. I checked my watch. Two-forty-four. I wanted to get going quite soon but I needed to catch up with Tara first. I knew she was busy combing the factory floors, building up the inventory she was producing. But I hadn't seen her for a while. She had passed through the dispatch room a couple of times, moving with a sense of purpose that I couldn't even begin to muster. Whenever she'd caught my eye she had flashed me her stock smile. Broad, with a hint of promise. There was something provocative about the smile, something provocative about her in general. She was one of those women who were very aware of the effect they had on men. But the thing was she always just made me feel insecure. And what made me even more uncomfortable were my suspicions that she was having an affair with Richard. I wasn't certain, far from it. But I got a sense of something, especially when they were around one another. Sex, attraction – what it was I didn't know. What I did know was that the uncertainty made me even more uneasy around her.

Moments later I heard the click of her heels coming down the staircase at the back of the room. As she came into view and strode towards her desk, I was reminded, as always, that if she hadn't become an architect there was no doubt she could have been a model. She looked like she'd stepped out of an advertisement for Burberry or a similar brand. Tall, almost my height, the short skirt and knee-high leather boots she was wearing showed off her long legs and shapely calves. A tight woollen sweater accentuated her small waist and perfectly sized breasts. She always wore her black hair straight, cut into a sharp, sleek bob that framed her face. And what a face it was: heart-shaped, with flawless olive skin, a slim Roman nose, full pink lips and deep blue eyes. No doubt about it, she was a goddess, of both Mediterranean and Celtic extraction. And whatever situation she found herself in, I imagined that she managed to look exceptional. Never a hair out of place. Always supremely confident. I realised that in some respects she reminded me of Richard and the irony made me smile. As she sat down in her chair she shot me a glance. 'What's up?'

'Oh, nothing. Just working on some ideas, doing some sketches, that sort of thing. How are you?'

'Not bad.' She looked me straight in the eye, direct, unflinching. Then her focus seemed to slip to somewhere beyond me. 'What are *those*?'

I turned to look and saw the shoes, sitting pert and pretty, on the corner of the desk. 'They're shoes,' I said, deadpan.

She was on her feet and beside me in seconds. 'Did you find them over there?' She gestured to the boxes.

'Sure did.'

'They're lovely,' she purred, picking them up and stroking the leather. 'Just my size. Can I have a pair too?' she added imploringly.

I thought about it for a second. What would it hurt? 'Take them,' I said. 'And help yourself to anything else.'

Her large eyes widened further. 'Are you serious?'

I nodded. 'All that stuff will get dumped in the end anyway. We won't be able to use it. So someone should. Go ahead, take whatever you want.'

Her face broke into a big smile. The first truly genuine smile from her that I'd seen. It suited her. 'Oh my God. That's brilliant. Thanks.'

I smiled back. 'Don't worry about it.'

She continued to look at the stilettos in her hand. 'You know, shoes are my absolute weakness.'

'Well, maybe this job just got a whole lot better for you.' As she began to walk back to her desk, I added, as an afterthought, 'Look, probably best not to tell anyone at the office that you're wearing the client's shoes. It's probably not the done thing.'

She turned mid-stride and saluted me. 'Don't worry, boss. I'm not one to bite the hand that feeds me.' Something about the gesture, the tone of her words, told me that moment of openness and complicity had passed. I felt a faint twinge of sadness.

For a moment I sat in silence before standing and putting on my jacket. 'Okay. I'm heading off. I've got some stuff I need to take care of. But you can carry on with the inventory, if that's all right. We need to get that complete as soon as possible.'

She nodded.

'Will you be okay here on your own?'

She raised her eyebrows and gave me a look. 'Of course,' she said.

'Okay, then. Don't stay too late.' I made my way to the door. 'I'll see you in the morning.'

'See you, then. Have a good evening.'

Back at my flat that was just what I was worrying about. Having a good evening. To distract myself I tidied up. I cleaned the bathroom, hoovered the carpets, put my clothes in the wardrobe and changed the bed sheets. Just in case. With that done, I set the table in the kitchen, then sat down, opened a bottle of wine and pondered my menu and its ingredients. I chopped fish, washed and sliced vegetables, blended garlic, ginger and spices and prepared as much as I could. Then I sat quietly and drank a glass of wine, studying the photograph on the wall behind the table.

It was a black and white collector's-edition print, the faint black scrawl of the photographer's signature visible in the bottom right-hand corner. Elmer Batters. I moved nearer. I never tired of looking at this image. Two feet, shot from below, were poised on the edge of a sofa. One foot draped over the other and black stiletto sandals, with thin high metallic heels, dangled tantalisingly from the toes, as if they were about to fall to the ground. The left foot was covered with a translucent black stocking through which the three smallest toes were visible. The right was bare but the toes were more obscured. There was a beauty, a symmetry to this photograph that usually calmed me. But right now it wasn't working its usual magic.

I drank another glass of wine and there was still no sign of Ophelia. I paced around the kitchen, then opened the French doors into the garden. I breathed the air tinged with the scent of hyacinths growing in pots on the patio. Then I went back to the table and sat down. I was a ball of anxiety. Finally, the doorbell rang. I checked myself out in the hallway mirror before I answered. I practised a smile. Keep it natural, relaxed, I told myself, and opened the door.

'Hi,' said Ophelia. Her hair was tied back and her skin looked paler than it had the day before. She looked tired and somehow smaller. 'I'm sorry I'm late. I've had a frantic day.'

'Don't worry about it. Come in.' I took her coat, hung it in the hallway and then wandered back into the kitchen. She took off her shoes and followed me. She was wearing a green blouse and a knee-length black skirt that showed off her slim calves and ankles. Her bare feet were a shock of white moving against the dark slate of the kitchen floor.

'Are you sure you've got enough trainers there?' She gestured back to the rows of shoes lined up in the hallway.

'Oh, yeah,' I replied, distracted. 'I just can't seem to stop buying them.'

'Wow. You must have about twenty pairs.'

I nodded and then added, 'I walk pretty much everywhere,' as if by way of justification.

When Ophelia reached the table I poured her a glass of wine. 'Cheers,' she said and took a sip. 'Hmm, delicious.'

'Good, I'm glad you like it.' I paused as I took another mouthful. I savoured the taste. It was delicious but I was going to have to pace myself if I didn't want the food to be a disaster. 'Do you want to sit down here,' I pointed to the table, 'while I get started on the food?'

'Sure, what are we eating?'

'I stopped at the fishmonger's on the way home and bought loads of stuff. So I thought we'd have fish curry. Sound okay?'

'Sounds wonderful.' She smiled at me again and took another sip of wine. The green blouse complemented her eyes and the paleness of her skin.

I swallowed and tried to get focused. It was a problem I'd been having all day.

'So you like to cook?'

I nodded. 'I love it. It relaxes me.' Just by saying the

word, something in me shifted. I felt less anxious. 'It's good to see you.'

'It's good to see you, too,' she said, smiling.

We looked at each other for a moment and then I turned, opened the fridge and took out the fish. I could feel her still watching me.

'So, your day was hectic. What happened?'

'Urgghh. Just a job that I'm working on. The location's dreadful, the set's a disaster. It's turning into a nightmare . . .'

As she talked I got started. I fried up shallots and aubergine and then added my blended paste of spices along with coconut milk and fish sauce. While the rice simmered on the hob, I added sea bass and salmon to the coconut curry. Then I dropped in some prawns, scallops and razor clams. In the final couple of minutes, I fried some samphire and spinach in garlic and butter. In short, I cooked up a storm. If she didn't enjoy this meal, I would eat my whole stockpile of trainers.

'This smells amazing,' said Ophelia, cutting through my thoughts. 'Can I help with anything?'

'You could light the candles on the table,' I said, handing her some matches. 'Then I think we're pretty much good to go.' I poured the curry into one bowl, rice into another and vegetables into a third and walked back and forth with the food to the table. Finally, I grabbed a couple of plates and sat down.

'This looks great,' said Ophelia, hovering over the food bowls and breathing in deeply.

'Well, I hope you like it.' I served her some rice and curry, then helped myself. Finally, I raised my glass. 'To you and to a better day tomorrow.'

'I'll drink to that.' She smiled. Then she nodded towards the Batters print on the wall. 'That's an amazing image, by the way.'

I gazed at the dangling stiletto shoes for a moment.

'Not many people are aware of the work of that photographer.' Ophelia was smiling at me in a knowing way.

I didn't really want to get into this conversation but it looked like I was going to have to. 'Maya, my wife, bought it for me a long time ago. I still love it, all these years later.' I smiled, waving my fork towards the image. 'For the record, she wasn't into feet as much as him.'

'I don't think many people were into feet as much as him.' Ophelia's eyes twinkled.

I laughed. 'No, I guess not. Maya used to say that feet tell stories, leave clues behind. Their mark upon the earth, if you like. She noticed them a lot.'

I crunched into a mouthful of samphire and felt its salty sharpness on my tongue. The last thing I wanted to do was get into another discussion about my wife. I wanted to leave all trace of her and the footprints she had left upon my life behind.

I looked at Ophelia, still studying the print. 'So,' I said, 'tell me more about yourself, your family, if that's not too nosy of me.'

The small scar above her lip twitched slightly and she hesitated for a moment. 'No, I don't mind telling you,' she said at last. She took a sip of her wine. 'Where to start, that's the problem.' She hesitated. 'Perhaps with my father.' She nodded, then smiled faintly. 'He was English, through and through, terribly eccentric. He grew up in London but the sea was always in his blood. And so, eventually, he became a marine biologist. Cetaceans were his thing.'

'Cetaceans?' I had no idea what she was talking about.

'From the Greek, *ketos* and the Latin, *cetus*. You can see I had it drummed into me as a child.' She smiled. 'For the uninitiated, it means whales, dolphins and porpoises.'

'Ah, I see.'

'They were his specialism. So we lived all my early life by the sea. Mainly on small islands or beaches.'

'Wow, fantastic. That's every kid's dream.'

'I guess so. And it was idyllic for a while. It feels very dreamlike now, you know, looking back. My father worked a lot. He always seemed to be out in the boat, or writing up reports or studies. So my mother mostly took care of me. I have wonderful memories of her. She was Italian, warm, beautiful, always smiling.' Ophelia paused and took another sip of her wine. 'She died when I was six. She'd been ill for a long time, but I was too young to know and of course no one told me. She had a heart condition which grew progressively worse.'

I stopped eating and looked at Ophelia. 'I'm so sorry.'

'It's okay. I don't mind talking about it. In fact, I like to talk about her, I like to remember.'

I nodded. 'Then tell me something about her.'

She thought for a second and laughed. 'Strangely enough, I remember her feet. They're one of my clearest memories.' She took a mouthful of fish and chewed slowly, savouring the memory in her mind. 'I remember sunlight on water, a twinkling blue and the impression of my mother's feet in the sand. Big and bold. Their outline was strong and smooth against the dampness of the beach.' She took a clam from her plate, pulled it open and ate it. 'And I stood in an imprint, looking down at my mother's toes. Then I bent over and followed their mark with my fingertips. Softly, gently.' She raised her eyebrows. 'I remember reciting a nursery rhyme.' Then she laughed, a slightly shrill, embarrassed laugh. I thought of her young, thin voice on the wind. 'This little piggy went to market. This little piggy stayed at home.' She pulled a strand of samphire from the bowl and held it between her fingers. 'I remember feeling safe in the sunlight, watching my mother walk ahead. I remember it clearly. The smell of the salt in the air. The taste of it on my lips. The suck of wet sand against my own feet. Now and then my mother turned and smiled at me, standing in her foot's imprint, delicately tracing in the sand. Then she would turn back and walk on. But I stayed exactly where I was until the tide came in and washed the footprints away.'

Neither of us said anything for a moment. Then I got up from the table and opened another bottle of wine.

'For some reason, I've been thinking about her a lot lately. I guess I never really ever stop thinking about her.'

Ophelia paused. 'It was incredibly difficult for her to be gone. Suddenly, to just be gone.'

I really couldn't imagine. 'It must have been terrible.'

She nodded, swirling the wine around in her glass, looking at it as she did. 'I feel the sense of loss, perhaps as much now as I did then. It reaches out to me.' She looked up suddenly and met my gaze. 'I'm sorry, that probably sounded ridiculous. It's hard to explain. The pull of what's lost.'

'Yeah. But I think I understand.'

She looked at me for a long moment and then she smiled. 'Maybe you do.'

'So what about your father? How did he cope when she was gone?'

Ophelia let out a sigh. 'He worked a lot. He had no choice. But now he was the one who read me stories, cooked and cared for me as well. In one way, I saw more of him than ever. But in another, I saw less.'

She paused. She looked like she was striving to find the right words.

'Something was different. He changed. He looked the same as my father. On the surface. But it wasn't him. Underneath, in the darkness, deep within him, he wasn't himself, he was someone else. Grief pulled him apart and filled him with emptiness. He wasn't the same man.'

I reached for my wine again and drained the glass. Then I refilled both our glasses. Now we were partway through the story I realised it was no fairy tale.

'For a while, we moved. I think that helped him a little.

We hopped from one continent to another, one country to the next: Greece to Australia, Fiji to California, Hong Kong to the Philippines. We moved six times in six years.'

I raised my eyebrows and let out a faint whistle.

'Yes, it was pretty insane. We were like nomads, rootless, forever shifting.' Ophelia had stopped eating and was looking at her hands, palms down, pale and flat against the dark oak of the table.

'I didn't realise it at the time but I know now that it was my father's way of trying to outrun the past, to stay one step ahead of the memories of my mother. I think he knew that if they caught up with him, if he let them in, they would fill up the empty spaces inside him and he would disappear under their weight.' She paused to take a sip of wine. 'But you can't run away from things for ever, can you?'

I sighed quietly and nodded. I had to agree with her. In the end, the things you ran away from always seemed to catch you.

'My father died not long after we moved to the Philippines.'

'I'm so sorry.' There it was again, another sorry. 'Really, you don't have to tell me this if it's too much.'

Ophelia smiled softly. 'Thanks. But, like I said, it was a long time ago. What difference does it make if I tell you now or later? It's the same story. It's not too hard to hear, is it?'

I shook my head as I pushed away my plate. 'So how did it happen?'

'We were living on the western island of Palawan in the Philippines. It's a stunning place, clear water, and jungle cascading right to the beach. And beneath the sea are nearly eleven thousand square kilometres of coral reefs. Activity near the reefs was what my father was interested in.' She paused. 'Anyway, one day he went out to sea and never came back. The weather was bad, he should never have gone in the first place, but there was no reasoning with him. There were terrific storms in the north and about a week after he went missing his boat was found washed ashore, mangled and broken up. There was no sign of him. The officials concluded that he had been thrown overboard and drowned.'

I didn't want to say again that I was sorry so I said nothing.

'So that was the way he died. The legally determined, authorised version, anyway. But I always felt that was only a part of it. On another level, he had finally surrendered to what had haunted him most and disappeared in its grasp. He was finally free. That's what I think.' Ophelia picked a prawn from the bowl and pulled it from its shell. 'So it's not a sad story. Not really.'

Maybe, I thought. Maybe not. The whole story seemed deeply tragic to me. But maybe she had to take solace where she could find it. That I could understand. 'But it must have been hard to handle when you were so young.'

'Hmm. I think for a long time I didn't understand it properly. I still imagined that my mother and father would come walking back into my life. I had problems working out what was real and what was not.' She laughed. Then she became serious once more. 'Even as an adult, it's hard enough. I still grapple with it from time to time.'

I nodded.

'I have always remembered what a local man in Palawan once told me. His tribe believed that those who died at sea were transformed into mythical creatures, sea nymphs and mermen of the deep who were made of the ocean and could swim like the fish. Once a year, for one night, they could return to the land and walk upon it like they used to.' Ophelia's eyes sparkled in the flickering candle-light. She looked beautiful. 'Do you think that could be true?'

'I don't know,' I answered finally. 'I guess it all comes down to what you believe in the end.'

'Yes, I suppose it does.' She smiled at me suddenly and there seemed to be a new lightness in her expression. 'So that's it. The whole story. I came to England then to be with my grandparents. The rest is history. So, tell me about the factory. What are you planning to do there?'

For a while we talked about the renovation and my ideas for the conversion. I told Ophelia about Tara, her abrasive confidence and her perfect breasts. We laughed and then fell into silence. As we picked at the remains of the food I wanted to say something else but I couldn't think of anything. Eventually, she put down her fork and looked at me.

'Do you ever dream?'

I stared at her.

'You know. When you sleep do you have dreams?'

'Sometimes,' I replied. 'But it's pretty unusual if I do. What about you?'

'Yes, I dream a lot. And a lot about my parents. Can I tell you something, something I don't really share that often?'

'Of course. You can tell me anything.' And as I said it I realised that I meant it.

'Well, I say it's a dream but it doesn't feel like a dream. It always feels very real. Like I am there, invisible but watching.' She paused, seemingly perplexed. 'But then I realise that I can't have been there. No matter how real it felt, it must have been a dream.' Pause. 'So, it's night-time, but out of the darkness a long beach appears, stretching on and on into the distance, so far that I can't see its end. The moon rises, large in the sky, and casts a pale reflection on the sea. Waves wash quietly against the sand.' Ophelia smiled faintly. 'Can you imagine it?'

I nodded.

'So, a woman walks along the shoreline. Slowly. From time to time she turns and smiles at the person following in her wake. Her feet make patterns in the wet sand. The person behind her follows her trail, touching the images she has left behind with his fingers. It's my father. He smiles at my mother. He has found her in this ancient place of memory and desire. He has come here for this one night in the year, to be with her in the moonlight, before his bones are returned to coral and his blood to salt water. As he follows her along the beach, gaining on her ever so slightly, my father also turns. Although there is no one there behind him, he looks with longing at the place that he has come from. A tear creeps down his cheek. Then he smiles, slowly turns and walks on.'

5

Chateau de Blois

June 1543

Catherine watched the flickering candlelight dance around her bedchamber. But she could not focus on the patterns of light and shade. Her gaze slipped and shifted to the green velvet curtains hanging down from the corners of the four-poster bed, then moved to the heavy embroidered tapestries against the wall beyond. But she could not connect with their beauty, their colourful splendour, could not hold any particular thought in her head. She was distracted, nervous, keen not to say or do anything that would intensify the distance she felt already between herself and Henri. She looked down at her hands, spread out on the bed sheets, and moved slightly on all fours to adjust herself. Hearing her husband manoeuvre himself behind her, she felt a bloom of desire hit her. Despite the ignominy of this position, she could not help but feel aroused. She turned her head to meet her husband's gaze, but his eyes were averted, his face devoid of expression. Then she felt him grasp her shoulder and, abruptly, push inside her. She squeezed her eyes tightly together, trying to imagine his face in front of hers, rapt as he stared at her, as she had seen him gaze upon another. She tried to imagine his breath, hot against her neck, his hands upon her breasts, his sweat binding them together, his need intense, urgent. And in the darkness behind her eyelids, beyond her sight, she could almost imagine it, could almost spin the shadows into reality. But, even there, something jarred. With each indifferent thrust, her fantasies became harder to sustain until finally they too slipped into darkness and dissolved entirely. She opened her eyes, felt the rhythmic slap of her husband's body against her own. The noise echoed like a shot in the silence that otherwise fell between them. Catherine closed her eyes once more and waited for it to be over.

Minutes later, his duty done, Henri withdrew from her, dressed in haste and left the room. The door closed behind him with a muted click. Perhaps less than twenty words had passed between them from the beginning of this act to the end. Catherine lay on her back with her eyes closed, wondering why, even now, she allowed herself to be subjected to this. She remembered the Doctor, Jean Fernel, with his prodding, poking fingers, exploring her, prising her apart. He had examined both her and Henri in an attempt to diagnose the cause of the apparent barrenness. Mercifully, he had declared that she was not infertile, simply that conception was proving difficult. Catherine's pride burned with the remembrance of what came next – that which caused her, even now in the emptiness of her bedchamber, to feel the blood sting her cheeks with shame once more. Henri's mistress had taken her aside and under the guise of solicitude, masquerading as sisterly concern, she had suggested a different approach that perhaps the Dauphin and Dauphine could benefit from. Try it à la levrette, she had urged. An alternative position might prove to be what was needed. Catherine could not be sure but thought she had detected the faintest trace of a smile at the edge of the woman's mouth as she pressed her point. Now, as Catherine lay in her darkened chamber, *having performed 'like a greyhound' as requested, she wondered if this was yet another game of the Duchess's to alienate her further from her husband's affections. For now, when they made love, he did not have to meet her eye, did not even have to face her.*

As Catherine rose from the bed, her hands rested lightly for a moment on her stomach. Then she put on her gown and made her way through the small chapel beside her chamber and into her study on the other side. As she walked idly around the room she rested a hand against the wooden panelling that lined the walls. Something in its touch soothed her. Perhaps it was the smooth solidity of the grain beneath her fingers. Perhaps it was the knowledge that she held of what was contained beneath the panels, in the secret compartments hidden in their depths. In some the ingredients for ancient pagan remedies were concealed. Mule's urine – a certain cure for sterility – she had drunk religiously upon the counsel of one of her alchemists, while she had taken a mixture of mare's milk, rabbit's blood and sheep's urine upon the advice of a second. She had tried all manner of dressings and poultices, purges, potions and lettings of the blood. For with each month that passed without a pregnancy her position had grown more and more precarious. There had been talk not too long ago of the repudiation of her marriage and her replacement by another. But she had found an unlikely ally in her husband's mistress, who had pleaded her case with Henri – her good nature, her gentleness, her youth and the fact that she would most likely bear children in the future when the time was right. And for the moment at least the matter seemed to have been dropped.

Catherine stopped beside the window and looked down into the courtyard below. All was quiet, serene. She placed her hand on the panel to the right of where she stood and prised open the secret compartment beneath it. A small vial, she knew, rested inside although she did not turn to look at it. It contained a white powder, innocuous enough, with the look of talc or flour. And yet its contents were deadly.

She thought of the Duchess again. Motivated always by self-interest it had served that woman's purpose to defend her, to champion the barren Dauphine's cause. After all, a new, perhaps more beautiful successor might not view the presence of an older mistress with such apparent calm and resignation. The Duchess's own position was in jeopardy. And so, with terrible irony, it seemed that the three of them – Catherine, Henri and his mistress – were bound together until a child was conceived. But after that, who could possibly know what would happen?

Catherine smiled in the darkness as she thought about the baby finally growing inside her. It was early in the pregnancy and she had managed thus far, through deception and guile, to keep it a secret. For with that discovery her husband's visits to her bedchamber would come to an end, she was certain. Tears pricked her eyes as she realised she would prefer the little she got from Henri to having nothing of him at all. And, as she contemplated the loss to come, tears fell down her cheeks. But she wiped them away. With a child, after all, came other possibilities. A growth in her influence and power. A decline, perhaps, in that of the Duchess. Who knew what could happen?

Her right hand, still resting over the secret compartment, now reached forward and her fingers caressed the vial of arsenic within. Yes, she thought, her smile returning, who knew what infinite possibilities lay ahead? Then she closed her eyes and thanked God silently for the child.

6

When I walked into the dispatch room the following morning
I saw Tara's handbag lying on her desk and her umbrella
sprawling sodden next to one of its legs. Her coat hung
limply behind the open door of the store cupboard close by.
So she was here already. It was early for her. I put my coffee
down next to the papers on my desk and slung my jacket,
wet from the rain, over my chair. It was then that I noticed
the note:

> *Come and find me as soon as you get in. I have a surprise
> for you!*
> Tara

I took a long, slow gulp of my coffee and wondered exactly
what it was that she wanted. I drank a little more and
then stood up. Normally I would have taken my time
before seeking her out. I might have looked over my papers
or made a few calls and only then gone to find her. In
short, I would have bolstered myself, prepared my Tara
defences. My armour and deflector shield. But today something was different. I was different. And no doubt all

because of Ophelia. I took her card out of my wallet and looked at it again. She had given it to me late the previous night just before she went home. Apart from her name, in white type in the centre, and her number beneath it, it was a square of black emptiness. I rolled the words around my tongue. OPHELIA GRAY. OPHELIA GRAY. Then I put the card away once more and went to find Tara.

Her note hadn't said where she would be but I didn't figure it would be difficult to track her down. I crossed into the finishing department where racks of completed shoes lined my path. The soft, sweet smell of the leather rose and wrapped itself around me like an old, familiar coat. As I walked, I seemed to catch the smell of Ophelia's skin on the air and an image of the kiss we had shared the night before flooded my mind. I thought of her lips, full and moist, and I closed my eyes as the vividness of the memory hit me. I blinked hard, tried to concentrate and walked briskly to the stairs. I ran up them two at a time and crossed the three sections on the first floor in turn. No sign of Tara. I stopped at the window and looked out at the park. In the dampness of the day, it looked greener than ever. The plane trees still stood like sentries on the periphery. There was no one there.

I turned back to the staircase and reached the second floor slightly out of breath. I looked around for a moment, then walked to the end of the factory floor and stopped. I was in the clicking department once again. But I still couldn't see any sign of Tara. Maybe she had popped out for a minute. But why leave a note and then take off? Plus her bag and coat were still here. I shouted her name and waited. My voice hit the walls flatly. I breathed in and waited some more. The clicking machines looked as if they, too, were frozen, waiting for an answer. Nothing came back but silence. So I took the stairs out of that department down to the first floor. As I walked its length, I called Tara again. The same flat voice. The same lack of answer. I coughed and then shouted her name, loudly this time. Nothing. Confused, I made my way to the staircase and back down to where I'd started. My coffee cup still stood on the table. My coat drooped idly on the back of the chair. I walked over to the door, turned round and looked across the room. Everything was as I'd left it five minutes ago. I called Tara one last time. Finally a muted noise responded to my call.

I froze momentarily. Then I moved to the centre of the room and called her again. The same small voice came back, but I was struggling to identify where it was coming from. I walked to the rear wall, turned and called again. Another muffled response. I looked to my right. Now I was pretty sure. Tara's voice was coming from the store cupboard.

I walked towards it, feeling mildly ridiculous. Was this some kind of weird game of hide-and-seek? She couldn't be hiding in the cupboard, could she? When I got to the open door I looked into the small rectangular space beyond. It was about twelve feet deep and four feet wide with a ceiling as high as the dispatch room. Narrow shelves ran all the way up and along the left-hand wall, packed with books, files, loose paperwork, swatches of leather, bits of apparatus and machinery. The floor was similarly crowded and towards the rear wall was littered with dusty cardboard boxes. I surveyed the chaos. There was no sign of my assistant.

'Tara, where are you?' I shouted loudly.

'Hey.' A subdued voice filtered out from the confines of the cupboard. 'You've found me out.'

I took a step forward and looked again into the depths, along the cupboard's walls and ceiling. No, I really wasn't sure I had.

'I'm not surprised it's taking you a while. It did me too.' Suddenly, a gap appeared in the right-hand wall. A long, thin strip of blackness. It continued to expand outwards, pushing against the floor. It was a door opening slowly from the inside. But the inside of what? I stood gaping. First I recognised Tara's hand, then her arm against the door and after a moment she emerged in full. She smiled naughtily. 'Well, hello. Welcome to my parlour.' With a flourish, she gestured to where she had just come from.

'What the hell?' My voice came out rather high-pitched. I was having trouble controlling it. And a little trouble with Tara popping out of the wall. 'What the hell?' I repeated, stuck for words. 'I don't remember seeing this in any of the plans.'

'That's because it's not marked on any of the plans. Come on down and see what you think.' And with that she turned and disappeared.

Incredulous, I watched the space where she had been for a second or two and then moved forwards towards the open doorway. It was something else, practically unde-tectable from the outside. I peered through the gap in the wall. I could make out the top of a staircase descending into blackness beyond. I was still standing, staring, when a voice jumped out at me from the darkness.

'Come on. The stairs are pretty dark but I've got candles down here.'

'Jesus, Tara. Are you crazy?'

I heard her laughter erupt from the darkness and then another 'Come on.'

A burst of anger rose within me. 'Look, you had no idea what was going to be down there. You could have hurt yourself.' I had a mental image of Richard reprimanding me for a complete lack of respect for health-and-safety regulations. Not to mention for endangering his lover.

'Yeah, yeah. Are you going to come down here or are you going to argue with me for the rest of the morning? Don't you want to see what I've found?'

I looked at the stairs. They were steep and wooden, with a painted handrail running alongside, presumably all the way to the bottom, although I couldn't see that far. I started to clamber down, counting the stairs as I descended into the darkness and holding on to the handrail as I went. It was ever so slightly sticky. One, two, three, four, five. My irritation with Tara was still fizzing inside me. Six, seven, eight, nine, ten. I kept stepping down the stairs, taking shallow breaths as I went. The air was stale as if this place had been shut up for a long time. It felt thick and cloying as I breathed. Eleven, twelve, thirteen, fourteen, fifteen. And slightly damp against the skin. Sixteen, seventeen, eighteen, nineteen, twenty. And with that my foot touched the floor at the bottom.

I turned around and looked back up the staircase at the pale rectangle of light that marked the doorway into the cupboard. It looked much smaller from here. The thought made me feel mildly uncomfortable. Then I felt a hand touch mine.

'Come on, slowcoach,' said Tara. 'Follow me.'

She led me down a narrow corridor to the left of the stairs and as I walked I stumbled now and again on the uneven floor. I couldn't see what it was made of, but I suspected that it was bare ground. There was an earthy smell that lingered. We walked for about ten paces and then my hand felt the frame of a doorway directly in front of me. It had the same mild stickiness as the handrail. We walked through it and then stopped.

'So, are you ready to see what's down here?' she asked.

'Yeah, I guess so.'

I heard a match being struck and then light pierced the darkness.

7

I blinked a couple of times, trying to see beyond the candlelight. But at first it was impossible, darkness crowding in around the edges of the solitary flame. Then Tara handed me the candle and lit a couple more. Suddenly light bounced off the walls.

We were in a small room, about twenty feet square, with a low ceiling that stood just over a foot above my head. The floor was earth. So I'd been right. The hairs in my nostrils twitched. The fusty smell was even stronger in here than it had been in the corridor outside and the room felt abandoned, forlorn. Its walls were bare and blotchy, paint having flaked in patches and dropped to the floor. In some places, the plasterwork had given way completely, revealing the old wooden laths beneath. There were no windows. Against the wall, furthest from where we stood, was a single bed complete with mattress. What looked like rust, eating its way slowly through the metal stand, was bright in the glowing light. Other than the bed, and a mouldering old yellow armchair in the corner to the right of it, the room seemed empty. I walked over to the bed and, suddenly nauseous, kneeled down, resting my hand against the mattress for support. For a moment my mind swam and I thought I might retch.

'Are you okay?' Tara's voice sounded lifeless, as if it was being sucked into the walls.

'Yeah. It's just the air in here.'

I stood up and turned around to face her. As I did so, I caught sight of something suspended on the wall furthest from the bed. It was a huge rectangular mirror, about six feet long and two feet wide, its thick silver frame tarnished in places, twinkling in the light. What had once no doubt been bright clear glass was now dark and deeply mottled. My outline was nothing more than a shadow, dully reflected in blackened silver.

'Seriously, are you okay? You don't look too good.' Tara hovered in the doorway. 'Maybe we should go back upstairs?'

'No, really, I'm all right.' The air was still sticking in my throat but that wasn't what was bothering me now. I walked towards the mirror. 'Strange . . .' I muttered to myself, looking over its surface.

'I know – it's creepy, isn't it? And what do you make of these?' She pointed to the top left-hand corner of the mirror. A pair of dark green leather shoes, with thick high heels, hung from a green velvet ribbon suspended over the mirror's frame. They were small and intricately embroidered around the toes with pale green silk thread. 'Strange place to leave your shoes, don't you think?'

'Very,' I mumbled as I reached out to touch them. They felt soft and smooth and even here, in this foul-smelling room, I could pick out the faint fragrance of the leather. They were still in good condition. Without thinking I slid my fingers inside the left shoe until it enclosed them snugly. Then I reached forward with my index finger and felt the soft leather of the insole. Within it was the subtle imprint of five small toes. An image of Ophelia on a beach danced fleetingly across my mind and then was gone. I blinked hard and tried to focus. I felt the imprint again.

'What are you doing?'

I turned my head and looked at Tara who was eyeing me curiously. 'I'm checking something.' I looked away as I slid my hand into the right shoe. The same imprint was there. 'To see if they've been worn. They have.'

'Yes, but not a lot. The soles are only a little scuffed.'

I turned the shoes over and sure enough they were lightly criss-crossed with grazes and scars. I ran my fingers over the lines and grooves and the logo branded in the middle of the sole. They had been made here at the factory. Yet they looked smarter than an average pair of shoes. The leather was sumptuously soft and the stitching on the uppers was elaborate.

I stared at them for I don't know how long until Tara cut in on my thoughts. 'So, there's more. Would you like to see another strange discovery?' She held out her right hand. Between her fingers was a piece of paper, an old scrap with ragged edges. I reached for it but at the same time I felt a quiver of unease. I had the growing feeling that we were handling things that perhaps we shouldn't. Things that were personal and private. And that we had stumbled into somewhere that perhaps we shouldn't have. I took a deep breath and tried to shake the feeling. On the side of the paper facing me there was nothing but a faint dark spot lying below the rough upper edge. I ran my finger over the mark and felt a slight stickiness. It must have been from where the note had been attached to something. I flipped the paper over. Here there was writing. Three lines stood out in the centre of the paper, in elongated green script.

> *I have heard, (but not believed)*
> *The spirits of the dead*
> *May walk again*

Around the edges of the paper, fragments of letters in the same green ink survived. It seemed that the scrap had once been part of a larger text. I looked at the words again. But I had no idea what to make of them.

'Where did you find this, Tara?'

'It was stuck to the mirror, to the bottom left-hand corner. Roughly there.' She pointed.

I moved forwards to look. While the surface was still dark, it was paler than the rest, with fewer thick inky marks. In the middle of this section there appeared to be two letters, etched into the surface of the mirror or just below it. It was difficult to say, due to both the darkness of the room and the discoloration of the mirror. I stepped nearer and bent in to take another look. Yes, they were definitely letters. Perhaps an ornate T and M, the long strokes of the letters intertwined. TM. It meant nothing to me. I touched the surface of the mirror gently, then stuck the paper back where it had been. It floated on the surface like shiny flotsam on a dirty pond.

'There's a marking on the other side, too.' Tara's voice was quiet.

I looked to my right and moved in closer to take a look. Sure enough, in the same style, was what looked like a letter H, with decoration between its vertical strokes. Again, I ran my fingers over the mirror's surface. Then I took a step back and frowned.

'So what do you make of it?' Tara said softly.

I turned to look at her and met her gaze. Her pupils were wide, as if adrenalin pumping through her body was dilating them. She didn't seem her usual confident self. 'I have absolutely no idea. About the room or the things here.' I paused. 'I mean, what is this place? It could perhaps have been an old coal cellar, although I'm not sure. Maybe it was just a storage space. Whatever it was, it seems to have been converted at some point into a strange hidden room to hang out in.'

'I'm with you there. I mean, what's with the bed?' Tara walked towards it, the familiar click of her heels noiseless against the earth floor. She tapped the leg of the bed frame with the toe of her boot. 'It's got to be sex, right?'

I had to agree. After all, why anyone would want to sleep down here was beyond me. I tried to think of other possibilities. But the sound Tara was making was distracting. I looked at her, at this beautiful girl tapping her foot against the edge of the bed. I studied the curve of her boots around her calves, traced the shape of her legs upwards until they disappeared under her skirt and I felt myself becoming aroused. A sudden rush of shock made me turn away. What was wrong with me? I blinked hard a few times and tried to concentrate, to focus. I took a couple of deep breaths. The fetid dampness of the air, sticking in my throat, seemed to bring me back to myself. Exhaling slowly, I looked at the mirror and tried to think. Clearly someone had brought it down here. But why? To hide it away? Or maybe to use it? But what purpose could there be in having a mirror that reflected practically nothing in a secret basement? I closed my eyes, suddenly tired and confused. The late night was catching up with me.

Tara's voice pierced the silence. 'What about the note and the shoes? They're bothering me.'

I looked around once again. At the room and everything it contained. It was all bothering me. Why were these things here? No escaping that their presence was deliberate. There was no other stuff in the room. But what the meaning was, presuming there was one, I didn't know.

'What do you think of when you see shoes like that?' Tara was back on her own line of questioning.

I shrugged.

'Well, they're pretty special shoes, right? Perhaps they belonged to someone special.' She walked back to the mirror and touched the edge of the note ever so lightly. '"I have heard, but not believed, the spirits of the dead may walk again." Hmm. What do you make of that? Is someone being haunted? Or wanting to be haunted but not believing it to be possible?' She paused for a second. 'Or is that just ridiculous?'

I looked into the mirror as she spoke, focusing on my shadowy reflection. Were we really talking ghosts? 'I don't know,' I said. My head had begun to ache. I moved it from side to side and suddenly some of the tension dislodged and evaporated. I smiled at myself. A dark distorted smile seemed to come back to me.

'What is it?' said Tara.

'I don't know,' I said again. We both laughed then, the sound slight and nervous. Our laughter, like everything else, was sucked into the walls and vanished. 'I can't make sense of any of it. And why isn't this place in the plans?'

She shrugged. 'Who knows? Maybe someone found it by accident and wanted to keep it private.'

I raised an eyebrow at myself in the mirror. 'So how did you find it if it's not marked anywhere?'

'I just stumbled on it.' Tara stopped. She too was looking at herself in the mirror. 'Courtesy of the great British weather. I got soaked on my way in. So I was hanging up my coat to dry behind the cupboard door and a couple of things in there caught my eye. Some bright-coloured shoes, matching leather samples. That kind of thing. I'd seen them before but never actually bothered to take a proper look. But today I did. I started to delve. I didn't think it would hurt.' The words hung for a moment on the air. 'And that's when I saw it. The door handle, hidden away at the back of the cupboard. But after I'd cleared away some stuff from the floor in front of it, it pulled open fairly easily.'

No kidding.

'Then I saw the stairs and thought I'd take a look at where they went. I found some candles and matches in the storage cupboard so I was away. And anyway, like I said, I don't mind the dark.'

I blinked hard. I didn't want to think about her descending into darkness not knowing where it might lead.

'I just thought it would be some normal kind of cellar.' Tara said it in a tone that implied she no longer thought that.

'Well, let's keep this place between ourselves for now until we find out more about it. Yeah?'

She nodded.

'So, what were you doing down here while I was looking for you?'

Tara paused. 'I don't really know. When I got down here I thought I wanted to get out as soon as possible. But then I came across the mirror and spent most of the time I was down here looking at it.' She reached out and touched its surface lightly with her fingertips. 'There's something about it.'

I nodded. For once, we were in accord.

She waited for a while. Then came the question I'd been wondering if she would ask. 'You feel it too, don't you?'

I looked at her. She seemed suddenly uncertain. But she met my gaze and held it. 'Yes, I feel it,' I said eventually.

We stood in silence for a few moments.

I looked again at my reflection, such as it was. My eyes stared back at me. They had lost all of their blueness and had deep, dark circles around them. Darker, I'm sure, than they actually were. Nonetheless, I felt exhausted. I didn't want to be underground any longer.

'Come on, let's go. I've had enough of being down here. I need some fresh air.' I walked through the doorway towards the stairs. 'And no more coming down here by yourself in the dark. Okay?'

'Okay.'

Standing at the bottom of the staircase I looked up towards the rectangle of light coming from the factory floor. I blew out the candle I was still holding, looked at Tara and then back at the stairs. 'Are you ready?' My voice bounced upwards, round and full. It was regaining its usual cadence.

'I'm ready,' she answered. Then she blew out her candles and plunged us momentarily into darkness once again.

8

We were quiet for a long time. Whenever I looked over at Tara she appeared to be hard at work, bent low over her laptop. But it was a front, I was sure. I suspected that she was as distracted as I was. I was sitting, papers spread out on my desk. But I wasn't focused on any of it. My mind was still in the underground room, flicking over its contents, trying to make sense of them. The presence of the mirror, in particular, was bothering me.

I went over the original blueprints of the factory once again and then the surveyor's drawings. I knew all the answers before I began but I did it anyway. Three floors. The shallow attic space. The thickness of the outer walls. Windows and doors clearly marked. No indication of a cellar. None whatsoever. Everything you'd expect, nothing that you wouldn't. I sighed and leaned back in my chair.

'All okay, boss?' Tara was staring at me. Her olive skin seemed paler than usual.

'Sure. I'm just distracted.'

'I know what you mean.'

She watched me as I got up from my desk and walked around the dispatch room. I looked out of the window but my eyes couldn't focus on anything. I blinked hard and tried to clear my head. Then I took a breath and before I'd thought through exactly what I was going to say, I turned back towards her and launched in. 'I've been thinking . . .'

'. . . about the room?'

I nodded. Clearly it was still on her mind. 'It might be an idea to try and dig up some more information on the factory's original owner and his family. Check out their history and the history of this place. It might lead to something on that cellar. If that's what it was. Who used it and what for? Something like that.' I paused, wondering how best to present it. 'I know, strictly speaking, this kind of research isn't really necessary. It's more that I'm interested to know, having been down there.'

Tara looked at me and nodded.

'Plus, if there is an interesting angle, then perhaps we can make that resonate in the conversion. It might even swing whether the space gets used or just sealed off and forgotten about.'

Tara didn't say anything for a while and I started to prepare myself for some resistance. When her answer finally came, it wasn't what I was expecting. 'Sure, I can do that. Richard has a lot of information on the factory. I'll start with that and take it from there.'

I smiled. 'Okay, great.' But with the mention of Richard, something occurred to me. 'Look, like I said before, do you mind not mentioning the room to anyone for the moment, until we find out a bit more?' I couldn't have said for certain why I was asking her to keep things secret from Richard, even though I hadn't referred to him explicitly. But for the time being I didn't want him to know about the room and, in particular, the mirror.

We stared at each other in tense silence for a few moments. Then Tara nodded. 'I've been thinking about the shoes,' she said, seemingly changing the subject. 'The shoes downstairs, I mean.'

I nodded as well. I too had been thinking about them. In my mind's eye I saw them through the darkness, dangling from a velvet ribbon over the edge of the mirror.

'So we know they were made here, right? The logo on the sole told us that.' Tara was looking at me intently. 'But they weren't run-of-the-mill shoes. They were beautiful, intricately stitched.' She looked down at her hands on the desk and then back at me. 'So, want to know what I think?'

'Sure,' I said. Shoes, after all, were Tara's thing.

'They're bespoke. I remember Richard telling me that they made one-off pairs for important customers. So I think I was right when I said they were for someone special.' She paused. 'And if I'm right on that then there would almost certainly have been a log of who the important customers were. Don't you think?'

I nodded again. 'It makes sense.'

'So, then it's a question of whether that log survived. There's enough paperwork still lying around so I'll see if I can track it down. And in turn the owner. That might tell us something, too. Give a different angle on the story.'

'Good thinking,' I managed to say, slightly shocked by

the orderliness of her reasoning when my mind was still somersaulting. 'If you really don't mind the research?'

'No, I don't mind. Besides,' she gestured towards the shoeboxes underneath the window, 'I owe you one for the free gifts.'

'Okay, great,' I said and smiled.

Tara nodded. She definitely wasn't her usual self.

'Are you okay? You seem a little off colour.'

'I'm fine. Just preoccupied.' She sat still for a moment and I wondered if she would mention it again. The feeling in the room. But it appeared that neither one of us wanted to revisit it.

Suddenly she jumped up. 'I think I need some fresh air and a coffee. Clear my head. Can I pick you one up while I'm gone?'

'No, I'm fine. But take your time. No need to hurry back.'

She looked at me and smiled. 'Thanks.' The click of her heels echoed as she moved around the room. So the sound, at least, was back to normal. Then she put up her umbrella, opened the door, and left in a flash of rain-spattered sunlight.

A few times during the course of the afternoon I thought of the mirror in the darkness of the room downstairs. Then a quiver of unease would travel down my back and settle coldly at the base of my spine. What was it about it that had unsettled me? But at the same time I felt a pull deep inside me to see it again. Part of me wanted to

73

ask Tara if she felt the same way. But I couldn't as she had gone back to the office. The other part of me, the part that wanted to dismiss it all as ridiculous and irrational, was relieved that she wasn't around to ask.

I got up from my desk and pulled open the outer factory doors. The afternoon was oppressive. Clouds hung low and threatening in the sky and the air was close, prickling with electricity. A thunderstorm was on the near horizon. I sighed, went back to my desk and began to shuffle papers around once again. It was then that I saw the pencil sketchings on my notepad. On a number of pieces of paper, I had drawn the markings I had noticed on the bottom corners of the mirror's glass. T and M intertwined. An H with embellishment. I wondered again what they could mean. Unable to concentrate on anything else, I switched on my computer and spent the rest of the afternoon carrying out internet searches on combinations of the letters alongside mirrors, engravings, darkened glass, antiquities. I searched anything and everything, but by the end of the afternoon I hadn't come up with anything concrete. I studied my drawings of the letters one last time. But there was nothing familiar about either them or their design. Rocking back on the legs of my chair, I closed my eyes and let the silence of the factory envelop me.

9

The rain was bouncing off the pavements as I left the factory and walked towards Ophelia's place. Still preoccupied by the discovery of the underground room and the mirror, I was only vaguely aware of the downpour splashing against my cheeks and neck. I crossed the park swiftly but as I reached the old bandstand something brought me to a standstill and I turned around.

The sun had now entirely disappeared from view and the evening was on its steady slide towards total winter darkness. The factory, closed up and empty, was little more than a silhouette against the deepening sky, illuminated faintly in the glow of the street lights, the fuzz of orange halos battling with the gloom. My eyes moved across the bricks and windows of the ground floor to the first and then the second. Then they came back to where I'd started. It was pointless. I couldn't see anything. And besides, what was I trying to see? My gaze flicked unsteadily over the factory windows once more. Up and down, to the left and right. But it was too dark. I turned and walked quickly towards the exit. As I stepped out of the park and closed the gate, my breathing was quick and my heart was beating fast. There was something there, I knew it. Beyond the darkness. I just didn't know what it was.

By the time I reached Ophelia's flat I was drenched. I stood outside the door, my finger resting lightly on the buzzer. But I didn't press it. Instead, I closed my eyes and leaned backwards, catching drops of rain as they fell. I tried to empty my mind, to think of nothing. As the seconds ticked by, my breathing slowed and returned to normal. I rang the bell and waited. The rain kept falling, running over my face and down my neck. I opened my eyes and looked upwards into the darkness. Black rain just kept on falling.

Then a voice rang out.

'Hello?' It was Ophelia. My heart did a different kind of leap in my chest. 'Hello?' the voice came again.

'Sorry, it's me. Soaked to the skin.'

'Come on up,' she replied and with a buzz the door swung open. 'Second floor.'

I took the stairs slowly, one at a time, leaving a dark wet imprint on the carpet with each step. A fleeting thought of footprints, of sand and sea, danced across my mind. As I climbed I took off my coat and shook my head, the motion flicking raindrops to the floor. I saw Ophelia standing in the doorway at the top of the stairs. Her dark hair hung around her face and she was wearing a black sleeveless dress, stark against the pale skin of her arms. It was high-necked and the material clung at her breasts and then fell in soft folds to her knees. She wore a pair of red shoes, a shock of brightness against her feet.

'You look terrible,' she said as I came to a stop in front of her. She smelled of roses and jasmine. 'Bad day?'

'You could say that.' I breathed her in. In spite of myself, of how I felt, I found I was smiling. I tried to pull her to me but she pushed my soaking body away, laughing. A strand of her hair fell across her face and I reached for it, my fingers pushing the stray lock behind her ear. I held it there, unable to let go. 'God, it's good to see you,' I said at last.

'You too.' And finally she leaned forward to kiss me. Then she pulled me through the door and closed it.

Ophelia took away my sodden clothes and while I waited for her I stood in my T-shirt and shorts before the fire, luxuriating in its warmth. The room before me was large and square, with two white leather sofas, perpendicular to one another, at the centre. At either end of them, two small chrome lamps resting on glass tables spilled soft light across the leather. Brown suede cushions were strewn on the pale carpet close to where I stood. Behind the sofas a dark wooden table was set for dinner. White roses stood in a vase at the centre and six candles in bright silver holders flickered light across the surface. Along almost the entire length of the room windows stretched from ceiling to floor and French doors opened onto what I presumed was a balcony. All I could see beyond them was a cold and dreary darkness filled with rain.

To my right, in the far corner of the room, was a set of double doors. They were wide open and led into a separate space that I presumed was Ophelia's studio. As in the sitting room, floor-to-ceiling windows dominated but blackout blinds were drawn on all of them. On a table in the centre were four computers which rested back to back, and on a wooden bench that ran along the side of the room were a series of printers of different sizes. A mass of ink cartridges and boxes of paper were scattered along a shelf above them and what looked like a large safe stood in the far corner of the room next to another door.

'That's where I keep my cameras,' said Ophelia, emerging beside me and gesturing at the safe. 'I've got lots of expensive equipment.'

'And a whole load of computers.' I took the glass of wine she was offering me. 'What do you need all those for?'

'For my location and shoot work. I use a digital camera and print the images off on the computers. It's also easy to colour balance, retouch and generally mess around on them. The blinds are down to keep it as dark as possible, so that I can see the images clearly. And through there is my darkroom.' She pointed to the doorway in the corner of the studio. 'It's where I develop my own prints. Not everyone shoots on film these days – in fact, few people do – although it is enjoying a bit of a renaissance. I keep it for the photography that I love; close-ups of people, portraits, that sort of thing. But that's definitely more of a hobby. I'll show you how it's done sometime.' And she smiled at me.

'I'd love that,' I said, moving towards the doorway of the studio and catching sight of a string of photographs on the wall above the printers. 'And what are these?'

'That's some of my shoot work. Have a look.'

I crossed the threshold and stood in front of them, a series of prints, ostensibly of shoes. In the first, a woman's head and naked upper body lay taut across the right-hand side of the frame. Long blonde hair fanned outwards around her expressionless face and her bright blue eyes had an unreal, glassy quality. In the left-hand side of the frame a black stiletto with a towering heel stood apart, almost as if at a safe distance from the body. I wasn't sure what I was supposed to feel about the supine woman pictured in the shot, but I found the fact that I wasn't sure somehow disturbing.

In another photograph pale legs, only visible between the knees and feet, were outstretched on a bright green sofa. One foot was clad in a glossy red stiletto heel, the other was bare and a viscous-looking red liquid dripped from the toes overhanging the sofa to the white floor below, where it collected in a thick pool. There was something unsettling and at the same time compelling about the image. I turned to look at Ophelia and raised my eyebrows.

'These are comforting.'

She laughed loudly. 'Just the look I was going for.' She took a sip of her wine and then smiled at me. 'Don't worry. They're supposed to make you feel unsure what you're seeing. Is it life, is it death, is it sex?'

'So they're snapshots. Literally half-told stories . . .'

'. . . laden with implication. Exactly.'

'Hmm,' I murmured. 'Explicit and inexplicit at the same time.'

'I'll take that as a compliment.' Ophelia paused and flicked through some images on the table behind where I was standing. 'I love the work of Guy Bourdin. Have you heard of him?'

I shook my head.

'He was a great fashion photographer. His images are seductive, voyeuristic – as if you're catching a glimpse of something you're not supposed to see. And often you're not sure exactly what you've seen.' She showed me a photograph of a partially open doorway through which a woman's torso, naked except for a sheer black bra, could be seen angled over the armrest of a chair. Her hair dropped downwards towards the floor and between her fingers, grazing the carpet, lay a bright pink flower. In the bottom right-hand corner of the frame, a man's finger was captured pressing the doorbell of the room. 'I mean, is it ecstasy or is it an assignation gone wrong? Who knows? But his shots often suggest something violent, something surreal. Some show women looking disturbingly like mannequins, perhaps even turning into mannequins.' Ophelia showed me a couple more images. In one, a mannequin's legs, seemingly amputated from below the knees, were clad in a pair of black stilettos and crossing a dark street. In another the same legs were climbing a set of stairs, wearing a pair of elegant grey high-heeled shoes. They looked bizarre. My face must have said it all.

'Yes, they're perverse,' said Ophelia. 'Glamour with a hint of danger. But fashion loves that combination. His images sold a lot of Charles Jourdan shoes in the 1970s.'

I turned to look at Ophelia's photographs once more. I could see the influence. Seductive but not easy to view. I looked at the sticky red substance dripping from the foot.

'The one on the end, with the red stilettos, is my own interpretation of the Red Shoes. You remember the fairy tale, don't you?'

I looked away from the picture as I tried to remember. I had known the story once but right now it escaped me.

'It's about a little girl who buys a pair of bright red shoes. But it turns out they're magical and dangerous and once she puts them on she can't take them off. They force her to dance and dance and dance. In the end she has to cut off her feet to remove them.'

I grimaced. 'That's nice.'

Ophelia nodded, beginning to laugh again. 'Cinderella has the same sort of thing. The ugly sisters cut off their toes to fit their feet into Cinders's shoes. Nothing like a bit of mutilation and violence for the sake of love.'

I stared at the red liquid dropping thickly down the foot in Ophelia's image and pooling at the bottom corner. I shivered involuntarily.

'Are you okay?'

'Yeah, I'm fine,' I lied. 'Just cold from the rain. Shall we go nearer to the fire?'

'Of course, I'm sorry. Let's sit down.'

I moved to the sofa and dropped heavily into the soft leather. It wrapped itself like a cocoon around my weary body. Ophelia sat down next to me and put her feet over my legs. I looked at the red shoes and paused for a second. A flash of bloody images crossed my brain but I blinked them away. One by one I slid the shoes off her feet slowly. They dropped to the floor soundlessly.

'Are you okay?' she asked again, settling herself into the sofa's cushions.

I nodded before swallowing deeply from my wine glass. The liquid slid smoothly down my throat and I felt something shift inside of me, something relax.

'So, tell me about today, then.'

I stroked Ophelia's left foot with my free hand and thought about my day. Where to begin? The story seemed to start underground.

'Tara found a room in the factory that we hadn't known existed. A cellar, not on any of the factory plans. The way to it, bizarrely enough, is through the storage cupboard in the room where we're working. From there, it's through an obscured doorway and down a dark flight of stairs.'

'Ooh. A Narnia-like entrance to another world?'

I was silent, thinking about that darkness once again.

'A hidden space, like a priest's hole?' Ophelia continued. I considered whether it might have been conceived as a secret place. It was possible but unlikely. 'I don't think it was specifically designed for that purpose although it's pretty well concealed. Now, at least. I think someone found it by chance and it became somewhere for them to go.'

'Hmm.' She nodded. 'So what was it like?'

I described the room and its contents briefly.

She raised her eyebrows at me. 'What a bizarre set-up – with the shoes and the note. It makes the mirror seem almost . . . shrine-like.' She took a sip of her wine. 'It has a feel of romance to it, don't you think?'

Maybe. I wasn't sure. And I had been thinking about it all day. But I was no closer to being able to explain the feeling I'd had. Or not adequately enough. 'There's something else,' I said. 'The room had a strange vibe.' I was quiet for a moment. 'I know that's not a very forensic way of putting it. But it just felt a little . . . off.'

'Off?'

'I really don't know how to describe it. It was similar to when you encounter something peculiar . . . when the hairs on the back of your neck stand up. You can't necessarily put your finger on what's triggered the reaction but you feel it. Unequivocally. You know what I mean?'

'I do.'

I looked down at the glass in my hand, at the deep plump redness of the wine. 'I couldn't shake the feeling of . . . of there being . . . something menacing, I suppose . . . I don't know if that makes any sense. But I felt it.' I paused. 'I think Tara felt the same thing, although we didn't talk about it explicitly.'

'So, did you feel threatened?'

'No.' I shook my head and then stopped. 'I don't think so, but it's difficult to say.' An image of the wooden stairs descending into darkness flashed across my mind and suddenly I could smell the room again. I blinked hard and took a large gulp of wine.

'Are you okay?' Ophelia was studying me.

'I'm fine.'

'It sounds strange and . . . unsettling.'

I nodded. 'It was. It even shut Tara up for the afternoon. And it takes a lot to do that.' We laughed and I shifted lower on my seat, trying to relax. But mentioning Tara made me think once more of the strong attraction that I had felt towards her in the room. Had she felt the same way towards me? I hadn't dared to ask. I looked at Ophelia who was staring at me intently and I felt a sudden rush of guilt. What had I been thinking? But that was just it. I hadn't been thinking anything. The feeling had appeared from nowhere. I closed my eyes and tried to clear my mind. But I couldn't. I kept picturing myself looking at the mirror, staring at its mottled surface. I was trying to see a reflection through the patchy darkness, the black and grey. But I couldn't see anything. I sighed and opened my eyes. The antique chandelier dangling from the ceiling was radiating watery light through its frosted glass droplets. 'I can't help feeling that I'm missing something,' I said at last. 'But I can't put my finger on what it is.'

'About the room, or the mirror, or what?'

'The mirror, I think. I just get the feeling that I'm not

seeing something.' I continued to watch the patterns of light flick across the ceiling.

'Can I take a look?' Ophelia's voice was quiet but purposeful.

'What?'

'At the mirror.' She paused. 'I'd like to see it.'

'Why?' My voice was calmer than I felt.

'I don't know. I'm intrigued.' She got up off the sofa and went to stand in front of the fire. Then she turned and faced me. 'So, what do you say?'

'I don't know.' I couldn't really think of a concrete reason to put her off. But I felt uncomfortable with the idea.

She was silent for a while, watching me. 'What is it? Why are you reticent?'

'I really don't know. Maybe it's what happened today. Perhaps I just feel a little jumpy. But I don't like the idea of involving you in it.'

I imagined the mirror large and looming on the wall of the underground room and anxiety rippled dully across my stomach. But at the same time I felt an uncertain excitement about seeing it again. And taking Ophelia with me. So what did that mean? I smiled to myself. It didn't mean anything. Except perhaps that I was going slowly mad.

'Hey, what's funny?'

'Oh, nothing. Just me,' I said, finishing off my wine. 'I think my brain has gone into overdrive today. Ignore me.' I put down my glass, pulled her to me and kissed her.

'So,' she said cajolingly, lying back down on the sofa, 'can we take a look sometime?'

I groaned. 'You're not going to let this one go, are you?'

She shook her head as she grinned at me. 'Come on. Humour me. You've sparked my curiosity. I really want to see it.'

'But why?'

'I don't know. I'd just like to see it. Come on . . .'

I looked at Ophelia's smiling face, her wide, curious eyes. And I felt I couldn't disappoint her. 'Okay, I'll take you to see it. I'm not saying when. But I promise I will take you.' Instantly, I felt the knot in my stomach, the one I hadn't even realised was there, unravel. I leaned forward and kissed her feet. Then my lips moved upwards, past her calves and inner thighs. I heard her sigh and felt her body shift under mine.

'Thank you,' she murmured. 'You won't be sorry.'

10

At some stage during the evening we moved from the sofa to the bedroom. Ophelia's hands sought out my face and pulled me to her. She kissed me intensely. Her breathing was quick and shallow. I unbuttoned her blouse and her bra and threw them onto the floor. She unbuckled my belt and pulled at my trouser buttons. For a few minutes we struggled to take off our clothes, and laughed at the collision of hands and teeth and lips. As I climbed on top of her, naked, I felt the softness of her skin beneath me, the swell of her breasts. She opened her legs and encased me, her feet pressing down against my back. As I pushed inside her, I heard myself groan, felt myself melt away. All thought and memory vanished. There was nothing left but feeling.

By eight o'clock the following morning I was heading back towards the factory. Dark clouds caught by the brisk wind scudded across the sky, bringing with them a cold, driving rain. I pulled up the collar of my coat and buried my face into it as I walked. The day was miserable, people ploughing through the wet, heads bowed, hastily dodging puddles and each other as they rushed to escape the weather. And yet, in spite of it all, I was upbeat and couldn't help smiling.

When I pushed open the inner doors of the factory, an intense smell of coffee greeted me. Tara, already at her desk, looked up and then pointed to her right, to a side table against the wall, on which rested what looked like a shiny new espresso machine.

'A small present for our humble offices.'

For a moment I simply stared. 'You didn't buy that, did you?' I managed eventually.

'No, of course not,' she replied dismissively, gesturing for me to sit down. 'I twisted Richard's arm, that's all.'

Her face was impossible to read as she said it but from her intonation I couldn't help thinking that there was something sexual about the comment. As I took off my coat and shook the rain from my hair, my head flooded with unwelcome images. I tried desperately to blink them away but they wouldn't budge. By the time I sat down, I had persuaded myself beyond any doubt that the coffee machine was a boon for some form of kinky encounter between them.

'Just an espresso, I presume?'

'That'd be great.'

I watched her as she fiddled with the machine. Clad in high ankle boots and skinny jeans, her legs seemed like they went on for ever. A tight-fitting black sweater similarly enhanced her upper body to perfection. Yet as I scrutinised her, there was a noticeable absence of the desire I had felt the previous day when I had been with her in the underground room. I was struck again by how inexplicable that had been.

Approaching my desk, she frowned as she offered me the coffee. 'Hang on a sec. I've never seen you arrive at work without an espresso in your hand. What happened?'

I reached for the cup and shrugged as nonchalantly as I could.

'Ah. Mr Carter,' she said in a tone of mock surprise and shock. 'You came a different route to work today, didn't pass your usual coffee shop.' She paused, smirking slightly, her eyes moving over me, no doubt registering the somewhat crumpled shirt that I'd worn the day before, the same pair of jeans and trainers.

'Okay, Tara.' I said it as sternly as I could, trying to indicate that this subject would not be discussed.

'I'm just saying, that's all.' She raised her hands in a gesture of surrender, then turned and made her way back to her own desk.

I watched her go, took in the slow deliberate walk, presumably cultivated from years of having the stares of men upon her. And in spite of myself, I found that I was smiling. She was funny, I'd give her that. I took a large mouthful of espresso, savouring its strong bitter taste, and turned back to the paperwork on my desk.

A couple of hours later I emerged from my drawings. I dropped my pencil on the desk, stretched my arms above my head and yawned. Turning towards Tara, I saw her quietly tapping away at her computer. 'What are you up to?'

She sighed. 'Inputting the inventory data I've listed so far. There's so much stuff here that it could get out of hand if I don't stay on top of it.'

'I'll bet.'

'And you?'

I looked at the vague designs spread out over my desk and wondered if she would be interested in looking over what I'd done. I had a feeling that her criticism would be damning – her ability to dismiss was legendary. But somehow today I felt I had the strength to take it on. As I thought about Ophelia again, I was hit by an intense memory of her body, the vivid recollection of the taste and smell of her skin. I waited for it to pass and then forced myself to refocus. 'Come and take a look, if you like?'

'I'd love to,' she said. She stood and moved over to my desk.

'I've only been thinking about things fairly abstractly,' I started, picking up the pencil resting on top of the pile of sketches, 'but I know that the client's big thing is light, and bringing as much of it as possible into the building. I think he envisages a great white dazzling space. Which no doubt could be beautiful.' I pointed with the pencil to the pitched roof shown in my first drawing. 'So that's easy on the top floor. I thought that it'd be cool to run glass panels along each side of the roof pitch, and intersperse them with white powder-coated steel. Something like that.

It'll flood the upper floor with light and give it different textures.'

I watched her eyes flick over the drawing, her head nodding.

'And on this one,' I pushed another piece of paper towards her, 'I've added a mezzanine to the top floor. The client said he'd love to have something like that, for a bed or some kind of quiet space. I've used a metal spiral staircase to connect the mezzanine to the top floor, reflecting the material of the old machines, a couple of which, the smaller ones maybe, I was thinking we could showcase on this floor; in niches or alcoves with some light funnelled down onto them.'

'Hmm. I like this,' Tara said, tapping her fingers over the drawings. 'I remember Richard working on a project a couple of years ago that used similar ideas to maximise the roof light.'

'Was that the launderette conversion in North London?'

Tara nodded and smiled.

I, however, grimaced. 'I really hated that project. The place was unbelievably dismal.'

'Not by the time you'd finished with it.' And she winked at me before looking down again at the drawings. 'You could also use some light tunnels from the top floor to bring light down to the first and ground floors.'

'Yeah. I thought about that. They're a great feature. And the lower floors have windows running along the outer walls on both sides so light really shouldn't be too much of a problem.'

Tara turned towards me, smiling. 'I really loved your Suffolk country-house extension, by the way. I heard that light really was a big problem there.'

'Right,' I said, surprised that she knew about it. 'That was a few years before you joined the practice, wasn't it?'

Tara nodded. 'Richard took me to see it recently. I think he's incredibly proud of your modern glass cube. And that it sits comfortably next to a very traditional turn-of-the-century farmhouse.'

I stared at her for a moment, trying to work out if Richard routinely took all our associates on forays into the English countryside to view our past projects or whether, as was far more likely, it was just Tara. Uncomfortable, I decided to skip over the confession, if that was what it was. 'Of course, the design was born out of practicality as much as aesthetics. The house was in shadow for the whole of winter because the sun didn't climb above the top of the forest that lay behind it. So we needed to steal as much light from outside as we could.'

'Well, it's very beautiful,' she said, looking down at my notepad on the table. 'Who's Ophelia, by the way?'

'What?' I said, shocked by the question.

'Ophelia,' Tara repeated, tapping her finger against a pencil doodle of the name on my notepad. I stared at it for a moment, stunned. Then I saw next to it, on the corner of the sheet, the pencil sketching I'd made the day before of the lettering on the mirror in the underground room – the intertwined T and M and the ornate H. I really needed to get a grip on my unconscious drawing habit. 'Who is she?'

'A fashion photographer,' I replied, deciding that it was probably better to give Tara something than have her question fruitlessly and therefore speculate.

She mouthed a mocking 'Wow!' at me and then smiled.

I couldn't help but smile back.

'And I take it you met her recently?'

I nodded and filled her in with the sparsest of details about how we met.

'Hmm,' she said again, the sound embodying scepticism.

'What is it?'

'Well, nothing good ever came from hooking up with someone you met in a park.'

'It didn't?'

'Nooooooo. Definitely not.' Tara paused. 'She's not a weirdo, is she? Hanging around green spaces, giving out implausible stories to strangers about lost camera lenses and waiting to entrap the most hapless of them into futile searches.'

I smiled and her laughing eyes smiled back.

'Well, so far she doesn't seem to be a freak,' I said.

'That sounds promising. But you wait. When you least expect it she may morph into just the lunatic you didn't expect, fucked up by all her parents' failings.'

I laughed but even as I did I remembered the story of Ophelia's mother and father. As she had said, their loss had affected her in a deep, painful way and its repercussions could still be felt. It was just that I hadn't so far been privy to those repercussions. But no doubt I would be in the future.

'Another coffee?' Tara called over her shoulder. She had turned and was walking back towards her desk, already moving on.

But the thought she had awoken sat uncomfortably with me for the rest of the day.

11

The first thing I became conscious of was the darkness, a blanket of heaviness around my shoulders. I was standing upright, that much I was aware of, but beyond that I couldn't tell. I turned from one side to the other, trying to see. But the blackness was total. I had no idea where I was. I tried to remember the last thing I had done, the last place I had been. But my mind was a blank.

It was then that I heard the sound. At first it seemed to come from far away, a faint noise, an echo of a woman's laugh. It moved gently around me and then disappeared. A moment later, it returned. Louder and nearer. Then it vanished once more. Seconds, minutes perhaps, passed in silence. I reached forwards into the darkness before me but I could feel nothing. Where was I? Fear had just begun to form a hard knot in my stomach when a faint light became visible. I blinked, unable at first to make anything out. But gradually it became clearer.

I was in a small room, with a low ceiling and an earth floor. A man was sitting in an armchair in the corner of the room. A candle, resting on the floor beside him, lit him from beneath. His head was inclined downwards, face obscured, his attention absorbed by what he held in the fingers of his right hand: a leather shoe with an ankle strap. Its style was old-fashioned, its leather dark green, the pointed toes matching the arc of the heel. It might have been embroidered with a paler thread, but as the light was dim I couldn't see for sure. For I don't know how long, the man sat in silence, his gaze held fast by the subtle movement of the shoe as he rocked it gently back and forth. Back and forth, back and forth, marking time in the half-light. Suddenly he hunched forward in the chair and cupped the shoe easily in his palms. I looked at him, at his large, rough hands softly cradling their precious cargo. But nothing about him was familiar.

Turning to my right, I caught sight of a doorway in the corner of the room leading away into pitch darkness. I couldn't remember coming through it or walking down the passageway beyond. So how had I come to be here? I looked down at my feet, at the earth floor beneath them, as if somehow they could provide me with the answer. Nothing came back but silence and the subtle smell of the damp ground.

I shivered, suddenly cold. Something about this place didn't feel right. Turning towards the doorway, I caught sight of a large mirror on the wall next to it. The silver glass was mottled with age, dark cobwebbed scars spreading out below its surface. Taking a step towards it, I searched for an image of myself through the darkness. Nothing. I took a step closer and looked deeper. But I couldn't see anything.

A sudden thud behind me made me jump. The man

had dropped the shoe to the floor where it lay on its side in the dirt. To the left of the shoe, I now noticed the corner of a bed. Upon its mattress, I could see a pair of woman's legs from the calves down to the feet. Moving to my right, I tried to get a better view of the woman. But no matter how much I turned, how much I moved, the perspective didn't change. I could see only her calves and feet and only from a certain angle. I stepped backwards, confused. It didn't make any sense. If I moved one way or the other, I ought to be able to see more to the left or right. I tried again. This time the candlelight flickered and suddenly the middle section of the bed was revealed. I could see a pair of pale thighs, the tops of which were roughly covered over with a white slip. I took another step forwards and as I moved the perspective changed again. The woman's torso came into view, the white slip tight over her stomach and breasts with tiny straps over her shoulders. It lay in folds at her armpits and her right arm fell, loose yet unmoving, off the bed to the floor, where her fingers grazed the dirt. Her left arm was flung backwards, seemingly behind her head, although I couldn't see that far. Her neck was slender and her collarbone stood out in the candlelight casting shadows over her pale skin. Something else, long and dark, was hanging loosely around her neck. But it didn't look like a necklace. It was too plain and the way it fell in cascades over her skin was too much like the folds of material. I looked harder, leaned in towards her, and realised that it was a green velvet ribbon.

As I was poised to take a final step forward, before I saw the woman's face, I looked back at the man. He was mumbling to himself, wringing his hands, and growing increasingly agitated. Suddenly he looked up. His eyes were puffy but catching sight of me they grew narrow and hostile.

'What do you think you're doing?' he said. His voice was low, indignant, the lines at the edges of his mouth hard. 'You're not supposed to be here.' He looked for a moment to his right, at the woman's feet. Then his gaze returned to me. 'What are you doing here?' he said again.

I opened my mouth to speak but then closed it. I didn't know how I'd got here, what I was doing or indeed where 'here' was. A cold sense of dread gathered at the base of my spine.

The man stood up. He was tall, much taller than me, his head almost grazing the low ceiling. He was dressed in an old-fashioned black suit, the trouser buttons of which were undone. He fastened them hurriedly and rearranged his waistcoat and jacket. Then he began to move towards me. His big hands swung casually at his sides as he walked. The movement was innocent enough and yet I felt a jolt of fear. Sweat beads pricked my upper lip as he drew level with me.

'Do you know who I am?' His dark eyes looked at me searchingly. Their irises were almost black.

I shook my head and turned away. I saw the doorway once more and regret ricocheted through me. I should have tried to get out of this place when I had the chance.

'You know I can't let you go,' he said. 'You know that, don't you?' He was so close to me now that his hot breath stuck to my cheek. 'It would be foolish of me, wouldn't it? After everything you've seen.'

I tried again to speak but still the words wouldn't come. I wanted to tell him that he was mistaken, that I hadn't seen anything. But the words caught in my throat, unspoken.

I took a step backwards and my foot hit the wall. My body followed and my head came to rest against the surface of the mirror.

'Going somewhere?' he said and then laughed.

Fear escalated inside me. I drew a deep breath, closed my eyes and tried to clear my mind. I knew there was a way out. There had to be. But the knowledge tumbled uncaught through my mind.

I heard the man's quiet words close to my ear. 'There's only one place you're going.'

And then I felt it. The intense struggle to breathe. I gasped, felt the pain in my chest as my lungs fought for air. I was suffocating in this darkness, in silence. As my body shuddered and everything around me turned black I experienced the sensation of falling. But I couldn't be falling, I thought, the wall was behind me. And yet I fell, consumed by the mirror, the room, and the darkness. So this is it, I thought. I am falling backwards towards the earth, falling towards death.

As I was about to hit the floor I felt the man's breath on my face once more, waited to hear his words close to my ear. But instead of his voice another pierced the darkness. Unexpected, dulcet. A woman's.

'Johnny,' it said quietly. 'Wake up.'

I opened my eyes, took a staccato breath and then sat upright. It was still dark around me, the day not quite having broken. But I could feel without seeing it that my body was drenched in sweat. It took me a moment to place where I was. But then the memories of coming over to Ophelia's the night before flooded back. I turned towards her body, lying beside me, convinced that it had been her voice that had woken me. But her silent, unmoving form told me otherwise. The alarm clock on the table beside her was flashing six o'clock. I breathed in and out deeply and lay back down. Then I heard Ophelia stir.

'You okay?' Her voice was groggy with sleep, not at all the clear voice that had brought me out of my nightmare.

'I'm fine. Just a bad dream. Go back to sleep.'

She was silent for a moment. Then she rolled towards me and propped herself on her side. 'What kind of bad dream?'

'A strange one.' I stared towards the ceiling. 'I was in a small room, dark and claustrophobic. It was the underground room at the factory, I'm pretty sure. I was watching a man play with a green shoe in his hands. I don't know what the significance of that was or if in fact there was any significance at all.' I paused for a moment, wondering if the shoe was, in fact, one of those from the factory. Old-fashioned, green. Most likely it was. 'Anyway, when the man caught sight of me, he got really angry. I was clearly not supposed to be there. And because I was there, I knew that I was going to die in that room.' My words were sucked into the dark, hovering silence. 'I felt tightness in my chest, something like suffocation, and then I was falling to the ground, to my death.' The intense pre-dawn quiet seemed to shift up a notch. I could hear my own uneven breath; Ophelia's was light and regular beside me. 'Then I woke up.'

Pause. 'So you didn't actually die in the dream?'

'No. I didn't die. But I knew that I was going to.'

Ophelia was silent.

'And to make matters worse, I couldn't get out of that place. In short, I was fucked. It was the typical nightmare scenario.'

Ophelia quietly put her hand on my chest. I could feel my heart beating fast against my ribcage.

'And this man from the dream – did you know who he was?'

'I'd never seen him before. But there was something about his eyes, something dark, unnatural. That was one of the things that was so terrifying about it.'

Ophelia shivered slightly by my side and shifted closer. I felt her legs brush against me, then her feet touched mine. Suddenly, I remembered.

'There were feet.'

'Feet? Well, that doesn't sound very scary.'

I smiled for the first time into the darkness. 'I could see a pair of legs on the edge of a bed, from the calves down to the feet. For a long time, that was all I could see. Just feet and legs, disembodied. Then, eventually, they panned out into a woman. But I couldn't see her face.'

Ophelia was quiet for a second.

'Was there any reason why the feet and legs in particular should have been in the dream? I mean, did they have any relevance?'

I tried to remember if there was anything distinctive about them. But I couldn't recall anything. I shook my head. 'No.'

'Then perhaps the legs were just a hang-up from our conversation the other night – about my work and Bourdin and that sort of thing. The cropped fashion legs. Maybe it's that?'

I nodded slowly. Now that I thought about it, it made sense. Still, it didn't help dispel my underlying sense of unease. I tried to breathe the vague anxiety away. But I couldn't. So instead I turned onto my side and faced Ophelia.

'It sounds to me as if this dream is a collage of the things that have been bothering you,' she said. 'The underground room and the things in it, the shoes and the bed, the images you saw at my flat. It got stored in your subconscious, jumbled up and played out in this way. Don't you think?'

'Yes, I'm sure you're right.' I closed my eyes once more. But after a moment the man's face formed again in my mind. I opened my eyes, blinked, and the image evaporated. 'I'm sure you're right,' I said again, as much to myself as to her.

Unwilling now to encourage sleep, I watched the dawn slowly breaking, transforming the bedroom into a twilight world of shadow. Long stealthy fingers of light crept underneath the curtains at the windows, mottling the walls as they shifted and dispersed the darkness. As I watched the moving patterns of light and dark I remembered the mirror.

'Anything else you want to tell me?' Ophelia's voice was a whisper.

I hesitated. Should I tell her that the mirror in the factory was also the mirror from my dream? Surely that would only pique her interest, make her even more desperate to see it. I made a snap decision. 'No,' I said, kissing her on the lips. 'There's nothing else.'

A couple of hours later I was heading back to the factory, feeling a little more like myself. But my mind remained unsettled by the nightmare. It was still early when I unlocked the doors of the dispatch room and the inside of the factory was dismal and dark. I switched on the lights and watched the fluorescent tubes flicker to life, dispersing winter shadows. I put my bag down on my desk and pulled out my work camera. It was a simple digital one that I used to take photographs of spaces before, during and after renovation. I turned the dial to the feature that would give good results in dimly lit conditions and slung it round my neck. Then I dug out two candles from the storage cupboard where Tara had left them and looked once more for the concealed door. I pulled it open, hearing as I did the soft groan of escaping air. It possessed the same fustiness as it had the last time. I looked down the staircase, into the utter darkness beyond, and considered abandoning my plan. But that would be ridiculous, I told myself. There was nothing to be afraid of. I took a step forward and began my descent.

A couple of minutes later, the candles were positioned on the floor at each end of the mirror and my eyes were growing accustomed to the dim light. No doubt about it, I thought, as I turned around and surveyed the room. This was the scene of my dream. My stomach formed a tight knot of disquiet.

I walked over to the edge of the bed and pressed down on the mattress. It was about half the thickness of the contemporary style and there were no signs of any box springs. I was sure it was Victorian, in keeping with the early history of the building. I looked more closely at the edge of the bed which had supported the legs in my dream. Now all that was visible there were ancient signs of rust upon the mattress, the same markings as those that were present on the metallic stand. I sighed and sat down. Despite its appearance and apparent dilapidation it actually felt quite sturdy. I bounced a couple of times on the frame and let out a short, quiet laugh. I looked around me, taking in the dilapidated nature of the room, the flaking paintwork on the wall beside me behind the armchair, the expanse of crumbled plasterwork on the wall below the mirror, exposing the wooden laths beneath. What the hell was I doing down here? The sooner I got this over with the better.

I stood up abruptly and positioned myself with the camera in front of the mirror. I wanted to get a clear, full picture of its overall size and shape and then close-ups of its surface and the corners with the letter markings. The candle flames rose tall and straight, steady in the absence of any draughts through the room, and cast a consistent glow over the mirror's surface. For a few minutes I snapped away until I was satisfied that I had produced at least some passable images. Then I went to pick up the candles and head back up the stairs. I stopped for a moment to look at the mirror as I had when I was last here. But this time I simply scanned its surface. The green shoes suspended over its left-hand corner, the note, white against the darkness, the faded lettering. Then I headed swiftly for the staircase. I needed to get back upstairs, I told myself, needed to get back to the task of designing the new factory layout.

A smaller voice inside me also whispered quietly. I needed to leave that darkness behind.

12

Chateau de Saint-Germain-en-Laye

July 1550

Catherine walked slowly through the darkening palace, her bare feet moving quietly over the parquet floors, amidst the settling shadows. Evening was approaching but she had only recently risen from her bed. She wore a richly embroidered dressing gown, the faint rustle of its black and gold silk, dragging along the floor behind her, the only sound that betrayed her presence. After a few minutes she was tired, out of breath, and paused to regain her composure. She could feel her body, bloated and heavy beneath the gown. Her fifth child, Charles-Maximilien, had been born only a few days earlier and she should have been resting. But she would not miss this spectacle for the world. She smiled at the thought of it and set off once again, her still-swollen feet bearing her closer to her destination. As she moved, she could feel herself almost salivating, so desperate was she to taste the humiliation of Henri's mistress. At the same time she wanted to wallow in the teasing delight of anticipation, to savour each and every moment of it.

Reaching an intersection she turned left and moved along the passageway. Before she reached the end of it she stopped. The entrance to the apartment was just around the corner. She listened intently, but she could hear nothing from the corridor beyond. Yet something told her to remain still, to wait. And then it came. Her smell. The odour of musk and rose-water, faint but present nonetheless. The King's mistress was there, just around the corner, sitting silently in wait. Catherine smiled and retraced her steps. Taking a key from the pocket of her gown she unlocked a nearby door and slipped through it. She found herself in a part of the palace that she had never visited before, an old storage room next to the apartment of Lady Flemyng, the Scottish governess. Lit candles had been placed upon the furniture that was there and a chair filled with cushions leaned against the far wall. So Catherine's ladies had been here already. She crossed the room, careful not to make any noise, and sat down. Instantly she felt relief, her limbs suddenly unburdened of her weight. Then she looked for the small hole that she had requested should be made in the wall.

Finding it, she moved her eye to the opening to take a look. The gesture triggered a memory that flashed unbidden across her mind. Her husband together with his older mistress. White limbs, slim and languid, intertwined with those of Henri, red lips, the sound of pleasure and passion and abandonment. She closed her eyes but she could still hear their decadent noise. It had been a long time, perhaps seven years, perhaps more, since she had spied upon this woman last. And yet the image which came uninvited into her mind was still so fresh, their unfettered noise so familiar. She opened her eyes and sat quietly for a moment chastising herself. This was no time to indulge in persecutory daydreams. This was a time to take consolation, to revel in the bitterness that her rival must now swallow.

Catherine returned her eye to the hole and focused on the corridor beyond. She blinked a couple of times until she could make out a woman's shadowy form sitting outside the doorway of the apartment. A smile played once more on Catherine's lips. Her hunger for the debasement of this woman was acute. But, as so often, she swallowed down the wanting and waited. Silence reigned. Catherine listened for sounds from the adjacent room. She could hear nothing but her heart twisted darkly in her chest as she imagined her husband together with Janet Flemyng, all flaming hair, pale skin and indiscreet laughter. She felt her jealousy bite, hot, black and poisonous as she pictured the scene. Yet this was nothing to endure, compared with the older mistress's continued dominance in all things.

Catherine looked upon the figure in the growing darkness of the corridor. That woman's composure was legendary and she looked serene in her present stillness. But Catherine knew that, in this moment, even she must be consumed with jealousy, with fear of this younger beauty who challenged her long-established pre-eminence. Catherine longed to see the mistress's eyes, to see the anguish reflected there, to see her share the emotions that ate the Queen of France alive day after day. In that moment, as Catherine looked through the hole in the wall, all her jubilant hatred was directed at this woman.

The sound of a door opening stirred both women. Catherine saw her rival stand, ready to confront whoever emerged from the room next door. For a moment there was the sound of two men deep in conversation. Then a subdued silence fell over the corridor. Catherine kept her eye firmly on the woman.

She heard a man's voice, the King's, finally pierce the silence. 'Duchess, what are you doing here?' His tone was full of surprise and embarrassment. Catherine knew that he imagined his mistress to be at her palace at Anet. He was unaware that when news of his dalliance had become known she had returned to Saint-Germain.

'I could ask the same of Your Majesty,' the woman uttered sharply in reply.

Catherine heard Henri mumble indistinctly, catching only the words 'talking to the governess' and 'there was nothing evil in it', and she smiled at the lame retort. She watched the woman, imagining the anger and mortification broiling inside her, and the urge to laugh out loud, to clap her hands and revel in the Duchess's pain, was almost too much to bear. But she contained herself.

The Duchess, however, could keep her composure no longer. Her voice was high and strained as she diverted her venom towards the King's companion, the Constable of France. 'Montmorency, how you disgrace yourself and betray your friends at Court. How could you encourage the King in this dishonourable liaison?' The Duchess took a breath and continued, her tone savage, 'It is not only shameful but impolitic conduct as you jeopardise the union of the King's son. He is to marry the child who has that woman for a governess. And now, after all, she is being raised by nothing better than a whore . . .'

She railed into the darkness while Catherine watched, eyes wide, transfixed by the display, only half listening to the spitting words of admonishment. She had never seen the woman lose control of herself, never heard her raise her voice. She heard the King's muted attempt at appeasement but it seemed only to fuel his mistress's fervour. Catherine drank down her incandescent fury, her hurt and betrayal. She smelled the Duchess's fear and inhaled it deeply. Slowly the insults diminished and the heat of the argument subsided.

'I wish neither to see you again in my path,' the Duchess declaimed in a parting shot to Montmorency, 'nor should you address a single word to me in the future.' With that she stalked away down the corridor, pursued by the King and, a few paces behind him, by the flustered Constable.

Silence seeped back into the vacuum left by the Duchess's loud, angry words. For a long moment Catherine continued to stare through the hole in the wall. Then, abruptly, she turned and slumped into the chair. Her body was on fire and she experienced a brief moment of relief as she felt the plump comfort of the cushions beneath her. Then, as she sat alone in the quiet of the candlelit room, a tear slid slowly down her cheek.

For this victory was a small one. She knew that now. No doubt it had been sweet to witness the mortification of the Duchess, but the sweetness was short-lived. It was not enough. It would never be enough. For that woman would suffer only a fraction of what Catherine suffered every day. The Duchess's pain would be transitory. The King, embarrassed by the exposure of his errant conduct, would reconcile with her and his dalliance would be forgiven. The woman's supremacy would ultimately remain untouched. In the end, it had all been for nothing.

Catherine rose, a bitter taste in her mouth. She breathed in deeply and then exhaled, trying to expel the sourness of her breath, and moved across the room towards the doorway, extinguishing the candles as she went. She was destined, it seemed, to be always thwarted, always defeated by that woman. There had been a time when, after the birth of her first child, she had fantasised that her own growing power and influence over the King might prove sufficient to dislodge the mistress from her position of authority. But it had not been so. With time the Duchess's influence, rather than waning, had only increased. Catherine felt her stomach churn with fury at the thought of it.

As she approached the far wall, she caught sight of her reflection in a mirror hanging there. She saw a face, swollen, thick about the neck and jowls, protruding eyes, fat lips. Her eyes widened as she studied herself and then, with a swift movement, she blew out the last candle in front of the mirror.

Standing in the darkness, she wondered whether it was in fact her face that she had seen. It did not seem to be hers. It was so far from the image that she longed to have – indeed, that she did have of herself. She thought of Henri's beautiful mistress again, supreme to the end, and imagined her reflection in the darkened glass.

The dull aching rage rose once more in her stomach. And as Catherine stepped out into the quiet night of the corridor she knew that, above all things, she would not rest until the Duchess was dead.

13

On Monday morning I arrived at the Shoreditch office well ahead of time for my meeting with Richard and Tara. I had to admit that I wasn't in the mood for it at all. But Richard loved to have regular project meetings even if there wasn't much progress to discuss. It was no doubt something to do with good management that I didn't even begin to understand. I preferred to just get on with it. Except that at the moment I didn't even want to do that. Since my nightmare, I was even more preoccupied than before with the underground room.

As I sat at my desk, half-heartedly catching up on admin, I saw Tara on the opposite side of the floor. She smiled and made her way over.

'Hi,' I said with as much enthusiasm as I could muster as she came to a stop in front of my desk.

'Hi yourself,' she said raising an eyebrow at me. 'Are you all right? You look shattered.'

'And Richard's meeting hasn't even begun yet.' I gave her a wry look. 'Seriously, though, I haven't been sleeping well.'

'Yeah? I'm sorry.' And Tara smiled in such a sympathetic

way that my usual barriers to sharing information gave way. Before I knew it I was giving her the abbreviated version of my nightmare.

'Ophelia's take on it was that it was all to do with the underground room and the things in it. They'd all become stored uncomfortably in my subconscious and chose this way to re-emerge.' I looked at Tara hopefully, wondering if she would agree. But instead I saw a frown cross her face.

'Wait a second,' she said, raising her hand. 'Just wait one second.'

I stared at her, waiting as instructed, wondering what was suddenly wrong.

'So you told Ophelia about the underground room?'

I nodded, not understanding.

'You told her.' The statement, no longer a question, still sounded like a challenge.

I nodded, more slowly this time, starting to grasp why she was becoming irate.

'When you specifically asked me not to tell anyone?' Then, lowering her voice, 'And one person in particular.'

I looked at Tara's face, her blue eyes narrowed, lips tight and thin. She was clearly furious.

'Yet you get to tell some random woman you met in the park a few days before.'

'Well, it's not quite like that . . .' I stopped, realising that this probably wasn't the best approach to take. 'I'm sorry, I wasn't thinking.'

Tara glared at me before turning on her heels and taking off in the direction of her desk.

I watched her stride away, feeling several sets of eyes upon me: people who had no doubt overheard the exchange. As I looked down, embarrassed, shuffling papers around my desk, I felt a stab of guilt. She was right to be angry. Without a second thought I had told Ophelia about the room and its contents and yet I had sworn Tara to secrecy on the subject. More than that, I had implicitly asked her not to mention it to Richard, who, it was looking increasingly likely, was the one person she might want to talk to about it. As I thought about it now, I couldn't work out why I'd done that. It didn't make any sense. And yet, if I was honest, I would still have preferred that he didn't know. I contemplated the matter for a few more minutes but it didn't become any clearer. What was obvious, however, was that I needed to clear the air. I got up and headed over to Tara's side of the office. I would make a heartfelt apology. I would grovel and get things back on an even keel. I would say that she could tell whoever she wanted to about the room. But when I reached her desk it was empty.

Half an hour later, I was sitting opposite Richard in his office. He was telling a story about something that had happened at the opera with his wife, a story that he clearly found highly amusing. But I was tense, preoccupied and only listening vaguely. I turned in my chair and looked again at the clock above the door. It was probably the fifth time I'd done it since I entered the room. Tara was fifteen minutes late for the meeting and there was still no sign of her. I felt a burgeoning guilt and, simultaneously, given the tenor of Richard's tale, growing annoyance with him on her behalf.

Before he'd reached the punchline, the door of his office swung open and Tara made her entrance, striding across the room, her cheeks flushed and expression purposeful. If anything, she looked more driven, more beautiful than usual. Anger obviously became her. I noticed that Richard abruptly abandoned the story of his wife and busied himself instead with the papers on his desk. As Tara sat down in the chair next to mine, she refused to meet my eye.

'So how's it going?' Richard said, looking from one to the other of us, smiling that easy smile of his.

'Fine,' I said neutrally.

'Fine,' Tara echoed.

'You've had a few initial thoughts, I understand.'

As I talked Richard through the first drawings I'd done and the potential designs I had in mind, I noticed Tara's left foot tapping impatiently against the office floor. I imagined her blue eyes flashing with barely contained rage. To try to defuse the situation I resorted to platitudes. 'Tara has had some great ideas, too,' I added.

Richard smiled. 'That's excellent.'

Tara nodded but didn't speak.

We talked through some more ideas. Richard suggested that I should have a word with various people in the office about new designs they were working on, and just as I thought that the meeting would wind up without major incident, Tara spoke.

'Perhaps we should also ask Ophelia for her thoughts. After all, she is privy to quite a lot of information.' For the first time, Tara turned and glared at me.

The look wasn't lost on Richard and the smile faded slowly from his face. 'Who's Ophelia?'

'It doesn't matter,' I said, closing my eyes and trying for a second to pretend this wasn't actually happening. 'It's irrelevant. Anyway, talk to me about the time frame. What are we really looking at in terms of drawings for a client meeting?'

Richard, clearly confused, looked from me to Tara and then back again. Deciding it was better to drop the issue, he indicated that we had three to four weeks to work up decent preliminary designs. 'Does that sound doable?'

I nodded. 'That sounds fine.'

'Tara?'

'Sure, that's good. I can finish the inventory and help Johnny work up his drawings. As long as he doesn't give me too much extraneous research to do.' And she turned and gave me that look again.

Before I could react, Richard was on it. 'Tara, that's enough.' He didn't raise his voice and yet it rang with authority. His smile had faded and he'd grown stern and challenging. I doubted that even Tara in her provocative mood would carry on now. 'Is there a problem here?' he continued.

I watched him, filled with something akin to admiration. He just wasn't one of those men you wanted to butt up against. You felt it instinctively. If you took him on you would lose. Even if you didn't lose the actual argument you would nonetheless lose something more intangible, more precious. There would be a withdrawal of collaboration or respect or approval. Somehow the contemplation of that was even worse than not winning the argument. It was invariably easier to back down.

Tara studied him for a moment, weighing up her options, and then her attitude simply evaporated. 'No, Richard,' she said, 'There's no problem, just a misunderstanding. I apologise.'

'Good, I'm glad to hear it. There's too much at stake here to allow personal issues to get in the way.' He laid stress on the word 'personal' in a way that wasn't lost on me.

The meeting continued for another ten minutes or so, but I could hardly focus or keep a thought in my head. Tara was the first to jump up and exit the room and I would have happily followed if Richard hadn't cornered me.

'So, interesting meet.' He was smiling and had regained his usual cool demeanour but I knew that underneath he was still bothered by Tara's outburst.

I nodded and shrugged my shoulders. 'It's nothing, Richard.'

'Maybe,' he said in a way that implied he didn't think so at all. 'But you shouldn't let her talk to you like that, Johnny. It's unprofessional.'

'Yeah, I guess. But it's her way, with me at least. I guess I don't quite have your gravitas.' While I didn't mean it to, this came out sounding somewhat snide.

Richard frowned. 'What's going on?'

'Nothing.' I laughed. 'Seriously, Richard. Like Tara said, it was just a misunderstanding.' As I thought about opening up fully about it, I realised that I couldn't. Or, at least, not without telling him about the underground room or that I'd asked Tara not to tell him about it. And I really didn't want to disclose either of those things. I closed my eyes, wondering how it had grown so complicated.

'And who's Ophelia?'

I thought about that for a second. 'She's my girlfriend,' I responded, seeing how the words rolled off my tongue.

'I see. And Tara has a problem with her?'

'No, Richard, it's not like that.' Although, strictly speaking, it *was* a little like that.

'Is there anything going on, Johnny?'

It was then that I knew for certain that he was jealous. The argument between Tara and me smacked to him of something more than it was. And being vague about its cause only compounded that for him. 'No, Richard, there's nothing going on. Nothing at all. It's purely a misunderstanding about work and that's it. It won't happen again,' I said with finality, more finality than I felt. But I wanted more than anything to kill this thing and get out of there.

Richard stared at me for a moment. 'Okay,' he said, clearly also wanting to move on. 'Sounds like we're all overreacting.' He smiled then but there wasn't any warmth to it.

I had almost made it to the door when he called out. 'Johnny.'

I turned to face him.

'We're not going to have a problem, are we?'

I stared at him. 'What do you mean?'

'Any flaky behaviour. The kind of stuff we've seen over the last few months.' Pause. 'Because this project is too big and important for any fuck-ups. And there are loads of other people dying to work on it.'

As I looked at him then, I felt my heart turning cold. 'No, Richard. There's not going to be any problem.'

I turned on my heel without waiting for him to respond, hating him in that moment for his thinly veiled threats. He reminded me so vividly of my brother, the last few times I had seen him, his reproaches and criticisms springing from an underground well of jealousy. I tried to focus on the rhythm of my feet crossing the office floor, pounding down the stairs towards the exit to the street. But my head was already filling with thoughts of my wife and her infidelity. I remembered the way it had touched and polluted every part of me, made me crazy and erratic, questioning myself and everything around me. More than anything I didn't want to feel that way again.

But as I pushed open the office door, heading out into the grey wetness of the day, that almost forgotten feeling – sick, powerless, evil – rose in my stomach once again.

14

I made a detour on my way back from the office to the factory. No doubt about it, I was putting off having to face Tara again. But, more than that, it was something that I felt I needed to do.

Instead of heading north off Old Street at the junction with Clerkenwell Road, I carried on walking. Dense clouds bloomed across the sky and rain was falling, cold and continuous. Cars sped through murky puddles, rear-ranging dirt across the city, and double-decker buses belched diesel fumes into the day. Dilapidated hoardings flapped with remnants of out-of-date adverts. They looked as grey, as jaded as the landscape. I shivered, buried my head further into the lapel of my coat and picked up the pace.

Reaching Hatton Garden I took a swift left turn and about halfway down headed right towards the familiar shopfront. The copper bell jangled from a string above my head as I pushed open the door. Stepping inside, into the dim interior, I was assaulted by the smell of beeswax and mothballs. The air was stuffy and smelt of age but after the chill of the outside and the cold discord of my morning it was homely and comforting, a welcome relief. As every conceivable space was crammed with furniture, I picked my way slowly across the shop floor, stepping behind a Louis XIV dresser, in front of a luxurious chaise longue, past a nineteenth-century washstand. I walked under Venetian crystal chandeliers, past the terrifying stuffed head of a wild boar, over mouldering Turkish and Moroccan rugs and eventually made it to the counter. That too was hidden beneath a jumble of paper and pens, numerous books and old tomes, a prehistoric-looking computer which I knew doubled as a cataloguer. Directly in front of me, a pile of cards to the side of the cash till told me that I was in the establishment of Alexander & Sons, Quality Antique Furnishings since 1919. I looked around, waiting, taking in the beautiful and eclectic pieces this place had developed a reputation for. Their style might be chaotic but the Alexanders could find you practically anything you wanted. And the knowledge of old Mr Alexander, not the founding father but his son, was unparalleled. When after five minutes there was still no sign of anyone I rang the bell, also located on the desk in front of me. Before the echo had rung itself out I heard sounds emanating from the back room: the screech of a chair moving against floorboards and a subsequent scuffle of feet.

'Just a moment.'

Even though I'd been expecting it, the tone of the voice still surprised me, sounding as it did like that of a man at least a hundred years old: soft, slightly cracking around the edges, yet at the same time imbued with a certainty and knowledge.

The second time it came, it was no more than a breath or a whisper, as if said more to himself than to me, 'I'll be with you in a moment.'

The shuffling grew louder until it reached the open doorway connecting the front of the shop to the rear. Then I heard the tinkle of the strings of glass droplets marking the partition and suddenly a tiny man stood in front of me. He couldn't have been more than four feet, ten inches tall and his frame was incredibly slight. Even clad in an old khaki cardigan and trousers, his arms and legs looked like matchsticks. His wrinkled head was almost free of hair, except for long wisps of white at his temples which were combed back around his ears. He looked ancient, and yet his eyes, magnified as they were by a pair of thick-lensed round spectacles, shone brightly even in the subdued light of the shop.

'Well, hello there.' The quiet tone was soothing. 'How nice to see you again, Johnny. It's been a while. How are you?'

'I'm fine, thanks, Mr Alexander. You're looking well.'

A small laugh. 'I can't complain. Keeping busy. As I'm sure you are.' He raised an eyebrow towards me. 'I take it you have a new job.'

I nodded.

'So how can I help you this time?'

Mr Alexander had become somewhat indispensable to me over the years. I'd met him early on in my career when

I'd been sourcing Regency furniture for a renovation project. Ever since then I had used him regularly – whenever I needed to buy or get advice on antique fixtures or fittings. So I told him briefly about the mirror and its markings. 'I was wondering if you could help me identify where it's from and perhaps who made it and for whom. I've tried some searches of my own on the lettering but they didn't reveal anything. So I took some pictures of it.' I removed the camera from my bag and placed it on the counter.

The old man looked at it and then back at me. 'Well, that all sounds very intriguing. Yes, let's take a look, shall we?'

I nodded, then clicked on the camera and flicked to the first image. 'So, this is the whole of the mirror. I know the background as well as the mirror is pretty dark, but I think you can make out the frame and the glass.'

The old man nodded and repeated 'Yes, yes' a couple of times.

I flicked through the next couple of photographs of the corners of the mirror containing the letters.

The old man leaned in to look more closely at the camera screen. He scrunched his eyes, scrutinising the images. Then steadily, softly, he said, 'I think that perhaps, Johnny, you have stumbled upon something very old indeed. If you could show me the rest of the photographs, just to be sure, then I can tell you what I think.'

'Of course.' I flicked through the images as the old man made quiet noises to himself. When I'd finished, he asked me to go back to the close-up shots of the lettering.

'Like I said,' he began, 'I think this mirror is extremely old, Johnny. I would guess that it was made towards the end of the sixteenth century.' He nodded. 'The reason I say this is twofold. Firstly, the extent of the degradation of the glass and frame. Secondly, the TM which you quite correctly identified. I believe these letters stand for Theseo Mutio.'

I tried to recall the name. Theseo Mutio. But I had never heard it before.

'Yes, yes. This is quite something.' The old man was squinting once more at the camera frame. 'Johnny, do you know anything about the mirror-making business in Venice?'

I racked my brain for a moment. 'I remember that Murano glass was highly sought after. It was the combination of elements in that particular area, I think – the seawater from the Venetian lagoon, the local wood for the firing process and the proportions of salt and soda that they used. It all led to a superior quality of glass and to Venice gaining a reputation ahead of competition from places like Germany and France.' I paused, my knowledge exhausted.

The old man nodded. 'Yes, yes. And it was a very lucrative business. So the Venetians, quite understandably, guarded their knowledge and their monopoly closely. It became a very cloak-and-dagger business,' he said, his enormous eyes winking from behind his glasses. 'Literally a matter of life and death. The Venetian authorities tried to prevent the movement of its glassworkers to countries that competed with the city. Of course, skilled craftsmen still managed to get out, to France for example. But the Venetians didn't let them go without a fight. There was blackmail, duplicity and murder. Corpses turned up from supposed bizarre accidents, there were rumours of poisonings and sabotage.' Mr Alexander nodded again. 'And it was during this period of much upheaval and unrest that Theseo Mutio went to France to work for King Henri II. He was commissioned to produce mirrors and other sorts of Venetian-style glass. A few years later his brother Ludovic joined him and together they made rather a success of it. For a time, at least. They had a factory in Saint-Germain-en-Laye, I believe, and their products were judged to be of the same beauty and excellence as work bought in Murano. However, in spite of the patronage and protection bestowed upon them by the King and Queen, the Mutio factory eventually faltered.'

'So what happened to them?'

The old man shrugged his shoulders. 'Impossible to say for sure. There's no mention of them in the last third of the century so no one really knows how long their experiment lasted or what ultimately did for it. What is clear, however, is that the Queen commissioned a not inconsiderable number of items from them.'

My brain tried to focus on the little French history I had once known. But I couldn't remember anything about Henri II, let alone his wife.

'The Queen was Catherine de Medici,' said the old man without looking up. He was frowning and pointing to the interlinking letters. 'You are quite right that there is a letter H here. And I think there are letters between its vertical strokes. Perhaps a letter C, for Catherine, facing the correct way, with another C, back to front, like a mirror image of the first. Two Cs, perhaps.'

I looked at the camera. Yes, it could definitely be a combination of H and C.

'Well, Johnny, I would love to take a look at it sometime, if you would permit me.'

I nodded but for some reason I didn't want him to. 'Of course, of course,' I lied. 'It's not clear what's going to happen to it yet. Whether it's going to be sold or kept or what. But I'll keep you in the loop and you can come over and see it. Sometime,' I said, fudging.

Mr Alexander nodded again. 'Well, any time, Johnny. Any time you want. It could be worth a fortune, you know. Something of this age and heritage.' And he winked at me. 'Where did you come across the piece?'

'In an underground room in the factory where I'm working.'

'Hmm. Underground.' The old man looked at the photographs again and then back at me with his wide eyes. 'That's a curious place to uncover something like this. But then again, it is a curious object. Are the pictures truly representative of it?'

I cocked an eyebrow at him, not really understanding what he was getting at.

'By which I mean is the glass really this stained?'

'Ah.' I looked down at the image on the camera and

the darkness of the mirror's surface seemed to ripple under my gaze. 'Yes,' I said, nodding.

'Hmm. Such deep mottling of the glass is fairly unusual – even in a piece as old as this.'

I looked at the image once again and felt faintly uneasy.

'It hardly even resembles a mirror any more.' He frowned, then clicked the camera off abruptly and pushed it back to me.

An uncertain silence hovered between us. I wanted to speak but didn't know what to say.

'Well.' Mr Alexander coughed lightly and rubbed his hands together. 'It's certainly a very interesting piece. And if I'm right then it's over four hundred years old. Quite remarkable. And do you know nothing of its history, Johnny?'

'No,' I replied quietly. 'Well, I know that the factory opened in 1864, so I guess it could have been there since then.'

'That still leaves three hundred years unaccounted for.' Then he fixed me with his big eyes and murmured quietly, 'Makes you wonder who's been looking into it all that time – and what they've seen.'

On my way back to the factory I made a diversion to the coffee shop. Sitting at my favourite spot, the fourth table back out of the five that ran along the length of the front window, I turned over Mr Alexander's parting words in my mind. They had touched on something that I had also thought. Or more than that, perhaps: something I had *felt.* What did you see when you looked into this mirror, this mirror that hardly resembled a mirror any more? I closed my eyes briefly as I tried to understand it. But all I saw was an ever-shifting blackness.

My mind moved away from the mirror and came back to the old man. As we were winding up our conversation, he had said that it might be difficult, given the age of the piece, to find out much more about it. Nonetheless, he would do his best. A personal interest, he called it. He still had contacts in the business that he could call upon and the markings would assist in tracking the mirror's movements before it came to the factory. I thanked him but secretly I knew it was a long shot. And besides, what would be the point?

As I waited for my coffee, I thought about the mirror maker, Theseo Mutio, making an object fit for a Queen. I imagined tin and mercury, lime and potash heated in a furnace until they formed a ball of molten glass. Then I saw the hands of Mutio, the alchemist, magically transforming them into solid crystal that produced reflections. But then, somehow, the glass grew almost too dark to produce an image. The mirror maker's initials shifted around in my mind. TM. Then they were joined by the intertwined letters, H and C, if that was what they were. The marks of a King and Queen. They too circled my mind, melded with the darkness of the mirror, and finally disappeared.

15

The following evening I was standing next to Ophelia in her darkroom. The red safelight cast a deep, hypnotic glow over the central space but barely penetrated the darkness at the edges of the room.

Ophelia took a negative and inserted it into the negative carrier. Then she placed the carrier in the slot below the light source of the enlarger. This was a strange piece of equipment on the edge of her workbench, which projected light through the negative onto photo paper on the bench below. With a click she turned on the enlarger and an image was reflected downwards. I saw her look at the timer before turning to face me.

'Well, the poisonings I knew about. Catherine de Medici was quite infamous in that department, wasn't she?' Ophelia checked the levels of liquid in the three trays in front of her and then her gaze shot back again to the timer. 'Yes, there were the famous poisoned gloves by which she dispatched her enemies and wasn't there once a decorated apple infused with poisonous vapours? It killed a dog, I think. By accident.'

I smiled into the darkness. 'I don't know about that.'

'And what about her chamber full of deadly poisons? Weren't lots of secret cabinets found in one of the rooms of her chateaux?'

I shook my head. I had no idea. But it seemed to fit with the general picture I'd been uncovering of her. Unable to get my conversation with Mr Alexander out of my head, I'd gone to the British Library and done some research of my own. 'I focused on sorcery,' I heard myself say. The words coming out of my mouth sounded bizarre.

'I think they omitted that part at school.' I heard the timer click off and the enlarger light went out. Ophelia took the exposed photo paper and placed it in the first tray. Deftly handling a pair of tongs, she gently pressed the paper in several places until it was covered by the liquid. Then she turned to me. 'So what did you discover?'

'Well, Catherine had been married off to Henri, the second son of King Francis I of France, when she was only fourteen years old. Only a few years later Henri's brother died, leaving him Dauphin, heir to the throne. So, as Dauphine, she was under great pressure, even more so than before, to conceive a child. And it didn't happen for her for a while. She tried everything, including pagan remedies and ancient magic. Eventually she did get pregnant. But who knows if it had anything to do with that.' I paused, watching Ophelia continue to move the photo paper beneath the liquid in the developing tray. 'So it seems that the origins of her interest in magic started there. But they certainly developed somewhat. Part of her entourage were the Ruggieri brothers, Tommaso and

Cosimo. They were renowned astrologers but also practised the dark arts – black magic and necromancy. That kind of stuff.'

'Really?'

I nodded. 'Catherine was supposed to have a talisman made of human blood, the blood of a goat and the metals of her birth chart. It wasn't unusual in the sixteenth century to have talismans, but that combination was a little odd.' I rubbed my eyes and watched the tongs in Ophelia's hands still shifting the paper in the developing tray. 'And after she gave up her chateau at Chaumont a number of items were found there that indicated occult practices having been carried out. Pentacles drawn on the floors, altars decorated with skulls, jars of powders and liquids, the remains of animal sacrifices. Lots of sinister stuff.'

'No wonder she became known as the Black Queen.'

'And then there are all the stories about her premonitions. Apparently, the night before Henri was fatally injured in a jousting match she dreamed of him lying stricken on the ground, his face covered in blood.'

'Creepy.'

'Hmm. She was said to have second sight. A number of those close to her recounted that she sometimes awoke from sleep screaming and predicting the death of a loved one.'

We both stood in silence for a while, the only sound the faint lapping of the liquid in the developing tray. In spite of myself, I couldn't help thinking of the nightmare

I'd had recently: the mirror, the man, the sensation of suffocation and falling. I closed my eyes, trying to blink the thought away. 'So, in light of all that, I guess it's not such a stretch to imagine her using mirrors for seeing and divination.' I paused for a moment. 'I read something else, and I don't know whether this is history or myth, that during her final visit to Chaumont, Catherine asked Cosimo to use a mirror in a darkened room to foretell the future. It was said that each of Catherine's sons appeared in turn and circled the mirror. Each circle was supposed to signify a year that they would reign.'

Ophelia nodded. 'Mirrors were often used to see the future. Witches through the ages, white and black, used them as a medium to see things, past, present and yet to come.'

I knew that, and even though I didn't really believe it I shifted vaguely on my feet, suddenly uncomfortable.

'Not much longer now,' said Ophelia, mistaking my movement for impatience. 'In fact . . .'

Sure enough, out of nowhere, an image was developing on the photo paper: a man's face, black and white, emerging from the darkness.

'Did you know that the ancient Greeks thought that looking at one's reflection in a mirror could invite death?' Ophelia's voice sounded suddenly strange in the darkness.

'No, I didn't know that,' I said.

'Something to do with the reflection capturing the soul. Lots of ancient cultures feel the same way about photographs. And when you think about it, in many ways, a mirror image is quite like a photograph. It captures an image of the self that isn't quite the self.'

Instinctively I thought of when I had looked into the mirror's surface with Tara. I thought about the darkened image hiding below the surface. A ripple of fear ran through me. I looked again at the photograph that was emerging in the tray: a man's unsmiling, monotone face, hard around the eyes. I felt something catch at the back of my throat and I swallowed hard. But my mouth was dry.

'My own special brand of dark magic,' said Ophelia, pulling the image from the developing tray with her tongs and placing it briefly in the next one along.

I swallowed again and tried to concentrate on the process.

'Do you remember me telling you that I like to take close-up photographs of people, portraits, that sort of thing? So this was taken in the park near the factory.'

Ophelia placed the image in the last tray, tilting it back and forth, moving the solution over the paper. I looked at the emerging face, feeling strangely disconcerted, and tried instead to focus on the movement, back and forth, back and forth. But my mind kept coming back to my reflection in the mirror, to my dream, to the sensation of falling.

'All done,' said Ophelia abruptly, lifting the photograph out of the solution. She walked to the sink in the far corner of the room and placed the image in a tray there, turning on the tap so that a soft trickle of water flowed into it. After a few moments she removed the photograph and hung it up to dry on the line that spanned the walls. The man's dark, unflinching stare, eerie in the red glow of the room, seemed directed at me. I stared back for a moment and then looked away, focusing on Ophelia as she moved the three developing trays off the central workbench. Then she headed back and stood silently in front of me.

I was just about to speak, to break the tension that I felt building, when she spoke.

'When are you going to let me see it, Johnny?'

I sighed. 'Not that again,' I said softly.

'But I don't understand. Why don't you want me to see it?'

I looked at her, this pale, delicate girl. 'It's not that,' I said, but as soon as the words were out of my mouth I knew they were a lie. Something about the prospect of her seeing the mirror made me uncomfortable. I wondered whether it was today's hocus-pocus talk. But I had felt the same way when we had last spoken about it. I didn't understand it and I didn't know how to explain it. I shook my head, confused. 'It's just a feeling. I don't know. It's probably ridiculous. Just wait a while, okay?'

She stared at me for a second and then looked away.

'Ophelia,' I said quietly, coaxingly, 'you're not angry with me, are you?'

She turned back to me and shook her head. But I sensed defiance in the movement.

'Hey, come on. Like I said before, you can see it. Just give me a little time. Please?'

Eventually, she nodded her head. 'Okay.'

I picked her up and sat her on the workbench in front of me. Then I pushed off her shoes, one by one, and took her feet in my hands, almost cupping them. I ran my left index finger under her right heel, over the high rise of the arch and across the ball of her foot to her toes. As my fingers traced them, one by one, I remembered the story she'd told me about her mother, walking along the beach in front of her while Ophelia crouched in the imprint made by her foot. *This little piggy went to market, this little piggy stayed at home.* I laughed softly, closing my eyes as I remembered.

'What is it? What are you thinking about?'

And even though my eyes were closed, I could tell she was smiling at me as she spoke.

'You,' I answered. 'I was thinking about you.'

16

After dinner we went to bed and made love. I fell asleep with my body curled around Ophelia and dreamed of a deep emptiness as if a black hole had sucked all the life out of my thoughts. I don't know how long I slept like this but I awoke suddenly, jumping upright as if in response to someone having just called out my name. I listened but I couldn't hear anything. I opened my eyes. It was still dark. I looked at the alarm clock. 03:17. The darkness was absolute and I wondered for a moment if I was still asleep. The room was freezing and the hairs on the back of my neck were standing to attention. I looked at the clock again. The same numbers flashed, marking time in the darkness. 03:17. But something wasn't right. I reached out to touch Ophelia beside me. Instead of her warm body, a cold emptiness greeted me.

I flicked on the bedside light and looked again. There was nothing but a space beside me. Everything else in the bedroom was exactly as it should be. The overflowing wardrobes to the left of the bed, the racks of shoes directly in front, the glowing lamp on the bedside table. I got out of bed, pulled on my jeans and walked towards the sitting room. As I passed the bathroom, I flicked on the light and looked inside. Nothing and no one. Next I tried the kitchen. But it was dark and empty. No Ophelia. At the threshold of the sitting room I listened intently, then called out her name. Nothing came back to me but silence. I stood there for a few more seconds and then moved forwards. The room should have been in darkness, but the curtains were open and moonlight spilled over everything. It cast a fluorescent blue glow over the walls and floor, shimmering over the dining table to my left and across the sofas ahead of me. I listened. But there was nothing. No sound. A deathly stillness hovered over everything.

Reaching the corner of the room, I looked through the French doors onto the darkness of the balcony. But it was deserted. There was no sign of Ophelia. I took a deep breath, letting my forehead rest briefly against the coolness of the glass. I didn't understand. Turning around, I looked into Ophelia's studio. It was in semi-darkness, the blinds lowered. For some reason, I called out her name once more, gently, but still desperate for an answer. Nothing came back and silence once more fell around me. But as I continued to look into the studio, one thing emerged. A pair of pale legs, blunt, truncated, rose out of the darkness from the image on the wall. They reclined on a sofa, a dark substance dropping from the paleness of the toes to the base of the picture. I looked, mesmerised for a second, before panic took hold.

I went back to the bedroom, trying to think. But my

mind couldn't make any sense of it. Where could Ophelia have gone? I rubbed my eyes and made my way to the window, looking down into the garden at the back of the house. Bare grass and a black poplar were illuminated in the moonlight. It was a typical London garden, unkempt and unplanted. I scanned the neighbouring plots. Nothing. I looked around the flat once again. I called her name. But it was pointless. She wasn't here.

I dressed quickly and on my way out of the flat went to pick up my keys from their usual place by the door. Only they weren't there. I hunted around in the hallway for a few seconds, then made a snap decision. It didn't matter. If I couldn't find her, it wouldn't be that long before I could get in touch with someone. I slipped my mobile phone into my pocket and by the time I left the flat I was running. I couldn't shake off an intense sense of foreboding. An image of feet and calves and viscous liquid flashed across my mind. I tried to sweep it away. Such thoughts were ridiculous, I told myself. I careered down the street, my trainers smacking hard against the tarmac. I breathed the air, cold and sharp, into my lungs. Maybe she couldn't sleep and went out for a walk. Maybe she was sitting in the park at this very moment. I took a left turn. The road was deserted and the light from the street lamps made little inroad into the darkness. A strong wind blew against me. The cold was intense. Why would she want to go out in weather like this? I took another left turn and tried not to think. But I started to become angry and irritated. Why the hell would she have left in the middle of the night? Who was this crazy woman? Then I felt a bloom of fear. After all, I hardly knew her. I didn't know what she was capable of doing.

I tried to put the thoughts from my mind. It wasn't helping. I just had to keep running. I was nearly there. A right turn and the park came into view. The way was second nature to me now. It was a short walk from the flat. Or a thirty-second sprint with a fist of ice in my chest. The railings loomed black and hostile. The signs rattled in the wind. Litter bounced down the street, dodged the iron rails and snagged in the bushes. I opened the gate and walked inside, breathing heavily, more cautious all of a sudden. I waited, looking into the wind. Then I called out her name. No reply. So I began to walk, to circle the park, moving under the trees and around the bushes. I took my time. I was vigilant. I covered every inch of ground. Strange, I thought. I had watched a scene very like this just a few days ago. But then a woman was looking for something she had lost. Now a man was looking for that woman.

I climbed the steps of the bandstand and looked around one last time. At the top of my voice I shouted her name into the wind. No answer came back. I waited. I called out once more. I waited again. There was no reply. Standing still, I listened to the hard sound of my breathing, in and out, in and out, in and out. I made a deliberate attempt to slow it down. I had to think. She wasn't at the flat, she wasn't here. So where was she?

As I looked around me the night tightened its grip on

the park, the moon disappearing behind dense cloud. Here especially, surrounded by trees, the darkness acquired a peculiar intensity. There were shades of deep violet and purple within it, lending it a richness like velvet. It was a darkness that you wanted to touch and yet which you knew would swallow your touch entirely. Standing here I thought about Ophelia. Where would she have gone on a night like this? And then it came to me.

I looked beyond the park's flower beds, hubs of churned earth covered over with a blanket of darkness, past the railings marking the perimeter and the road that lay beyond, a circle of concrete and tarmac, white and yellow lines. I looked past the street lights sparkling at the border of the park, as faint and fragile as fairy lights. On the far side of the road, shadowy houses, terraces towering four storeys tall, formed almost a full circle around me. I turned, looking upwards, looking as I had just a few days earlier for the interruption in their Georgian symmetry. There it was. The factory. I suddenly knew with complete certainty that that was where she had gone.

I moved swiftly in the darkness from my vantage point on the bandstand towards the gate nearest the factory doors. They opened with a loud squeaking noise that set my nerves further on edge. I made my way quickly to the outer doors of the dispatch room and, sure enough, the large padlock and chain we used when the factory was empty were gone. I pulled at the doors and they swung open easily. The ordinary lock had also been opened. Only Tara and I had keys for these doors. And my keys had disappeared.

I entered the dispatch room and closed the door softly behind me. Moonlight poured through the windows, irradiating everything with a soft light. I could see the shoeboxes piled against the factory wall, the tables where Tara and I worked during the day. Only, bathed in that unearthly light, they didn't look the same. They seemed suspended in a different time and place. As I moved slowly across the room I felt like a deep-sea diver hundreds of miles below the surface, crossing the sea floor in a silence almost as deep as the ocean, my movements slow and pronounced. I almost didn't feel like myself.

Peering inside the storage cupboard, I saw that the inner door was wide open. Without hesitating, I moved towards it and looked down the staircase. An orange glow, as if from candlelight, climbed the stairs. Relief flooded through me. She was here, she was safe. But by the time my feet touched the bottom of the stairs I felt another emotion rise within me. Turning towards the underground room, I caught sight of Ophelia standing in front of the mirror, a candle on the floor at each end of it. She was wearing a long coat over what appeared to be a white nightdress. Her feet were bare, her shoes discarded on the floor beside her, and her right arm hung inert at her side. Her left was holding a silver locket that she often wore, sliding it up and down the chain from which it was suspended. For a few moments I watched her staring into the darkness of the mirror, a look of longing on her face, oblivious to everything around her, including my presence.

'Ophelia?' I said at last. My voice when it emerged was a hard whisper.

She jumped and turned abruptly towards me. Her face looked waxen, ghostly in the candlelight.

Neither of us said anything for a moment. I just stared at her.

'You scared me,' she said at last. Her voice didn't sound as if it belonged to her.

'What are you doing?'

She looked around her and nodded distractedly. 'I'm sorry, I couldn't sleep. So . . . I . . . I came here.' She sounded unsure. 'I'm sorry,' she said again.

'Stop saying that,' I snapped, suddenly letting it out. I felt enormously, irrepressibly angry with her. 'What are you doing? It's the middle of the night.'

'I'm . . . I just wanted to take a look.' She bit her lip and looked as if she was about to cry.

I wanted to move towards her but somehow my feet didn't budge. 'It's three o'clock in the morning, Ophelia. And you took my keys and came here. After everything I said.'

She nodded, then walked over to me silently. 'I'm sorry if you're angry. I didn't mean to upset you.'

I looked at her face, her pale skin and the dark circles under her eyes. I traced their lines with my fingers and felt the fury slide out of me. She looked exhausted. 'What is it?' I asked.

'It's nothing.'

'It isn't nothing. What are you doing?'

She stared at me but didn't say anything. Instead she pulled me to her and held me there for a long moment.

'Ophelia, what is it?'

'I don't know,' she said at last. 'I don't know how to explain it. Perhaps it can't even be explained. Not rationally. But I was dreaming . . . and then I awoke. Or I thought I awoke. And then . . . I was here.' She paused. 'I don't even remember getting here. Not properly.' She looked down at her bare feet and then, taking my hand, walked back to stand in front of the mirror.

The silver was spattered with blotches of black and dark grey, radiating across the surface like the bloom of ink drops when they hit water. I tried to focus on my face. There was only the vaguest of reflections, blurred, leeched of colour. The blue of my eyes had vanished, the pink of my skin had disappeared. I was a black and grey silhouette. A shadow. My gaze shifted and came to rest on the spot in the bottom left-hand corner where the initials were: TM. Then it moved to the other corner and sought out the others: H and C. Raising my eyes slowly upwards over the surface of the glass, I could see Ophelia's dark reflection staring out towards me.

'My father didn't like mirrors,' she announced abruptly.

Yeah. I was with him there.

'He hated to see his reflection. He didn't like the idea of it. This other him, one identical to him and yet not him, staring back from across an unbridgeable divide. He used to joke about it, quote Newton's laws of physics. A reflection is only refracted light. But I don't think he believed it really. There was something else, I'm sure of it.' She paused. 'Anyway, there were never any mirrors on the walls of the places where we lived. Not after my mother died.' She stared at the mirror's surface. 'Strange, then, that looking into this mirror made me think of my father.' She breathed heavily in and out and then, out of the corner of my eye, I saw her turn towards me. 'I'm sorry, Johnny. You were right. I should never have come here. I don't know what I was thinking.'

'It's okay,' I said, without facing her. 'Forget about it.' But even as the words fell out of my mouth I felt the anger rise within me once more. She was right, she shouldn't have come here. I tried to let it go, concentrating on the image of myself in the mirror. The black eyes, the dark lips. I smiled but something hard was reflected back at me. I looked at my lips, fascinated. 'It's okay,' I said again, more to myself this time than to her.

'Johnny?'

Her voice sounded very far away.

'Johnny?'

'Hmm.' This time I turned to face her.

'Come on, let's get out of here. You were right. There's something . . . I don't know . . .' She looked around the room and then back at me. 'Are you okay?'

'I'm fine.'

'Are you sure?'

I looked at her face then, paler than usual in the candle-light and I felt a heady, overwhelming rush of desire.

'I'm fine,' I said, pulling her to me. 'More than fine.'

I kissed her deeply, my hands behind her neck, holding her to me, then moving under her coat, over the thin white cotton of her nightdress to her breasts. They were full and warm beneath my fingertips. Squeezing tightly, I felt her nipples harden. I heard her moan, felt her hot breath against my ear. My hands slid down her body, over the taut skin of her stomach, downwards and between her naked thighs. Feeling her wetness, I grew harder, shifted my hands to her hips and lifted her. She wrapped her legs around me and I pushed her backwards against the wall, against the mirror. Her hair fell dark against the darkness of the glass, her skin white, almost luminous against it. I looked at the arch of her long neck, ran my fingers over the skin, felt the fast throb of her pulse beneath the surface. My body flooded with desire. I inhaled deeply, watching my reflection in the mirror as I felt her hands grappling with the belt at my waist. She smelled of roses and jasmine, and her smell and that of the room sank inside me into the darkness. I closed my eyes. And then I was inside her. I heard her gasp, murmur something to me, but what the words were I couldn't tell. As I pushed deep into her, I felt something, besides desire, stir inside me. What was it? It rose in my stomach, blooming like ink on water, like the marks on the mirror's surface. I opened my eyes and their reflection stared back at me, black, hostile from within the dark glass. Then I knew that what I felt was anger. Anger at her. My hands were once more around her neck, her pulse beating, strong against them. I became more aroused. As I pushed her harder, quicker against the wall, I heard her voice again, but still the words were not clear. I closed my eyes, closed my ears, surrendered to the turmoil inside, and in an explosion of anger and lust came hard, deep inside her.

Then, for a moment, there was nothing but darkness.

17

Chateau de Chaumont

November 1552

Catherine shivered in the chill of the room, conscious of the dark silence hanging thickly, sticking to her, a heavy shroud around her shoulders. She tried to remember how long she had been standing like this. But she could not. She had heard the last small gasp of the wick as the candle extinguished itself. Then she had smelled smoke on the air as the fumes rose. It had caught in the back of her throat, hard and sooty, before eventually dispersing. But she had no idea whether that had been seconds or minutes ago. She tried to peer through the darkness, to see her reflection in the mirror that she knew was in front of her. But she could not. Neither could she see her hand when she raised it towards her face, nor where it finished and the darkness began. And standing in this cold black room, where time had ceased to have any meaning, she began to feel a strange sensation, almost of suffocation. As if the darkness was taking hold of her. Just as panic began to rise, as she was about to call out, she caught a flicker of light once more.

Immediately her breathing stilled and the rapid beat of her heart slowed. Through the half-light she could see the reflection of Tommaso in the mirror, his silhouette behind her, bending over a new candle.

Cosimo, close to him, was marking out a pentacle on the stone slabs. The liquid he daubed onto the floor looked thick and black, no doubt the blood of some animal. But in the flickering candlelight Catherine could not see clearly. Perhaps that was for the best. She watched Cosimo, his movements confident and swift. When the pentacle was finished he placed a glass jar at each of its five points. One, she knew, contained earth, another air, a third water. Then he placed the candle in the fourth, the symbol of fire. The fifth remained empty – awaiting the spirit that would fill it.

Catherine swallowed, her mouth suddenly dry, and shifted her focus from the brothers back to the mirror. She looked over its thick silver frame. It was a beautiful piece, that was for sure. And that thought made her fury rise once more. She thought about Henri's mistress, with her skin, so white, so pale. She thought of the elixirs prepared to keep her young, the liquid gold she drank to preserve her youth. She thought about her vanity and her greed. She thought about her licentiousness. And Catherine smiled to herself. She had waited so long – so long on the sidelines, in the shadows – for the moment that would soon arrive, when Cosimo would perfect his craft. But that moment was almost upon her. The moment for her revenge to bite.

She was stirred by Cosimo's voice, calm, low, commanding, speaking in tongues that she did not understand. She continued to look into the mirror, avoiding her own reflection as instructed, waiting. Suddenly there was a change, a shift in the room. Cosimo ceased talking and an unquiet silence loitered in the spaces where his words had been. The darkness seemed to become fluid, moving around the room, moving tighter around Catherine, suppressing the candlelight. The hairs on her forearms rose. Fear bloomed within her as the darkness tightened its grip. Then she could smell it on the air, the stench of her own sweat. And she knew with absolute certainty that there was something to be afraid of within this new-found darkness. The dead were among them.

Her eyes flickered momentarily towards the reflection of the fifth jar on the floor behind her. But terror forced her to look away before she could focus. Instead, she made herself raise her gaze and stare directly ahead into the mirror. For the first time that night she allowed herself to see her reflection, to look into her own eyes. Through her rising fear she tried to remember what Cosimo had told her. 'Keep your eyes upon yourself alone once the ceremony has begun. Concentrate on your own gaze and when I tell you place your hands upon the mirror's surface.'

Catherine felt the knot in her stomach tighten as the mirror appeared to quiver and shift. She stared at herself, at her own eyes, yet the more she looked at them the less they appeared to be her own. She stared at her face but again she failed to recognise it. She willed herself to smile, to dispel the fear and tension, and although she was sure that she had not, could not, she was equally sure that the reflection which she saw smiled darkly back at her.

She opened her mouth to speak, but before she could do so she heard Cosimo's voice behind her, compelling her to touch the mirror. She hesitated, almost frozen with fright. His voice came again, authoritative in the darkness. And this time she did as she was told. For a moment she felt nothing. Then a tingling began in her fingertips. It spread slowly throughout her fingers and into her hands. And as she watched herself in the mirror, as she heard Cosimo's voice chanting once again behind her, she felt all her anger and rage, all her fear and hatred, all her frustrated desire and longing flood out of her. A *moment later, exhausted, her hands fell from the mirror's surface and she stumbled backwards. Tommaso rushed to her aid, supporting her, as she closed her eyes and waited, just as Cosimo had instructed, for the incantation to be over.*

As Catherine stood in the darkness she thought of her husband once more. She had done all for him: sacrificed everything, almost forgiven and almost forgotten. But she had not forgiven those closest to him, those who were corrupt and who defiled him in turn. She thought of his whore again. This had been done for her. It was time for retribution.

It was time for a gift tinctured with vengeance.

18

The days were passing swiftly. Yet we seemed more stuck than ever in the frozen heart of winter. The nights were long and dark, the days, barely lighter, were bitter and overcast. Every day I trudged to the factory longing for the clarity of blue skies and the onset of spring. And every day I was disappointed.

In this time my ideas for the renovation, also seemingly frozen, had hardly developed at all. Day after day I stared at my drawings, frustrated by their lack of progress, by my own inertia, yet seemingly impotent to change either. I tinkered, amended and redrew but nothing substantive or complete, nothing wholly satisfactory ever seemed to evolve. I ended every day more confused about what I wanted, more unsure of what to present to the client. I began to think that it was a subconscious unwillingness on my part for the project to end, a deep-seated reluctance to leave the factory when the time came and return to the office. But perhaps I was just overthinking. At the end of the day, perhaps I was simply preoccupied with other things.

*

The sound of Tara's footsteps beside me disturbed my meandering thoughts. We were walking back to the factory after another project meeting with Richard. Surprisingly, notwithstanding the stasis of my ideas this one had gone better than the last. Richard had shown some concern at the lack of development but as I had promised him results within the next few days it hadn't become a bigger issue. The fact that I didn't feel my promises were worth much was a source of considerable anxiety to me. But I was keen to avoid a restatement of the lack of faith that he probably still felt. So there was a sense that neither of us was being fully truthful but that we had both settled upon an uneasy truce.

I exhaled deeply into the biting air and focused on the dull thud of Tara's boots against the tarmac. At least the spat I had had with her had blown over. I had apologised for my behaviour and she had done the same – saying that she had overreacted and was sorry and embarrassed that it had spilled over into our meeting. With that, the air was clear and now it was almost as if it had never happened. Almost. But I had been careful since then to avoid mentioning Ophelia to her – and, more specifically, to avoid revealing that Ophelia had now visited the underground room. As my mind turned once again to thoughts of the mirror, I became aware of Tara's voice, echoing faintly beside me.

I turned towards her. 'Sorry. Did you say something?'

She nodded and then smiled. 'It doesn't matter.' She paused for a second and then carried on. 'You seem miles away. Is everything okay?'

I shrugged. 'Sure, it's fine. I was just thinking about the mirror in the underground room at the factory. That's all,' I added as if it were nothing.

She turned towards me. 'What about it?'

As I had with Ophelia, I had told her about my visit to Mr Alexander and the discussion I'd had with him about the letter markings on the mirror's surface. But we hadn't spoken about it since then.

'I went to the British Library a few days ago. I wanted to check on the intertwining H and C letters. It started to bother me that we didn't know for sure that that's what they were.'

'And?'

'And it seems that they were probably not intended to be Cs at all. They're most likely Ds.'

A barrage of horns interrupted me as two white vans advanced towards one another from opposite ends of the street. Each was hurtling along kamikaze-style, taking more than its fair share of the oncoming-traffic lane. Their tyres screeched as they braked violently and swerved inwards, hurling dust and grit into the air. Tara looked up, observed the chaos of the street indifferently, then looked down again. She said nothing.

'So Henri II,' I continued, when the volume of street noise had returned to normal, 'like most kings of the time, had a number of mistresses. But there was one he adored more than all the others: Diane de Poitiers or the Duchess of Valentinois. She was almost twenty years older than him but she was his mistress throughout his adulthood.

Between them they created a monogram, combining the letters H and D.'

Tara nodded but again was silent.

'It was apparently a symbol of their love. It's been found on objects associated with them – the panelling of their bedchamber at Diane's chateau at Anet, for example. Ironically, the layout of the letters also makes it possible to decipher a letter C within them. Or maybe this was purposeful – who knows? A sop to Catherine.'

Tara, staring down at her feet, now spoke. 'It's possible. But did you know that Cs were also associated with Diane? They're crescent moons, the symbol of Diana, the hunting goddess. And they too were incorporated into lots of architectural features – floor stones, wall engravings, buildings and such – during Henri's reign.' Tara looked up at me and smiled. 'You're not the only one who was intrigued enough to do some more research.'

I nodded. 'Clearly.'

We walked along in silence for a few moments, taking a right turn into the factory square. The park came into view and the noise of the main road began to recede.

Tara was the first to speak. 'So do you think the mirror even belonged to Catherine, then? Or was it actually Diane's?'

I shrugged again. 'Who knows?'

'I think it's more than likely that it was Diane's. She was always receiving gifts from Henri, gifts that should rightfully have been given to his Queen. When Henri's father died, both his long-term mistress and his widow had to return all the jewels they had been given by the crown. Henri gave Diane the key to the treasury and told her to take whatever she wanted.'

I shook my head.

'He also gave her the Chateau of Chenonceau – a palace that Catherine had always wanted for herself and claimed had been promised to her.'

'Yeah. I read about that,' I said, coming to a standstill in front of the factory. 'She had a pretty rough time of it, all things considered.'

I pulled the keys from my jacket pocket and unlocked and pushed open the heavy outer doors. Tara went before me, turning on all the lights, switching on her computer and then busying herself with the coffee machine. I sat down at my desk and stared hopelessly at the array of designs spread chaotically across it. To avoid dealing with them, I took my camera from my desk drawer and flicked once more through the images of the mirror that I'd taken to show Mr Alexander, the ones that showed the TM of the mirror maker and the interwoven lettering on the bottom right corner. H and C. Or, more likely now, H and D. After a few moments I closed my eyes and rubbed the lids. 'I don't even know why I'm so interested in this,' I said, more to myself than to Tara. But, hearing me, she crossed over to my desk.

'I didn't know you'd taken these,' she said, grabbing the camera from me and scrolling through the images. Then she removed the SIM card from the camera and took it back to her computer. After a moment she called out,

'You might want to come and take a look at this. You don't really get a true sense of it when you see it on the camera.'

Glad of the distraction, I got up and headed over to her. When I saw the picture of the mirror on her computer screen, with the colour and contrast sharpened, the difference was staggering.

The mirror's metallic surface was dark, but the subtle gradations of its mottling were clearer: dark silver here, lighter silver there, unfathomable darkness blooming in patches elsewhere. The silver frame was easily distinguishable from the glass and faint tarnished patches were discernible on it. What I had not been able to see when I looked at the image on the camera, but could clearly see on Tara's computer screen, was my own dark reflection evident in the mirror.

'Wow,' I said. 'That's amazing.'

'Yes, that's you.'

I focused on the shadowy blur, dark and elongated, that had been caught by the camera. I blinked and looked again. Was that really me? As I stared at it, I felt a subtle ache of disquiet in my stomach. The same feeling that I had had intermittently since the first discovery of the mirror and the underground room.

Tara broke in on my thoughts. 'When did you take these?'

I took a breath and tried to think. 'A few weeks ago.'

She pursed her lips, still staring at the screen. There was something hypnotic about the image. 'And have you been back down to the room since then?'

I paused, wondering if I should tell her the truth. That not only had I found Ophelia there one night alone, but that we had subsequently been back there together, perhaps three, maybe four times. But I wasn't sure that she would understand, wasn't sure that I would be able to explain adequately. That alongside the disquiet that I felt when I thought about the room, there was a small kernel of excitement, growing in the darkness inside, pulling me back towards that place: a stronger, more powerful urge than the one to stay away. So while I wanted to tell her, I didn't. And the lie slipped out of my mouth. 'No,' I said. 'I haven't been back.'

Tara nodded and said nothing.

'What about you? Have you been down there since you found the room?'

I thought I sensed a moment's hesitation before she shook her head. 'No,' she said quietly. 'I haven't.' Then she turned to face me and looked me directly in the eye. 'And I haven't told Richard about it, either.'

I hesitated, unsure what to say. I knew that I didn't have any right to ask her not to talk to him about it but something in me still baulked at the idea of him knowing about the room. I felt a wave of anxiety flow through me as I imagined him walking around the cellar, examining the mirror and then wanting the room discussed and drawn and analysed in project meetings.

'I haven't told him,' she said again.

As I continued to meet Tara's unflinching gaze, my fear passed and another feeling rose in me. Something resembling relief. I was sure that she was telling the truth. I nodded and then gave her a slight smile.

'But I think someone has been visiting the underground room. In any event, someone has been coming in and out of the factory – and they haven't been locking the doors properly.'

'What?' I said, not understanding.

'Someone has been surreptitiously visiting here. And both you and I know how to lock the doors properly. So who do you suppose that could be?'

For a moment I stood there silently with Tara watching me. 'It's not Ophelia,' I said eventually. 'She wouldn't do something like that.'

'How do you know that? You hardly know her. You have no idea what she might do.'

'But I know that she wouldn't do that.' I said it loudly, stridently. 'You must have made a mistake.'

'I didn't make a mistake.' Tara's face had a defiant look to it.

'Well, then there must be some other explanation.'

'Like what?'

'Like . . . Richard came over or someone else from the office. I don't know.'

'Well, I do. I already asked. Richard said that no one had been over since his first visit here with you.'

'In that case there must be another explanation.' I said it with a conviction I didn't by any means feel. 'There must be.'

'Okay,' Tara said, turning back to her computer.

'When you've worked out what it is I'd like to know.' The image of the mirror – dark, resplendent – was still in sharp focus on her screen. We both stared at it for a moment before I turned and walked back to my desk. I was suddenly weary, overcome by tiredness. I sat down heavily and surveyed the disorder of my drawings once again. Taking a breath, I began rearranging them, grappling with the unwieldy pile of sketches, then, when I had finished, rearranging them again. After twenty minutes, there was no more structure or clarity among them than there had been before. I sighed and looked up to see Tara watching me.

'You look exhausted,' was all she said. 'When was the last time you got a good night's sleep?'

I shrugged. I couldn't remember.

'Maybe you should go home, work from there?'

I shook my head. 'I work better here.' It was the second lie to slip easily out of my mouth.

'Okay,' she said, and then added sceptically, 'I hope you make progress.'

'Thanks,' I said, knowing that was unlikely. I closed my eyes and tried to clear my head. But my mind was in turmoil. I kept thinking about what she had told me. I thought of me and Ophelia in the underground room together. Then I wondered if Ophelia could be visiting it alone. I didn't think so but it was possible. After all, she had access to my keys and she had done it before. I sighed. I didn't want to believe it. But if it wasn't her, then who was it?

I turned and looked at Tara, tapping away at her keyboard, busy once more with her work. Her words about Ophelia echoed in my head.

'You hardly know her. You have no idea what she might do.'

19

We made our way down into the underground room, candles in our hands.

I watched Ophelia move ahead of me, studying the mirror for a moment or two, gently touching the surface of the glass before placing the candle she held on the floor. Then she unhooked the green shoes from the corner of the mirror. The ribbon rested lightly over the fingers of her left hand, and she swung the shoes slightly as she walked around the room. I placed my own candle upon the floor and then turned to watch her, walking in the candlelight, rocking the shoes back and forth, back and forth, in her slim, pale fingers. I couldn't stop watching her: there was something provocative, flirtatious about the action that made me smile. Finally, she sat down on the bed and slipped off her own shoes. She looked up at me, said something and laughed. The sound bounced indolently around the room but I couldn't hear it properly, nor the words that she was saying to me. It was all I could do to keep my eyes on her, on this beautiful creature now lying back upon the mattress, her feet visible against its edge in the candlelight.

I watched Ophelia slide the ribbon out from beneath the straps of the green shoes, watched them fall, released, against the dirt floor, watched her weave the soft velvet of the ribbon between her fingers. As I continued to look at her, at her face tilting now towards me, speaking to me in the half-light, I felt a huge surge of arousal. I walked over to the bed and knelt on the floor beside it. As my hands moved up her legs, under her skirt to her thighs, she sat upright in front of me. I felt her pull impatiently at the buttons of my jeans, adjust herself and slide on top of me. I closed my eyes, buried my head in her neck, inhaled the strong smell of her and the room: roses and jasmine and earth. I heard her voice and the sound of her laughter, felt her taking each of my hands in turn and tying them behind my back. I felt a sudden pinch around my wrists, tight and soft at the same time. The ribbon. As I realised what she had done, I heard the sound of my own laughter. It sounded odd, unlike me, as though it came from a long way away.

As she put her arms around my neck and pushed down hard on top of me, my bound hands sought support from the floor. In the darkness of my mind's eye, as I felt myself inside her, I longed to search out an image of myself in the mirror. Longed to see something clear beyond the vague blackness of eyes and mouth and hair. I felt the need deep within me to connect with it. My reflection. I opened my eyes and looked at Ophelia moving against me, green eyes flashing, breathing hard, wild in her aban-donment. It was then that I felt it again, the intense uncurling of that feeling, blooming deeply within, erotic, angry, irrepressible. As I looked at her, I struggled hard to release my hands from the ribbon. I wanted, more than anything, to feel her skin beneath my fingertips, to feel the subtle beat of her heart. But the ribbon held fast and eventually I surrendered to the darkness.

Time had passed. I had no idea how much. Maybe half an hour. Equally it could have been ten minutes or an hour. The surface of the mirror flickered and pulled the light towards it. I looked to my right and there was Ophelia, at my side in the shadows. Her bare feet were just visible in the candlelight. The sight of them made me smile. I took her hand in mine and, as I did so, I caught sight of the bruising on my wrist that was beginning to show. My hands ached as if in response, imagining the pull, the restraint of the green ribbon against them. I pictured Ophelia above me, moving, writhing in the darkness and as these thoughts crowded into my mind, I felt another surge of anger and arousal. I closed my eyes and took a deep breath, tried to calm myself. I breathed in and out deeply a few more times, connected the air outside to the air inside, the darkness outside to the darkness within. And I began to feel calmer. I imagined the dark air of the room moving deep inside me, bringing me peace. Then I imagined the darkness inside taking over completely, my self disappearing. I opened my eyes and looked again into the depths of the mirror. The darkness now seemed almost fluid, different from before. I looked again, deeper, but I couldn't see myself. Intrigued, I concentrated, sought out my reflection. The black irises that should have been blue. As I continued to look, I finally found them. So I concentrated and looked into my eyes. I squinted to focus more clearly in the darkness. But something was different. I focused harder and the reflection became clearer. I blinked and looked hard again.

I saw a vision in the glass, clear for the first time, a dark, distorted version of myself. My eyes were possessed of a deep haunting blackness, staring intensely at me, focused, determined. My face was distended, the skin tight over a thin, skeletal face, my cheekbones sharp. My lips in the mirror parted and smiled at my self standing in the underground room. They sneered at me and the face followed suit, depraved, corrupted, carnal, yet undeniably powerful. I stared, horrified yet hypnotised by my reflection.

A second later the face vanished.

20

I jumped as if I'd been given an electric shock, stumbling several steps back from the mirror. I took a couple of short, stifled breaths and then my eyes flashed across its dark surface once again. But I could no longer see what I had seen a moment before.

Turning towards Ophelia, I saw her looking at me, stunned, mouth open slightly, as if she too had been given an electric shock.

'What happened?' she said in a whisper.

'I don't know,' I managed to get out eventually, struggling to button my jeans and fasten my belt. 'I don't know what just happened. But I need to get out of this room.' My gaze flickered briefly towards the mirror, then I turned on my heels. I raced up the stairs, vaguely aware of the sounds of Ophelia following behind me.

Minutes later, sitting opposite each other at Ophelia's kitchen table, a bottle of Jack Daniel's in the space between us, neither of us spoke. We didn't even look at one another. I took a long slug of my drink. My mind was jumping around between conviction and disbelief at what I had just experienced. Or thought I had experienced. And I kept coming back to the same place. I wasn't sure what I had seen. At the end of the day, I just didn't believe my own eyes.

'I want to know what happened in there,' Ophelia said at last. Her eyes were dull and had dark circles underneath them. She looked like she hadn't slept in a fortnight. She took a sip of whiskey, looking at me as she swallowed. Then she rolled the glass between her fingers, slowly back and forth. Her skin looked pale in the kitchen's artificial light. Even paler than usual. It gave her an air of intense vulnerability. I felt something twist in my stomach.

'Are you okay?' I said, reaching towards her across the table.

She looked at my hand but continued to roll the glass between her fingers. 'Yes, I'm okay. I'm just anxious, that's all. What happened back there?' She was staring at me, her eyes wide.

I hesitated, trying to assemble my thoughts. 'I thought I saw something. My own reflection. Someone else's. I couldn't say for sure. The whole thing happened in a matter of seconds.'

'I'm not sure I follow.'

I wasn't sure I followed, either. That was the whole point. 'Well, one moment I felt like I was looking at my own eyes. And then they weren't mine any more.' One moment they were ordinary, simply corrupted by the darkness of the glass, and the next they were simply corrupt. There was a world of difference, it seemed to me, between the two states. 'And then my whole reflection didn't feel like my own,' I added.

'So whose was it?'

'I'm not sure, but someone else's.' I paused. At least, I hoped it was.

Ophelia sat upright in her chair and stared at me incredulously. Neither of us seemed to be able to think of anything to say. 'What were you thinking about when it happened?' she said finally.

'Nothing in particular.' The words flew out of my mouth but I knew they were a lie. I had been thinking about darkness, connecting to it, breathing it in. Suddenly I felt cold. Perhaps those thoughts had in some way influenced what I saw. If I saw anything, that is. I took another shot of whiskey and felt its warm rush down my throat.

Ophelia was watching me closely. 'Were you scared?' she said eventually.

I looked down at my hand around the whiskey glass and noticed that it was still shaking slightly. I nodded. 'Although I think it was more shock than fear. And now I'm not even sure I saw anything.' I shook my head and then I reached out my hand to her again. This time she took it. 'Are you okay?' I asked her.

She looked at me for a long moment, then let go of my hand, grabbing the Jack Daniel's bottle and refilling our glasses. 'I don't know,' she said. Then she tipped her head back and downed her shot of whiskey.

'Did you see anything?' I ventured.

Ophelia looked back at me but she was silent.

I wanted to ask her more, to know if she had gone back to the underground room by herself after the first time. But she seemed withdrawn, upset, and I knew by now that it was better in such circumstances not to press her. So instead I bent over and stroked her hair. 'Look, I'm exhausted. I need to sleep. But I'm aching for a shower. Will you join me?'

She looked at me then and smiled. For the first time since we had returned. 'Thank you,' she said quietly.

'What for?'

'For not pushing me.' Then she got up from the table and made her way to the bathroom.

When I turned on the television a black and white film from 1954 was on BBC2. *The Barefoot Contessa*, starring Ava Gardner. Now I loved that movie, in particular the scene where Gardner, playing sex symbol Maria Vargas, dances a sublime barefoot flamenco for Rossano Brazzi. Ophelia had never seen the film so we lay in bed drinking whiskey and watching a spellbinding and mostly shoeless Vargas until we couldn't stay awake any more.

Ophelia fell asleep first, her body angled towards me, her hand cupping her cheek. I looked at her face, luminous in the flickering blue light of the TV. The worry lines that had etched themselves into her face during the day had dissolved with sleep. Her skin was smooth, childlike once again. I turned off the television and, facing her, lay in the darkness waiting for sleep to come.

But, despite my weariness, sleep wouldn't come. Instead

my mind circled around the events of the last few weeks: the discovery of the underground room, my nightmare, and now the face staring back at me from the depths of the mirror. The face that was and wasn't mine. Just thinking about it all made my stomach twist with anxiety.

I shivered and drew a little closer to Ophelia, reassuring myself of her presence. I stroked her hair and let my fingers run gently over her face. She was still, the flow of her breathing shallow, uninterrupted. As I watched her, my stomach twisted even more tightly. Who was this girl? Could I rely on her? Something told me in my gut that I could but I had been trusting my gut much less of late, distrusting even myself and my motivations. I thought of the mirror, shadowy in the darkness of the underground room, and an image of the face I thought I'd seen there flashed momentarily across my mind. But I pushed it away, down into the darkness inside. I was overwrought, oversensitive. I needed to put all that aside, all the distractions that I seemed to spend so much time dwelling upon. I needed to forget about Catherine, Diane, Henri and the mirror, suspend all thoughts of the underground room. I needed to sleep and work. I needed to concentrate on my drawings and show Richard that I could do it. I needed to pull myself together. Or my life was going to unravel. A fleeting image of my wife Maya floated across my mind. But I pushed it away too. I pulled Ophelia closer, inhaling the smell of her skin, the scent of her hair against the pillow. I could trust her. I knew it. So close to her, my mind calmed and my breathing slowed. I could almost hear the wings of sleep beating against the darkness and moving ever closer.

I opened my eyes and even though the room was still in shadow I saw her green eyes looking back at me. So she was awake too. I smiled at her, closed my eyes and tried to turn over. Only I wasn't lying down. I wasn't in bed. I was somewhere else.

I opened my eyes again. The woman was sitting opposite me, watching. Candles arranged on the floor beside her spilled soft light over us, making the green of her eyes twinkle. Her dark hair hung in thick tresses almost to her waist and she was wearing a long, black dress with sleeves down to her wrists. Her hands were intertwined in her lap, her thumbs circling one another in a repetitive gesture, perhaps of anxiety. Incongruously with the rest of her appearance they were red and rough. I looked at her face again. She was young, in her early twenties perhaps, but already an absolute beauty, as if she'd just walked out of a painting by Rossetti. Her skin was smooth and pale, she had a long, straight nose, high cheekbones and lips that were pink and full. But her most distinguishing feature was her eyes. They were green, deep emerald around the pupil but much lighter towards the edges of the iris with flashes of yellow and orange. They were deep-set, a pronounced oval shape framed with long, thick lashes. The combination of her features gave her a look that was hard to describe. It was the oddest combination of innocence and knowingness. She seemed shyly youthful, yet something about the eyes gave her a provocative, almost feline quality. The more I looked at her, the more I had the feeling that I had seen her before. Something about her was familiar. But I couldn't remember where I knew her from. Or, in fact, whether I knew her at all.

The silence between us had just begun to make its presence felt when she spoke.

'Hello, Johnny.' Her voice was calm, confident and if she felt any nervousness I couldn't detect it. 'I'm very pleased to make your acquaintance at last.' I smiled. She had a funny, old-fashioned way of talking. Bizarrely enough, I felt that if she had been standing she would have dropped me a small curtsy as she introduced herself. The thought had only just formed when her lips parted and she laughed, revealing bright white teeth. Then she leaped to her feet and bobbed down in front of me, her left knee grazing the floor. 'Yes, I might just have done that, sir.' She stressed the last word, pointedly.

I stared at her. It was as if she had looked into my mind. And then mocked me with what she saw there.

She laughed again, girlishly. 'I'm sorry. I shouldn't be acting in such a manner. Especially since we've only just been introduced.' Then she smiled at me. It was a beautiful, intoxicating smile.

In spite of being wrong-footed – quite how, I didn't know – I smiled back.

She sat down opposite me once more and scrutinised me. 'Now, are you quite comfortable?' she asked.

I nodded without thinking and then instinctively looked down at myself. I was sitting in an armchair, dressed in an old-fashioned three-piece suit and tie. I frowned. Where on earth had I acquired this from?

'Don't trouble yourself about that now,' she said, as if reading my mind again. 'It's something for you to dwell upon later.'

I looked at her, perplexed and suddenly uncomfortable. I felt the itch of the stiff cotton shirt, the tightness of the tie knot at my neck.

'You will have to come back to it. We don't have much time here now.' She smiled softly again. 'I've got some things I want to say to you.'

I looked at her face again, trying to place it. 'Do I know you?' Instantly I regretted the question. A better one would have been, 'Do you know me?'

Strangely, she answered the question I hadn't asked. 'Yes, I know you, Johnny. But more importantly right now, do you know who I am?'

I shook my head.

'Not even a glimmer of recognition?'

I shook my head again but with less certainty this time. As I had thought before, there was something familiar about her.

'Well, you have seen me. But perhaps it was too fleeting a glimpse.'

Her green eyes flashed and I wondered again if it was them that were familiar.

But she shook her head. 'It doesn't matter. All I wanted

to do now was introduce myself properly. I'm here to help you, Johnny.'

I looked at her but had no idea what she meant.

'Perhaps that doesn't really mean anything to you yet?' She smiled again but shook her head slowly. 'Never mind. I just wanted you to know that I will be here for you when you need help.' She cocked her head and looked at me, suddenly concerned. 'And you *will* need some help, before too long.'

I nodded, still not understanding. I had no idea who she was, what she was talking about or what I was doing here. Wherever 'here' was. For the first time, I looked around me properly. As I had noticed before I was sitting in an armchair. Now I saw that the woman in front of me was perched on what appeared to be the edge of a bed. Apart from these two items of furniture the room was empty. In the corner, behind me, was a doorway and beyond it I could just make out a hallway disappearing into darkness. I looked around me again, my curiosity suddenly pricked. The yellow velvet of the armchair upon which I sat was dull and faded, the mattress on the bed in front of it was stained and worn. I looked at the walls, their flaking plaster and paint, at the dank earth floor. Then I turned back to the woman still sitting upon the bed. 'Where am I?' I asked, already thinking that I knew the answer.

She shook her head gently and her earlier easiness and humour seemed to have evaporated. 'It's really not important.' But something about her tone inclined me not to believe her.

'What are you doing here, then?' I was suddenly curious to know why a beautiful young woman would be in this dreary, dark place.

She looked at me, no doubt sensing my bewilderment. 'Waiting,' was all she said.

'Waiting for what?'

She didn't answer.

'Well, how long have you been here?'

She hesitated before speaking. 'A long time. But it doesn't matter.' She gripped her legs and hugged them to her body tightly. 'For now I simply need you to know that you can trust me. Do you understand?'

Well, as it happened, I didn't. In fact, the whole situation felt completely beyond me. I couldn't get a handle on it. I looked at her again, perched on the edge of the bed, her bare feet poking out from beneath the hemline of her dress. And then, suddenly, it came to me. Of course. I was dreaming. I was stuck somewhere in my own unconscious with my memories of the Contessa, of dark-haired barefoot beauty Ava Gardner. In reality, I was still lying in bed next to Ophelia. Sleeping. This woman wasn't real at all. This was all unreal. That was why she knew so much more than me. Why she could read my thoughts. I smiled.

She, however, frowned. 'It would be a mistake for you to think that. I can read your mind because I'm dead.'

I stared at her, shaken by her revelation. 'But I don't even know who you are. How can I be expected to trust you?'

The young woman nodded and paused. 'So then you need to find out about me, Johnny. Find out who I am. And trust might flow from there.'

'But can't you just tell me about yourself?'

She laughed. 'Well, so far you don't seem to be very receptive to what I've got to say. So I think it might be better if you found it out for yourself. And besides, if you think about it, really think about it, Johnny, you know where to look.'

'Then you're real.'

She nodded.

I sighed. 'So I'm not dreaming.'

She shook her head. 'No. Or, at least, not in the way you think.'

'Okay,' I said uncertainly. I sighed and looked down at her feet once more. I studied her toes and felt a sudden urge to reach out and touch them. Maybe touching her would tell me if she was real or not.

'It won't,' she said. 'It won't.'

The candles that were laid out on the floor around us flickered as if a door had been opened somewhere close by and a draught had disturbed them. Instinctively, she looked behind her to the doorway which led out of the room.

'Look, Johnny. I don't have much time. Like I said before, I'm here to help you. There is danger in your future.'

'How do you know that?' I paused, suddenly confused again. 'And why do you want to help me?'

'Let's just say that there are some similarities in our

situations.' She paused. 'And I feel for you.' She smiled at me again then, that beautiful big smile of hers.

I smiled back. But the gesture felt hollow. The truth was that I didn't know what she was talking about.

'Start with what you know, Johnny. The rest will follow from there.' Then the woman stood up. She was tall, her body curvaceous beneath the black dress. 'I have to go now. But I'll be seeing you again. In the meantime, I'll be watching you.'

Then she turned her back on me and started to walk away.

'Wait,' I called after her. She continued to move towards the doorway in the far wall. 'I don't even know your name.'

She stopped, turned her head for a second and smiled again. Then she carried on into the darkness and disappeared.

21

I opened my eyes. The light of the alarm clock showed six o'clock. So it was morning and I had been asleep a long time. Yet I felt exhausted as if I had only just lost consciousness and was already awake again. I lay still, eyes closed for a while, and then looked at the clock a second time. Just after six. No mistaking it. Another day had come around. I yawned heavily. Ophelia was still asleep on her side, facing me. She was breathing silently, as quiet and unmoving as death. Calm, still slumbers. Something about that thought pricked at my drowsy brain. I looked at her face again and, perhaps sensing that I was looking at her, she opened her deep green eyes.

My brain was suddenly alert, all my recollections crowding in on me. 'I had the strangest dream last night,' I muttered.

Ophelia yawned by way of response.

'There was a beautiful young woman in it – Pre-Raphaelite features, long flowing hair. I had a very cryptic conversation with her.' I propped myself up on my right elbow as my narrative got into its stride. 'She had green eyes.' Images from the dream cruised through my brain, like a seamless progression of movie stills.

'Really?' Ophelia's voice was deadpan as she leaned over to take a drink of water from the glass on the bedside table.

'Hmm. It was odd. She told me things but at the same time didn't really seem to tell me anything.'

'Sounds like a typical annoying dream scenario.' She turned onto her back, her hair spreading out over the pillows.

'Just what I was thinking,' I said, distractedly. 'One thing she did say was that there was danger ahead and that she wanted to help me.' I felt a flicker of unease as I thought of the woman in the dark room. 'She had bare feet,' I murmured, wondering if that fact was somehow relevant.

'Bare feet?' said Ophelia and began to laugh. 'I'd say your subconscious is playing with you again. The movie, Ava Gardner. It's pretty self-explanatory, wouldn't you say?'

I thought about it and nodded.

Ophelia turned onto her side and faced me intently. 'I do like the fact, however, that your subconscious operates through a beautiful Alma Tadema type.' She winked. 'And what were you doing during her cryptic conversation with you?'

'I was dressed in a Victorian three-piece suit and sitting in an armchair.' I laughed softly. Saying it out loud made the actuality of the dream sound even more ridiculous.

'Oh. That's somewhat disappointing, I have to say. I

thought it might be a bit racier than that.' For a moment we were both silent, then she raised the duvet and looked at my naked body beneath. 'So, did anything else happen in this dream, then?'

As she continued to look at me I felt myself becoming aroused. I tried to think myself out of it. 'No, it wasn't like that at all. I was in a small, dark room. In fact, I'm pretty sure that it was the underground room.' I frowned, thinking of the furniture: in all respects it had been like that in the factory cellar. 'And the woman, I just felt that she was looking out for me.' I frowned again. The dream seemed so much like a dream in the retelling and yet I really hadn't experienced it that way. 'There was a tangible quality to it. To the dream, to her.' I stopped for a second. 'She did keep telling me she was real. And that I should try to find out about her.'

'I'll just bet she did!'

'Ah, this is hopeless. *You*'re hopeless.'

By now Ophelia had pulled up the duvet and vanished underneath it, her stifled giggles rising to the surface intermittently. In spite of myself, I found that I was smiling. I felt her fingers move down my chest and around my hips. Then she pushed me onto my back.

'You should take this more seriously,' I said, working my head into the pillows. 'Maybe there's something to it.' As I said this I felt her run the tip of her tongue over my cock, slowly, up and down, and then her lips closed around it. Her mouth felt deep and wet and I became hard immediately. I closed my eyes. My head began to spin. I could only think of the wetness of her mouth enclosing me. I took a deep breath, exhaled slowly and surrendered.

Afterwards, as I lay in bed, I studied Ophelia as she moved around the room getting ready to leave. I watched her as she picked up her clothes, as she looked at her face in the mirror, as she ran her hands through her dark hair and tied it in a ponytail. I watched her as she stood beside the armchair facing the bed, getting dressed. She pulled her trousers over her feet and up over her pale calves and thighs all the way to her waist, where she pulled absently at the zip. Then she put on a bra, threw on a shirt and buttoned it from the bottom, slowly, to the top. There was something erotic about her movements, vague and yet deliberate, as if she were performing them to thrill me. But there didn't appear to be anything conscious about them; she seemed entirely unaware that I was watching her. As her hands continued their slow journey upwards, I noticed the dark mole below her left breast and felt the need to reach out and touch it. Just as I was about to lean over to her from the bed, she raised her head and something held me back. She had a strange look on her face, the same look that she had when she gazed into the mirror in the underground room. As if she was staring at somewhere far away in the distance, a place filled with longing, the lines at the corners of her eyes sharp with the effort of looking. As I continued to watch her, her gaze met mine for the briefest of moments. Then she turned away and finished buttoning her shirt. When she raised her face again, a moment later, the look was gone. The woman smiling at me now was the Ophelia that I knew, the one that I recognised. But I could not forget that look.

An hour or so later, as I walked absent-mindedly towards the coffee shop, I couldn't get her out of my head. She had looked so different in that moment in the bedroom, so remote, that it almost didn't appear to be her face at all. She had seemed so far away from me, an insurmountable distance that I would never be able to cover, no matter how long or how hard I tried. And yet this Ophelia that I didn't recognise was a part of the Ophelia that I did, as much a part – if not more, perhaps – as the Ophelia that I knew. A sudden jolt of anxiety and fear shot through me. What did the look signify? I had no idea. And yet why was I surprised by this? I had met her only a few weeks ago. I was still getting to know her and while I had got a little under her skin that was probably all I had done. Yearning to know someone and actually knowing them were, after all, two very different things. As I trudged along through another grey day, rain spitting down from above, I began to wonder how much I would ever understand her. I mean really, truly understand her. The more I thought about that, growing to know her, the more I thought about whether we ever came to know anybody. Truly. Completely. People we thought we knew, sometimes intimately, could act totally unpredictably and surprise us. At the end of the day, when we tried to know someone, maybe we did no more than scratch the surface of their personality, no matter how long we spent trying to navigate the depths.

By the time I reached the coffee shop I was beginning to get a headache. A dull throbbing had started up behind my left eye. I ordered a croissant and a coffee and leaned against the counter while I waited, listening to the music pumping out from an old radio next to the espresso machine. I started to hum along. It was 'Don't Stand So Close to Me' by the Police. My wife loved that band. And she had loved that song. Thinking about her now, I wondered whether, after five years of marriage, I had known her. Really known her. I thought about that for a second and a frighteningly long list formed in my head. I knew that she cried easily and often about many things, and cried a lot if she was reading a Raymond Carver story. I knew the intricacies of her sometimes schizophrenic personality, her irrational anger and that it was better to leave her alone when she was blue. I knew her favourite foods. I knew the pleasure she got from eating foie gras and the guilt that she would feel afterwards. I knew she was a terrible liar but that she also couldn't be trusted. Yes, there was no doubt, I knew a whole lot of things about her. But how much did I really know her? I had no idea what hid deep down inside, in the recesses of her brain, small and perhaps insignificant, the parts of her that she disclosed to no one, that she scarcely admitted to herself. After all, what did she dream about, alone in the darkness? I really had no idea.

Lost in this thought, I became only gradually aware of

a hand waving in front of my face and pointing to a double espresso in a small paper cup on the counter. A little foam hovered on the top. I raised my eyes and stared straight into the smiling face of the waitress. I smiled back, apologised for being miles away and fumbled in my pocket for cash.

'Everything all right?' She nodded towards the steaming coffee but her tone seemed to suggest that she was talking about something else.

I looked at her closely but she just continued to smile her edgeless smile. I nodded and stirred some sugar into the cup while she opened the till and fiddled with the money. While I waited, I felt my head begin to throb in time with the beat from the radio. 'Every Breath You Take'. It must have been the Police dedication hour or something. In spite of the pounding in my head, I started to sing along under my breath. Now I loved this song. It was right up there for me. Alongside 'Roxanne'. Finally, the waitress handed me my change.

'Is there anything else I can do for you?'

'No,' I said, pocketing the coins while I looked at her, 'Thanks.'

'Okay.' And with a smile she moved down the counter and on to the next customer.

I stared into the space left by her departure and at my reflection in the mirror on the wall. I watched my mouth moving in time to the music. 'I'll be watching you,' said my lips in the mirror, mouthing the words of the song. I stopped singing and for a moment watched the reflection of me standing in the coffee shop. Several days' growth of black stubble clung to my chin and in contrast the skin above it was incredibly pale, as if it hadn't seen the sun for a while. My eyes were ringed with dark circles, my hair was unkempt and even my clothes looked dishevelled, as though they hadn't seen the touch of an iron for a while. I stared at myself for a little while longer before focusing again on the words of the song. Then I picked up my coffee and headed towards the door, my trainers squeaking softly against the linoleum floor. As I stepped back into the rainy day I thought for the first time since I had woken up about the words of the green-eyed girl, words that I had forgotten until now.

I'll be watching you.

22

'What are you doing?'

Tara's voice seemed to travel from a long way away before it reached me as I stood, motionless, at the far end of the factory's ground floor. I turned to look at her advancing form and shrugged my shoulders. I had no idea what I was doing.

When I arrived at the factory I had been entertaining a vague notion that something there could shed some light on my dream of the woman with the green eyes. On who she was or on something connected to her history. I didn't know what I thought I could discover; only that I could discover *something* if perhaps I looked in the right place. Now, as I saw the reality of Tara striding towards me, I realised how ridiculous that notion seemed. I turned back to look at the machine in front of me, pieces of plastic tubing with what looked like metal interiors scattered on a workbench beside it.

Tara stopped beside me and I sensed her gaze moving over the items before us. She was quiet for a moment or two and then she exclaimed, 'I've just realised what this machine is. Do you know?'

I shook my head.

'It's for making stilettos.' She picked up a piece of tubing from the workbench and handed it to me. 'It makes these, a plastic-encased steel tube.'

I ran my fingers over the elegantly tapering shell. 'Now that you've said it, I can see it.'

'It's called a spigot, I think. Ooh, it's amazing to see these at this stage, before they're covered in leather. Before they're beautified.' And she smiled widely at me. 'Before these machines were invented, wood was used to make the heels.'

She took one in each hand and trotted them over the surface of the bench, making a click-click sound.

'But wood simply didn't have the strength of plastic and steel. So the heels wore down very quickly and beyond a certain height were prone to snap. Four inches, I think, was about the max. Still, there were a lot of beautiful shoes around at this time. Roger Vivier, for example. Have you heard of him?'

I shook my head.

'He was known as the Fabergé of footwear. The Empress of Iran ordered over a hundred pairs of his shoes a year.'

'Is that so?'

'And Charles Jourdan. Know him?'

I nodded. I remembered his name from the conversation I'd had a few weeks earlier with Ophelia. Thinking of that, my mind began to fill with images of truncated legs. A second later it flitted to the nightmare I'd had of the underground room. In the next moment came flashes of another dream. A woman with green eyes, a pink, plump mouth, opening and forming words. *You have to find me.* Then Ophelia with a distant look on her face, her thoughts closed to me. I shut my eyes, trying to still my mind, but saw only reflections of my own face, almost unrecognisable to me.

'Imelda Marcos had heaps of Jourdan shoes.' Tara chattered on. 'There was a lot of experimentation at this time, people like Ferragamo, Perugia, all trying to achieve the most attenuated heel. The end result was this.' She pointed to the machine. 'These radicalised shoe design. By the end of the 1950s a five-inch heel was pretty standard – ultra-thin but reliable, less prone to breaking. Thus was the stiletto born.'

She looked at me for a moment, before holding the plastic heels in the space between us. Then, without speaking, she raised her right hand to my neck until the heel rested lengthways against my throat. I felt it hard against my Adam's apple. 'Did you know that the word "stiletto" is derived from a knife, a sharp blade?' Without losing eye contact with me, she went on. 'It was first favoured by Renaissance assassins and later by the Sicilian underworld.' She moved her hand around my neck and I felt the heel dig into my throat. 'So while stilettos are glamorous, sexy, they're also synonymous with death.' She made a noise as of a throat being slit. 'So you'd better tread carefully.'

For a moment we stood in silence, staring at each other. Then Tara laughed and dropped the plastic heels back onto the table. They wobbled before coming to rest.

Involuntarily, as I watched them, I ran my fingers over my neck. My voice, when it came, sounded curt, irritated. 'How do you know all this stuff, Tara?'

'Well, as I've said before, shoes are my thing.' She was quiet for a moment. 'Are you okay? You seem a little . . . tetchy.'

I turned to face her. 'I'm tired and I've got a lot on my mind.'

'I'm sorry,' she said.

'Forget it.' In the big scheme of things, it was the least of my worries.

'Anyway, I didn't come to talk to you about stilettos. I actually came to tell you something quite different. Something much more mysterious,' Tara whispered conspiratorially.

'Well?'

A moment's silence.

'Someone died here.'

It took a second for me to register what she had said. 'What?'

'You heard correctly.'

I nodded, still not really having taken it in.

'It came up in my research.'

'What?' I said again, not understanding.

'You know, the owner of the factory, the green shoes, secret rooms, that sort of thing.'

'Oh, of course.' Pause. 'So how did it happen? An accident? With the machinery?'

Tara shook her head. 'No, it didn't happen that way.'

'Then what?'

'Hmm. Not sure. Even the coroner seemed uncertain.'

'The coroner?'

Tara nodded.

'Right,' I muttered. So we were looking at a sudden, violent or unnatural death.

'Look, I think it's better if I don't try and precis the information. There's a file here that I found in the storage cupboard when I was digging around. I think it's about the investigation. Or at least part of it. Plus there's some extra information I uncovered that I've added in at the back.'

I nodded. Without really wanting to know the answer I asked the question anyway. 'So who was it? Who died here?'

'James Brimley. The second Brimley to run the factory.'

23

Night was closing in. I was lying on the sofa in my sitting room, cushions piled under my head. I had come home alone, needing some quiet time to myself, undisturbed. The TV flickered in the corner of the room, the sound down low. But I wasn't watching it. Instead, I had just begun to leaf through the file that Tara had given me. I filled up my wine glass from the bottle beside me on the coffee table and took a mouthful.

The first things I came to were two newspaper clippings, each containing an obituary of James Brimley.

James Arthur Brimley passed from the sorrows of the earth September 25, 1898. He now rests from the labours of a well-spent life and his family will find consolation in contemplating his purity and virtues – in the pious and firm-grounded hope that he has gone to the eternal rest and that in the fullness of time, when it shall please God to call them, they will join him in that abode of peace where the wicked cease from troubling and the weary are at rest.

Full of Victorian religious hyperbole and sentimentality, it shed no light whatsoever on the actual cause or location of death. I turned to the next one.

From The Times, September 28, 1898

James Brimley, Director of Brimley & Co, shoemakers, departed this life September 25, 1898, aged 39 years.

Born September 2, 1859, the first son of Eleanor and Jack Brimley. From an early age he manifested a keen interest in the industry founded by his father, often accompanying him to the factory in its nascent years when it operated out of premises at Spercer Mews, Clerkenwell, and when its workforce was comprised of far fewer individuals than at present.

From 20 years of age, James worked alongside his father at the Company's newer premises at Percival Square, Clerkenwell, having learned both the practicalities of shoe-making from the factory floor and the requisite enterprise necessary to develop and encourage the business. Renowned for his diligence, it was commonplace that he would spend long hours at the factory. However, he was equally known for his radicalism. A frequent traveller abroad, particularly to France and Italy, he was always keen to examine any new methods of manufacture and design emerging in shoemaking on the Continent.

Upon reaching 33 years of age, he succeeded his father as head of the business, and under his steady control it continued to flourish. In the short time he headed the Company he amassed not inconsiderable wealth for his family. A quiet, knowledgeable man, he was an esteemed member of the business community.

His death was sudden and without illness and our thoughts and prayers are with his family. A doting husband and father, he is survived by a wife, Elizabeth, 32 and one child, Thomas, 12.

It was certainly less pompous than the first obituary and contained numerous details about James's life. Frustratingly, however, there was little information about his death.

Turning the page, I came to a coroner's report, dated 28 September 1898. It was a long document recording the results of the inquiry into James's death. This was more like it. I sped over the introduction and focused on the section in which the coroner summarised the statements he had obtained from James's father, Jack, and James's wife, Elizabeth.

Jack Brimley indicated that his son's state of mental health had been rapidly deteriorating over the summer months of 1898. This was a particularly troublesome time in the business with problems concerning the delivery of several large and important contracts hanging over the factory. It may have been that these pressures were exacerbating factors in his decline. In any event, there were sustained bouts of depression and anger, increased periods of absence from home and a predisposition towards solitariness. Nonetheless, the family were shocked when they heard of James's death. They had never suspected that his unhappiness was so deep or would lead to such a drastic step.

According to the coroner, Mrs Elizabeth Brimley's account followed in the same vein.

Her husband's moods had become increasingly erratic and bleak over the summer months of 1898 and while James was present at the family home, albeit less and less frequently, he often sought silence and his own company. On occasion he would drink to excess. But in general he was a quiet man and remained so until the end.

I turned the page and came to the end of the coroner's report. Here he set out his conclusions on the case.

At approximately 11 o'clock in the morning, on Sunday 25 September 1898, the body of James Brimley was discovered on the premises of Brimley & Co., shoemakers. The deceased was found by his father, Mr Jack Brimley.

An examination of the body on site, made in daylight, indicated that there were grazes to the underside of the deceased's hands. In addition, there were marks around the neck, possibly from being bound with rope. However, the body was otherwise externally unharmed and no implements were discovered at the scene which could have produced the markings. Given the peculiarity of this, notice was given of the need for a post-mortem to be carried out.

Prior to the post-mortem, strangulation was the assumed

cause of death (given the pattern of markings around the region of the neck) and suicide the suspected method. However, when the examination was carried out, it was found that the larynx was undamaged and there were no fractures to the bones in the neck. There were no indications (beyond the bruising) of self-violence. Death was, in fact, natural. The deceased's heart appeared simply to have arrested.

The time of death was difficult to establish but was determined, given the state of rigor of the body, to have occurred sometime in the early hours of 25 September.

I dropped the file onto my chest and rubbed my eyes with my fingers. Poor old James. That was one hell of a strange way to go out. Dead in the factory, covered with bruises of unknown origin, inflicted by some unknown instrument. I reached for my glass and took a long, slow slug of wine, thinking about where in the factory his body might have been found. That was another thing that was unclear from the report. It could have been anywhere. Maybe the room where Tara and I worked day after day. Maybe the underground room. I shivered ever so slightly. No, if it had been there it would surely have been mentioned.

I put down my wine and focused once again on the file. The next document was a handwritten note, the script small and difficult to read. Flicking through it, I concluded that it was a private note of the coroner's, made after he had conducted his initial site investigation and consulted with the witnesses.

It began with some general observations on the state of the body after discovery. This was what I could decipher.

25/9/1898 James Brimley (39). Body discovered on ground floor of shoe factory (place of work) by father, Jack Brimley. Found facing upwards, arms and legs spread apart, eyes open. A tall man, 6 feet 7 inches, and of solid, muscular physicality, approximately 280 pounds in weight. His clothing was neat, indicating no sign of violence or altercation.

A rough sketch of the dispatch room was drawn underneath this statement, with a cross indicating where the body had been located. Just metres from the cupboard and the entrance to the underground room.

Time of death? Body shows signs of advanced rigor. Contusions around neck – but no bindings present at the scene. Not present when deceased last seen at family home (wife corroborated). Otherwise, no markings to the eyes, face or neck. Light grazing to palms and traces of earth in cuts and under fingernails – deceased crawled on all fours before death? From where? Evading assailant? But no signs of struggle in the surrounding area of the factory floor. No signs of forcible entry or intrusion. Presence of body only sign of disturbance.

There was no mention of the underground room in this section of the note. So the doorway must have been closed or surely it would have been commented upon. And yet,

James's body had been found very close to it. Maybe James had been in the underground room. That could, after all, explain the presence of earth on his hands. I thought about the cloying smell of the room, the dampness of the earth floor. My palms became moist. Maybe he had crawled up the rough wooden stairs on his hands and knees into the main part of the factory. That would explain the grazing on his body. But why would he do that? Drunk, maybe. Or incapacitated in some other way.

My eyes refocused on the section of text where the coroner had speculated about James's injuries and the presence of a third party. Maybe he was trying to get away from someone. But who? There had been no sign of struggle or forced entry at the scene and his clothes were undisturbed, not indicative of a fight having taken place. What could James have been doing in the underground room, if indeed he had been down there? I felt a slight tingle journey up my spine as I thought, not for the first time, about the mirror. I looked back at the page to see if there was any mention of it. But there was none. There were no further conclusions.

I flicked to the next page in the file. First was a death certificate, then a burial order, followed by a short article dated 1 October 1898, concerning the outcome of the coroner's investigation and the details of James's funeral. It seemed he was finally buried on 30 September 1898, in a quiet private ceremony at Bunhill Fields. I glanced over two small photographs which lay beneath the text. The one on the left was a small black and white picture of James alone. The one on the right, more faded, was presumably one of him and his family. I brought the page closer and looked again.

The first image showed James, a tall, imposing man with a handlebar moustache and a beard. He stood incredibly upright, looking straight into the camera, dressed in a smart suit and waistcoat and resting his weight upon a cane. He looked stiff, starched and somewhat uncomfortable. His shoes shone brightly, his black hair was slicked back away from his face, which was unsmiling. He had dark brooding eyes. The photo was captioned *Man of Industry* and was dated 24 May 1896, more than two years before his death. He did indeed look the epitome of Victorian industriousness: sleek, serious and expensively entrepreneurial. I looked more closely at the photograph, at his eyes once again. There was something about them: the heavy lids, the irises quickening darkly beneath.

Beside this image, the second one focused on a group of individuals. A certain grainy quality to the photograph, and around the central figures, made it difficult to see anything exact. Below it the caption read *James Brimley and family, 27 September 1898*. I brought the image closer towards me. James, dressed in a black suit and tie, stood rigidly upright behind a seated woman and child. They must have been his wife Elizabeth, who was also dressed conservatively in black, and his son Thomas, who looked like a miniature version of his father. They all stared ahead at the camera. I focused on the woman, trying to make out the details. But nothing beyond the generality of her features, her dark hair and eyes, the overall shape of her face, was discernible. The same was true of the son. But one thing was clear – a certain tension in the demeanour of all the subjects. The whole party were sombre, dour and unsmiling, and a mood of intense unhappiness seemed to hover tangibly over the image. I looked again at James. He was clean-shaven now and his once jet-black hair appeared to have wisps of grey running through it. But beyond the obvious contours of his face, his eyes, nose and mouth, I couldn't decipher anything.

I looked at the image once again. Something about it wasn't right. I turned back to the coroner's report, looking for the exact date of James's death. When I came across it – 25 September 1898 – I knew exactly what was wrong with the photograph. It had been taken two days after James's death.

'It's a Victorian death portrait,' I said aloud.

Now that I knew it, it seemed so obvious: the extra formal arrangement of the subjects, even down to the dead man standing upright to reinforce the idea of his being alive. I knew that such photographs were a way of remembering the life of the deceased. And yet, simultaneously, they were also a direct acknowledgement of death.

I focused on the image once again. But it was too small to make out any more than I had done already. I got up and went to the cupboard in the kitchen to retrieve my magnifying glass. I often used it for work to look closely at plans or drawings or to sharpen up old documents. It ought to enlarge the photograph enough to clarify the characters a little more.

I sat back down on the sofa and looked at the image through the glass. Sure enough, now I could see the faces of the subjects more clearly. I saw Thomas, wide-eyed and uptight. No wonder, poor kid. The idea of such photographs was pretty morbid, if you asked me. Elizabeth, while she didn't look as strained as her son, had a taut intensity about her face which suggested that she wasn't relishing the experience either. I turned my attention back to James, to his greying hair, his shaven cheeks. As I looked, more closely now, at the black eyes staring out at me, my heart began to thud hard in my chest.

I looked at the eyes again. They were deep wells of darkness and even death hadn't quite obliterated the hardness at their edges. I swallowed and felt the fear explode in my stomach. I looked over James's face once more but there was no way I was mistaken. I had seen this man before. I had met him.

The dead man in the picture was the man I had encountered a few weeks earlier in my nightmare.

I sat bolt upright, my head spinning. Then I got up from the sofa and poured myself another glass of wine, my hand shaking slightly as I did so.

I took a long, slow mouthful and tried to make sense of things. But they didn't make any sense. The man from my nightmare was James Brimley. And even though I hadn't known what he looked like until now, I had seen him already in my dreams. I frowned. How could that be?

I took another mouthful of wine and tried to think. James Brimley. He was born in 1859. He had been a Director at the shoe factory where I now spent my days working. We had no doubt trudged over the same floor-boards, taken in the same scenes, maybe both been down to the underground room. I blinked hard. It was difficult to take in. He had been real. He had had a wife and a child and had died in 1898. And yet I had dreamed about him long before I had found out any of this.

I tried to remember the nightmare. There had been the man, James, holding the green shoe in his hand, the mirror, dark against the wall, and the feet and legs and body on the bed. Then there had been his intense anger at my intrusion and the sensation of suffocation and falling. Now James, the man from my dream, had entered my real life. I thought of the strangeness surrounding his death, the positioning of the body close to the under-ground room, the mirror in the darkness beneath. I shivered and downed the rest of the wine in my glass.

Pouring myself another, I looked at the open file on the coffee table. I knew there were pages still unread but I was unsure now if I wanted to continue. I couldn't begin to imagine what they might contain. Instead, I tried to think about eating something. But the thought left me nauseous. I wasn't hungry and, besides, it was late. I paced up and down the room thinking, trying to make sense of things. Finally I walked over to the television in the corner of the room and turned it off. Even though the sound hadn't been on loud, the room was plunged instantly into deep silence. It spilled over me and somehow brought with it calm. I walked back to the sofa and lay down. I stared at the file open beside me on the coffee table but I couldn't summon the energy to reach across to it. The will to continue reading had now completely deserted me. Instead I tried to relax and let the quietness take control.

24

The sound of the telephone woke me, shattering the comforting silence of my sleep. It set my nerves instantly on edge. I attempted to open my eyes but they were cemented shut. Lying still for a moment, I tried to remember where I was. My whole body was cold, aching and my mouth felt as dry as a desert.

The insistent grating of the telephone continued. Turning onto my side, I prised my eyelids apart. I was still on the sofa in the sitting room. Late-morning sunlight streamed through the windows, illuminating an empty red-wine bottle, a half-empty glass and a yellow file on the table beside me. A trail of wine had snaked down the length of the glass and formed a deep purple circle around its base on the table top. I breathed in deeply, closed my eyes and surrendered momentarily to the dull thud of a hangover forming in the recesses of my brain. As I lay there, incapacitated, the harsh ringing of the telephone suddenly stopped. It left an ominous silence in its wake, a silence that seemed to be speaking to me. I opened my eyes again, grabbed my watch from the coffee table. 'Shit,' I yelled and jumped up.

*

Half an hour later, I sprang out of a cab and ran towards the doors of our Shoreditch office. I felt sick as I sprinted up the steps to them two at a time. As I moved towards Richard's office, I found myself hating, not for the first time, our open-plan arrangement. Multiple stares rose from the paperwork on various desks and followed my progress as I marched briskly across the floor. I began to sweat and the colour rose in my cheeks. Why on earth hadn't I taken five more minutes to brush my hair and find a clean shirt? I really hadn't thought this through properly. As I passed Tara's desk, she leaped up and walked with me.

She looked concerned. 'I tried calling you. Where were you?'

I shrugged, not replying.

'Look, do you think it's a good idea to go and see him in this state?' She indicated my crumpled appearance.

'Yeah. I think it's better to just deal with it now.' Although, to tell the truth, I didn't know whether it was. I didn't really know what I was doing. Only that this seemed better than the alternative of turning round and leaving across the open-plan office again.

As we reached Richard's door Tara's hand intercepted mine. She held the handle closed for a second. 'Are you sure it isn't better to go home, take a shower, come back later with some drawings? He really wants to see some progress, Johnny.' Tara was looking at me, her eyes pleading. I noticed then, for the first time, that she too looked tired. 'Wouldn't it be better if you could offer him that?'

She was probably right but something in me didn't want to turn back. Besides, I wasn't sure that I could offer Richard any progress, now or later. I smiled. 'Don't worry. It'll be okay.' And I moved her hand out of the way and turned the handle.

As I stepped into Richard's office the first thing I noticed was the sunlight pouring in through the windows. The blinds had been lowered but the light still shone unforgivingly across the room. I blinked as I walked through it, imagining myself in high definition, a tired, bedraggled spectacle with untidy hair and clothes. Again I regretted my earlier decision not to simply turn on my heels and leave. But now it was too late. I was in full view, exposed by the glowing winter brightness. I was vaguely aware of Tara following me, closing the door behind us, and of Richard rising from the chair behind his desk and muttering something to me. But what it was I didn't hear. I came to a halt and when I saw Richard gesture to a seat I felt my knees bend in reflex. Only when I had been sitting for a moment or two did I notice Hajime, one of our senior associates, standing beside Richard's chair.

'Hi there,' I said to him. I heard my own voice clearly, so the acoustics at least seemed to be back to normal. 'It's a little bright in here, don't you think?'

He nodded and smiled, but even in my somewhat dazed state I noticed how uncomfortable he seemed. I turned my attention back to Richard who was now seated once more, staring down at his desk.

'Hi, Richard,' I began. 'Sorry I'm so late for our meeting. Am I interrupting anything now?'

'No, no, no,' he said, but his tone seemed to imply that he was somewhat at a loss. He looked from me to Tara and then back again, without his usual display of certainty.

'Is everything okay?' I ventured.

'Yes,' he said, eventually, taking a breath and running a hand through his hair. This seemed to embolden him. 'In fact, perhaps it's better that you're here now.'

'Okay,' I said but added nothing more. The intense sunlight seemed to heighten the tension in the room and I felt a quiver of unease in my stomach.

'Look, Johnny . . .'

As soon as I heard the words I closed my eyes. I knew what was coming. For some reason, an image of the mirror flashed across my mind.

'. . . I don't really know how to say this. So I'm just going to say it.' Then Richard paused, as if in doubt about whether he was in fact going to say it. He cleared his throat and, in spite of myself, I felt for him. He was nervous and it can't have been a feeling that sat very easily with him. 'Things don't seem to have been heading in the right direction on this project for a little while now. I think perhaps you might even agree?'

He paused again for a moment and I thought about contradicting him, jumping in with some upbeat statements about my ideas and drawings, saying that the finished designs were just around the corner. I thought about telling him that he'd got it completely wrong. If he'd only give me a little more time there'd be something exceptional coming his way. But when I opened my mouth to speak no words came out. Something in me couldn't do it. I couldn't muster the capacity to lie. So instead I closed my mouth again and let the unexpected winter sunlight wash over me, bright and cleansing. I looked at him and simply waited for what was coming next.

'Well,' he soldiered on, 'given that we're now behind on the timetable and there's no real concrete sign of drawings that can realistically be shown to the client . . .' Richard hesitated for a second, perhaps waiting for an interjection from me that didn't come. 'I really feel I have no choice but to reassign the factory project.'

He rushed out the last few words. Still, their meaning was clear enough. He was firing me from the job. I had dreaded being given this news, had felt it hanging over me, heavily, for a couple of weeks. But now it had actually been delivered I felt surprisingly little. If anything, relief spilled through me. I turned to Hajime and really saw him for the first time. Of course, that was why he was here. Our talented Japanese associate. He was diligent, ambitious, unkempt but in a stylish sort of way. In short, he was everything that I was not.

I followed his averted gaze, unable to meet mine, to the table in front of him and Richard. It was only then that I noticed the photographs of the factory, its spaces, its light, its machinery, the pile of surveyors' drawings, the few rough pencil sketches. I took a breath and looked out of the window into the sunlight. Then my gaze returned to the desk. Yes, there was no mistaking it. There were pictures and documents concerning the factory renovation. So this had been a done deal before today. I felt a slow uncurling of anger in my stomach. Whatever I might have said to Richard, however I might have tried to redeem myself now, it would have been too late. The process had already started. They had begun to carve up factory floors, eager to get their hands dirty on the job.

I looked at Richard, at my friend, who had made no real effort to speak to me about his concerns. And I felt fury take hold of me, fury directed at him. In that moment I wanted to yell, to scream into the sunlight, to say everything I'd ever held back. But as the words failed me, as I sat silently, I felt the momentum of my anger shift. Towards myself: I had let this happen, I had not raised my own anxieties with him but rather had sought to keep him in the dark about them and had asked others to do the same.

I turned to look at Tara, feeling the regret swell and tangle inside me. She had tried to warn me, to help me and even when I hadn't listened she had stood by me, by every bad decision I had made. And she had lied to Richard for me. I looked at her face, pale, stricken. Perhaps this was a shock to her too, something she had not been expecting quite yet. Yet it had all been heading inexorably to this point.

I smiled at her as I stood up, somewhat shakily, and pushed the chair away from me. 'Tell me just one thing, Richard. Has Hajime been to the factory already to have a look at things? Perhaps he's been a few times, when Tara and I haven't been there?'

After a moment or two, Richard nodded and had the decency to look embarrassed. 'I'm sorry, Johnny, but I had to take steps . . . in case . . .' His voice petered out.

'I understand. Tara noticed that someone had been coming in and out. She just didn't know who it was.'

I turned to look at her but she didn't see me. She was facing Richard, a furious expression on her face. So he had kept her in the dark about his plans. I had to hand it to him. He could be a ruthless bastard when he wanted to be. 'Funny,' I said to myself, moving towards the door.

'I'll need your factory keys back, Johnny. You won't be needing them now.' Richard's tone was impassive, his voice composed. 'I'm sorry to ask it but . . .'

I stopped and turned back to face him. I studied his chiselled face, the set expression, his brown eyes, the hardness at their edge. He didn't look like he was sorry.

I felt the anger rise within me again. I looked out of the window and saw a rush of dark clouds across the sky, casting a pall over the city. The next moment the brilliant sunshine vanished from the room. As I pulled the factory keys from my pocket, I noticed a bitter taste in my mouth. I swallowed and tried to clear my head. But it was then that the images hit me. A mirror in the blackness, a man, James Brimley, a man from my dreams, dead upon a factory floor. The green eyes of a girl, the blackness of a queen. The images tumbled through my mind, disconnected. Then I saw the keys sitting in the palm of my hand. As Richard reached across to take them, it took all my strength, all of my composure not to snatch my hand away. A dark reflection flickered in front of my eyes and vanished. Then Richard pocketed the keys.

I smiled at him for a moment. A brief, tight smile filled with hate. Then I turned on my heels and left.

25

That evening I was sitting at Ophelia's dining table, having just recounted the sorry story of being fired from the factory project. A half-empty bottle of red wine sat in front of me. I took a large mouthful from my glass and wondered for the hundredth time how it had happened. Even now, having gone over the details with Ophelia, it all still felt somewhat unreal. I looked at the silver candlestick next to the bottle of wine, at the white candle, cascades of wax clinging to its side. I frowned. Somehow the candlestick looked different today from the way it had looked the last time I was here. And yet it was the same candlestick, I was sure. Perhaps it was simply that everything looked different now. Jaded, tainted.

I pulled off a piece of wax, rolled it into a small white ball and placed it next to the yellow file open beside me on the table. I stared at it for a time, then took another large gulp of wine. It seemed like the best thing to do in the circumstances. Closing my eyes, I rubbed my fingers across them. I was tired, I needed some rest. But in the darkness behind my eyelids I saw an image of the keys of the factory sitting in the palm of my hand, my offering to Richard. My eyes snapped open and my anger, which had abated somewhat, rose ferociously once more. I came back to the question I had been asking myself all day. Which of these two scenarios was worse? Being sacked from the project or being evicted from its premises?

'Here you go.' Ophelia was making her way back into the room, carrying a sandwich. She moved the bottle of red wine and set the plate down on the table in front of me. 'Now eat this. You can't just drink.' She ran her fingers through my hair and kissed me on the cheek. Then she sat opposite me again.

'Thanks,' I said, but simply looking at the sandwich made me feel queasy. I pushed the plate towards Ophelia with an apologetic smile. Then I refilled our wine glasses.

'You really should eat,' she said, but without much conviction. We sat for a moment or two in silence. 'So what I can't work out is why Richard wouldn't have discussed his issues with you first. It's all very draconian, especially as you're supposed to be his friend.' Ophelia frowned, narrowing her eyes.

I simply nodded. I had been thinking about it all day and the only conclusion I could come to was that he was still angry with me over Tara. Whether he knew it or not, that had probably had a bearing on his decision-making. Kill two birds with one stone. Get me off the project. And get me off the project in which she was involved.

'It doesn't make any sense,' Ophelia continued.

Except that perhaps it did. The old green-eyed monster had raised its head again. With that thought, something else came to mind. Instinctively my right hand reached for the yellow file open beside me, my fingers resting against the roughness of the paper.

'What is that, by the way?' Ophelia pointed to the file. 'You keep touching it. Are you making sure it's real?' And she laughed.

But, ironically, she was right on point. 'Funny you should say that.' I smiled. 'It's a file that Tara prepared for me. I read some of it last night but I haven't had a chance to tell you about it.' The events of the day flashed in fast-forward through my mind and again I had a sense of the unreality of things. I stared at the candlestick to see if that helped. It didn't. But the coolness of the paper under my right hand, the solidity of the table beneath it, soothed me. 'It's mostly about James Brimley, one-time boss of the factory.' I took a breath. 'And the investigations into how he died there.'

'Oh,' said Ophelia, her laughter all gone.

'Do you want me to tell you about it?'

'Only if you want to.' She looked at me as she took a sip of her wine. 'It's been a bit of a day for you, after all.'

Images of the meeting cascaded through my brain. Then leaving the Shoreditch office, pounding the streets for a while trying to make sense of things, ignoring calls from Tara and finally heading home. Finishing reading the file had turned out to be a welcome distraction – even if there were other unexpected things within it. 'No, it's fine. Really. It takes my mind off today, at least.' I thought of Richard's outstretched hand once more, reclaiming the factory keys, and my mortification and fury rose again. I took another gulp of wine, swallowed it down and began the story of James Brimley's death.

As I talked about what Tara had uncovered, Ophelia watched me, her green eyes calm, collected. Only when I paused for breath did she interject. 'So James was found dead in the dispatch room?'

It was less of a question than a statement, but I nodded nonetheless. Then I showed her the drawing that the coroner had made, the cross marking the place where the body had been discovered. 'Tara and I must have walked over the spot hundreds of times.'

Ophelia looked at me and shuddered. 'Creepy. And the circumstances of the death were creepy, too.'

'Right. And yet the coroner concluded he died from natural causes . . .'

'But . . .? Aren't you convinced?'

'There's nothing conclusive. It's all circumstantial stuff like scuffs on his hands and marks on his neck. There's nothing really to suggest suicide or some kind of wrangle with an intruder. There's nothing really to point to foul play.'

'So what are you thinking?' Ophelia's eyes had narrowed again.

'I don't know. I really don't. But something about it doesn't stack up.' I thought about my nightmare again. That didn't stack up either.

'What is it, Johnny?' Ophelia said.

I sighed. 'Do you remember me telling you about the nightmare I had? A few weeks ago?'

'Of course I remember.' She paused. 'The one in which you thought you died.'

I pulled the article with the photographs of James from the file and placed them in front of her. 'Turns out that he was the man from my nightmare.'

'James?'

I nodded.

Ophelia stared at me for a second, uncomprehending.

'I know, I know. It's a head fuck.'

'So, let me see if I've got this straight. A man who you see in a dream turns out to have actually existed.' She paused. 'And to have worked in the place where you now work.'

I nodded again. We were both silent for a few minutes, each caught in our own thoughts.

'It's . . . well . . . I don't know.'

'Exactly. I started to wonder if I was going mad.' I paused for a moment and took a deep breath. 'And then today it got even weirder.' I flicked through Tara's file until I came to the right document. I pulled it out and placed it in front of Ophelia.

Her gaze shot downwards. She cursorily examined the page and then looked back at me expectantly. 'What is it?'

'It's a photocopy of a page from an old log, a ledger.' It was handwritten, like the coroner's report, but the writing was larger and clearer. 'Women's names, as you can see, run in alphabetical order down the left-hand column. Marjorie Ashton, Mary Audley, Irene Bailey,

Sarah Burnham, Eva Dooler, so on and so forth down to Katherine Irvine. The middle rows document shoe sizes, colours and styles, including a summary of the shoes' main features. The final three columns running down the right-hand side detail the not inconsiderable sums paid for the items, the addresses and dispatch dates. These, as you can see, are all in 1898.'

Ophelia looked up at me and shrugged. 'So?'

'When Tara and I first went into the underground room, she was particularly interested in the green shoes that were down there. She was sure that they were hand-made and that we could identify who they belonged to if she could just find the records. She was certain that there would be a log somewhere in the files littering the place detailing orders and who had placed them.'

'And this is the log?'

I nodded, tapping my finger on the page. 'This is a list of women who ordered handmade shoes from the factory in the first two quarters of 1898.'

This time Ophelia looked properly down the list, her gaze moving over the descriptions of the shoes until she found them. Dark green leather, tapering heel, ankle strap, embroidered uppers, pale green thread. Then, reaching the name alongside it, she said it aloud. 'Amelia Holmes.'

I closed my eyes as the words seemed to rise off the page and take shape, moulding themselves into the contours of a woman. I nodded and pulled the final piece of paper from the file. 'When Tara discovered that the shoes belonged to an Amelia Holmes, she obviously wanted to know more about her. I have to hand it to the girl, she's a genius at uncovering information. She found an old newspaper article which you can read in a moment. First, just take a look at the photograph at the bottom of the page.'

Ophelia scanned the picture and gave a quiet whistle. Even in a poorly reproduced photograph from an old newspaper there was no question about it. The woman, Amelia Holmes, was staggeringly beautiful. She was smiling conservatively, her mouth closed but raised at the corners and the striking nature of her eyes, even in black and white, was evident.

'Wow, she's a looker,' said Ophelia, tilting her head to get a better look at the image.

A moment passed in silence as I too looked at the photograph. I took in the eyes, imagined their irises of green and yellow and orange. Then I said it. 'She's the woman I told you about before. The woman from my dream.'

26

'How is it possible?' Ophelia was staring at me, wide-eyed. I imagined her mind in free fall, trying once more to make sense of something nonsensical.

I reached over to the newspaper article and ran my finger over the name. 'She existed, too.' She had been as real, as substantial as Ophelia and me.

'Incredible.' Ophelia shook her head. 'And like James you saw her in a dream before you knew she existed.'

I thought once more about my dream of Amelia Holmes, when I had spoken to her in what I presumed was the underground room.

Ophelia pointed to the name in the log once more. 'And James's factory made the shoes for her. So there was a connection between them.'

I nodded. 'More than you know.' I reached over the table and tapped the newspaper article. 'Why don't you read this now?'

'Okay,' she said, although the look in her eyes was unsure.

The Chronicle, 15 October 1898

Local Girl – MISSING

Amelia Holmes, of Bethnal Green, has now been missing for over three weeks. She was last seen by fellow workers of Brimley's shoe factory in Clerkenwell at approximately six o'clock in the evening on 23 September, in Percival Square. However, she has neither been seen nor heard from since.

Amelia (b. 3 April 1879) is the eldest of five children born to Grace and Branwell Holmes, Grace Holmes having died of consumption in May 1897. Since that time Amelia has worked in the assembling department of Brimley's. It was while leaving the premises of the factory that she was last seen.

No trace of Miss Holmes has been found since her disappearance. Her father commented that: 'She is a very loving daughter and sister. When her mother died she selflessly stepped into her shoes and took care of us all. A warm, generous-hearted and considerate girl, she would not have gone anywhere of her own free will without telling us. I appeal to anyone with any information about her. She is much missed.'

For a few moments Ophelia simply stared in silence at the piece of paper on the table. 'So she actually worked with James,' she said eventually. 'The connections between them just keep growing.' Then silence resumed. No doubt, as I had done myself when I read the article, she was trying to piece things together.

'So I've been thinking about this for a while,' I ventured. 'Want to know what I've come up with?'

Ophelia nodded, rubbing her temples. 'My head's in a scramble. I can't get any of it straight.'

'Okay. Let me try.' I took a slow breath and began. 'So these are the facts we know. Amelia Holmes was born in the East End of London and lost her mother in 1897 at the age of eighteen. This clearly marked a change in the fortunes of the family and not just emotionally. With five children and with one less parent working, without question the family would have needed more money. She had to get a job. So in May Amelia went to Brimley's factory to make shoes.'

I could see Ophelia looking at James's log, at Amelia's name written there. Picking up my thread, she continued. 'And there she would have met James. The rather dour but dashing new boss.'

'Hmm.'

We looked at each other but neither of us said what the other was no doubt thinking.

'And, if nothing else, there is at least one sign, I think, which points to a certain . . . closeness, shall we say, between them.'

'The shoes.'

I nodded. 'Exactly.'

'Yes. She's poor, working in a factory to help sustain her family.' Ophelia tapped the article about her disappearance. 'So what was she doing with a pair of expensive hand-crafted and stitched shoes? It doesn't add up that she'd have bought them. She'd have had to save for them for an eternity. And her money would have been going home to the family, surely.' Ophelia flicked back through the log, scrolling down the column indicating the amounts paid for the handmade shoes. 'Johnny, there's no amount written down in Amelia Holmes's column for the green shoes.'

I nodded again. I had noticed it when I first looked through the log. 'There's no delivery address listed, either.'

'So it makes sense that they were a gift from him to her. A gift from one lover to another?' Ophelia tilted her head and looked quizzically at me.

'Well, let's not get ahead of ourselves. We don't know that.' But even as I said it I doubted myself. The image from my nightmare of a woman's body on the bed in the underground room flashed through my mind: the slip, crumpled and sweat-stained, the pale uncovered thighs.

'That's true,' Ophelia said, wrinkling her nose. 'But something about an affair feels right, wouldn't you say?'

I nodded.

'And besides, you found the shoes in the basement, which puts one or other or both of them down there. And it just happens to contain a bed.'

Her words made me think of something Tara had said about that. 'I mean, what's with the bed. It's got to be sex, right?' Yes, it probably was sex. Another image of the sated, spent body in the underground room flashed through my mind.

'Let's put that aside for the moment,' I said. 'What we know is that Amelia began work at the factory in May 1897 and disappeared a little less than a year and a half later, in September 1898. She literally vanished on her way home from work one night.'

'Right,' said Ophelia.

'I did an internet search on her disappearance after reading the news article that Tara found. But it didn't bring up anything at all about it. And I'm guessing, because there's nothing else in the file, that Tara didn't find anything, either. So I think it's unlikely that Amelia ever reappeared or was found.'

We were both silent for a few moments. Finally Ophelia spoke. 'So, maybe the affair, if there was one, ended badly. She could have left, unable to bear the thought of seeing him day after day.'

I thought about it, but something about this version of events didn't ring true. 'The whole point of her taking this job was that she wouldn't be far from her family. They were important to her. So I don't buy the idea that she would just leave if an affair went wrong. That can't be it. She'd just change her job, surely.'

'Hmm. Right. But might she have fled if she got pregnant? Rather than face the shame.'

That made more sense, I had to admit. After all, pregnancy outside marriage was a big deal back then. Still, something didn't resonate for me. 'But she loved her family. So even if she'd taken off, why wouldn't she at least tell them that she was alive? It doesn't make any sense.'

'Yeah, you're right.' Ophelia studied the missing-person article once more. 'Her father clearly thought that something untoward had happened to her. "She would not have gone anywhere of her own free will without telling us." So maybe she was abducted or killed on her way home.'

I nodded. There had been a number of notorious murders in this period of Victorian history and it was one of the explanations that made the most sense to me. I paused, as my mind flooded with the darkest possibility. 'And, of course, there's the other thing.'

Ophelia nodded but didn't say anything.

'James killed her. And masked a murder with a disappearance.'

'Right.'

For a moment we sat in silence while Ophelia flicked through the pages of the file. 'Only a short time after Amelia's disappearance James is discovered dead at the factory.'

I nodded. 'He was found on the Sunday morning. Two days after she disappeared.'

'And the coroner concluded that he'd died of natural causes.'

'Right.'

'But let's assume for a second that the coroner's wrong.'

'Okay.'

'Maybe James killed her and then, driven mad by what he had done, he killed himself.'

'I thought about that, too. But then, how did he commit suicide? He didn't strangle himself, even if he tried, and there's no evidence to point to anything else. He had a heart attack.'

Ophelia nodded and was quiet for a second. 'What if Amelia killed James, left the body at the factory and then disappeared?'

I had considered that as well. 'But he was so much bigger, so much taller and stronger than her. I just can't see how that could happen. Or, if she managed to kill him somehow, how it could leave no trace.'

'Hmm. And if he'd been in the underground room, as seems likely from the coroner's report, then she'd have had a real struggle on her hands to get a body weighing 280 pounds up the stairs and into the dispatch room.'

We fell silent again for a moment before Ophelia raised her next question.

'But the timing is weird, don't you think?'

I nodded as I pulled another piece of wax from the candle and rolled it into a ball. It was weird as far as the eye could see.

'I think it's most likely that Amelia was killed by James. And that scenario explains why the green shoes stayed in the basement. Surely if she was planning to escape to a different life she'd take the most beautiful things she possessed.'

I bowed my head in agreement.

'But instead the shoes remained in the underground room.'

For an instant I was descending the cellar stairs, moving into the darkness, seeing the green shoes hanging from the velvet ribbon on the corner of the mirror. What exactly had happened to Amelia and James? I couldn't shake the feeling that, whatever it was, it was connected to the mirror. Lost in this thought, I only gradually became aware of Ophelia repeating my name.

I coughed. 'Sorry. I was miles away.'

'What were you thinking about?'

I wondered for a second if I should tell her or not. But it was only fair. She too had stared into its darkness. And might do so again. 'I was thinking about the mirror.'

'What about it?'

I paused, then decided to bite the bullet. 'It was in my nightmare too.'

'Oh. You didn't tell me that before.'

'Didn't really see the point.' It was a light, white lie.

Ophelia looked at me. 'What do you think it means?'

'I don't know.' But I was sure it meant something. And that thought was plaguing me.

'Well, whatever it means, it's bizarre. You dream about two people before you know who they are. Then it turns out that they were connected to one another, possibly, perhaps even probably, in the most intimate of ways. Then there are the shoes, also in the dream, at first seemingly unconnected, that turn out to tie them together even further. So the mirror must be connected too. And the underground room. All the things in the dream are there for a reason.'

I nodded. I was sure she was right. I was just struggling to make the connections.

'I'm sure there's more information at the factory that could help clarify things. It's just a question of finding it.

But now I have no way of getting in.' I had told Ophelia of the ignominy of having to hand my keys back to Richard.

As I smiled at her sadly, she reached across the table, took my hand in hers and for a few moments simply stared at me. 'Well, I guess every cloud has a silver lining,' she said finally.

I looked at her. 'What do you mean?'

'Well . . .' and then she stopped. 'Johnny, if I tell you this, you have to promise not to get angry.'

'Why would I get angry with you?' At the moment, the only person I could imagine directing my anger towards was Richard.

Ophelia smiled. 'Just promise me, okay?'

'Okay,' I said and kissed her hand.

'Well, a little while ago, one weekend when you had left your keys at my flat . . . I can't remember where you'd gone off to . . . anyway . . .' Ophelia stopped and took a deep breath. 'I had another set of your factory keys cut.' She rushed out the sentence and then fell silent.

For a moment I simply stared at her. I was having trouble understanding what she'd said. 'Why?' I said eventually.

'I don't know. I really don't. I suppose I thought I might need them.'

'Why?' I said again.

'I don't know,' Ophelia repeated.

'Have you ever used them?'

'No.'

I stared at her, into her deep green eyes, but I didn't know if she was telling me the truth or not.

'You have to believe me, Johnny. I've only been there once without you. You know about that. Since then, since the keys were cut, I've only been back with you.'

I nodded, trying to make sense of it. But I couldn't. I couldn't understand why she would do such a thing. Unless it had always been her plan to use the keys without my knowledge.

'Are you angry with me?' Ophelia's eyes were pleading.

'No,' I said, my voice surprisingly calm. 'I'm not angry.'

'And, as it turns out, it's a good thing, isn't it?' She smiled. 'Now you can still get into the factory. We can still get into it.'

'Yes, I suppose.' I paused, trying to think. 'Thank you,' I added, but I couldn't bring myself to smile.

'You'll need to be careful, of course.'

I nodded. The last thing I wanted was to be found trespassing on the premises. If Richard caught me there I had no idea what he might do. Strangely enough, the thought made me smile.

'What is it?'

'Oh, nothing.'

Ophelia looked at me for a long moment. Then she stood up, taking the uneaten sandwich and heading towards the kitchen. 'You haven't forgotten that I'm leaving for that shoot in Yorkshire next week?'

I turned to look at her. 'No, I haven't forgotten.'

'Will you be okay while I'm gone?'

The look of concern in her eyes made my coldness evaporate. 'Yes, I'll be okay,' I said, smiling.

'And no more strange dreams, okay?'

'Okay,' I said.

But instead of moving she simply stood there looking at me. Then she gave voice to a thought that had been bothering me for some time. 'Johnny, do you even think they were dreams?'

I shrugged. I really wasn't sure of anything any more. But if they weren't dreams, then what were they? I thought of Amelia and James again, of the underground room, the darkened mirror hanging on the wall, its cipher on the bottom right-hand corner. I thought of a Black Queen, her witchcraft, her visions and premonitions. Then I thought of the past and the paths of history that lead to the present.

27

Chateau de Fontainebleau

June 1556

Catherine lay in her bed, completely still, settled upon a mound of silk pillows. They felt soft and smooth against her skin, more sensitive today than usual. Her body was sore and weak, exhausted from the birth of twins and the slightest ill-considered movement brought her pain.

Dark damask fabrics hung at the open windows and when caught by the warm wind they bloomed inwards into the chamber, scattering patterns of sunlight across the ceiling. She knew it must be a bright, beautiful day outside, but she did not turn her head to look. Instead, she continued to stare upwards, her gaze following the dancing pools of light over the panels of gold leaf and cobalt blue. It should have been a happy day, she thought. But it was not. The doctors had said it would be unlikely that Victoire, the firstborn child, would last beyond a few weeks. And Jeanne, the second, was already dead, her mangled, broken body, pulled from Catherine's womb, already in the ground. Tears slid silently down Catherine's cheek. She heard the voices echoing over and over, telling her that she had nearly died, that her life was something to be grateful for, that God was to be praised. But in this moment, remembering, she was not grateful and she could not praise.

The curtains blew into the room once more, caught by the strong breeze. It carried with it the sound of children's voices, her children's voices, from the garden below. They were playing, shouting and laughing. As she listened she heard Edouard-Alexandre, his voice ragged, out of breath, calling for his sister. She heard the patter of his small feet, running. A moment later she heard him reprimanding Claude for cheating. She broke into a smile as she listened and her heart bloomed. Thank God for Edouard-Alexandre, for her beloved children. A moment later another voice floated into the room. It was a woman's, one that she recognised instantly, subdued and asking the children to be quiet. She called them by their nicknames, affectionate names used by Catherine and the King, names that Catherine believed only she and the King should use.

Instantly her small moment of contentment vanished and her mood changed. The rising hatred she felt was almost suffocating. She listened for the voice again, certain that if she heard it she would screech in anger, unable to suppress her rage. But the breeze carried nothing more. She breathed deeply and tried to compose herself. But her heart constricted inside her. Was there nowhere, nothing, sacred from this woman's polluting influence? She turned abruptly onto her side and felt a searing pain in her abdomen. The force of it caused tears to spring to her eyes but she did not care. The physical pain was a welcome distraction from the emotional turmoil she had to endure at the hands of this whore day after day. She poked her nose into affairs that should not concern her, prodded with her grasping tainted fingers at things that were treasured, private, held dear. If only Catherine could be rid of her. But it was too dangerous for her to meet a death that could be traced back to the hand of the Queen. She was, after all, still protected by the King.

A knock on the door disturbed Catherine's thoughts. She pushed herself upright, wincing in pain as she did so, and settled herself once more on the pillows.

'Come in,' she said a moment later.

The door opened slowly to reveal Cathelot, her female jester. For a moment the two women simply looked at one another. Then the dwarf closed the door behind her and moved across the room. The ringing of the bells on her jester's hat echoed dissonantly through the subdued chamber. Catherine watched as she approached, in her usual red and gold attire, and something in the incongruity of her dress, so usually associated with mirth, made her heart weep. When she reached the edge of the bed she scrambled up onto it like a child and, sitting beside Catherine, took her hand.

'How are you, my Queen?' Her voice, usually so joyful and full of laughter, was curiously muted.

Catherine said nothing for a moment, not trusting herself to speak. Finally, when she was certain of her composure, she answered. 'I am rallying, Cathelot, I am rallying. I am better simply for seeing you. It has been a while.'

Cathelot nodded. 'And I am sorry for my absence, my lady. I have been back for a little while now. But I did not wish to disturb you so close to the birth. In the circumstances, I could stay away no longer.' Pause. 'I am very sorry about the little one.'

Catherine took a deep breath. 'I must count my blessings, Cathelot. I have eight children alive.'

'Yes, my Queen. But no doubt you still feel the loss keenly.'

Catherine looked at her, at this woman who knew her better than most, and fought back her tears once more. She raised the dwarf's hand to her mouth and kissed it. Then she moved to change the subject.

'And what news of the King, Cathelot? How fares he?'

'He is well, Your Majesty. Much relieved now that you are out of danger.'

Catherine smiled. 'And how does he pass the time?'

'He has spent much of the day outside with the children. They are now all retired to the nursery.'

'And her . . . ?' Catherine remembered the voice of the woman floating through the window of her chamber.

'Much the same, my lady.' She felt her servant's hand tense within her own.

'Do you have news?' She looked Cathelot directly in the eye and found something evasive there. 'What is it?'

'Your Majesty, I do not think that now is the time. You need to rest and recover. You need to be peaceful.'

Catherine looked at her favourite again, at the pained expression on her face, the concern wrinkling her brow. She was loyal beyond all others to her Queen. And yet she was also trusted by the King, by his mistress even, and in that blessed position could wander freely where others could not. 'I thank you for the love and care you have shown me, Cathelot. I know the depth of your devotion and allegiance. Know that I could not have asked of anyone else what I asked of you.' She paused and smiled. 'But I am strong, more resilient than you can imagine. So know that whatever it is you have to tell me, I can bear it.'

Cathelot stared at her for a few moments. 'Very well. Then know that I did as Your Majesty requested during your confinement. I accompanied both the King and the Duchess of Valentinois to both Anet and Chenonceau.'

Catherine nodded. These were the palaces where she considered *it most likely that the object would have been kept. It had not been present in the mistress's chambers in the other chateaux – Catherine had had those checked by her* dames d'honneur *– but these residences, belonging to her, were more private; where she and the King were most often together alone. Thinking of it, Catherine felt a jealous stab in her chest. She closed her eyes to the images of ecstasy that flooded her mind and thought of the mirror and where it might now reside.*

'I searched both places thoroughly, Your Majesty. I found my moments when she and the King went out hunting or riding.'

Catherine felt a light-headedness taking her over. 'And did you find it?'

Cathelot nodded, but her demeanour was morose. 'I found it. But it was in a place that I believe, that I am sure, no one visits. It is kept in a bare cellar at Anet, Your Majesty. Hidden, locked away. It moulders in the dark.' She paused before she went on. 'She knows, my lady. Or if she does not know, she senses.'

Catherine stared at Cathelot for a long moment. Then she murmured, 'Thank you for your honesty.' She closed her eyes and leaned her head back into the pillows beneath her. But now they felt like needles pressing into her skull.

'Are you all right, Your Majesty?' Cathelot's voice was tinged with concern.

'I am fine,' Catherine mumbled. 'Now please leave me.'

'Are you sure? I do not feel comfortable doing so.'

'I am sure. Please go.'

'Very well. But I will visit you later, my lady, if it pleases you.'

Unable to respond, Catherine squeezed Cathelot's hand and then released her. The bells tinkled mockingly as the dwarf crossed the chamber floor. When Catherine heard the door close, she opened her eyes and for a moment was supremely still. Then her tears began to flow, tears that until now she had fought against. Now she wept with a silent, unquenchable grief, for the gift that had been given and then hidden away, for the death of her plan that had never come to fruition. She wept for her thwarted love, her plight to be always second to a woman whom her husband championed, a woman who had to cajole him to sleep with his own wife. She wept for the death of her child and the one in all likelihood that would follow in its wake.

She wept for the stillbirth of all her dreams and ambitions.

28

It was a cold, dark Saturday morning.

I was sitting in the coffee shop, drinking my third espresso, distractedly making my way through the *Guardian*. Ophelia had left the previous evening for her photo shoot and in her absence I was contemplating going to the factory. It was still early and I didn't expect anyone from the office to be there at this time, if at all on a weekend. I skimmed the contents of a review of some play at the National and turned the page. It was a report of a woman's body found in the basement of a Central London block of flats. She had been missing for a couple of months. A man wanted for questioning by the police had, it seemed, left the country some time ago. I closed my eyes, rubbed them and an image of a different woman's body, reclining on a bed, flashed across my mind. I blinked to get rid of it and continued flicking through the newspaper. But I couldn't concentrate on the articles. Eventually I folded up the paper and put it down on the table. Then I drained my coffee cup and headed out into the day.

I listened to the slap, slap, slap of my trainers as I

crossed the road. The movement was quick and even, the asphalt hard against my feet, sturdy and supportive. I mounted the pavement and concentrated once more on the smoothness of the beat, the equable rhythm. Slap, slap, slap. A concrete beat on a concrete surface. The icy wind buffeted the trees, tossed torn newspaper print along the pavement, whipped up a sandstorm of gritty air. Bodies loomed towards me and just as quickly receded. Voices flooded into and out of my brain. It was an average day for a London winter. Cold, loud and windy.

I shivered and turned off the main road into a side street, colliding with another pedestrian in the process. I felt the elbow hard against my ribs and instinctively closed my eyes, as if somehow that would dull the impact. But in that moment, that split second of darkness, my head flooded again with thoughts of Amelia. Amelia Holmes. A woman who had also walked on dirty pavements, breathed and existed in a London not all that different from my own. What had happened to her?

My eyes snapped open, bringing me back to the grey of the here and now. What was it she was trying to tell me? I remembered my dream of her, her parting words. 'Find out who I am,' she had said. 'The rest will follow . . .'

I turned left at the next road junction, made a right into the square and the factory came into view. I traced the outline of its windows as I approached, as I had done many times before. My gaze moved over the bricks and glass of the ground floor, then the first and second in turn. It was all dark. So no one was here yet. I unlocked the outer doors and pulled them open defiantly. Then I made my way in.

Standing in the stillness of the clicking room, I began to feel with more certainty that something here, something in the factory, could tell me about Amelia. That something here was connected to her. I had felt the same way after my dream of her, when Tara had found me on the ground floor in front of the stiletto machine. The notion back then, however, had been vague, unformed. It was a general inkling. But now I felt a more powerful conviction. After all, this place and Amelia were intrinsically linked. Something here could tell me something. I was sure of it. I just wasn't sure what.

I had started my search in the storage cupboard. There were all kinds of records there. But by and large it was general factory paperwork, papers that made for the smooth running of a business: lists of customers, invoices, remittances, order forms for materials, that kind of thing. And a whole lot of financial data: accounting information, reports, projections, forecasts and suchlike. It was entirely mercantile, dry. Even the newspaper articles I came across were about the business – its times of prosperity in the late nineteenth and early part of the twentieth centuries and its subsequent period of decline. But there was nothing that focused on either James or Amelia.

I had moved upwards through the factory, scrutinising each floor as I went. But all paper records seemed to have been located in the dispatch room. On the upper floors

I had discovered nothing beyond the carcasses of old machines, rotting under layers of dust. And finally I had concluded my search in the clicking room, where I now stood, staring into its silence. Reaching forwards, I pushed the metal beam of one of the clicking machines. It let out a hollow metallic groan as it rocked back and forth, a sad, aching noise that reverberated along the length of the room. I put out my hand and, bringing the movement of the metal to a stop, silenced the noise. The stillness regrouped around me.

I looked along the factory floor, past the rows of sewing machines, the leather scraps and samples littering the floor, over the benches of tools and patterns, to the giant machines of the sole-cutting room. My gaze flickered over it all, then came back to rest where I stood. What was I doing here? I smiled and almost laughed out loud. I mean, really. Sneaking around the floors of the factory, following an oblique hunch that something here could tell me something. It was ridiculous.

I picked up a knife resting on a piece of black leather on one of the workbenches. I touched its point which, in spite of its age, was still incredibly keen. It was a clicking knife, kept sharp by the whetstone that lay alongside it. I ran my fingers over the stone. It was coarse and grainy. Although the knife didn't need it, I felt a sudden compulsion to sharpen it, pushing the blade up and then pulling it down the rough block. I repeated the movement a few times before stopping. Then I pulled a pattern from an adjacent workbench and, placing it on the leather, made an incision with the blade along its length. The knife moved easily, slicing through the material in a single fluid movement. At the end of the cut, the knife clicked against the wooden bench. A subtle clicking sound. I repeated the movement over a different area, following the contours of the pattern. The same click finished the cut. I did it again. The same clicking noise. It was hypnotic, satisfying. *Click, click, click.*

A few minutes later I had cut out the shape of an upper from the leather. I smiled at my handiwork. A little rough – I didn't quite have the skill of a clicker. But a good assembler might have been able to make something of it. I turned to look once more down the factory floor. The four rows of sewing machines lay in front of me, receding along the length of the assembling room. They were abandoned now but at one point the place had been full of women, Amelia among them. A scene flashed across my mind – women working away, stitching and sewing in a black and white world. I frowned. Where had I seen that? I gazed along the factory floor, trying to remember. Then I turned and looked down the stairwell. As my gaze took in the bank of photographs, dense and tightly packed on the wall opposite me, I suddenly remembered. I had looked at a picture of such a scene, capturing the women workers of the assembling room. I had seen it on the first day I had visited the factory with Richard. I walked down the stairwell, my eyes moving over the rows of photographs until I found the image again. *1898* said the caption beneath it. *Workers in the Assembling Room.* It pictured four rows of women, each seated at a sewing machine, stitching. They were dressed in black, with white aprons over their dresses, their heads bowed, focused on their work. All, that was, except for one. Her head was raised slightly, distracted by something, and although she wasn't facing the camera directly it was clear that she was a beauty. I smiled. I remembered now. I had focused on her the last time I had looked at this photograph. Long thick hair, refined features – she stood out from the crowd. Only then I hadn't known who she was. Now I did. It was Amelia.

I followed her gaze in the shot and saw for the first time that it was directed towards a man. The only man in the photograph. I didn't remember him. He was tall, well built, dressed in a black suit, ostensibly supervising the industry of his workers, making his way between the benches. While he was still very much in the background of the image, his head was tilted towards the woman, the merest hint of a smile on his lips, the camera seeming to have caught the very moment their eyes met. There was something profound about the timing of the shot, something quintessentially romantic about the look. Half given, half disguised. And if you knew nothing about them perhaps it would have looked like nothing. A supervisor doing his rounds, a young woman looking askance, both distracted during working hours. But now I knew that it was James and Amelia.

With trembling fingers, I reached forward to unhook the photograph from the wall. It came away easily in my hands but I could feel the back of it, loose and moving, clearly not well attached to the frame. As I brought it downwards, away from the wall, the back shifted and fell away, clattering against the wooden floorboards. Several pieces of paper also fluttered to the ground. They came to rest by the side of my foot.

When I bent down to pick them up, I saw that they were letters.

29

Venice, Italy
1898

My darling,

How I have missed you. Believe me when I tell you that you have been almost constantly in my mind — a mind which tortures me with visions of you. I remember your beautiful mouth and I long to kiss your lips, I imagine your skin and ache to touch it, to feel its smoothness beneath my fingers. I wish, beyond all things, that you could be here with me. Especially now, in Venice. I have found the weight of your absence almost impossible to bear, and have had to force myself to engage with others, to focus on everyday matters.

Now, as I sit at the writing desk in my hotel room, overlooking the city, I find a rare moment of peace. And in this quiet space I can tell you what has transpired whilst I have been gone from you.

We have spent the last two days in Stra with our exemplary host, Signore Giovanni Voltan. He is a charismatic, driven and determined man and his vision, as you know, in its scale and imagination, is an exciting one — through increased mechanisation to replicate in Italy the shoemaking processes he learned in Boston. We visited his new premises, reviewed his proposals for mass production and I, for one, am convinced that his plans will put this village in the Venetian hinterland firmly on the map.

This morning, however, leaving industry behind, we rose well before dawn and traversed the 20 or so miles from Brenta to the edge of the Venetian lagoon before daybreak. Giovanni had promised that this way we would enter the floating city by boat as the sun was rising. It is the only way to arrive in Venice, he said.

And he was not lying. Out of the darkness of the lagoon, shrouded in fog, the sun rose, a pale yellow disc. And it was in this sudden quickening of morning light that an amphibious city seemed to climb right out of the water. How I wish that you could have been here with me to see it. Suddenly houses and chimneys, churches and domes crowded around us, jostled for space along the banks of narrow canals. We followed their twists and turns, left, then right, moving deftly, quietly beneath bridges, below washing hanging suspended in the air above us, past the windows of palaces now glinting in sunlight. My darling, it was quite mesmeric.

Since we set foot upon dry land, my brother Thomas and I have been compulsive sightseers. It is a bitter-sweet distraction for me from my thoughts of you. We visited the Doge's palace, climbed the Campanile, taking in the tremendous views over the city, drank coffee in St Mark's Square and then wandered around until we got lost.

This afternoon, Thomas had wanted to spend time at the famous art gallery, the Accademia. I couldn't stand the thought of being shut up inside, admiring paintings, when the day had turned out so bright. I wanted to be in the sunshine. And besides, I quite relished the idea of being alone with my thoughts. So I dropped Thomas at the gallery and arranged to meet him back there later in the day. I could then wander through the backstreets of the surrounding area. We hadn't visited the Dorsoduro as yet and I spent a good hour simply ambling around. It is famously picturesque, the artists' quarter, full of small galleries and studios, scattered liberally on narrow streets alongside the canals. I must confess that I wasn't paying attention to where I was going. What I do remember is that I had just left a gallery filled with beautiful watercolours of Venice and had continued to head east in the direction of the Salute church. I passed over one bridge, caught sight of another ahead, and followed it over to the right into a narrow alleyway. I now had no idea where I was and the foot traffic had thinned to nothing. Not to be perturbed I tried to keep moving east. However, the alleyways of this area continued to narrow, the houses to grow taller, so I could no longer use the white dome of the church as a marker.

As I was about to turn back to attempt to retrace my steps, the alleyway opened up into a tiny piazza. A ruined church stood in its corner, beside a stagnant silted-up canal. Slates were falling from the church roof, it was pockmarked with blown bricks, its foundations decaying, sliding into a watery grave. Opposite the church was a small antiques emporium. I examined the window, surprised to find such a place so far off the beaten track, and decided to venture inside — as much to get directions as to look around.

I pushed open the door and a chime above it sounded into the darkness of the interior. I heard a woman's voice from within greet me in Italian. But there was no sign of her. As I looked around the shop, waiting for her to appear, I saw that it was stacked full of old Venetian mirrors, what I took to be antiques. In fact, the more I looked, the only things that I could see were mirrors. Just as I was completing a circuit of the establishment, the woman appeared from a room at the side. She gabbled at me in incomprehensible Italian and I made my excuses, no doubt in the same! Then I asked if she spoke English. Smiling, she said that she spoke a little.

This was in fact a lie as her English was very good. She told me that the shop dated back to the fifteen hundreds when it had been famous for selling the finest Murano glass. Her family had once sold to the most prestigious households in Venice and in addition had exported to Europe. Over the last two hundred years or so, with the decline in the industry, the shop had become more of a sideline. But no one in the family, given its long history and connection with glass making, could bring themselves to close it completely. So it limped on, towards the turn of yet another century. Besides, she said, people still knew the family name and sometimes sought them out, particularly if a certain artefact was wanted. We are still excellent at sourcing the finest or most idiosyncratic pieces, she told me. If you were to tell me a piece that you wanted, a piece that you had heard about, my cousins, I can guarantee, could track it down for you. It is something of a family gift, this ability to recover the lost things of the past. I often think that that is where our only skill lies these days, in finding and gathering old pieces to us.

We talked for a long time, exploring the cavernous reaches of the shop, the woman showing me the best items that she had. Beautiful antique mirrors, some with the glass still clear and bright, others more marked with age and deterioration. But there was a certain beauty to them all. Just as I was thinking that I should be getting back to meet Thomas, my eye chanced upon a mirror, secreted away in the corner of the room. It was, one might say, of simple design in comparison with some of the highly decorative pieces. It was a rectangular shape, with a heavy silver frame, the glass very much stained and blackened through age. Indeed, we laughed as I tried to see my own reflection in its depths. It took me some time but I eventually found myself within its darkness. When I enquired about this mirror, the woman laughed and told me an odd little tale. It was made, she said, by a famous Venetian craftsman, Theseo Mutio, at the end of the sixteenth century. She showed me his initials in the bottom left-hand corner of the mirror. It was believed, the woman said, that this piece had originally been commissioned by King Henri II of France for his mistress, Diane de Poitiers. But by accident it fell into the possession of the Queen, Catherine de Medici, who believed it was intended as a gift for her. When the King realised the mistake he ordered that the mirror be given to Diane and also branded with the couple's cipher — the conjoining of the letters H and D — in the bottom right corner. Furious, Catherine handed over the coveted gift but its lustre began to fade and eventually it became tarnished by a darkness that spread below the surface. Nobody could explain it but, according to the story, Diane never used the mirror after Catherine gave it up. She did not wish to destroy it and thus upset the King, but neither did she want it near her.

When the woman finished her tale, we stood in silence for a few moments, each lost in our thoughts. I looked at the overlapping letters H and D still visible beneath the mirror's dark surface. Is it true, I asked? After all, it sounded like a tall tale. She shrugged and let out a quiet laugh. Who knows? It's just a story that my grandfather told me once. I smiled and nodded, asking if she knew how the mirror had come to make its way back to Italy from France. But she shrugged, once again indicating that she didn't know. That, she said at last, was as lost in history and myth as the true story of the mirror.

What I do know, said the woman, looking at me with a confidential air, is that the mirror has come to us now through tragedy. It was most recently owned by the Tornaquincis of Rome, descendants of Catherine de Medici. Sadly, the whole family was killed one night in a fire. It was not known how it started but not one of them escaped the blaze. The mirror and a few other artefacts were the only things to survive.

Is that why it is so stained and blackened? I ventured, letting my fingers glide over the glass. After a moment the woman answered. It's possible, I suppose. But I do not think so. The darkness seems deeper than damage by fire and smoke. And she too let her hand linger on the mirror's surface.

For a few moments we stood in silence, each lost in our own thoughts. The mere existence of this object seemed incredible after what the woman had told me. Perhaps it was this touch of the miraculous that appealed. Perhaps it was the odd heritage of the piece: the idea of the King and his mistress and the doomed giving of a gift of love. Perhaps it was the romance of Venice, perhaps it was thoughts of you. Perhaps it was even a combination of all those things. But something pulled at me as I looked into the darkness of that mirror and, with an impetuosity that is rare in me, I decided to have it. More than anything I wanted it for you. When I told the woman I intended to buy it, for a moment she looked faintly taken aback. I thought that she might try to dissuade me. But then she smiled and said she would have it delivered to my hotel. I said goodbye to her and thanked her for her time and her stories. We shook hands warmly and parted.

As I left the little piazza, heading back the way I had come, I had a strange experience. The light was fading and Venice was taking on a different hue. The air felt colder and thicker, the canal side streets crowded in upon themselves, their height seeming to topple down upon me, pressing against their narrow edges. And I felt, suddenly and distinctly, a menace in the watery heart of this city and the sensation of something closing around me. A shiver rose inexplicably throughout my body. As if, as they say, someone had walked over my grave. I took a breath, trying to calm my nerves and closed my eyes. In that moment, in my mind's eye, I was again upon the lagoon we had crossed that morning, but alone this time, with the fog marching in. Only it was no longer simply benign, but moulding itself into ghostly forms. Their cold damp fingers reached out to me and I felt their touch against my skin, their wet clutches closing around me.

Somehow I forced myself to open my eyes and spurred my body into motion, running, almost tumbling, along the tiny alleyways. Before I knew it I turned a corner and was back in the midst of a crowd. I recovered myself a little and continued walking. I turned another corner and the Accademia came into view, Thomas standing beside it, looking at his watch, then chastising me for my lateness. It was all so suddenly mundane. In the chatter that followed, that feeling of intense fear vanished as quickly as it had come. But, even now, much later, when I revisit it, I cannot understand it, cannot begin to comprehend where it came from. Perhaps it was mere overtiredness on my part. Perhaps my longing for you is making my mind excitable, making me feel things which do not truly exist. Whatever it is I know that I cannot wait to see you again, to be comforted by your presence, to feel you within my arms.

By the time this letter reaches you, I will no doubt almost be home, destined before your eyes have long taken in the words off the page to see them for myself. I have missed you beyond measure.

Yours always

James x

30

'What are you *doing* here?'

The words bounced off the walls, loud against the hush of the factory. I jumped to my feet, my heart beating wildly, to see Tara advancing up the staircase towards me. Her expression was strained, her skin not quite as radiant as usual and her perfectly bobbed hair, ordinarily so sleek and stylish, was tied back in a rough ponytail. She still looked beautiful, but also tired and tense. However, as she halted in front of me, I noticed there was a twinkle in her eye.

'Hi, Tara.'

'Hi yourself. How the hell did you get in here?'

I shrugged. It was probably better if she didn't know.

She narrowed her eyes but obviously decided to let it pass.

'So, how are you?' I asked.

'Hmm. Not bad,' she said, an edge of petulance to her voice, 'considering I'm here at the weekend. Making up for lost time, Richard calls it.' And she gave me a pointed look. 'But I'd say it's more to do with the fact that Hajime hasn't yet been quite as fantastic on this job as he imagined he could be. Richard hasn't told me that, of course. It would involve losing face, after all. Admitting he made a bad decision with you.' Pause. 'Plus he and I aren't really talking at the moment.'

'Oh. I'm sorry to hear that,' I said, trying to disguise the tremor of jubilation in my voice.

'No, you're not,' said Tara, smiling at me. 'Anyway, enough of that. How are you?'

'Oh . . .' I paused, wondering in fact how I was doing. 'I'm okay, I suppose.'

Tara studied me for a moment. 'No, you're not.'

'No, I'm not.'

'Serves you right for not returning my calls.' She frowned at me, but there was still a hint of a smile on her face. 'So just what are you doing here, Johnny?'

I took a breath and wondered what I should say. But there was no question of not telling her everything. 'I read your file about James and Amelia.'

'Oh, that. You're still interested in it after everything that's happened?'

'It's got under my skin, if you know what I mean?'

Tara looked at me and then nodded. 'Weird stuff, huh?'

'Weird and annoyingly incomplete.'

'Yeah. I did my best, but I couldn't find anything else.'

'That's what I thought. But something told me there was more to the story here at the factory. So I came back. And I found these.' I lifted up the pieces of paper I was still holding.

'What are they?'

'They're letters. Two of them. I've only got through the first one but it made for pretty interesting reading. Want to see?'

Tara shook her head and instead of taking them looked down at her watch. 'Why don't you tell me instead? Hajime's on his way in and I wouldn't want him to find you here.'

We made our way up the stairs and into the clicking room as I summarised the contents of the letter. When I had finished, Tara remained silent for a moment, leaning against one of the clicking benches and absent-mindedly picking at a piece of leather. 'So the mirror did belong to Diane after all, if you believe the story that the woman told James. And it came here via Rome and Venice. On the heels of tragedy.' She paused for a moment. 'Where did you find the letters?'

'Behind this photograph.' I moved towards her and showed her the picture of Amelia in the assembling room.

'Wow. Look at the two of them.'

'Hmm. What do you think? Lovers?'

Tara continued to look at the photograph. 'Well, from what I found it would seem so. He gave her the green shoes and we found them in the underground room. So they were probably down there together sometime. And now this photograph and the letters. It has to be, right?'

An image flitted across my mind. It was James, in the armchair and playing with the green shoe in his hand. Another followed, this time of the woman's body on the bed in the cellar. I was becoming increasingly sure that it had been Amelia.

'Do you think he killed her, Johnny?'

As Tara uttered the words I saw the body, supine on the bed, and wondered, for the first time, if it was dead. I blinked to clear my vision, then shrugged. 'It seems fairly likely, wouldn't you say?'

She nodded. 'But if his death was natural, something odd still seems to have happened.'

I thought about it again: the bruising around James's neck, the grazing on his hands. The heart attack he had ultimately suffered. These were the facts. But how did they fit together?

Tara dropped the piece of leather she had been stroking and picked up a clicking knife from the workbench. She stared at its sharp blade. 'And if Amelia was already dead and he was down in the basement, what was he doing down there alone?'

'That I don't know.' But as I said it I thought of the Italian woman's tale of the mirror. Of the darkening of the glass after Catherine had had to relinquish possession of it. James was right. It sounded like a tall tale. But these days I wasn't quite my old sceptical self. A fleeting image of my darkened self, the self I thought I had seen in the mirror, appeared momentarily in my mind and then glided beyond view. I looked at Tara again. She was still holding the clicking knife, but was now flicking it between her finger and thumb.

'You should be careful with that,' I said. I looked at the

blade and remembered how easily, how cleanly it had sliced through the leather when I had used it earlier. 'It's amazingly sharp.'

She made a face and pointed it at me. Then she laughed and placed it back on the workbench.

We were both quiet for a few seconds.

'How's Ophelia, by the way?'

Surprised by the question, I looked up. 'She's fine.'

Tara paused. 'Look, I think I owe both you and her an apology. I made assumptions about who was coming into the factory and I was way off base. I'm sorry.'

I smiled. 'Apology accepted.' But, as I thought of Ophelia having the factory keys cut, I wondered if in fact Tara had been far off the mark.

'So, do you think she and I will ever meet? I'd like to get to know her.'

'Really?' I said, frowning.

'Yes, I mean it. I think I've been a little harsh where she's concerned.'

'Well, perhaps,' I said, and smiled.

Tara watched me for a second before moving on. 'And you should probably call Richard. I know he regrets how things turned out. You should clear the air. Try and get back on this job.'

'Richard can call me if he wants to patch things up.'

'Okay, fair enough. But I thought you'd be glad to get rid of Hajime. Stop him sniffing around your territory.' Tara's tone was teasing but it made me think of the underground room. Sooner or later, if he hadn't already,

Hajime would stumble upon it. I felt the rise of an angry feeling in my chest again and I pictured Richard, hand outstretched, demanding my keys. I breathed hard and tried to calm myself.

'Johnny.' Tara's voice seemed to come from a long way away. My eyes slowly focused on her. 'Look, you'd better get out of here. Hajime will be here any minute.' And she looked at her watch again. 'In fact, he's already late.'

'Okay,' I said, pocketing the letters and photograph. When I reached the top of the stairs I turned. 'Thanks, Tara. I'll keep you posted if I find out anything else. Take care of yourself.'

'You too.'

And, as she raised her hand in goodbye, I turned and left.

31

Paris, France
1898

My darling,

I have struggled in my time here to erase you from my mind
for even a moment. Know that I miss you terribly, with an intensity
that I find hard to bear. I catch glimpses of you everywhere:
in a dark-haired woman walking ahead of me along the bank of
the Seine, another turning down an alleyway in Saint Germain,
a third darting behind Notre-Dame and away from me. Always
the woman's face is just beyond my gaze, her turn an instant too
early for me to see her clearly. And yet each time I am convinced
that it is you. Even though I know that it cannot be. I am haunted
by you. I seem to catch the scent of your skin on the air as I
walk beside the river, feel the echo of your touch in the graze
of the wind, hear your dulcet tones in the rustling of the trees.
I long to hold you again, to be with you in the flickering flame of
candlelight.

I can hear your quiet laugh as you read this and the gentle
reprimand you might utter to me. 'You must concentrate on the
task in hand. You must learn what you can. It is, after all, only

a few days that you will be gone.' As I remember this, that we shall not be parted for very long, I can once more breathe without you. I can think clearly and still my heart. And in this short-lived space of calm, I can take pause, write of things other than you and recount a little of what I have seen here. I know, after all, that you long to be privy to what I am seeing.

Well then, I must write of Signore Pietro Yanturni. I imagine you sighing at the mere mention of his name and the fine crea-tions it conjures in your imagination. While he has not proved himself to be another Giovanni Voltan in his welcome, I have to confess that I am not much surprised by this. His reputation as a recluse precedes him and I did think that perhaps my intro-duction by our own dear Henry seemed a little tenuous. Nonetheless, he has been cordial to me and opened up his enterprise without suspicion. I suppose that even the most mistrustful of individuals must be aware that our ventures are so different that it is clear there is nothing to fear from me. My products are mundane in comparison with his and any ambitions I might have pertaining to truly exclusive handcrafted pieces remain just that, whereas his ambitions have already taken off and gained flight. As you know, Pietro works alongside the designer Jacques Doucet, of the fashion house of Doucet, and his works are masterpieces of intricacy and finery. But to see them first-hand, rather than in sketches or photographs, and appreciate the materials used is enough to make you reel: eleventh- and twelfth-century velvets, Renaissance silks, rare feathers, brocades of gold and silver. His creations are incredible extravagances and I have come to understand that his customers have no say in what their shoes will look like or even what materials will be used. It is a matter for his discretion alone. And yet he has a clientele clamouring to pay him $1000 per pair and to wait two to three years for delivery! He has created a truly astonishing enterprise and it makes me laugh to even think of trying to replicate it at home.

His approach to his clients is also novel. Today, having allowed me (after a little hesitation) to be present during a fitting with a customer, he requested that the woman walk up and down the room in front of him in her bare feet so that he could see how she moved. This was crucial, he told me, in assessing what kind of shoe would be appropriate for her. I assumed he took into account her height, her ordinary sway and motion, the natural incline of her feet, although he didn't give me any detail about what he took from the exercise. For perhaps fifteen whole minutes we watched her feet rising and falling as she walked, slightly self-conscious at first, then more confident as time went by. After this exercise, the woman was instructed to sit down and Pietro began to make plaster models of each foot. I knew that they were the first step towards production of his exquisite shoes, 'lasts' upon which he would mould his delicate fabrics and materials.

I watched Pietro work his magic, his youth suddenly dazzling to me — twenty-four years old and already shining. Focused on the plaster, drying around the small, tender foot of the woman, I suddenly caught a glimpse of myself, saw my reflection, as if in a mirror. I was a dark shadow and, while I appeared virile, when I looked closely everything vital was stripped away. I was desiccated, a shell, and in the place of my heart sat a deadened empty space. My mind was flooded momentarily with dark imaginings. I was overcome by anger and fear.

A sudden desolation possessed me in that moment, incongruous in my opulent surroundings, watching a young woman's dream come alive. I felt that I, by way of distinction, was trapped in a nightmare, heading towards loss and death.

I cannot explain it. But in that moment I felt utterly bereft.

It is perhaps bizarre, having sampled the extravagant delights of this Paris fashion house and admired the exquisite craftsmanship executed within its walls, that I long to see my more humble factory once more, to walk along its floors, inhale the fragrance of wood and leather, hear the familiar whirring of its machinery and explore its depths once more with you. In short, while I have enjoyed my experiences here, I am plagued by bleak visions and I ache for what is familiar to me.

Perhaps it is only my mind, my imagination, susceptible and sensitive in its parting from you. I try to shrug off this melancholy but know that I, jealous of everything that is near you, the air that you breathe, that hangs around you and touches your skin, long to be with you again.

Until then, I remain your most devoted

James x

The darkness of the winter's afternoon had closed in, pressing against the French windows of my kitchen, against the brightness of the overhead lights.

Sitting at the dining table, I had just finished rereading the letters. I looked down at the sheets of intricate script, the green ink on the yellowing white of the pages, the faint smell of mouldering age loitering in the air around them. The letters were real. Still, I found it hard to believe. They were miraculous, an unexpected prize, another window into the world of James and Amelia. His passion for her was intense, consuming, as were the unsettling emotions he suffered as a result of his absence from her. So James had bought the mirror as a gift for Amelia. When he got it back to England, he had, presumably, taken it into the factory's basement where it seemed their secret trysts took place. I thought of the mirror on the wall in the darkness, the green script of the letters and the same green script of the note floating on the mirror's surface. So it too had been written by James.

I stood up, turning to look out of the French windows. I tried to see the dull green of the grass through the darkness, the boundary wall beyond it. But I couldn't make out either. The only thing I had a clear view of was my own reflection in the window pane, dark against the artificial lights of the kitchen. I stared at myself: black hair uncombed, deep circles under sagging eyes, stubble flecked with grey. I looked wrecked. Rubbing my cheeks and staring at myself in the glass, I thought about James's vision of himself as he watched the plaster dry on the foot of Yanturni's customer. The stretched skin, the dark, skeletal face. I was instantly catapulted back to the underground room and what I myself had seen, or thought I had seen, in the mirror. I wondered if James, like me, had caught this image of himself in the mirror's depths and whether that had triggered the anxiety he had so clearly felt in Paris.

I turned my back to the window and stared once more

at the letters in my hands. The dates were imprecise, only the year ascertainable – 1898. So had their affair begun then? Or even earlier than that? In 1897, perhaps? The tone of the correspondence indicated that there was history, attachment between the two of them. Whichever it was, did it really matter?

I folded the pages and placed the letters back on the dining table.

32

Ophelia's green eyes were looking at me. I smiled and closed mine again. For a moment I thought of nothing, the dull stupor of sleep still hanging over me. Then, as consciousness crystallised, I remembered. I hadn't gone to Ophelia's tonight. She was on her photo shoot in Yorkshire. I had come home to my flat and spoken to her about the letters from here. So the green eyes looking at me didn't belong to her. Which told me instantly where I was and who was facing me.

'Hello, Amelia,' I said and opened my eyes.

Her shy but smiling red lips greeted me. 'Hello, Johnny. It's very nice to see you again. I hope you don't mind me disturbing you.'

I shook my head. 'No, I don't mind,' I said, sitting upright, noticing as I moved that I was back in the low-ceilinged dark room, in the armchair, dressed once more in the old-fashioned three-piece suit. The tie was unbearably tight at the neck and I reached for the knot, trying to make myself more comfortable. Amelia watched me in silence as I struggled. The candle, flickering on the floor beside her, cast shadows across her face. Tie loosened, I relaxed a little, and looked at her properly.

She was sitting opposite me, just like the last time I'd seen her, but now her feet were curled under her body. Her dark hair was tied back at the nape of her neck and she was wearing the same black dress as before. It was the dress that I now knew she had worn day after day – her factory uniform, if you like. The dress captured, beneath a white apron, in the photograph of the workers from the wall of the factory.

'How are you feeling, Johnny?'

I looked down at the three-piece suit and the tie once more. 'Uncomfortable,' I replied. 'But I think I know where you're going with this. I've thought about it a few times since I was last here. I am literally in James's clothes right now, right down to his factory-made footwear.' I jigged my feet vaguely, eyeing the elegant beige brogues that they were modelling. I tried to remember, and couldn't, whether I had been wearing them the last time I was here. Dragging my gaze away from my feet, I looked back at Amelia. 'I'm in James's shoes, I think you'd say, in both a literal and a figurative sense.'

'Indeed,' she said, and smiled. Then, suddenly serious, 'And so you'd better tread carefully. You know what happened to him.'

I thought about it and realised that technically I didn't. I only knew the ultimate result: that he'd died in suspicious circumstances, not how it had happened. That remained unclear. But what I did know was that I didn't want to go out the same way.

'No, indeed,' said Amelia. 'So you need to keep going, keep uncovering information.'

I nodded but I felt suddenly disheartened. What I'd found out so far seemed pretty bleak.

'You're right.' Amelia cut in on my thoughts yet again. 'But let's concentrate on what you know. That will help.'

I paused for a moment. 'Well, I know you went to work for James Brimley in May 1897. After the death of your mother.'

Amelia looked down at her lap, smoothing her dress across her legs. I looked again at the rough redness of her hands, so incongruous with the perfection of the rest of her. No doubt about it, it was not the destiny her parents would have chosen for her, nor the destiny perhaps that she would have chosen for herself.

'I had celebrated my eighteenth birthday the month before I went to work at Brimley's. On 3 April, in fact. My mother was still alive then and she had baked me a cake.' Amelia smiled and looked at me, the twinkle in her eyes almost childlike. 'A towering sponge filled with cream and jam. A Victoria sponge, I think you call it, after Queen Victoria. I remember that more than anything. My father carried it into the front room of the house, my mother following behind him. Her steps were short, like her breath, while her hair and her skin were grey. She was very ill by this time.' Amelia's voice cracked and she waited a few moments before resuming. 'The cake was laden down with candles and I looked at them so that I wouldn't have to look at her illness. I wanted to cry, seeing her so weak and shrunken, but instead I smiled. I tried to look happy to give her some comfort. She died soon afterwards. On 14 May.' She stopped again and swallowed. Her voice when it came was ragged. 'I was close to my mother. I loved her very much. But grief was hard for me. With so many younger brothers and sisters around, it was difficult to show it. The eldest, Betty, was ten when my mother died. And Bertie, my youngest brother, was only two. So I didn't get to express how I felt that freely. I couldn't walk around weeping or shouting, giving vent to my sadness or anger. The children would have become too upset.'

A tear fell silently onto her right cheek.

'Are you all right?'

She nodded. 'But at the time I wasn't. And I had to push it all down, inside, everything I felt, and only examine it briefly in the quiet time I had alone. Which wasn't much, I can tell you. I had to step – or jump, rather – into my mother's shoes, into the role of carer for the children. So, naturally, I didn't have the luxury of proper mourning. And holding on to, suppressing all those feelings of sadness, made me miss her presence all the more. Does that make sense?'

'Of course.'

Amelia paused. 'Anyway, my first day was 30 May 1897. I remember it so clearly, the feeling of desolation. My mother's death was still raw, still weighing down upon me. And in this frame of mind I arrived at Brimley's on an unseasonably cold Monday morning.'

She paused again, holding out her palms, raised, for me to see. 'It might seem an odd choice, a shoemaker's. Hard on the hands for one thing, constantly cutting and sewing by hand and machine. I had wanted to be a governess. I loved reading, you see, wanted to teach. But after my mother's death none of that seemed to matter. Family friends tried to interest me in other positions – maid, domestic servant, seamstress. And others said any menial role was nonsensical for a girl of my obvious talents.' She turned her head to the side, narrowed her eyes and batted her eyelids. 'But I wouldn't listen to anyone. I had made up my mind. And the one thing that Brimley's had that the others didn't was that my mother had worked there. So in an odd sort of way I felt that I would be connected to her, would be closer to her even, if I was there. That somehow I would be happier. And they were delighted to have me, to help the family. She had been so well liked and regarded, you see. My dear mother, Gracie Branwell.'

Amelia smiled palely and then took a deep breath. 'So, frozen to the bone by grief and weather, I arrived. I opened the door of the dispatch room in a flurry of wet wind and half stumbled, half ran inside, my hair streaming around my face, my clothes sodden. I must have looked a fright. Like a banshee or something similar.' She laughed, girlish all of a sudden. Her eyes were bright, shining with recollection. 'And that was the first time I saw him. He was talking to Miss Perkins – Minnie, the bookkeeper – who worked closely with him. They had their backs to me but when the door clattered open and then slammed shut, they both turned, startled by the noise, and simply stared at me. Miss Perkins was a shy thing, pretty and dark-haired. She looked horrified by my arrival, bursting into the factory like that. No words were exchanged between any of us and for what felt like the longest time they simply looked at me.'

Amelia halted briefly, as if she was remembering it. 'Mr Brimley's was a deep, penetrating stare. As if he had peered into my soul and seen everything exposed that I had hidden there. He looked at me with those dark, serious, deep-set eyes of his, and then he smiled, walked towards me and began to speak. Not about anything in particular – the weather, the wet, the state of the buses. It was mere chit-chat, entirely banal. But he said it in a way which was very soothing. Then he steered me towards Minnie and asked her to take care of me, to see that I didn't come down with a cold on my first day. I think those were his exact words. She did as he said, but reluctantly. My appearance shocked her that day and she would have liked nothing more, I am sure, than to send me on my way again. But if we were not allies in the beginning, we became so later.'

She smiled but with a sad look in her eyes. 'But from my first moment there, Mr Brimley – James – looked after me. Without fuss or overdue concern, he quietly took control of my welfare. And looking back, as I did many times later, I think the connection between us was forged then. In that first moment of meeting. Maybe something in him recognised the deep well of pain inside me. Maybe something in him tapped into it and felt a little kinship with it. Whatever it was, he never made reference to it explicitly.

'But he told me later, much later, that, even though he didn't know it then, looking back his heart was lost at that point, in that moment when he turned, amid the wind and the rain, to see that a beautiful, desolate girl had washed up on his shore.'

33

'We didn't speak about my mother much. But every day he would come and talk to me. Quietly, in that reassuring way of his. And gradually, over time, I came to depend on him and would look forward to exchanging a few daily words. I would hear him first, his firm, confident step moving across the assembling room; the solid rhythmic click-click of his heels against the floorboards.'

I thought of the photograph of Amelia that I had found, the image of her gazing towards an advancing man. I smiled.

Amelia smiled back at me and nodded. 'Later I began to notice a change in the way I felt. It wasn't a sudden change of mood, more a gradual happening. But I began to notice that when I heard his footsteps my heart would flicker slightly, lightly, the merest murmur of butterfly wings in my chest. That was the beginning.' Amelia's eyes shone and her cheeks had become a little flushed. 'And then later still I found out that James felt the same way.' She paused, clearly revisiting the moment in her mind. 'It was one evening when I was working late for some extra money, hand-stitching a pair of bespoke shoes, the only person still at work in the assembling room, or even on the third floor. I became aware all at once of the sound of James's approaching footsteps. It took me by surprise. I was not expecting him at this hour and, for the first time in our history, I was overcome with embarrassment. I didn't look up, struggling to get a grip on my emotions, certain that my first words – if I could get them out of my mouth, that is – would betray my passion for him. In any event, the footsteps stopped. I was still stitching, pretending to be absorbed in my work, my heart pounding furiously, the blood beating hard beneath my skin.

'I became conscious of James speaking, saying my name quietly, once, then again. And so eventually I had to look up. I remember that he seemed far away. He was very tall, you see, and he towered over me as I was sitting on my chair. He must have felt the distance too because he knelt down almost immediately, still looking at me as he did so. And for the first time since the day of our meeting, I felt that his eyes were burrowing into my soul, looking into the depths of my being, unearthing my secrets. I was aware that he was speaking to me, but I don't remember anything he said. I was only conscious of his lips moving, seeing their pallor, their dryness. He kept pausing to lick them and his eyes had an uncertain, wide look to them, as if he was a little afraid. It occurred to me then that he was nervous. I had never seen him like this, in all the time I'd known him and so I knew that whatever he was saying, it was important, definitive. That it would somehow change things between us.

'And then I knew, without needing to hear it from him, just how he felt about me. I smiled at him then and in the sudden gesture something opened up. The restraint which had been sitting there, marking the distance between us, evaporated. James stopped speaking and looked at me for a second. Then he handed me a large box. As I took it from him, my fingers brushed against his and I blushed deeply. I felt the heat of the blood in my face and for a second I paused, perhaps aware that if I went any further, this mix of emotions, guilt, embarrassment, excitement, desire would stain and mark me for ever after. I paused, only for a second, and then I made my choice. I ripped the lid off the box and looked inside.' She paused and smiled at me. 'But you already know what was in there, don't you, Johnny?'

I smiled back and then nodded slowly.

'The most beautiful pair of green shoes. You may not know this but they were very fashionable at the time. Henry Maybury made them. He was employed by James at the factory and his designs were quite something. The pointed toes echoed the sculpted heel, the leather was soft and luscious and the embroidery intricate, complementing the colour of the uppers but also interspersed with lighter threads. James said that the shoes were inspired by the bewildering beauty of my eyes, their vast array of depth and colour. His words, not mine.'

Amelia stopped and flushed lightly once more. 'I remember that I was unable to speak at first, unable to really absorb his words, his gesture.' She paused and smiled. 'I remember holding the shoes in my hands, staring at them. James took them from me, put them on the floor beside him and unlaced my work boots. His fingers moved deftly, with certainty. Then he slid the boots off my feet slowly, one by one, and replaced them with the shoes. I don't know how he knew but somehow they were a perfect fit.

'I think in that moment I felt, overwhelmingly, all that he had done for me. He had helped me so much after the death of my mother – slowly, over time, he had put me back together piece by small piece, through the repetitive, small gestures of every day. And this knowledge circled down and around me in those moments in the assembling room.' Pause. 'Perhaps it was in that moment that I was lost. But I resisted for a long time after that. He was unhappy with his wife, I knew that. They were companions who didn't much like each other's companionship any longer. They lived separate lives and yet they didn't separate. James loved his son, and wanted to keep him near. But it was difficult for him, I know that, to remain with Elizabeth.' She breathed out slowly. 'Quite how much I didn't realise until the very end.'

I coughed and reached for my necktie again, running my fingers around the collar. 'So, that's how it all began?'

Amelia nodded. 'The shoes. Exquisite, expensive beyond most women's wildest hopes. But of course I couldn't really wear them anywhere. If I had they would only have attracted suspicion. And if my father had seen them, he would have had a fit.' She laughed. 'He'd have thought I had spent a whole year and a half's wages. And some of his, too. So they had to remain in the factory. I don't think James gave it a second's thought before he had them made; that I really wouldn't be able to wear them. He had only been thinking of the best gift he could give to me. Something that he knew I would love and treasure. And so, tragically, they became something to hide. In fact, they became an embodiment of everything that was between us: symbols of love and friendship. But ultimately hidden, shrouded in darkness.'

I thought instinctively of the underground room and the first time that Tara and I had gone down there, when we had seen the green shoes hanging suspended from the velvet ribbon over the side of the mirror. Then it had seemed strange to find them there, unfathomable that such beautiful things should be trapped, mouldering in the dark. Now it made perfect sense.

'How did you find the underground room?'

'James discovered it. It had originally been a cellar, used very occasionally for storage. But it wasn't a convenient place. It had a steep, narrow staircase and no proper lighting, so it had rarely been used. Then James's father had constructed the storage cupboards in the dispatch room, one of which was around its entrance. So while it was never boarded up, people forgot about it. But James remembered it.'

I nodded. Much of this was as Ophelia and I had thought.

'So, as I said, that was the beginning. What I didn't realise was that it was also the beginning of the end.' The candlelight beside Amelia flickered and jumped, a sudden bright splash of light. I looked around the room for the first time in a while, absorbed as I had been by Amelia's tale, and noticed that it was much brighter than before, light spilling in around the edges. Amelia frowned.

'What is it?' I asked, sitting upright.

The candle's flame began to judder violently even though there was no draught. 'I have to go.' She stood up abruptly, poised to leave. Her black dress, in sharp contrast to the growing light behind her, made her look like a dark shadow. It reminded me of something I had been meaning to ask her.

'It was the mirror, wasn't it?' I felt my voice rise. 'That ended things, I mean.' Suddenly the candle flame rose higher, taut and straight, as if it too was straining to hear what, if anything, Amelia would say.

She nodded. 'But it's not all as you think. I'm sorry, Johnny. I cannot tell you what you do not know. Keep looking.' Then she smiled at me. 'I will help you when the time comes.' Then she turned and disappeared into the light.

As the brightness continued to grow, the room seemed to fill with a rush of noise and air. I felt a heaviness in my head, which permeated down through my body. My eyelids fluttered and closed, then fluttered open again. As I felt my body move in and out of unconsciousness, my last thoughts were about the mirror.

34

The sunlight streaming through the French windows stirred me.

I lifted my head off the wooden table and winced. My neck was strained and stiff and my head pounded. In front of me stood a half-empty bottle of red wine, a stained wine glass, and the photograph of Amelia and James from the factory wall surrounded by the letters it had concealed. I surveyed the scene momentarily before leaning back in my chair and rubbing my eyes. I remembered reading the letters again late last night at the dining table but I didn't remember falling asleep.

Through the windows, the garden looked sad and ravaged. A stunted tree stood at its far end and the grass, touched by winter's lifeless fingers, was browning in clumps. But the sun peeped tentatively over the boundary wall, flooding the patio with bright white light and giving heat to the pots in front of the glass. The hyacinths and daffodils, already sprouting greenery, looked well on the way to flowering. Perhaps spring was coming after all.

I yawned and stood up, the Batters print above the table catching my eye as I moved: the beautiful black and white symmetry, the stockinged feet, one above the other, the tantalising, dangling stiletto shoes. I smiled and closed my eyes. But instead of that image another formed in my mind. Green shoes suspended over the edge of the mirror. With that came the recollection of the dream I had had and then Amelia's parting words to me. *You need to keep looking.*

I frowned as I headed into the kitchen. As I thought about it all, the banging in the back of my head intensified. I opened the fridge and took out coffee, spooning it absent-mindedly into the espresso maker. I filled it with water and put it on the hob. I poured milk into a pan and began to heat it. I would look over Tara's file again. Maybe something I hadn't noticed so far would jump out at me. I thought again about James and Amelia, and their love affair. I thought of the first time they had met, of their connection. I thought of his intensity, his gift, their complicity, their love. What had happened to them? What exactly had happened to undo it all? I knew that it was somehow connected to the mirror. I felt it with certainty. Catherine had done something to it. Perhaps she'd touched it, as the Italian woman had suggested, with the darkness she seemed so familiar with. Perhaps she'd given it some kind of arcane power. I thought of it in the basement of the factory, waiting in the darkness.

Perhaps waiting for me, as it had waited for James.

By evening, I had trawled through Tara's file twice more and uncovered nothing new. My eyes flitted lazily over the text, now familiar to me, but kept drifting back to the photographs contained within an article about James – the death portrait, which was always fascinating to me, but also to the one of him standing upright and alone, dressed in his customary three-piece suit. It was not the first time that I had stuttered and faltered over these images. There was something familiar about the dark, brooding eyes, something which I had previously put down to the fact that I had seen this man before in my dreams. The earlier shock of that discovery had eclipsed everything else, including the feeling that I was now experiencing, that I had, in addition to the dream, recognised this man, this photograph, from somewhere else.

I got up from the table and grabbed my coat and keys. I had to get back to the factory as soon as possible. I looked at my watch. Ten to seven. It was unlikely that anyone would be there at this time on a Sunday evening. But I would be cautious, nonetheless. With that I pulled on a pair of trainers and left, slamming the front door shut behind me.

When I arrived at the factory it was in darkness. If anyone had been there during the day, they had now departed. The square was deserted, but still I opened the outer doors cautiously, checking over my shoulder a couple of times. But all was quiet and still. Turning on just a few lights, I made my way to the stairs at the opposite end of the floor, climbing the stairwell until I was standing in front of the bank of photographs. My gaze moved over the prints: a group of machinists, smiling, a small gathering of bearded, sombre men, a man in a flat cap, smoking a pipe outside the front of the premises. Scouring the rows, I eventually came to the one I was looking for and felt a tremor of excitement in my stomach. It was entitled 'Director' and dated 24 May 1896. It showed a solitary man with dark eyes that glowered at the camera. I placed the image from the article in the paper next to the one on the factory wall. No doubt about it, it was the same photograph. And the man in both pictures was James Brimley.

I reached forward and unhooked the image from the wall, leaving a pale empty square in its place, outlined by dust trails. It didn't look as though the photograph had been removed since it had been hung there. I turned it over in my hands, my fingers trembling with anticipation, and unhooked the clasps that held the photograph in its frame – just as I had done with the one of Amelia and the factory workers. Slowly, deliberately, holding my breath, I removed its back and looked inside.

I was instantly disappointed. There was nothing there except the photograph and the sheet of glass in front of it. I sighed. I had been so sure that I was on the right track. That, just as with the photograph of Amelia, there would be letters behind it. Replacing the picture frame, I hung the image back on the wall. James Brimley stared down at me once more, his shoes shining brightly, his black hair slicked back away from his unsmiling face. I took in the three-piece suit. The suit that I had seen many times before, in photographs, in my dream of James and more recently on myself, during my conversations with Amelia. I looked at James's eyes again: the heavy lids, the irises dark beneath, and the merest wisp of an idea began to form in my brain that perhaps I did, after all, know where to look. I stared at the photograph, at the deep-set eyes. I had seen their brooding darkness, before, and not only in my dreams. I had seen them when I looked into the mirror. They were the same eyes that stared back at me, as if they were my own.

I turned and made my way down the stairs and across the ground floor. My head was suddenly filled with the idea that the mirror could tell me something. I paused for a moment in the storage cupboard, taking two candles and a box of matches from the ones that Tara had found there. Then I pulled open the door to the underground room and, before I could change my mind, began to walk down the stairs. The darkness was intense and I struck a match and lit a candle as I walked, trying not to break the rhythm of my strides. Seconds later, I reached the bottom of the stairs.

I stood stationary for a moment, the darkness of the corridor pushed back by the small pool of yellow candle-light around me. I struck another match and lit the second candle. The flame leaped high and the darkness seemed to recede even further. I turned momentarily, looking back up the stairs to the dull rectangle of light formed by the doorway at the top. As always, it looked very far away. I swallowed, the thick smell of dampness catching pungently in my throat, and not for the first time in this place I fought the urge to retch. I opened my mouth and took a shallow breath. I repeated the action a couple of times. Then, turning slowly, I made my way into the underground room. My steps were hesitant, the light blooming ahead of me and giving me a vague sense of comfort. The mirror loomed large against the wall to my left-hand side.

I placed the candles on the floor, one level with each end of the mirror, moving slowly and purposefully. I told myself that if my actions were conscious, deliberate, nothing could happen to me. There was nothing to be afraid of. I breathed in deeply, looked up and stared at the surface of the mirror, at its deep grey mottling, its ink blooms of darkness, its initials, markers of lives gone by. I tried to put everything that I knew, or thought I knew, out of my mind, resolving only to focus on myself and my reflection. I looked over the murky surface, searching for my eyes, and eventually found them.

As usual, the glass corrupted my image. The blue of my eyes was leached of colour, dyed black. I took a step forward and looked at the rest of my reflection, holding my breath. I smiled and I could just about discern a dark smile coming back at me. I continued to look at my eyes, my face, waiting for something to happen. The seconds ticked past and once or twice I heard the soft click-clack of my watch, its hands turning in circles, marking time in the darkness. But beyond that there was nothing. I was in a noiseless room, looking for a spark of something I had seen before that would perhaps lead me somewhere. I concentrated and watched my own black eyes. The more

I watched, the more I studied myself in the mirror, the less I felt any connection to the face I saw there.

I sighed. This was not the way I had felt the last time I was here with Ophelia. Then I had felt an almost overwhelming mixture of emotions. Now I felt strangely disconnected. I smiled again and the dark face in the mirror smiled back. I looked at the face, intrigued and repulsed. But it was just my face darkened and twisted by the mottled surface. A rush of frustration flooded through me. I wasn't feeling anything. So what was I doing? It was pathetic, ridiculous. With a sudden rush of irritation, I punched the mirror's surface hard with my fist. Its whole frame juddered and rocked back and forth, creaking on the ancient metal chain suspending it from the wall. The release felt good and I struck it again. The same judder and creak, the same moaning sound as the mirror rocked precariously against the wall.

And then a different sound, almost the fluttering of butterfly wings. I thought of Amelia and, a second later, of James. Then the sound was gone and with it the fleeting thought. I took a step back from the mirror and looked around me. Had I heard something fall to the ground? I stooped to grab one of the candles from the floor and, as I did so, my hand grazed a piece of paper beside it. I picked it up, certain that it had not been there when I had arrived in the room. It must have fallen to the floor when I hit the mirror. The paper felt warm to the touch. I opened it up, raised it closer to my face and saw that it was a letter, written in green ink.

35

London
August, 1898

My darling,

    I am sitting at my desk in the drawing room in Bloomsbury Square, pen and paper in hand, and my son Thomas is playing nearby in front of the fire. Elizabeth is visiting friends from church, and so we men are quite alone in the house. I hope you know that I would never say these things to hurt you, that I would never seek to remind you unnecessarily of my domestic circumstances. But the darkness of my thoughts is almost overwhelming and you are the only one with whom I can share them.

    For the last half an hour, perhaps, I have been staring at my son, my beloved son, playing with his thaumatrope. I am sure, my darling, that you must have come across such an object when you were a child. It is, you will remember, a disc with an image drawn on each side, held on opposite ends of its circumference by pieces of string. The disc is rotated to wind up the strings and then released. As the strings unravel the disc spins quickly and the two pictures on its sides appear to combine into one. It is a simple type of optical illusion. The pictures are interchangeable and so

Thomas has been amusing himself with an assortment. The first had a bare tree on one side, its leaves on the other. When the pictures are spun, a tree complete with leaves appears. Or seems to. The next picture had a bird on one side and a cage on the other. As you can now imagine, when the pictures are spun the bird appears to be in the cage. Similarly, we have had flowers and a vase, producing flowers in a vase.

As I watch my son now, the picture he is spinning has a man on one side of it. This man looks neat and innocuous. His hair is short and straight and he is clean-shaven. Bland, one might even call this man. On the other side of the picture is wild hair, dark eyes and large eyebrows. Bizarre, I'm sure you'd agree, when looked at in isolation. But when the picture is spun, the innocuous man is transformed into a creature resembling a devil (no doubt inspired by Mr Stevenson's Dr Jekyll and Mr Hyde). At first I found it rather bewitching to watch. However, as I continued to do so, time and again witnessing the transformation of the man into a monster, the more peculiar yet pertinent this image seemed to me. And I have become possessed, truly possessed by fear.

I think it all began in Venice.

No, I know it all began in Venice. With the mirror and the feeling I had in the evening beside the canal. Everything seems to have stemmed from there.

Can you ever forgive me?

It is ironic considering the way I felt back then, in the beginning . . . I remember quite distinctly my true delight in having discovered a mirror belonging to Henri II. I had felt pure and unfettered excitement at having retrieved such an object from obscurity and at the prospect of bringing it home to you.

282

Somehow it felt appropriate to me that it should be your gift. I don't know whether this was my attempt to redeem a thwarted gesture of the past or something else, misplaced and misconceived. Whatever, looking back, I can see that from the beginning my happiness was almost instantly polluted, replaced by unsettling feelings, destructive of my contentment.

I remember clearly that after I had brought the mirror down to the basement and we had admired it and looked into it I felt compulsion and excitement. Something stirred inside me, largely desire. I had thought that that was occasioned by my reunion with you, and that alone. But I know now that that was not the case. Alongside my felicity, I always felt twinges of unease; that there was something else that hovered alongside my ardent emotions, something that penetrated into the darkness inside me. And while I rationalised and discarded this uneasiness, something lurked in the back of my mind, a haunting seed of doubt. There was something that disturbed me when I looked into the mirror, what I saw, what I felt. And yet every time I tried to name it, to see it for what it might be, it seemed to shift into something else, something less potent, and my rationality overpowered my fear, transmuted it into neurosis, a thought not to be trusted.

As time went on, the excitement, if anything, intensified. But alongside it the other emotion was also growing, deeper, darker and more haunting than before. It became increasingly difficult to fight, to ignore, to displace with platitudes about overreaction. I felt it seeping into the dark crevices of my body and I wanted to scratch it out of me, to tear it from my insides. But I didn't know how.

Sometimes now I feel almost overcome by a desire to tear at my skin, to do harm to myself, to rip this thing from me. I feel it ever reaching out to me in the darkness of my dreams, whispering in my ear, polluting my thoughts. And in truth when I feel it, when I hear it, I am very afraid.

I have tried to overcome this, to discard it once more as a fiction, generated from some obscure hysterical part of myself. But I know that it is not. I know it beyond a shadow of any doubt that I might have had.

For some reason, I felt a need to let you know my feelings. When you are not with me, I find myself alone in the darkness, quite alone but for the murmurings plaguing my senses. Can you hear them now?

It used to be that I dreamed of you at night, of the smell of your hair, the touch of your skin, the beauty of your eyes and face. Now my dreams are gone and only nightmares plague me. One in particular is current. It begins very much like the scene I have described to you today. My son and I are in the drawing room of the Bloomsbury Square house. I am writing letters at my desk while he plays with his thaumatrope in front of the fire. I sit and watch him, see the twirling images mingling and separating before my eyes. And while I feel very much as if I am present in the room with him, in the peace of our home, I also know that I am not there. That really, truly, I am in the basement of the factory, in the shadows, quite alone, with the darkness whispering in my ears. A part of me is trapped here, and always will be, unable to escape. I feel almost beside myself in my loneliness.

I am more alone than I have ever been in my life.

36

'You're becoming quite the detective, Johnny. First you find letters behind a photograph in the factory and now you find one behind the mirror in the underground room. What will you uncover next?' Ophelia's tone was teasing but I knew from the silence that followed that that wasn't all she felt. Static crackled down the line intermittently.

'Where exactly are you? The reception is terrible.'

'Not surprising. I'm where people always do fashion shoots: in the middle of nowhere, in the wilderness, very cold, very remote.'

I nodded but didn't say anything. The static detonated, a sudden burst in my ear, before settling down again. I shifted in my seat at the kitchen table, running my finger around the rim of my coffee mug. 'So what do you think about them all?'

'Well.' She paused as she thought about it and I could hear the shouts and laughter of other people in the background at her end. 'I know the ones from abroad aren't precisely dated but I think the change in tone is pretty noticeable across the whole lot. He goes from intense and emotional in Italy, perhaps missing his mistress with just the right amount of ardour, to more effusive and neurotic in France, to eloquent but clearly delusional back in London. I think they were probably written in that order.' Pause. 'Do you think he was even in his house when he wrote the last letter?'

'I don't know,' I said quietly. But I had thought exactly the same thing. Could he have actually been in the underground room, simply imagining that he was with his child in Bloomsbury Square? I shivered once more at the thought of it. But it was certainly possible. Especially given what else I had found. 'There's something else . . .'

'What?' Ophelia's voice was terse above the background noise.

'I found some other notes pushed into the lining at the back of the mirror.'

'Really?'

'Maybe ten or so. After the first letter fell I thought it was best to check what else was there. They're just musings.' I paused as I looked at the stack of scribblings scattered across the kitchen table – pages spattered with patches of green ink, littered with surreal doodles. 'And none of them are dated. But I'm guessing they were written after this last letter. He seems to have completely lost touch with reality by the time these were penned.'

There was silence on the line. I could feel Ophelia's hesitation. 'Can you . . . can you give me an example?'

'Sure.' I picked one from the table. 'A lot are just random words. Eyes. Darkness. Death. Hell. But this one is a little more coherent. If that could ever be the right word to use.' I cleared my throat.

'"I have heard you calling to me. In the darkness. You are coming for me. I know I can't escape from here. From the darkness. From the demons and the dead that call out to me. I hear their voices, echoing. I see their faces reflected in the place where mine should be. They are coming for me, creeping out of the shadows, touching me, their dirty claws around my neck, dragging me down.

'"Don't leave me here. In the darkness.

'"Alone."'

I coughed slightly. 'And there are lots of others in the same vein.'

'I see.' For a moment we both listened to the static crackle on the line. 'I wonder if he wrote them all in the underground room, when he heard the darkness talking to him.'

'That's what I'm thinking.'

'Jesus.'

I thought of James's dead body on the factory floor. Was he driven mad by his delusions, haunted, literally tortured by his imaginings, doing harm to himself, dying of anxiety and fright? I shivered as I thought about it. 'I think the note that was left on the mirror was written around the same time.'

'Yes – it never seemed to make much sense, did it?'

I shook my head, thinking about its words. *I have heard, but not believed, the spirits of the dead may walk again.* I swallowed, but my mouth was dry.

'Johnny, are you okay?'

'Sure. I'm fine.' Pause. 'I just can't wait to see you again. I've really, really missed you.'

'Me too. It feels like for ever. And not just because I'm watching models tromp around a moor in the snow in stilettos.'

Thinking about that made me laugh. 'God, I miss you,' I said. Almost immediately I thought of James pounding the streets of Paris, pining for Amelia and professing his love for her in his letters. A sudden anxious feeling grew in my stomach and I wanted more than anything to get off the line. Perhaps if I denied what I felt I could deny a lot of other things too. 'Well, I guess I'll let you get back to work.' The static hissed and spluttered over my awkwardness.

'Okay. But I'll see you tomorrow. Five-thirty in Shoreditch, right? The place I mentioned before.'

'Of course,' I said. 'I remember.'

'See you there, then.' Pause. 'Hey. Try not to think too much about all this, okay?'

'I won't,' I said, conscious of the denial that my words were steeped in.

Ophelia said something else but I couldn't catch it. The static bloomed, exploded and finally the line went dead.

I stared at the phone as I hung up, overcome by an inexplicable sense of desolation. Suddenly I felt very alone.

37

The sound of the telephone woke me. I opened my eyes but I had no idea what time it was. I lay in bed for a moment or two, listening to the insistent ringing. Then I got up and staggered towards the kitchen.

'Hello.' My voice was curt, still a little croaky from sleep. I coughed and looked at the clock on the wall. It was one forty-seven p.m. Jesus. Mid-afternoon. I had to try to start keeping more regular hours.

'Ah, hello. Johnny, is that you?'

The voice was unexpected and I struggled for a moment to identify it. 'It is. Is that Mr Alexander?'

'Indeed, indeed. I hope I haven't caught you at a bad time?' And then, before I could answer: 'I have some rather interesting information about your mirror.'

The animation in his voice made me feel queasy and I sat down. On the kitchen table in front of me were scattered pages – the ramblings of James and the picture of him and Amelia. I looked at it all and realised I was a little fearful. Mr Alexander could tell me almost anything and I would believe him.

'The information came to me through one of my old acquaintances,' he began.

I nodded into the receiver. I remembered what he'd said. But I hadn't ever expected that anything would come of it.

'It turns out that a friend of mine in the business has come across your mirror before.'

My heart did a silent somersault in my chest.

'Indirectly, of course, given that it's probably been down in that cellar for over a hundred years.'

I nodded again but said nothing.

'Johnny, are you there?'

'I'm here, Mr Alexander.' But my voice was quiet and unwilling. It felt as if it was being dragged out of me. 'Just surprised by your news, that's all.'

'Well, yes, it *is* rather surprising. I was speaking to Nathaniel Raven, that's his name, on another matter just today. Nat has an antiques business in the City. Leadenhall Market. When we had concluded our business I thought I'd mention your mirror. Just on the off chance, you know. But when I told him about the initials of the mirror maker on the left-hand side of the glass and the lettering opposite it rang a bell for him. Especially when I remarked upon the darkness of the silver. He knew that he had come across something to do with this mirror before.'

Mr Alexander paused and I waited silently for him to get to the point. I felt my hand tense its grip around the receiver and beads of sweat begin to form on my upper lip.

'As it happens, he deals largely in antique prints and photographs so I couldn't understand how he would have come across a piece like yours. But here's the thing. In his line of business he does often come across letters, notes and suchlike, alongside the images or prints – particularly if they are recovered straight from houses after the death of a family member. By complete chance, some letters that came into his possession, dated sometime in 1762, had made reference to this mirror. A strange coincidence, don't you think?'

'Very.' Although even as I said it I was aware that what Mr Alexander had just told me didn't feel remarkable or odd at all. It felt like information that had always been destined to find me.

'Nat no longer has the letters but he broadly recalled their contents. Largely because it was such an unusual tale. Shall I go on?'

'Yes, please.' The words came out of my mouth but if I was honest it was probably the last thing I wanted to hear. I felt my body tense.

'The letters came from Louisiana,' said the old man, his voice assuming the same wistful and yet authoritative quality that it had had on the day I'd visited him. 'They were sent in mid-1762, I think. Nat couldn't recall when precisely, but he knew it was while the state still belonged to the French. It was ceded to the Spanish shortly after-wards, in a secret treaty made in September of that year.'

In spite of the way I was feeling, I smiled to myself. Somehow Mr Alexander always made me feel like I was in a history tutorial with him. How he knew all this stuff I had no idea.

'The letters were sent by a Frenchwoman, the wife of a plantation owner, to her friend in Paris. They gave an account of some peculiar happenings on a neighbouring plantation in Southern Louisiana. The owner, a Frenchman, had moved out to America to attempt to make his fortune in tobacco. It was suggested that he was of some gentility, having shipped out a plethora of beautiful furniture, including armoires, dressers, chaises longues, lavish paintings, prints and – a particular favourite – an antique mirror, quite blackened with age and with engraved lettering on its surface. He was, apparently, singularly proud of this last item and extremely enamoured of the fact that it had once belonged to Henri II.'

He paused for a moment as if allowing this information to penetrate. 'Anyway, this man's wife, uninterested in living in a remote colony of France, stayed at home. And, perhaps as a result of this, there were rumours before too long of an affair between the man and one of the slave women on his plantation. Apparently the French woman dedicated a number of pages to a thorough discussion of the inappropriateness of this behaviour. Most of the French out there at the time were devout Catholics, you see.'

Mr Alexander coughed delicately and then resumed his story. 'Nat recalled particularly that one letter told of a peculiar event that took place on the Frenchman's plantation in the summer of 1762. It had been a rainy night, the tail end of a hurricane making its way inland, accompanied by thunder and lightning and howling winds. The slaves on the plantation said later that they thought they had heard raised voices and loud noises coming from the house. But they couldn't be sure and ultimately put it down to the clamour of the storm. However, the following day the Frenchman was found dead on the floor of his sitting room, beneath the mirror, his body marked in various places. The slave girl who had become his lover was nowhere to be found.

'Rumours abounded for weeks. Black magic – conjuring – was prevalent in the American South and was suspected particularly when a man died in mysterious circumstances. And there were plentiful stories about the girl. Among which that she had bewitched him and stolen his soul, disappearing on the night of his death never to be seen again. A trail of her muddy footprints was apparently found circling the wooden floors of the house leading from the doorway to the body and back again.'

As I listened to Mr Alexander's voice, my gaze flicked upwards to the Elmer Batters print on the wall above the kitchen table. I looked at the stockinged feet, the shoes hanging precariously from the toes. For some reason they made me think of Amelia.

'Another tale had it that the girl had disappeared some time before his death and that he, driven mad by her abandonment, had killed himself. Others said that he was a dark and powerful magician and had sacrificed her long before his own demise. The stories abounded, each more fantastical than the last. But whatever the tale, all were united in one thing. Something ominous had happened in the house that night.'

Silence followed. I was sure that Mr Alexander was waiting for me to say something. But I had nothing to say.

'Nat said that it was a scandal for quite some time. It appalled the letter writer, in any event, that much is for sure. That's no doubt why he remembered it.'

No doubt.

'The letters also said that the Frenchman's estate was packed up and shipped back to France. So the mirror probably ended up back in Paris sometime in 1762. But who knows where it had been before – or, indeed, where it went after?'

Well, I knew that by 1898 it had made its way to Venice. What I didn't know was whether its journey had been accompanied by tales as bizarre as the one from Louisiana or as tragic as the one from Rome. An image flashed through my mind of the slave girl's footprints of mud patterning the floor of the Frenchman's plantation house. The next moment I thought of Ophelia and the story she had told me about her mother's feet marking the sand. Delicate, transitory imprints formed before the tide washed them away. I closed my eyes and breathed deeply. Could the story I had just heard in any way be true? Could any of the things that Mr Alexander had told me have actually happened? A month ago I'd have laughed and dismissed it out of hand. But now I was not so sure. It seemed believable enough, at least parts of it, given what

I knew of James Brimley's death. And what I now knew about the manner of his demise.

'Johnny, are you still there?' Mr Alexander's voice contained a tinge of agitation. Not surprising. I couldn't have sounded like myself throughout the whole of the call.

I forced my voice into breeziness. 'Yes, I'm still here. Sorry. I was just thinking. I don't suppose your friend happens to remember the name of the Frenchman or the woman writing the letters? So that we can try and verify the facts – if, indeed, they are facts.'

'I'm afraid not. It was the first thing I asked him as well. I've told you everything he could recollect. And he can't remember what happened to the letters, either. He had a quick look around for them but to no avail. I'm sad to say that the most likely outcome is that they ended up getting thrown out. It happens a lot in our line of business.'

I could imagine. Dealers must come across hundreds of letters that don't have any monetary value. Worthless personal histories thrown out with the rubbish. There was something tragic about it.

'Anyway, I thought I'd let you know, Johnny, simply because it was such a strange story. And given that the piece itself is so strange.' Mr Alexander's marvel at the strangeness of it all seemed to hang suspended on the line for a moment or two. 'But it's just another tall tale, I suspect.'

'No doubt about it.' Trying to make light of it, I managed a small laugh. But it lacked any heart.

38

After Mr Alexander's phone call, I was haunted by visions of bodies lying unmoving across wooden floorboards. When I thought of the Frenchman, images flashed across my brain accompanied by the sounds of wind and rain and cicadas, a Deep South melody. When I imagined James, the only herald of his death was silence, punctuated intermittently by the creaking of the factory floors and the whistling of its ancient pipes. In the darkness around the edges of both visions, I saw the mirror.

To escape these thoughts, to distract myself, I got dressed and left the flat. I had no idea where I was going but I needed to get out, to walk, to try to clear my head. I set off, heading south in the vague direction of where I had agreed to meet Ophelia later that afternoon. Crisscrossing backstreets and avoiding main roads, I tried to keep my mind blank, to avoid thinking any more. The wind was cool and light, the air and the calmness of the day soothing. I passed blocks of flats, shops and parks, the signs of urban life all around me. Yet everywhere seemed still and deserted. Out of necessity I crossed Old Street and then continued moving south, keeping away from the crowds and the thrum of the traffic. I listened, but beyond the occasional car passing by, the odd screech of tyres or children, everything seemed subdued. The only signs of vibrancy were the tattered plastic bags which rose on the air and then, caught by the push of the wind, rolled down the street, peculiarly colourful man-made tumbleweed.

After ten minutes I emerged onto City Road. It was busy, people jostling one another, passing back and forth, going about their business. As I was poised to cross the main road, something brought me to a halt. It was the sign for Bunhill Fields, emerging now on my right. I had come across its name recently. Only I couldn't remember where. I stopped and stared at it as I thought about it. I racked my brain. Then it came to me in a flash. James Brimley had been buried in its graveyard. I had come across the information in an article about his death. For a moment, I stared at the sign and the green space beyond. Then I made my way through the gates.

I had visited Bunhill Fields before and knew that it contained the graves of several famous individuals: William Blake, Daniel Defoe, John Bunyan. It was a beautiful, romantic space, a walled burial ground which also contained a large public garden. It was filled with mature trees – oak, lime and ash – and interspersed with small pathways that meandered amongst the graves, many of which were packed closely together and others which were enclosed behind railings. I ambled past the gravestones until I found what I was looking for: a small, insignificant plot in a corner. The headstone was slant-faced, traditionally Victorian, and made from granite. It had sunk somewhat into the ground and was now obscured by moss and lichen, making the inscription a little difficult to read. Beyond his name, James Arthur Brimley, and the dates below it, 2 September 1859 – 25 September 1898, there was nothing to be instantly gleaned. I knelt down and rubbed the stone until the inscription became clearer:

To a devoted son and father. May he rest in peace.

Short and sweet. There was no reference to his wife and I wondered if this was deliberate.

I rubbed away at the lichen on the top of the headstone until an indented line of crosses appeared, which ran along the top edge of the rectangle. I continued to rub my fingers over its outer edges until a full border of crosses was revealed. I ran my fingers over them to be sure, but they were definitely crosses. And there were lots of them.

I looked over at the gravestone to the left of James's, the only one nearby. It too was tired and overgrown, almost entirely covered in moss, ivy snaking densely across its surface. But through the foliage I could just make out the name on the headstone: Michael Cleaver. So James's wife was buried somewhere else.

'What, pray, are you doing? Not desecrating graves, I trust.'

I looked up to see Ophelia approaching, looking at me quizzically.

I jumped to my feet, laughing, and walked to meet her.

'Not unless you count cleaning up a grave as desecration. Hey, stranger.' I pulled her to me.

She studied me for a moment. 'Johnny, you look tired.' And her fingers moved gently over the lines at the corners of my eyes. 'Have you been sleeping?'

I shrugged as nonchalantly as I could. 'I've been missing you,' was all I said. And only now, as I held her, did I realise how much. Holding her tightly to me, I kissed her, the smell of rose and jasmine enveloping me. I had missed the touch of her lips, the smell of her skin, the comforting sensation of her body against mine. 'Welcome back. How was your trip?'

'It was fine. The usual.' She shrugged. 'What are you doing here?'

I laughed. 'I might ask you the same thing.'

'I was walking up City Road to meet you when I saw you come in here. I called out to you but you didn't hear me. So I followed you in.' Pause. 'And now I see why. Our old friend James.'

I nodded. 'One of the articles I read about him said that he was buried here. I remembered as I was standing on the road. So I thought I'd take a look.'

We both stared at the headstone for a few moments.

'The chain of crucifixes around the edge is a bit over the top, don't you think? Overkill even for the Victorians.'

'Perhaps someone was worried for his soul.' The words were barely out of my mouth before a barrage of images of dead bodies on bare floors once more flooded my brain. I blinked hard and then closed my eyes, but in the darkness there I thought of James again, in the underground room, rambling on about death and what evils lurked, waiting for him. When I opened my eyes I found Ophelia looking at me. She squeezed my hand softly and smiled. 'Are you okay?'

I nodded quickly and tried to forget it all. I looked back at the headstone.

'I feel sorry for him,' said Ophelia. 'He dies . . . oddly, to say the least, jabbering and deranged, and then ends up here, in this corner of a cemetery. I can't help feeling that he was being hidden away.'

I looked at where we were standing, on the very fringes of the churchyard, hard against the boundary wall. He certainly wasn't in pride of place at the centre. And his headstone was hardly one that distinguished itself. There was certainly some disparity between this and the bold claims about his popularity, at home and in the world at large, in the literature at the time of his death.

Ophelia looked around her, at the other crumbling, dilapidated headstones, worn down by sun, rain and the movement of the earth, overgrown with ivy, brambles and creepers. 'I love graveyards,' she said finally.

I looked at her and frowned. 'What?'

'There's something sacred about them. And I don't mean that in a religious way. They are places dedicated to love, to remembrance, where you can feel close to someone long after they are gone. That's why they're so affecting.'

Now I began to understand. 'Where's your mother buried?'

'She's not. She was cremated and my father and I scattered her ashes into the sea. I think my father thought it was the right thing to do, given the life we'd led at that point.' Ophelia turned to look at me. 'And as you know he died at sea. So they're both buried in a pretty expansive grave. I suppose that's why I like the idea of a small plot. Somewhere contained to go.' She tilted her head as she continued to look at the gravestones. 'I remember once seeing an exhibition of photographs. They were taken in Jewish cemeteries in Eastern Europe in the early twentieth century. They showed families, individuals, children and adults pictured alongside the graves of their loved ones. I remember two men in bowler hats standing beside the grave of their father. A woman leaning casually against her mother's headstone. And a young girl reclining, almost seductively, along the length of her lover's grave. She had laid flowers there and they matched the ones she had in her hair. So you see. It's not unusual: people love to have a place to go. Graveyards are as much about the living as the dead.'

I nodded. 'So do you have anywhere that you go to remember your mother and father?'

'No. Nowhere.' Ophelia shook her head slowly. 'But I have photographs that I carry with me. Pretty much all the time. So I remember them that way.' Reaching to her neck, she unclasped the silver locket she always wore and showed me the images inside. Both were black and white. The left-hand photograph was of a woman shot with a close camera lens. It captured her face and not much more. She had dark wavy hair, full, oval lips and twinkling eyes. She was beautiful, all luminous skin and cheekbones and an enigmatic smile, much like Ophelia's. In the image on the right, the same woman appeared with a man, their two heads together, touching, caught in laughter. The man had dark hair, a large nose and distant eyes. Eyes that he had passed on to Ophelia. There was an intimacy to the shot that was captivating.

'They're beautiful,' I said.

Ophelia twisted the locket around to face her and smiled. 'Yes, they are. I often think that it was these pictures of my parents that made me want to become a photographer. To capture lives, moments like this. And it's probably why I take so many close-up shots now. Perhaps trying to capture these moments again.' She looked at the photographs for a few more seconds. 'I've been missing them more than usual at the moment. Strange.' Then she closed the locket with a quiet click and dropped her hand to her side.

'Why haven't you shown me these photographs before?' I asked.

She paused for a second. 'I don't know. These in particular are intensely personal to me.' And her hand reached up instinctively to take hold of the locket once more. 'Perhaps I wasn't ready. But I've shown you now.'

I smiled, reaching for her hand and taking her fingers in mine. 'It's good to have you back.'

'It's good to be back,' she said and leaned forward to kiss me.

As we turned to head out of the cemetery in the

fading light, I caught a final glimpse of James's grave from out of the corner of my eye, its surface an ostentatious loop of crosses. I wondered if they were intended as symbols of love and redemption. Or whether they were trying to guard him from something much darker and more damning, something which lurked hidden, unseen.

39

The Louvre

July 1559

Catherine sat in the corner of the room in silence. Her eyes were red, her face puffy. She had been weeping. But now she was quiet, her mind blank, made up of nothing. She found the emptiness comforting and luxuriated in its darkness. Her eyes flicked to the left and saw the walls shrouded in black brocade. Black cloth was spread upon the floor and across the windows where it blocked out the light. Looking behind her she saw the bed, covered with a black sheet, and in front of her an altar dressed in the same manner. Candles burned at each end of it, the only light to pierce the darkness of the room. For a split second she couldn't remember where she was or why the room had been decorated like this. Then in the next instant she felt it rising, almost in slow motion. The unthinkable. Her whole body stiffened and with a sudden painful fury the remembrance came. The knowledge that he was dead and the violence of his passing.

She inhaled ragged breaths as the images flooded through her. A still, hot day in June, sunlight glinting off the armour of two men. Her husband, resplendent in the saddle, charging his opponent time and again, their jousts clashing repeatedly. She saw herself begging him not to continue, just as she had begged him that morning not to partake of the games that day, warning of her vision of him lying stricken on the ground. But he had laughed, said that it was sport and that he did not believe in predictions. The furious noise of the crowd had rung in her ears as the men advanced upon one another one last time. Then there was only the sight of wood splintering against metal, piercing a broken visor and penetrating a skull. And a dying husband, bleeding from his eye and his temple, lying prostrate in the dirt.

Catherine closed her eyes and her sobbing began again. Now, in this moment, she could not imagine that there were points of forgetful calm, small oases of time in which there was no knowledge that such a thing had happened. Now, in this moment, there was only desolation, entire, complete. There was only emptiness in the place where she should have felt her heart beating.

Minutes later the force of the emotion left her. She wiped her eyes and sat unmoving for a moment. Then she reached for the hand mirror beside her on the chair. Looking at her face, even in the darkness, she could see enough. The high forehead, bulging eyes, the sharp, pointed nose, the protruding lower lip. Her face was not attractive – it never had been. Her body was short, fat, after years of child-bearing. The mare of France, they had called her, and her eyes pricked with tears of a different nature. For years she had hidden her feelings inside this body, disguised her anger, her hatred and her longing beneath an expressionless plain face. She had been overshadowed, surpassed in almost every respect and the love she had longed for, that should have been hers alone, had been given instead to a harlot. Donec totum impleat orbem (Until it fills the whole world), their motto, the words dedicated to their love, that had been lauded over her without shame, had stuck in her throat for over twenty years. But no longer.

She stood abruptly, the mirror still in her hand and paced the floor of the chamber. In the darkness her cheeks and her pride burned. With her husband gone, his whore had no more standing. She, Catherine, would banish her from court and from memory, as effectively as she had banished her from his funeral bed. She smiled as she remembered her first taste of power. He had called out for his mistress day and night and she, Catherine, had prevented her from entering his chamber. He had died without a last sight of her.

She stopped in front of the altar and raised the mirror once more in front of her face. A dark smile played upon her lips. It reminded her of a different time and an altogether different mirror. She had tried, always, to give him the strength that his whore had stripped him of. To allow him to break the bonds that tied him to her. What was it that had so ensnared him? She had driven herself half mad in the contemplation of it. Catherine remembered the holes in her bedroom floor that had been made what felt like a lifetime ago, and the sight through them of the pale skin, the long, slender limbs entwining him. His mistress had fashioned herself on Diana, goddess of the hunt, and he had allowed her to spin the myth around them. It was degrading. That he, like Actaeon, had stumbled upon her naked beauty in the forest and that in retribution for being so caught she had had his heart ripped out. Why had he allowed such a belittling story to be not only told but celebrated? And she, Catherine, had had to tolerate it. How was it that a crescent moon could eclipse a Queen?

She looked once more into the glass and saw her own reflection there. In disgust she hurled the mirror against the wall. It smashed into pieces and then fell, disappearing into the darkness at the room's edges. She had tried to make him strong. She had given him the power to reverse that woman's spell and also avenge his mistreated wife. But the gift had never been put to use and the whore, wiser than she appeared, had hidden it away in fear. She had triumphed once again. But no more.

Catherine turned and walked towards the window. She could, of course, demand its return as she had demanded the return of the crown jewels and would, before long, demand the offering of Chenonceau. But perhaps there was a better way. She smiled again as she placed her hands upon the black cloth which covered the glass in the window. She remembered the tingling in her fingers, still remembered acutely the sensations that ran through her that night in the darkened room with Cosimo. Perhaps it was better for it to remain at large, passed down into posterity. Her smile broadened as she imagined her vengeance, her revenge exacted upon those whores that fornicated with men tied to others, women who failed to give heed to God's ordinances. If she had failed with Diane, she would succeed with others. Her curse had been to love: theirs would be the same.

As she turned from the window and resumed her vigil at the darkened altar, her mind was set. Donec totum impleat orbem. *It would become her motto now and it would symbolise not her love but her revenge passed down, far and wide.*

Until it filled the whole world.

40

Ophelia and I were ensconced in a cocktail bar in Shoreditch.

It was a great place that I'd been to a few times before – an eclectic space with exposed brick walls decked with a mixture of anatomical drawings and ancient tapestries, filled with antique pieces, giant Chinese vases, a myriad of chandeliers and wooden toy horses suspended from the ceiling, even a hippopotamus head jutting out of the wall. We were in a corner, a life-size wooden swan sitting on the table alongside our drinks, a grandfather clock ticking softly beside us. I had just finished telling Ophelia the story that Mr Alexander had recounted to me that morning.

'Of course, it doesn't seem as if there's any written record of these events,' I went on. 'The man who told the antique dealer about the letters couldn't find them. He just remembered the story. And we all know how that works. Memory and imagination don't always stick to the facts.'

Ophelia pulled a face. 'Nonetheless, the similarities between what happened there and what happened to James are weird.'

I nodded, looking at the giant swan. 'Right.' It was true. I hadn't mentioned James, or what had happened to him, to Mr Alexander. And I couldn't imagine that he would have known about such things. So she was right: the similarities, seemingly coincidental, were strange.

'And both narratives featured a woman who had disappeared.'

'Do you think the slave girl ran away from the plantation on the night of the storm or do you think she was already dead?'

I shrugged. 'Beats me.' But what had happened to her had been bothering me since Mr Alexander had first told me the story. The thought triggered an image of footprints, patterns of mud across the Frenchman's house, leading to his body beneath the mirror. I closed my eyes, imagining him staring into its rippling darkness. And that in turn made me think of something else.

'You know, you've never told me what you saw in the mirror. If you saw anything, that is.'

Ophelia looked at me for a second before speaking. 'No, I didn't tell you.' She smiled faintly and I sensed a reluctance in her to talk about it. A moment or two passed. 'It made me think of my parents,' she said at last, looking at me. 'Strange, don't you think?'

After she'd shown me the photographs in her locket earlier today, it wasn't a total surprise. She always played with the locket when she looked into the mirror. But she was right, it was strange. I reached for my drink, catching sight as I did so of the mutilated hippopotamus. Its head, jutting surreally into the corridor of the bar, seemed suddenly ominous, otherworldly. I took a large mouthful and swallowed. The alcohol shot into my system and I felt a momentary rush. 'Will you tell me exactly what you saw? In detail. I'd really like to know.'

'Okay,' said Ophelia. Then she took a deep breath. 'Well, at first, I saw nothing. It was all darkness, the darkness of the mirror's surface. But the deeper I looked, the more I concentrated, if you like, the more the darkness seemed to clear – or, at least, I appeared to be able to see through it.'

I nodded. I knew what that was like.

'The cloudy greyness, the blotchiness of the surface, vanished and instead a landscape started to form, the landscape of my dream. The same dream I've had since I was a child, the one I told you about.'

I remembered it clearly.

'First I saw my mother walking down the beach, then I saw my father following.' She smiled. 'It was strange. As I looked at them through the mirror, I felt as if I was standing behind both of them, as if I too was on the beach. I could almost feel the sand between my toes, taste the salty tang of the air. And yet I also knew that I was not on that beach, that I was apart from them, separated somehow, watching. But I had the inescapable feeling that I could be part of it if I chose, if I only chose to cross over into it. Do you understand what I mean?'

I nodded, although I wasn't sure that I did.

'I saw the curve of the beach, bright in the moonlight, clouds floating over the sea, dappling its surface with patches of deeper darkness. The stars were bright in the sky. I saw my mother turn, smile at the person behind her, my father, touching the imprints she had made in the wet sand with her feet. And I felt an intense joy, an over-whelming happiness, that I had found them again. My mother and my father. And then my father also turned, looking back to the place he'd come from.'

Ophelia smiled faintly, then a slight frown crossed her face.

'What is it?'

'I've had this dream for years, Johnny. Since I was a child. Ever since my father's death. It has always been the same. Exactly as I've just described to you, as I described to you before. The next thing that happens is that my father turns back and begins to follow my mother once more. It's the way it's always been.' Pause. 'But the last time I looked into the mirror with you something new happened. Something unexpected. My father saw me. I've never felt that before. In my dreams I always felt that I was an observer, not a participant. But clearly this time he saw me. I was present. Or at least there was the tantalising possibility that I could be. He smiled at me and beckoned me to go, to join them, to cross over and be with them. Then I saw my mother turn, from further up the beach, and wave at me. She too was gesturing for me to come to them, to follow in their footsteps.' Pause. 'And, in that moment, I felt the longing inside me bloom and explode. It was almost too much to bear.'

I stared at Ophelia, not quite sure what to say next. For a moment, for a reason I couldn't quite pinpoint, I felt scared.

'Don't worry, the feeling's nothing new,' Ophelia said lightly. But she didn't meet my eye as she said it and I wasn't sure that I believed her.

For a few moments neither of us said anything, each caught up in our own thoughts.

'I found myself thinking a lot about Amelia while I was away,' said Ophelia, seeming to change the subject. 'About her disappearance, about what happened to her. And now something else has just occurred to me. What do you suppose she thought of when she looked into the mirror? What do you think she saw?'

'I have no idea,' I said. But again, I felt a quiver of apprehension in my stomach.

'I have an idea,' said Ophelia, her voice quiet but resonant against the hum of the conversations in the bar. 'I think perhaps she thought about her mother.'

That night Ophelia went to bed early, wiped out by her journey. But my brain was anything but tired. At first I paced around her sitting room, thoughts tumbling through my head. Then, when I couldn't stay up any longer, I lay in bed beside Ophelia's slumbering form, longing for my mind to be still and aching for a sleep which wouldn't come.

When I closed my eyes I saw the mirror, a mirror touched, polluted somehow, by a Black Queen. Then the image of a dead body flashed beneath my eyelids. But whether it was James or someone else, I couldn't tell. I opened my eyes, feeling my heart racing in the darkness and sweat prickling against my skin, marking the bed sheet. Closing my eyes again, I saw the dead beckoning, gesturing to those who were still alive, and in the thick darkness around me I struggled to breathe, unsure whether the feeling was in my dreams or in reality. I heard the torrential downpour of warm rain, pounding the dark, rich earth of Louisiana but in the next moment it became the swift, heavy drumming of my heart in my chest. I tried to slow it down, to calm it to a strong, rhythmic beat. I tried to move away from panic and back to myself, to forget everything that haunted me now. Loss, death, madness, the mirror, shapeless haunting forms at the edges of my vision. I closed my eyes to all of it and concentrated on my breathing.

Whether I slept or not I couldn't be sure, but my mind was filled with a dark and dreamless emptiness. Out of this, I awoke suddenly. The hairs on my arms were standing to attention and the room felt cold. But it was quiet. For a moment I remained motionless, listening. All I could hear was the quick, shallow breathing of Ophelia beside me, but as the room was in darkness I couldn't make out her face. I flicked on the lamp and looked at her again. Her eyelids were flickering and she looked as though she was dreaming. I moved closer to her, still studying her face. She looked beautiful as she slept. Suddenly she opened her eyes. When she saw me looking down at her she opened her mouth.

Then she began to scream.

41

The sound was shrill, intense, shocking in the quiet of the night. Instantly I sprang away from Ophelia and at the same time she sat upright, increasing the distance between us. Then, as quickly as it had begun, the screaming stopped.

For a moment a profound silence reigned as we stared at one another. Ophelia's eyes were wide, terrified, her mouth open as if poised to scream again. More than anything I wanted to prevent that.

'Ophelia, it's me. What's the matter?'

'Johnny?'

'Yes, it's me.' Instinctively, I looked at myself, standing naked in the middle of her bedroom. 'It's me.'

Still she looked uncertain.

'What is it? What's going on?'

'Am I dreaming?'

I looked at her blankly. 'No, you're not dreaming,' I said uncertainly.

'No?'

'No.' I shook my head, unsettled by Ophelia's continuing bewildered gaze. 'What's the matter?' I said again, equally bewildered.

Ophelia stared at me for a moment or two longer, then turned her head to look around her. She seemed to take in the bedroom, the familiar racks of shoes, the open wardrobe, the desk next to the window, the photographs on the wall beside it. For a few moments she said nothing, simply looking around her – presumably at the familiarity of it all.

'Ophelia, what's going on?'

She turned to me for the first time with something that resembled recognition, wrapping her arms around her and hugging herself tightly. 'I had a nightmare,' she said at last. She nodded and frowned, took a deep breath and let it go slowly.

I walked over to the bed and sat down next to her. 'Are you all right?'

She looked at me, clearly still distressed, and shook her head.

'It's okay,' I said, noticing her hesitancy as I leaned forward to take her in my arms. 'It's okay,' I said, again. At first her body felt awkward, resisting my embrace, but eventually, as I continued to hold her, I felt the tension drop away. 'Are you all right?'

She nodded. 'Yes, I am now. I'm sorry, I was confused.'

'It's okay. It doesn't matter.' I ran my hands over her hair, again and again, trying to calm her with the repetitive movement. 'Shall we go and get a drink?'

'Yes, good idea. Something strong.' And for the first time since she had woken she smiled.

*

Ten minutes later, sitting in the warmth of the kitchen, we had drunk two glasses of Jack Daniel's each. I was pouring us a third when Ophelia finally spoke.

'It was the weirdest thing. You know those dreams where you're aware that it's a dream?'

'Sure.'

'But it feels very real. Not dreamlike at all. And you can't wake up.' She frowned and reached for her glass. 'I remember it all clearly. Probably because it wasn't new to me.'

'What?' I really wasn't following what she was saying. 'You'd had the dream before?'

'No.' She shook her head. 'I'm sorry. I'm not making much sense. But perhaps I should just keep going?'

'Okay,' I said, downing my drink.

'It began with darkness. I was surrounded by it. At first I thought I had just woken up and it was the middle of the night. I remember raising my hand in front of my face but I couldn't see it. It was pitch dark in the truest sense.'

I looked at Ophelia, beginning to feel uncomfortable.

'Then I realised that I was standing upright, not lying down. I swung my arms at my sides but I couldn't detect any movement. Just as I was about to panic, I began to see candlelight in front of me. As the flame grew I was able to see where I was. Do you know?'

I nodded, slowly, unwillingly. I was beginning to feel sick. 'You were in a small room with a low ceiling, a mirror on the wall to your right and a doorway next to it with a dark passageway beyond.'

'A mirror in which I could see only the very faintest reflection of myself and a passageway which I felt I would never be able to reach.' Ophelia licked her lips, which I suddenly noticed were pale and dry. Her eyes were wide, afraid. 'And as I stared into the mirror trying to see something, something in me knew that I should try and get out of the room. That something bad, something terrible had happened there. And yet I couldn't. Something else stopped me. I could feel it quite distinctly. An overwhelming desire to stay.'

I nodded again. Strange as it was, this was all familiar territory for me.

Ophelia took a deep, uneven breath. 'Suddenly I heard a noise and I turned to see a man sitting in an armchair, his head tilted downwards. On the floor at his feet was a green shoe. He had obviously dropped it and was distressed, muttering and rubbing his hands together. But I couldn't see his face. I remember trying to but I couldn't.' She paused for a moment and took a sip of her drink. 'Then something came into view on his left. All of a sudden. It was bizarre, very cinematic, like the flickering and then unfolding of a film. I saw a pair of feet, perched on the edge of a bed.'

Ophelia's voice cracked and I thought I saw tears begin to well in her eyes. 'At first I wasn't able to look beyond the feet and calves. No matter how hard I tried. And all I could think was that it reminded me so much of what you had told me about the dream you had. And that demonstrated to me that it was a dream and that I was

conscious of that. Then I saw the feet again, so familiar.'
Ophelia looked at me, her eyes wide, intense and glistening.
'Finally I was able to make out legs, then a torso and
chest. It was a woman's body, unmoving.' Ophelia put her
hand to her neck instinctively and reached for her locket.
She rubbed her fingers over its smooth silver for a moment
or two before continuing. 'And just as in your dream, I
couldn't see her face. But it didn't matter. My heart filled
with a sense of dread and foreboding. I knew her anyway,
this woman, and I knew with a sudden certainty what
had happened to her. Just as I was about to run from the
room, the man looked up and caught sight of me, watching
him and the woman in the basement. After all, that's
where it was.'

She looked at me straight and I nodded.

'And he was suddenly incredibly angry at my presence
and what I might have seen take place in that room. He
challenged me, asked me what I was doing there, then
stood up and approached me. He was dressed in an old-
fashioned black suit, with a waistcoat and jacket, and I
knew, just like you said to me about your dream, that if
he reached me there would be trouble.' Ophelia hesitated
as she looked at me. 'And I tried to will myself awake.
Like I said, I knew it was a dream, and that I should in
theory be able to exert control over its outcome. But as
the man came to a stop in front of me, very close in front
of me, I knew that I had no control over this. The outcome
had already been written.' Ophelia stopped and looked
at me, tears in her eyes. 'And like you, I knew I should

have tried harder to escape that place while I had the chance. Now I knew it was too late. He was going to kill me.' Her voice petered out.

I stared at her for a second, shaking my head. 'I'm sorry. It's horrible, I know. Are you okay?'

She nodded and took another sip of whiskey. 'Yes, I'm okay. I didn't see it, or feel it. I woke up. But I knew how it was going to end.'

I stared at her. So she had had exactly the same sensation as me even though I too hadn't died in the dream. I shook my head again. I didn't understand it. It didn't make any sense. 'It's strange that you should have had a dream like mine – how can that be?'

Ophelia shrugged. 'I don't know.' Pause. 'Anyway, it wasn't identical to your dream.'

'No? Sounds pretty similar.'

'Similar, yes. But it was different.' Ophelia took a deep breath. 'Your dream was about James and Amelia. You didn't know it at the time, but it was them.'

I felt a creeping uncertainty rise up my back. 'Yes. Yours wasn't about them?'

'No. It wasn't.'

My throat felt suddenly parched. I picked up my glass and then realised that it was empty. Replacing it on the table I saw that my hand was shaking slightly. 'Who was the man, then, the man seated in the chair?'

Ophelia paused. 'It was you.'

'Me?' My speech stuttered to a halt as I struggled to grasp the implication.

Ophelia nodded and bit down on her lip.

I knew I had to ask the question even though I didn't want to. 'And the woman on the bed?'

Ophelia nodded, confirming what I already knew. 'It was me, Johnny.' Her voice faltered and then regained itself. 'It was me.'

42

We stared at each other for a long time before I finally broke the silence.

'So you were lying in Amelia's place on the bed?'

Ophelia nodded.

'Are you sure?' I was grasping at straws, I knew, but I couldn't help it.

'Of course. I knew it from the moment I saw the feet on the bed. They were my feet, Johnny. I'd know them anywhere.' She added quietly: 'I'm sure.'

I nodded, trying to take it in, this picture of Ophelia inert on the bed in the underground room.

'And before you ask, it was definitely you in James's place. In the chair and . . . later.' She exhaled hard, refilling her glass once more. 'And do you want to know what else I knew?'

I nodded, although I wasn't sure that I really did.

'I was dead, Johnny.' The words fell heavily into the gap between us at the table. 'The Ophelia lying on the bed was dead.'

I took a deep breath and closed my eyes. I tried to

think. But nothing came other than the obvious. 'How do you know?'

'I just know. In the same way that I knew that the body on the bed was mine, I also knew I was dead. I felt it.'

The matter-of-fact way in which she said it made me shudder. I opened my eyes and looked at her face. At the green eyes, intense, serious, at her red lips, parted slightly as she breathed harshly. I thought of her dead body lying motionless on the bed, underground in the darkness.

Suddenly Ophelia spoke. 'I think Amelia was dead, too. In the dream you had of her.'

My mind shifted instantly to the same dream of Amelia, moving upwards from her feet and calves, over her thighs and body, halting at the green ribbon draped around her neck. It had looked like a necklace, so innocuous. But perhaps it had been more than that. 'How are you so certain?'

Ophelia shrugged. 'A feeling. Plus the symmetry of the dreams. Everything matches except the people. So if I am dead, she is dead.'

I took my glass in both hands, needing to anchor myself around something small and real and concrete.

'James killed Amelia. In that basement. I think that's what Amelia has been trying to lead you to. That I am following in her footsteps and you are following in James's.'

I paused for a second before I spoke. I wanted to make sure that this was the inevitable, unavoidable conclusion. 'So in this dream you just had, you think I killed you?'

Her green eyes looked at me, still serious. She nodded. 'And there's something else. Do you want to know?'

I looked at her sombre face and had to admit to myself that I really didn't. I was still reeling from what she'd just said.

'I asked you a little while ago if you thought the dreams you'd been having were in fact dreams. Or if they were something else. You didn't answer me but I still knew what you thought. You didn't think they were dreams. Not really, not truly. Did you?'

I looked at her, at her pale, earnest face. 'No, I didn't.'

'Well, I don't think this was a dream either. It was definitely something different. It was a vision, Johnny. It was a premonition of what's coming.'

I stared at her, heard her voice, the utter conviction in it, and in that moment all I wanted to do was laugh. To give myself release, to dismiss as ridiculous everything she was saying, to dispel her fears with hilarity and then move on, together. But I also realised that I couldn't do that. We had come too far down this path together. In that moment of uncertainty, when I longed to hear laughter, I heard another sound instead, strange, haunting, strangled. It was a moment or two before I realised it was coming from me. I coughed and the coughing brought an end to the other sound.

'Sorry,' I said, grabbing for the bottle of Jack Daniel's and pouring us both another shot. 'I'm just feeling a little . . .'

'Weird? Join the club.' Ophelia reached for her glass

and downed its contents. 'But I think that's the way things are meant to pan out. I really feel it, Johnny. Unless we stop it.'

I nodded vaguely, but my mind was on something that had been bothering me since she raised it. 'Do you really think that I could hurt you, Ophelia?' As I said the words aloud, an image of myself in the underground room came into my mind, the green ribbon tied around my wrists as I had sex with Ophelia. As I thought about it now I could feel it digging into my skin, cutting into my flesh as I struggled to free myself from its grip. I stopped short and looked into her eyes. Then I realised that she hadn't answered me. 'I could never hurt you,' I said, and even though Ophelia nodded at me I knew we were both thinking of the times we had been in the cellar together.

I sighed deeply and poured Ophelia another drink. We sat in silence for a few minutes, each caught in our own dark thoughts.

'I'm scared, Johnny.' Ophelia's eyes were wide, her face paler than usual. She looked as scared as she no doubt felt. Looking at her now, something twisted deep inside me. More than anything I wanted to protect her.

What I was most scared of was that I wouldn't be able to do that.

43

My breath plumed into the night air like smoke. It was bitterly cold, the sky clear, not a cloud in sight. I tried to see stars, but as ever they were obscured by the light of the city. I exhaled deeply and another breath bloomed into the night. I was like a man on fire.

Pulling my mobile from my jacket pocket, I dialled the number before I could think better of it. For what felt like for ever I was forced to listen to the intermittent ring, punctuated with emptiness. But just as I was about to hang up, she picked up at the other end.

'Johnny?' The voice didn't sound sleepy, but there was a tone to it that I couldn't quite place. Perhaps it was repressed anger that I was calling so late.

'Yes, it's me.' Pause. 'I'm sorry, Tara. Did I wake you?'

There was a crackle on the line. 'No, amazingly, you didn't. Is everything okay?'

It was then that I placed the tone. It was concern. She was worried about me. 'I'm okay. I just needed to talk to you.'

'At three a.m.?'

'Yeah, I'm sorry,' I said again.

'Don't worry about it. I wasn't sleeping.' There was a shuffling noise on the end of the line, as if she was getting up from somewhere and moving around. 'Okay. I'm sitting down. Talk to me.'

I didn't really know where to start. But today's developments seemed like a good place. First I told her about Mr Alexander's phone call and the letters that his colleague Nathaniel Raven had once had. Then I described James's solitary grave in Bunhill Fields, away from family and friends, and the last letters I had found behind the mirror. Finally, although it was most on my mind, I told her what Ophelia had seen in the mirror and what she had dreamed that night. When I was finished, the line fell silent.

'Tara, are you there?'

'I'm still here.' Her voice was quiet and I guessed that she was trying to digest the information.

'I ran some computer searches on the Frenchman just now, looking for anything that could add to or clarify what Mr Alexander told me. But I couldn't find anything.' The Frenchman's history remained a yawning blank. 'So then I came back to the factory.'

I heard Tara sigh. 'Johnny, you're crazy. You went there in the middle of the night?'

I nodded into the darkness. 'And I took down every photograph from every wall and checked behind every image. I thought there might be more letters there.' I sighed, remembering my disappointment. 'I was so sure that there was something else out there that could tie all these strands together. But there wasn't anything.'

'No. I think the factory has given up all its secrets to us, Johnny.'

'What makes you say that?'

'After we met there the other day, I did another complete trawl of all the paperwork. I'm pretty sure there's nothing left there now that we haven't seen.'

So that was it. We were at a dead end. Literally, if dreams were to be believed. I shivered in the cold night air.

'Where are you? You sound like you're freezing to death.'

'You're not far off. I'm in the park opposite the factory.'

'Johnny, you're crazy,' Tara said again.

I smiled. She was probably right. After all the strange things that had happened, I was probably well on my way to madness. But sitting in the quiet stillness of the park didn't seem like the craziest thing in the world for me to do right now.

'You should go home. Try and get some rest. You must be exhausted.'

I was. And overwrought. But home was the last place I wanted to go.

'Look, don't worry about finding more information. I've got an idea and I'll follow it up first thing tomorrow. You go home and go to bed.'

'I don't want to go bed.' The words came out in a slew of fear and anger. Sleep wasn't what I wanted these days. I was too plagued by what I saw when I closed my eyes.

I heard Tara sigh and I thought for a second that she

might lose her temper. But her voice when it came down the line was calm.

'No, I can understand that. I really can.' She paused for a moment. 'Johnny, can I tell you something?'

'Of course. What is it?'

Tara paused again and I wondered if she would go on. When she did, her voice was soft but it made me flinch nonetheless. 'I've seen something in the mirror too.'

I was silent for a moment, trying to take it in, trying to fight back my anxiety and rage. 'Didn't I ask you not to go down there alone? It's dark and dangerous.' The words reverberated loudly in the quietness of the park. As silence descended once more I heard a dog bark in the distance.

'Yes, I'm sorry. You did say that, I know. But it was when I was searching the factory for information. That last time a few days ago.' She paused. 'It's the only time I've been back down there since you and I found the mirror.'

I sat silently on the park bench, wondering if she was telling me the truth.

'Look, when haven't I been honest with you, Johnny?' Anger had now entered her voice. 'And besides, I hardly think you're in any position to lecture me. You've clearly been going there with Ophelia. Ritually.'

She was right, of course. I was being incredibly unfair. 'I'm sorry. I'm just worried, that's all.'

Tara sighed. 'It's okay. I get it.'

'So do you still want to tell me what you saw?'

I heard her swallow and then take a breath. 'I saw my grandmother.' Pause. 'I was very close to her when I was growing up, but she died when I was small. And yet I saw her. In the mirror.' Her voice sounded incredulous. 'Or I thought I saw her. I don't really know. And while it was oddly comforting, imagining her, seeing her, whatever you want to call it, it was also kind of frightening.'

I felt the rock of anxiety that had been building in my stomach harden. 'Why was it frightening?' I asked.

'It was a general feeling, at first. It was an old memory, you see. And that in itself was bizarre. I mean, how was it that I could see that reflected there?' Tara paused, thinking. 'My grandmother called out my name. Just my name at first. And then she came into view, walking down her garden path in her pink slippers like she always did, like I remember her doing when I was a child.' She laughed. 'It was both wonderful and disquieting just to see her. She called me Tara-bell. Exactly as she did when I was little.' She stopped, hesitating before continuing. 'And that was frightening. Not the simple fact of her calling out to me. But the way she did it. Or started to do it. She was gesturing, beckoning, as if indicating that if I wanted to join her I could.' She paused again. 'That's truly what made me afraid. It wasn't just a memory that I was reliving – I was seeing a memory that had been tampered with. One that was suggesting the possibility of being with her.'

I nodded. It sounded very similar to what Ophelia had told me she'd seen. The dream of her parents, the dream that had been altered.

'I don't know what it means,' Tara went on. 'But the way the memory has been twisted feels fundamentally wrong, perverse. It's suggesting something that cannot be, should not be, and therefore must be false.' Pause. 'The mirror's evil, Johnny. It should be destroyed.'

'I know. I've been thinking the same thing all night.'

'So what are you going to do?'

'I'm not sure. But I might just go down there with a sledgehammer and smash it to bits.'

'Works for me,' said Tara, her tone becoming lighter instantly. 'Well, if you need an assistant just give me a shout. I'd be more than happy to help out.'

'No, I'll do it alone, when I'm ready.' My tone was unexpectedly sharp. 'Understood?'

'Understood,' she said.

But immediately I felt a needling doubt. I had been saying to myself for the last hour or so that I would go down into the basement and destroy the mirror. It was the only way, I had concluded, to make sure that no one came to any harm – myself, Ophelia, Tara, or anyone else who came into contact with it. Yet still I sat here in the park, having done no such thing. Every time I tried to act upon it, something stopped me.

I heard Tara's voice, seemingly coming from far away. 'Johnny?'

I didn't answer.

'Johnny?'

I heard my name again. 'Sorry, I was miles away.'

'Are you okay?'

'Yes. I'm fine.'

'Okay. Then you should go home. And don't worry about Ophelia. I know you won't hurt her. If anything, I'd say she's much more likely to turn on you.' Tara's tone was playful. She was trying, I knew, to lighten the mood. But I couldn't connect with it at all. I stared at the plane trees, their branches rippling in the gentle night-time breeze. As with almost everything, it reminded me of the mirror.

'One last thing. Promise me you won't go down into the underground room again,' I said.

'I promise. Now go home and get some rest.'

44

Two days later, Ophelia and I were sitting opposite one another at her dining table. We had just finished dinner and our empty plates and glasses lay scattered on the table. I reached for the red-wine bottle sitting between us and poured the last of its contents into my glass. Having consumed most of it, I was feeling a little drunk. But I was enjoying the sensation, taking the edge off or even blocking out as it did so many of the things I didn't want to think about.

As I raised the glass to my lips I became conscious of Ophelia looking at me.

'What's wrong?' I said. Things hadn't been quite right between us since the dream she'd had. The dream in which she thought I killed her. I closed my eyes and tried to jettison the thought from my mind.

'I could ask you the same question.' The scar above her lip twitched slightly, the way it always did when she tightened her mouth, when she was angry or irritated with me.

I could feel a fight brewing and it was the last thing I wanted. So I tried to avoid it. 'I'm sorry, I'm preoccupied.

I've been thinking . . . well, you know what I've been thinking. Ever since your dream the other night . . .'

She nodded.

'I've been trying to work out what to do.'

'Me too.'

'I spoke to Tara about it.'

Ophelia interlinked her fingers and rested them on the tabletop. 'You did?'

'She thinks that I should destroy the mirror.'

'And what do *you* think?' Ophelia was leaning towards me, her body language betraying her eagerness to know.

'I think I agree with her.'

Ophelia was studying me closely. 'But I can sense some hesitation in you. What is it?'

I shook my head. 'Nothing. I know it has to be done.' I said it with a certainty that I didn't by any means feel. 'Tara had the same experience as you, you know. She felt, saw, whatever the right expression is, that her grandmother was calling out to her. I think the word she used was . . . beckoning. She said it didn't feel right. As if something was at work beneath the vision. Offering something that was unreal.'

Ophelia stared at me, her face a mask. It betrayed nothing.

'Did you feel the same way when you looked into the mirror?'

For a moment she remained silent, motionless, and then she shrugged. 'I don't know, Johnny. I can't say with any clarity whether I felt that. What I felt, what I always feel when I see them, when I think of them, is an intense, an overriding sense of loss, of longing.'

I nodded. That was what she'd always told me.

'So what are you going to do, Johnny?' I thought I heard a tremor of agitation in Ophelia's voice.

'I'm going to destroy it.' I looked at her. 'Something sinister is at work. I don't know exactly how but I know no good can come from it.' The dark, distorted reflection of my face flashed across my mind. It was a powerful face, but it was not my own. 'I'm going to do it tomorrow, alone.' I thought of my feelings, the heady wash of emotions I felt when Ophelia was with me in the underground room. When I had gone there alone, for some reason I'd felt much calmer, my senses less impaired. Perhaps I'd have more prospects of success alone.

'Okay,' said Ophelia. 'It's probably for the best.' Then she smiled at me as she stood up and began to clear the table. It was an automatic smile, swift, momentary, mechanical and I felt a flicker of unease again in my stomach.

'Ophelia, are you okay?'

'I'm fine. Just tired. You should get some sleep too, Johnny. You look exhausted.'

I looked at her and nodded. 'One last thing. Promise me you won't go down there again. For whatever reason. Let me deal with this myself now. Alone. I think it's safer that way.'

'Okay,' she said. 'I promise.'

45

We went to bed. Ophelia fell asleep in my arms and my body curled around hers, enclosing her, holding her to me.

When I awoke some time later, I felt sluggish, my brain slow, still affected by the wine, and there was a dull pounding in my head. I groaned and flexed my body. It was then that I noticed the absence of Ophelia within my arms. I strained my ears, listening for her quiet sleeping breath beside me. I couldn't hear anything. I opened my eyes but it was still dark and I couldn't see. So I flicked on the bedside light and looked. Sure enough, her side of the bed was empty. Instantly, I remembered having woken a month or so ago in almost exactly the same circumstances. Then I had also discovered Ophelia gone. My heart felt heavy, began to sink under the weight of knowing. I looked around the room, hoping. But she wasn't there.

I got out of bed and pulled on my jeans. As I passed the darkness of the bathroom I flicked on the light. A spill of yellow incandescence flowed over my feet and made me feel a little less tense. But I was still conscious of my heart, a dead weight in my chest. At the doorway of the sitting room I stopped and listened. But everything was silent. It was all so familiar, like going through the motions. I stood stationary for a few more seconds and then moved forwards.

The moon cast a shimmering blue light across the room, over the dining table and sofas, rippling over my feet in waves as I walked across the pale carpet. I looked for any sign of Ophelia but there was none. The room was empty and quiet but for the faint noise that penetrated from the road below, the whir of street cleaners, the mewing of cats. I opened the French windows and looked out onto the deserted darkness of the balcony, a sudden hollow fear in my stomach. I closed the doors and readied myself.

Walking back to the bedroom, I was conscious of the fact that I had not once shouted Ophelia's name. Last month, when this scene had played out in an almost identical way, I had called out to her constantly. Then I had thought that nothing could feel worse than not knowing where she was. Now I realised that there was a feeling much worse than that. It was knowing with certainty where she had gone.

I dressed quickly, pausing at the threshold of the flat. Was it really the right thing to do to go after her? Was she safer alone, given everything that had happened, everything that she thought might happen? Was it better, after all, to sit here and wait for her to return? I hesitated, torn. But I wanted to be with her, near her. I wanted to bring her home. I didn't want to imagine her alone in that darkness. A darkness where I felt almost anything could happen. It was dangerous.

As the word formed in my mind, the decision was made. I left the flat and began to run. As my feet hit hard against the asphalt, I thought of Ophelia. Why had she gone there without me again? I felt a surge of anger at her impetuosity. After everything we had agreed and she had promised. Perhaps she hadn't believed that I would destroy the mirror and had taken it upon herself to do it. I bridled at the idea, felt a flush of annoyance. Then, almost simultaneously, I felt sympathy for her. After all, I had hesitated to take action. So should I leave her to it now? No, I needed to go to her. It was a dark and dangerous place.

I turned left and the factory came into view. Just a little further and I would reach the door. Then I would be only moments away. I could find Ophelia and we could go home. As I came to a standstill, I noticed that the outer door was unlocked. So she was here. My hand reached for the handle and as it did so I heard a small voice echo inside my head: *You are dark and dangerous too*, it said.

For a moment, I stood stock-still. The quietness of the night around me was profound. There was no wind, nothing fluttering in its grasp, no music or people, not even the comforting rustle of the branches of the trees. A deep stillness reigned. I listened for the voice once again, but there was nothing. Suddenly, against the silence of the night, my mobile rang, in my jacket pocket, screeching, loud. I pulled it out, nerves raw, and saw that it was Tara. The phone also showed two missed calls from her earlier in the evening. Whatever it was, whatever she wanted, I couldn't deal with it right now. I switched the phone to silent and pocketed it again. Then I shook my aching head, pulled open the door and walked inside.

Soft moonlight poured through the windows. Almost violet, thick and heavy around me, it spilled over the floor. I looked down the length of the factory, took in the silhouettes of shoeboxes stacked high against the walls and beyond them the shadowy masses of ancient machines receding all the way into the heeling department. In the corner, in the glowing light of the window, I could make out the stiletto machine that Tara and I had stood in front of not so long ago. I felt the invisible press of something cold and sharp at my neck and my hand reached up instinctively. *Tread carefully*, said another voice in my head. Then I heard a burst of laughter, loud and melodic. I spun around but there was nothing, no one, there. I pressed my fingers to my eyes and took a deep breath. *Calm down*, said my own voice in my head.

I turned, making my way towards the storage cupboard, my trainers moving silently over the place where James Brimley's body had been found. I tried not to think about what had happened there but a quiver of anxiety shot through me, followed by a sudden bombardment of images. The director, unsmiling with dark eyes. A beautiful woman gazing at him as he walked the factory floor. The tidy green script of love letters filled with longing and desire. A woman's sated body, a velvet ribbon around her neck. The chaotic green ink of madness and decline.

I blinked rapidly, trying to focus. I wished I hadn't drunk so much wine, that my head wasn't so agitated, my body so wired. No distraction, no thinking, I told myself. I had to do what I came to do. To get Ophelia and leave. Just that, nothing more. I took the last few steps to the storage cupboard and saw that the inner door was open, the unmistakable orange glow of candlelight climbing the stairs beyond. As I began to descend, a memory bloomed out of the darkness, a nursery rhyme from childhood that I had recently heard. By the time I reached the bottom of the stairs my head was filled with it. *This little piggy went to market. This little piggy stayed at home. This little piggy had roast beef. This little piggy had none. And this little piggy went wee wee wee wee all the way home.* I heard a child's voice reciting the rhyme, carried as if on the sea breeze. It was followed by a woman's. *Come home*, it said, *come home, my darling*. Then both vanished under the sound of the sea.

I took a deep breath and tried again to still my mind. *Think of nothing*, I told myself, *think of a deep black emptiness*. I don't know how long I stayed there trying to think of nothing. But when I felt I was ready I turned towards the underground room.

Just as I had expected, Ophelia was standing in front of the mirror, candles on the floor at each end of it. She was staring straight ahead, unmoving, totally absorbed. In the fingers of her right hand she held the locket that had her parents' photographs inside, sliding it up and down the silver necklace that she always wore. I looked at her bare feet, her shoes on the floor beside her and her coat slung over the white nightdress underneath. I had witnessed this scene, been a part of it, once before.

It was an exact echo of the first time we had come to the underground room together. Now, the last time we would be here, I was determined it would play out differently.

I took a couple of steps forward so that I was almost level with the edge of the mirror.

'Ophelia,' I said quietly, so as not to alarm her.

She didn't move, still entirely unaware of my presence.

I looked at her face and something inside me melted. Certain now why she had come here, I could give her a little more time. Give her time to say goodbye. I looked around the room, at the bed along the far wall, the armchair at its right-hand end. I blinked away an image of Amelia's body, her arm falling away from her onto the earth floor. But as soon as it was gone another followed. James sitting in the chair, holding a green shoe in his hand. I frowned. I still didn't understand it. I turned to look at the shoes, hanging by the velvet ribbon over the corner of the mirror's frame. Instinctively I reached out to touch them. The leather was soft, delicate. I unhooked them from the mirror and brought them closer to my face. I inhaled deeply. After all this time, they still possessed a faint fragrance. I slid my hand into the left shoe. Sure enough, the five-toe indentation was there. I smiled and closed my eyes. I pictured a beach, a child with her hand in the imprint of a foot, a woman turning in the distance, the smell of salt on the air. Then I saw Amelia's feet on the bed in the underground room – and a moment later they became Ophelia's.

My eyes snapped open. We had to get going.

'Ophelia,' I said again, louder now.

This time she turned towards me. But she hesitated a moment before she spoke. 'I didn't recognise you, Johnny. You look different somehow. What are you doing here?'

'I might ask you the same question.'

She looked back at the mirror, then down at her bare feet and the nightdress and coat. 'I remember dreaming. The same dream . . . you know. And then I wanted to come here.' She frowned. 'Don't be angry, Johnny. I just had to come.'

I nodded. I wasn't angry. I thought I understood. 'It's okay. You wanted to see them again. One last time.' I nodded towards the mirror.

Ophelia gazed back at it again. 'Yes, perhaps.'

I looked at her, still holding the locket in her right hand, running it up and down the silver chain. In spite of myself, I smiled. 'Did you know that you always do that when you're thinking of your parents?'

Ophelia looked down at her hands and then back at me. 'No, I didn't.' She smiled too.

'I think if I'd realised it earlier I might have understood a little more. Those moments when you were so distant when I watched and wondered where you were. You were giving me clues the whole time.' I gestured to her locket. 'But I guess that's what coming to know someone is all about. It takes time.' Yes, I thought. It takes time to know someone, to know their motivations, their innermost thoughts. And who could have guessed back then that the dead were my biggest competition. I smiled again as I thought about it. But something else twisted deep down inside me.

I looked back at Ophelia. She was scrutinising me properly, perhaps for the first time. I saw her gaze take me in: the messy hair, the dark eyes, the crumpled T-shirt and jeans. 'Johnny, what are you doing here?'

I stared at her, not understanding. 'I came to get you. I didn't like the idea of your being here on your own.'

She nodded, looked down at my hands and then back into my eyes. 'I thought you didn't want us to be here together at all.'

'Well, no, obviously.' I felt a sudden flash of annoyance. 'I did say that, of course. But you came here. And I thought, having weighed it up, that it was better for me to come and get you than not.'

Ophelia looked back at the mirror once more. She was still for a long moment and then she nodded.

'Are you okay?'

She turned back in my direction, flashing another look at my hands. 'Yes, I'm okay. I think I'm beginning to understand.'

'What does that mean?' Again I experienced a spark of anger. What was she talking about? I for one didn't understand.

'Johnny, what are you doing with the shoes?' Pause. 'And the ribbon?'

Now it was my turn to look down at my hands. In my left I held the shoes by their ankle straps, in my right I held the velvet ribbon, manipulating it like a string of rosary beads. The gesture was innocuous enough and yet for some reason the question made me defensive. 'Nothing,' I said, sharply. 'I'm not doing anything. What's the matter with you?'

'Nothing,' she said, but I knew she was thinking something that she wasn't saying. 'Why don't we go upstairs and talk about it?'

I stared at her. All of a sudden that was the last thing I wanted to do. I ran my thumb and forefinger along the ribbon in my right hand, feeling the soft crush of the velvet. It was reassuring to the touch. 'No,' I said. 'Tell me now.'

Ophelia hesitated and I thought I saw a flash of panic cross her eyes. 'Okay, then. Bear with me. I'm just trying to get it straight.'

I stared at her, my irritation no doubt apparent.

'Will you keep your eyes on me, Johnny, while I tell you what I'm thinking? Will you focus on me entirely?'

I looked at her then, really looked at her, at her dark hair hanging down, at the beautiful green of her eyes. My heart softened. I smiled. 'Of course I will.'

'Good.' She took a deep breath and exhaled. The sound was jagged, rasping. The sound of fear. 'So you remember the dream of my parents?'

'Of course.'

'And that it's been the same since childhood.'

I nodded.

'But when I see it in the mirror, the ending is different.'

I nodded again. None of this was new. We had talked about it before.

'It bothered me from the first time I saw it. I couldn't understand how it could be. That the dream was precisely the same but for this one crucial difference. But now I think I understand it. Like Tara said, the mirror is suggesting that a different ending is possible. That the dream it showed me could be reality.'

Ophelia paused. I didn't say anything, trying to understand. The silence closed around us, intense, suffocating, and I squeezed the shoes in my left hand.

'Johnny, are you following?'

I shook my head. 'Not really. It's a dream – different ending or not. You know it's not real, don't you?'

She looked at me, her eyes glinting in the candlelight. 'I know that it could be real, Johnny. You've come to realise by now, haven't you, that sometimes dreams are more than dreams?'

I thought about what I had seen lately – James sitting in the chair in the underground room, Amelia upon the bed or engaged in conversation with me – and I nodded. But I still wasn't quite there.

'The dream can end in one of two ways. The way it normally ends. The way I always envisage it. My parents walk away and I remain here. Or the way the mirror is suggesting. That I go to join my parents.'

I frowned, my stomach tightening. I felt my body tense, my hands clench. 'But then one choice is life, and the other death?'

Ophelia nodded, glancing down at my hands.

'But that's not a real choice, Ophelia. It's perverse.'

'Yes, of course. It's a choice that only something dark and tainted would suggest.' She paused and looked at the mirror again.

I turned to look at it for the first time, remembering what Tara had said. That it was evil. I looked at it closely. Yes, no doubt about it, it was dark and dangerous. *You are dark and dangerous too*, said that small voice in my head again. I squinted, looking into the mirror's depths, searching for my reflection. But before I could find it I heard Ophelia's voice calling my name.

'Johnny. Johnny. Please look at me. Look at me.' She sounded desperate and, like the voice in my head, very far away. 'Johnny,' she said again louder, sharply, and brought me back in an instant to her. 'Try to concentrate on me,' I heard her say.

I nodded, turning to face her.

For a moment or two there was silence between us as she stared at me. 'Are you with me, Johnny?' she said finally.

'Yes, of course.'

Nonetheless, she continued to stare at me. Eventually she started talking again. 'I've really struggled to understand it. But I think I finally get it. Like you, I felt this attraction to the mirror. But at the same time I feared it, felt that there was something menacing, something that I should stay away from. I realise that both of these sensations are generated by it. On the one hand there's the pull of the mirror – its darkness, its power, its magic, whatever you want to call it. It seems to offer you something, the offer of the thing that perhaps you want most in the whole world. It's mesmerising, seductive, you want to feel it, to taste it. You want to go on tasting it. You want to give in to it. But on the other hand you feel revulsion, the tug of your own instinct, the will to resist, to fight it, to remain wholly yourself, however flawed, however incomplete that might be. Because what you have is real and you want it to survive.'

I stared back at Ophelia, thinking it through. I had been struggling for a while now to come to this realisation. But in the end this was it. And Ophelia had made the connection.

'And now I fear that I've made my choice, by default; by coming back here, by giving way to the mirror one too many times. Perhaps I've chosen what the mirror wanted, the mirror's version of events.'

I frowned, still not understanding. 'You've chosen death? How?'

But even as I asked the question, I felt a sinking feeling in my stomach. And then something twisted deep down inside me.

Ophelia continued to stare at me for a moment. Then her gaze drifted downwards once more to my hands. 'You know how, Johnny.'

I thought about the dream that Ophelia had had a few nights ago. An image of her feet flashed across my mind. They were unmoving on the corner of the bed. Terrified, I tried to blink everything away, to clear my mind. But this time the images stubbornly persisted. Then I heard the small voice in my head again. *This is the choice the mirror's been guiding you to all along. Life or death*, it said. *She has made her choice. Now you must make yours.*

I tried to banish it, to close my ears to the sound. But the voice wouldn't be banished this time. I heard it again, the voice that I had struggled with, small but persistent, speaking from the heart of darkness inside me. *But you know what happens. You have known it all along.*

Then it waited for a moment before delivering the final blow.

You kill her, it said.

46

I knew Ophelia was talking, I could hear her voice, remote, in the background, speaking to me. But the sound seemed somehow to have slipped, to have become fluid, to have stopped obeying all the normal rules. I felt it slide, uncaught, around the room, whirl around me for a second and then trickle through my fingers. I looked down at my hands but I didn't recognise them. They looked big, the fingers thick, not like my own. I wondered if I still had my own face and was just about to turn and look into the mirror when I heard Ophelia shout.

'No, Johnny. Don't do that. You promised me, remember?' She was staring at me, her eyes wild, pleading. But her words made me think of something else.

'And *you* promised *me* that you wouldn't come down here. It seems that your promises aren't worth much.'

'I know – I'm sorry. But like you said, I was coming to say goodbye. You know that, don't you?'

She was looking at me intently but as I stared back at her I wondered whether she was in fact being honest.

She took a step forwards and reached out to me. 'Can we get out of here?'

I looked from her hand to my own, holding the green ribbon between two fingers. 'Why?' The words came out of my mouth but they didn't sound like me.

'Because I choose you, Johnny. That's my choice. Not the mirror's choice, my own. You have a choice, too.'

I looked at her, but I no longer saw her face. Instead I saw Amelia standing there. She was wearing her black dress. Her hair fell long and loose down her back, wild and beautiful, and her feline eyes were wide – frightened, perhaps.

Ophelia's voice punctured my thoughts. 'You believe me, don't you, Johnny?'

'Stop saying my name,' I yelled. 'I don't like it.' Somehow it didn't sound right. I raised my right hand up to my head, which was throbbing, and as I did so I saw the ribbon dangling between my fingers. For some reason, it made me remember something that had been bothering me. 'You actually think that I could hurt you, don't you?'

'No, of course not.' The tone was heartfelt but Ophelia's eyes betrayed her.

'You actually think that I could kill you. You think that is my choice, don't you? Your life or your death. And you think that I've chosen death.'

Ophelia shook her head but I could see the tears that had started to fall down her cheeks. Something about it made me angry and I felt a bloom of irritation burst inside me. I took a step forward towards her, dropping the shoes I'd been holding onto the floor. They hit the ground with a dull thud. The sound made me think of something but I couldn't remember what it was.

I took another step forwards, Ophelia crying out now, speaking to me, but I shut my ears to it all. Instead, I turned and looked into the mirror. I had been fighting this moment for so long that to surrender to it finally produced an intense release. I sought out my reflection, the darkness of my eyes, and found them almost immediately. Then I looked deeper and smiled and my grey lips curled, the gnarled leer grinning back at me, my stronger, darker, more virile self. The self I had longed for.

I stared at my reflection, different from me and yet the same. It was tantalising, mesmeric. In that moment when I caught sight of that vision of myself, I thought of a woman's feet walking across the floor of a Paris fashion house. Was it a memory or something that I had merely read about? I tried to remember but I couldn't. The thought was followed by a bloom of fear, of sudden terror, that she would leave me alone. I frowned. A strong man wouldn't let her leave. I shook my head, looking at my face in the mirror. The dark, distorted reflection shook its head too. No, I couldn't let her leave, leave me alone. I had to make her stay here.

I turned towards Ophelia, now standing against the side wall. I took another step towards her.

'Johnny, is it you?' Her voice was small, plaintive.

'Of course,' I snarled, but I didn't feel quite like myself. My head felt thick, my body awkward, as if not quite comfortable within its own skin. I stared at her, saw her gaze dart to my hands. I looked down and saw that I no longer held the green ribbon in my right hand. It was now taut between both hands. I smiled and took another step towards her. 'You know I can't let you go. I can't let you leave me.'

I heard her sob, saw her body shudder. 'I don't want to leave you.'

'Stop lying. It's why you're here, after all. Well, you're not going to leave. I won't allow it.'

We were face to face now, staring into each other's eyes. Ophelia's skin was pale and her hair had fallen down one side of her face, across her cheek. I let go of the ribbon with my left hand to push the strands behind her ear. A memory clawed its way up from the darkness inside: a woman smiling in an open doorway, dressed in black, red shoes on her feet. I closed my eyes and inhaled deeply, feeling the memory move through me. It smelled of rainwater, jasmine and roses. I opened my eyes and looked at the woman in front of me.

'Ophelia?'

'Johnny?' she replied.

For an instant we simply looked at one another, connected by memory. The next moment I felt a searing pain in my crotch. I buckled under the weight of it, staggering backwards, sensing rather than seeing Ophelia dart away from me. As I grabbed blindly towards her I felt an anger rise within me, heard a furious yell escape my lips. Then the darkness took over. My hand clawed frantically in her direction, catching her nightdress, and I heard a ripping sound as I pulled it towards me. I fell to the ground, twisting around, pulling her with me, grabbing at her legs, her arms.

We each struggled for a moment, she trying to escape, me trying to detain her, a writhing mass of limbs, breath, spit and blood. Then I was on top of her, grabbing and grappling with a fury matched only by her own. My hands were around her neck, feeling the rapid thud of her heartbeat. I closed my eyes and listened to it, to its reassuring sound, the fast throb of her pulse beneath the surface. It was intoxicating. *Boom, boom.* I felt the ribbon's velvet crush against her neck. Then out of the darkness came another sound. Loud, terrifying, like the wail of a banshee.

'JOHNNY!'

The noise reverberated around the room, thudding through my brain, dislodging the hypnotising sound of the beat. My eyes sprang open and I was suddenly alert. I looked down to see Ophelia beneath me, pinned to the floor by the weight of my body. My hands, holding each end of the green ribbon, were pulling it tighter and tighter around her neck. Her nose was bloody, her lip cut, her arms, flung above her head, marked and grazed from the dirt floor, her hair spread out chaotically around her head. Her eyes were closed.

'Johnny!'

The noise came again, but not as loud this time. I looked up to see Tara standing over me. She was dressed in black. Her face looked thin and pale in the candlelight, the skin around her eyes dark.

'Let her go, Johnny.' Her eyes stared at me coldly.

A moment passed without any movement from either of us.

'Let her go,' Tara repeated slowly.

I looked at her and a smile uncurled on my lips. 'No.'

For a moment she was savagely still, staring at me. Then I saw her arm move towards me fast and felt something smash against my skull.

I wavered momentarily as I registered the impact of the blow, then felt myself falling sideways onto the floor. I saw Tara then, watching me, a green shoe in her hand. And I saw, behind her, the candle lying sideways, its flame licking the exposed laths in the wall, threatening to grow, to envelop everything, including the mirror.

I blinked hard, trying to think. But in that moment time lost all meaning. When I reopened my eyes both Tara and Ophelia had disappeared. The flames had grown and I was struggling to breathe. I remembered the dream I had had – it seemed like such a long time ago. The sensation of falling and slow suffocation and death. *So it has come to pass*, I thought. *That dream has, after all, come true.*

Then the darkness took me again.

47

It was the voice that roused me.

At first it seemed to come from far away. A strange voice, whispering in the darkness, calling out to me. It brought me back to myself, to an awareness that I was lying on a floor that smelled of stale earth, my body hot and sweating, my head throbbing. I tried to open my eyes but I lacked the strength to do it. So instead I listened, trying to place exactly where I was. And then I heard it, again, echoing through my mind. A woman's voice.

'Johnny, wake up,' it said.

Something about the voice was familiar, although it didn't strike me as a voice that I heard every day. Nonetheless it galvanised me into action. There was an urgency to it that made me want to comply. I opened my eyes. The vision through my left one was blurred, obscured. But what I saw, nonetheless, brought me to with a jolt. A few feet in front of me the wall was on fire. The mirror, still suspended from it, was covered in flames. They licked its dark surface, dancing over the inky stains, melting the grey glass into liquid fire. The heat it generated was intense, burning my face and body.

I tried to move but even shifting my head a fraction caused me to wince in pain. My left eye was wet, my head tight and swollen and when I brought my hand to it I felt a sticky substance there. Blood, I was sure. And, in that instant, I remembered.

An image of Ophelia's battered face flashed across my mind. I saw the bloody nose, the cut lip, saw myself pinning her to the earth floor, anger and horror in her eyes, and I shuddered with the remembrance of it. An image of the green ribbon floated through my mind. Was she alive? Did Tara make it here in time?

I opened my eyes, barely aware that I had closed them again, and looked again at the mirror, dripping molten silver onto the floor. I heard it creak and groan amid the crackling flames, watched the smoke drift downwards in thick curls, over its surface and towards the ground. I tried to move. I had to get out of here. There wasn't much time. Shifting slightly, I caught a sudden flicker at the edge of my vision, the shadowy form of a woman. I opened my mouth but I couldn't speak. I was having difficulty breathing. I felt my eyes closing and knew in that moment that I could fall asleep and never wake again. I could surrender my body to the darkness and drift into oblivion. As I slipped towards unconsciousness, my last thought was of my dream, of suffocation and falling. Had it all been leading to this? I wondered. Had it all been leading to this moment, here in the underground room?

Through the darkness I heard the sound of footsteps

against the earth floor. Then I heard the voice again, floating through my mind.

'Johnny, wake up.'

I forced my eyes open. I saw the outline of a woman once more. I tried to blink the blood away and looked again.

The shadow seemed to shift, moving closer towards me until I could clearly see her feet below the hem of her long black dress.

'Amelia,' I said. 'Is it you?'

As she knelt beside me, her face came into view and I saw that it was her. She smiled at me then – that big, beautiful smile of hers – and stretched her hand out towards me. I reached for her, but she stepped towards the staircase. Then she waited once more. I could feel her as she stood there, watching me, willing me to move. And, somehow, I felt I couldn't disappoint her. I dragged my body along the floor, feeling the agony of each breath. The weight of my head seemed immense, unbearable as I pulled myself forwards, following in her footsteps, pain ricocheting through me. Perhaps I slipped in and out of consciousness. Moments of darkness were followed by the blinding brightness of the underground room as I watched it burn. But I felt her presence beside me, always just beyond my reach, willing me forwards.

At the bottom of the stairs I paused, a searing pain in my temple. I tried to breathe through it but with each lungful of air the smoke seemed thicker and more dangerous. Fear moved through me in waves. But I saw Amelia ahead of me, calmly beckoning to me and carefully, one step at a time I followed.

The smoke funnelled around us, forming a column ascending upwards. I felt its thickness in my throat and I tried to take tiny breaths. Slowly, painfully, I inched my way upwards. I watched the smoke plume grey and purple in the flickering light around me. I closed my eyes, imagining myself looking upwards to the rectangle of light above, the door to the storage cupboard growing larger with every move I made. And as Amelia and I climbed higher, I began to entertain the tantalising possibility that I might actually make it out of here.

As I dragged my body over the last step and through the doorway, moonlight filled the dispatch room. It made me think of Diana the huntress, and in turn of Diane, the one whom the curse had been cast to entrap and the one who, ironically, had escaped unscathed. As I pulled myself further into the room, the smoke thinned and my breathing eased. A moment later I lay down in the middle of the floor.

Amelia knelt beside me and I saw her face clearly for the first time, her deep-set oval eyes, green with flecks of orange and yellow across the irises. For a moment we just looked at one another. Then she smiled.

I smiled too, realising this was goodbye. I knew somehow that I would not see her again.

A welter of pain shot through my body and instinctively I closed my eyes. When I reopened them she was gone. Slowly I eased my head left and right, trying to look around me, beyond my body on the floor of the dispatch room. As I did so I realised that I was lying more or less in the place where James's body had rested more than a century before. Would I meet the same fate as him? I really didn't know.

I closed my eyes again and took a deep breath, in and out. I thought of Ophelia and Tara out there in the darkness somewhere. And I prayed for them to be safe, and to know that when I'd acted as I had I was not myself but under the influence of a dark spell. I prayed for help to arrive soon or for the flames beneath me to miraculously die down. As I prayed I listened to the quietness of the night, across the silent east of the city.

And eventually from somewhere in the distance I heard a siren's approaching wail.

48

I opened my eyes. I was lying in a narrow bed, bright artificial light pouring down upon me from fluorescent strips in the ceiling. It hurt my eyes and I closed them again. I licked my lips. They were cracked and sore. I tried to open my mouth to say something but I couldn't. My throat was parched and made me want to cough. Blips and beeps sounded quietly but continuously close by and beyond them I thought I heard subdued voices, the faint echoes of people coming and going, of life milling around me. But the sounds came to me as if from far away, fragmented, distorted.

For a few moments I lay still, feeling the uncomfortable press of tight crisp sheets against my body. I felt bruised and exhausted. I opened my eyes again and blinked against the light. Shadows came into and out of my vision. But as focus came I saw Ophelia sitting in the chair opposite my bed. At first I couldn't tell if I was dreaming. She was dressed from head to toe in black and the blood from her face had been washed away. The only outward sign that betrayed what had happened at the factory was the cut across her lip. She had her feet pulled under her body and was staring out of the window into the night.

Sitting on her right was Tara, dressed in the same black clothes that she had worn at the factory. She was holding Ophelia's hand. I felt my heart constrict. They were safe. Tara was staring vacantly into the middle distance but, as I continued to watch her, her gaze shifted towards me. For a moment we simply looked at one another and then she smiled. But as she did so a tear fell slowly, silently down her cheek. I returned her smile. Perhaps I understood a little of what she was feeling. Happiness that we had all made it out of the factory that night; sorrow that some of us almost hadn't. I saw her rise from her seat and silently leave the room.

I turned back to Ophelia and as our eyes met I saw hers fill with tears.

'Johnny,' she said.

I nodded, feeling as I did a throbbing pain in my head.

'I thought you were dead,' she said, coming over to the bed. She sat down next to me and took my hand in hers. 'Tara carried me out of there. Then she took me back to my flat. We called for help on the way. We couldn't think of what else to do. I tidied myself, changed my clothes and then we came here. But so much time passed before they got to you. And when you arrived here you were unconscious. I thought you were dead,' she said again. Tears pricked her eyes. 'Can you ever forgive me for leaving you?'

'Can you ever forgive me for trying to make you stay?'

I raised my hand to her face and ran a finger gently over the cut on her lip. 'I'm so very, very sorry.'

Ophelia nodded gently and we were both silent for a moment.

'They can't figure out how you escaped. How you managed to get up the stairs with your injuries and with the smoke.'

Her words brought to mind the paramedics who had arrived at the factory fire.

'But I just don't understand how it was possible for him alone,' they had said.

I wasn't alone, I had wanted to say. But they would put it down to delirium, seeing ghosts, spirits where there was only smoke and mirrors. I smiled. Perhaps it had been a dream, perhaps not. But Amelia had been with me during the fire.

As they'd raised me onto a stretcher to take me to the hospital I thought I had seen dirty, sooty footprints across the floor of the dispatch room around the place where my body had lain. The prints were small, delicate, from the feet of a young woman. Then a tide of firemen moved into the space and the footprints were washed away.

Ophelia's voice brought me back to the here and now. 'What happened?' she asked hesitantly, as if part of her wasn't sure she really wanted to know.

I smiled at her. 'I had a strange dream,' I said, and as my eyes closed and I slipped again towards unconsciousness I thought I heard the soft sound of dirty, sooty footsteps making their way across my mind.

*

'The basement was gutted. But the rest of the place is still intact. A little smoke damage only, they say. They think it was an accident. A bumbling architect falling down some dark cellar steps, the candle she was carrying starting a blaze.' Tara winked at me and smiled.

I shook my head and although there was pain it was subsiding. A severely fractured skull was the diagnosis, but I would live. 'I can't let you take the blame for it, Tara. Don't worry, I'll square it with Richard.' I had a feeling that things might get back to normal now. I pictured the flames licking the mirror's surface, the molten glass dripping onto the earth floor, and felt that perhaps the power the mirror had once possessed had finally been destroyed.

I closed my eyes for a moment and an image of slave feet leaving footprints of mud behind in the darkness danced across my mind. How many others, I wondered, had been caught by the mirror, driven to murder by an ancient hate? But I would never know for sure. I thought of Catherine, the thwarted Queen, her frustrated love and desire, her betrayal and rage. Somehow she had poured these emotions into this gift that was not meant for her and let them sit waiting there, in darkness. Patiently waiting, as she had done, for her moment of vengeance. And in the end it had caught up with me.

I opened my eyes and raised my left hand so that I could see the third finger. The pale circle of flesh remained there, a marker for the moment. Even though my wedding ring was gone, I was after all still married. I heard Tara's voice in my head, our last conversation about the mirror. It is evil, she had said. And she had been right. But its evil, its power, was only unleashed on those who shared the same love as Henri and Diane. Catherine had waged war on the love of men and their mistresses, pulling the women towards it with images of what they most loved and driving men mad with lust and fear that they would lose what they most wanted. Her revenge had flowed through the centuries. The Frenchman and his slave. James and Amelia. Ophelia and me.

'But I still don't know for sure what happened between James and Amelia.' I said it out loud, even though it was more to myself than anyone else.

'Ah, well, I think I can help you there.' Tara stood up and pulled something from the pocket of the black jeans that she was wearing. 'I would have told you sooner, only you never return my calls.' She smiled and put it down on the table beside my bed.

'What is it?' I said, straining to turn my head to see.

'It's a letter,' she said.

I gazed at her. Another letter. I swallowed, feeling the dryness of my throat. 'Where did you find it?'

'After we spoke the other night, I got in touch with Mr Alexander. I wanted the number of Nathaniel Raven. I remembered you told me that he often came across letters in his line of work, letters accompanying other items, often retrieved from house clearances. If you remember, James's Bloomsbury house is on the market. While it hasn't sold yet, its contents are being cleared. I persuaded Nat to go there with me – to give me some antique collector's credentials, if you like – and we went through it from top to bottom, looking for anything that might help. We found this along with Elizabeth's personal, private possessions.'

'Elizabeth. James's wife?'

Tara nodded. 'It was amongst her papers, diaries. Things her son kept untouched after her death and his son in turn left undisturbed. She obviously wanted it kept safe, undisclosed.'

'What does it say?'

'That we drew a lot of the wrong conclusions from what we found. And that if we'd found it earlier, some of this could perhaps have been avoided.' She made a sweeping gesture towards Ophelia and me. 'Still, after I'd read it and I couldn't get hold of you on the phone, I came to the factory. If I hadn't, things might have turned out very differently.' She shivered. 'Anyway, read it Johnny, when you're ready. It explains a lot.'

I nodded. But the pounding in my head was starting to intensify.

'Are you okay?' Tara said. 'You're looking a little pale.'

'I'm fine,' I lied. 'You've got a great right hook, by the way.'

She grimaced. 'I think it's time for me to get out of here. But when you're better let's go out for a drink. The three of us. When I said to you that I thought we should hang out, I didn't mean in these sorts of circumstances.' She smiled at me, then leaned over and kissed my forehead. 'I'm sorry about your temple,' I heard her whisper.

'I'm sorry about everything,' I whispered back. I stared

at her and for a moment worried that I might cry. 'Thank you.'

She shrugged. 'You know, of course, that you owe me at least a few pairs of shoes for this. But in the meantime rest and get better.' Then she turned, said goodbye to Ophelia and left.

As silence fell after Tara's departure, Ophelia came to sit beside me on the bed. 'You look tired, Johnny.'

I nodded. I was exhausted. But I wanted to fight sleep a little longer. I looked at Ophelia, at her beautiful eyes, her lips, her skin and I noticed that she wasn't wearing the locket that held the photograph of her parents.

'Where's your necklace?' I asked.

'Oh. I took it off. After the fire.' Then she paused. 'I thought it was about time.'

'Are you sure?' I asked.

'I'm sure,' she replied, smiling at me. 'I love you.'

'I love you too,' I said.

And as sleep descended upon me I felt Ophelia take my hand in hers.

'Talk to me,' I said. 'I want to hear your voice.'

'Okay,' she said. 'Let me tell you a story.'

49

23 September 1899
Rose Cottage
St Just
Cornwall

Mrs Brimley,

I have spent a year deliberating whether to write this letter, whether it is better to disclose things which have been hidden or to leave the past in the past. I confess that still I do not know. But I find myself, perhaps out of conscience, putting pen to paper nonetheless. Please forgive me if it transpires that I am disclosing things you would rather not have known. Many of them will be painful to you.

My name is Amelia Holmes. I know that it will be familiar and no doubt a shock to read it now. As you will recall, both from the fact that I worked at your husband's factory and from the newspaper reports at the time, I disappeared a year ago on the evening of 23 September 1898. But I had not, as was suspected at the time, been abducted and killed. Rather, my disappearance was connected to the events of that night, events which I feel, after much reflection, I must recount to you now.

It was a Friday evening. I, and the rest of the girls of the assembling department, left the factory as usual at around six p.m. We chatted outside, giggling and laughing over the gossip of the week, and then we dispersed to begin our respective journeys home. As I began my usual walk, everything appeared as normal. Except that everything, for me at least, was far from so. After a while, after I was sure that no one would see me, I retraced my steps and made my way back to the factory.

I apologise for what I am about to tell you now. I was returning to meet your husband. He had shown care and concern for me since I began work at the factory the year before. And for a long time it remained just that: pure solicitude and kindness. But I am ashamed to say that from this grew something more. By the summer of 1898 there had been a shift in emotions. We each knew the other's feelings plainly and James had, a number of times, asked me to meet him after hours at the factory. I, terrified by what might happen, had always refused, always sought to fight what I felt. After all, it was wrong, sinful. But that night I could contain my emotions no longer.

I returned to the factory determined to surprise him. I waited, watching from the bandstand in the park, hidden and out of view, until it was dark. I knew, as always, that Mr Laver — the manager — and James would be the last people on the premises. And that when Mr Laver left he would lock the outer doors even though James was still inside. It had been the same routine since I arrived. What no one else knew, besides James and myself, was that James had given me a key to the doors.

After I saw Mr Laver leave I allowed some time to pass. Perhaps even then I was suffering a crisis of conscience, still in two minds about what to do next: about what would happen if I crossed the park, if I let myself in, if I allowed myself to be alone with James. I don't remember exactly what was running through my mind. What I do know is that even in my wildest imaginings I could never have anticipated what came next.

I remember unlocking the factory doors and making my way into the dispatch room. It was quiet and empty, only partially lit. I crossed the ground floor and climbed the stairs. But both the first and second floors were in total darkness. As I retraced my steps, I began to have doubts. The darkened factory was eerie, strangely unfamiliar. Perhaps it would be better if I simply went home. James, after all, was not expecting me and did not appear to be there. But as I turned to leave I heard the sound of voices. They were muffled, obscured and for a while I simply listened, trying to place them. Finally it dawned upon me. They were coming from the underground room. I remembered then that James had told me about this place; a private space that only he used, that only he really knew of. I moved to the top of the cellar stairs and, looking down, saw the flicker of candle flames. In that instant, as I looked down into the darkness, my heart flickered too. It told me to leave, to leave that darkness well alone. But the sound of the voices pulled at me. One belonged to James. But who was the person he was talking to? Before I knew what I was doing I found myself descending the stairs.

As I moved deeper into the darkness James's voice became clearer. He was arguing with a woman and her voice sounded animated, upset. I knew that I should turn around and go home — every instinct told me so. Yet something else pulled me towards that room, towards the darkness. I tried to imagine the scene beyond the threshold of the doorway, but when I reached it I was totally unprepared for what I saw.

James was sitting in an armchair in the corner of the room, in a dishevelled state of semi-undress. On a narrow bed, across from where he sat, lay Minnie Perkins. Miss Perkins, the book-keeper. A white slip was all that covered her and even this exposed her thighs and calves. Around her neck, and cascading down over her breasts, was a piece of green velvet ribbon. For a moment or two I simply stared at them, stunned, disbelieving. But as I began to realise what I was seeing, what I was witnessing, I noticed something else. In his hands, James held a green shoe which he was rocking back and forth. The sight made my eyes fill with tears. It was one of a pair that he had had made for me.

For I don't know how long, I stared at James, in the armchair, playing with the green shoe. I could not bear to look at Minnie's face, so instead I gazed at her bare legs on the bed. These images will haunt me for ever. In my distraction I caught only snippets of their argument, only phrases and recriminations. She was upset, chastising him for holding the shoe, for thinking of someone else when he was there with her. I heard her shouting about letters that he had sent to her, letters filled with love and longing. What had happened to that feeling now? He retorted that their affair had long been over, that she should leave him alone, stop taunting and tempting him. I looked away then, embarrassed, as the words circled dreamlike, unreal around me. It was only when they stopped, when silence descended, that I looked back at them and saw that my presence had been discovered. Horrified to find myself in the middle of this scene, I was nonetheless frozen to the spot. I couldn't move. I noticed that James, now standing, had dropped the shoe onto the floor and was moving towards me. His face betrayed his guilt and devastation, his fear and regret. And, in spite of myself, I felt tears spring to my eyes. He began to apologise, to say he was so sorry for this discovery. How disappointed in him I must be. But he had given up hope that I would ever be with him. His tirade against himself continued. But I could not utter a word. I stood stock-still, silent. And with every second that passed, with every word that I failed to utter in response, he grew more agitated. I was only vaguely aware of Minnie rising from the bed behind him, arguing still. But I didn't hear what she said. All I knew was that suddenly he began to grow angry. And as I watched him, watched his face grow harder, I could have sworn that his eyes grew blacker too. All of a sudden he advanced upon me, demanding to know what I was doing there, what I had seen. In that moment I grew scared. I felt my blood run cold as he towered over me, so much taller, so much stronger than me, his large hands suddenly threatening, moving towards me, driving me backwards until my body hit the wall. Fear pulsed through me. Minnie must have felt the same because I heard her shouting to him to stop. But I do not think he caught her words, do not think he recognised either her or me. And at that moment I felt terror for the first time.

What happened next passed in a series of broken images, lost, caught out of time. I saw him turn upon Minnie, shout at her that this was all her fault and that she would pay. He advanced upon her but she was quick, agile and she darted behind him, the green ribbon suddenly in her hands. Then it was around his neck, tightening in her grip, pulling him backwards and down to the floor. There was a struggle and for a few moments the writhing and twisting of fighting bodies. But Minnie was no match for him, even though he was severely weakened, winded. He pushed her away, and she struck her head against the wall. And I knew, in that moment, that if I did nothing, if I did not intercede, she would die.

Before James could recover, before he could stand, I grabbed the mattress from the bed. It was the only thing in the room that I, in my panic, could see to use. I pressed it down upon the full length of him, leant the weight of my whole body upon his face, starving him of air, slowly suffocating him. At one point I thought that he might overpower me, but with my legs pinning his arms to his body I managed to restrain him. I felt him kicking, squirming beneath me, but I held fast for as long as I could. Eventually, exhausted and breathless, I let go. For a long moment there was nothing. I stared down at the mattress beneath me, unmoving and then I realised. He was dead. And I had killed him.

As if in the slow unfolding of a dream, I became aware of Minnie standing beside me, talking. She was dazed from the blow to her head and I could hear an edge of hysteria creeping into her voice. I told her to be quiet, to get dressed and to let me think.

I put the mattress back on the bed and tied the green shoes, my green shoes, together with her ribbon, hanging them from the left-hand corner of a mirror on the wall. The mirror was black, discoloured and I remember Minnie shouting that it had started all of this, that it was evil. I put her words down to delirium and tried to silence her. But still she talked. She picked up some letters from the floor, letters, it seemed, from James to her. I have to get rid of them, she repeated over and over. I cannot have anything that ties him to me now. In her agitation I had no hope that she would dispose of them properly. So I took them from her and put them in my pocket.

Finally we turned to James. What were we to do with him? Minnie wanted to leave his body in the cellar. But something in me baulked at that. I couldn't abandon him to that darkness or to the risk that a long time might pass before someone discovered his body, by then rotting and unrecognisable. So between us, heaven knows how, and with much struggle, we carried his body up the stairs and into the dispatch room.

And there, in the shadow light, with James's body lying on the floor beside us, we came up with a plan. No one, it seemed, knew of his and Minnie's affair. They had concealed the indiscretion well. So I told Minnie that she should go home and try to calm herself. When the factory reopened after the discovery of the body, she must return to work as if nothing had happened. It was the best way, I thought, for her to escape any suspicion. I, on the other hand, would flee. I had been the one who had occasioned James's death. So if the conclusions of the police were that James had been murdered, it seemed only fair that they should come after me.

Minnie argued with me for some time. She said that we were both responsible, that we should both remain and stay silent.

Who knew what conclusions the police would draw? And, after all, it had been self-defence. But in my heart I did not see it that way. I had killed the man I loved and if anyone should be punished for that crime it was me. If I managed to evade the punishment of prison then a heavy sentence would be imposed upon me by separation from my family.

After much debate and persuasion, Minnie finally agreed and left. Then I finished my business in the factory. I hid the letters that James had sent to her behind a photograph in which he and I were clearly visible, looking at one another. If they were ever found they would point to an affair between him and me and would implicate me, rather than Minnie, in respect of the murder.

I went back to the underground room, checked everything there, then climbed the stairs and sealed the door. In my heart, I hoped it would never be opened again. Then I looked properly, for the first time since his death, at James. My eyes filled with tears as I saw the marks around his neck already beginning to show, the unforeseen brutality of the green ribbon. I straightened his disordered clothes, kissed his lips, held his grazed and dirty hands in mine one last time. Then I left the factory for ever. I locked the door and left everything behind me in darkness.

With a little money in my pocket, I fled London straight away. For weeks, I feared my discovery or the unveiling of our plot. So much depended on Minnie, on what conclusions the police drew. But as time went on, it appeared that we would not be discovered. Minnie must have played her part well and we were assisted by the coroner who, beyond the superficial marks of the ribbon, found that there were no indicators of violence done to James. The cardiac arrest, no doubt the result of the suffocation, looked natural. And as the door to the factory was locked, and James alone and in possession of his keys, there was no reason to suspect that there had been a third party at the scene. And rather than appearing incriminating as I had supposed, my disappearance was taken for something else entirely — that I had been the victim of murder myself.

To avoid discovery I had to change the way I looked, the colour and cut of my hair. But avoid it I have. Over time I have made my way here, far away from London, from the people I love and cherish. But that is a small price to pay for what I did.

Since that night my life has been filled with regret, and the knowledge of what happened weighs very heavily upon me. I am punished every day by the remembrance of it. And I feel that part of me, the soul of the nineteen-year-old girl I was that night, has been lost, will be trapped for ever, in the darkness of the factory, unable to escape what was done that night.

And so it is no coincidence that this letter comes to you on the anniversary of your husband's death. If, when you have read it, you wish to hand me over to the police, so be it. They will be able to find me at this address.

But I ask you one last thing. If you send them for me and the events of that night are exposed, the underground room opened up for evidence and exploration, I beg you not to allow the blackened mirror there to be released into the world. Both Minnie and James spoke to me of it, words that I put down to her hysteria and James's tiredness and distraction in the final months of his life. But before I left that room for the last time that night a year ago, something compelled me to look into that mirror, to gaze into its tainted blackened silver, to watch and wait until something emerged from the darkness. I will not tell you what I saw. But I began to understand that perhaps there was foundation in their anxiety that the mirror had perhaps played a part in the events of that night.

I know that these words themselves sound hysterical, defy belief. But I do not ask you to believe me. I only ask you, beg of you, that you leave it closed up, sealed off for ever.

Amelia Holmes

Acknowledgements

I would like to thank everyone who has read drafts of this novel and, in particular, Sarah Masarachia, Sini Downing, Sophia Martelli and Blaise Hesselgren for their honesty and encouragement. Your comments were invaluable.

Thanks to my agent, Luigi Bonomi of LBA, always inspiring and full of ideas, and to everyone at LBA and ILA for their hard work. Many thanks to Rosie de Courcy without whose passion and insight (and plentiful yellow stickers!) this book would not be what it is. And much appreciation to my fantastic editor Jenny Geras – who took up the reins with energy and enthusiasm – for her keen eye and light editorial touch.

Big thanks to Angela and Rachel, who buoyed me up when I needed it. Most of all, thanks to my Mum and Dad for their unwavering faith and support and to Parvais, who held my hand every step of the way.

THE POWER OF READING

Visit the Random House website and get connected with information on all our books and authors

EXTRACTS from our recently published books and selected backlist titles

COMPETITIONS AND PRIZE DRAWS Win signed books, audiobooks and more

AUTHOR EVENTS Find out which of our authors are on tour and where you can meet them

LATEST NEWS on bestsellers, awards and new publications

MINISITES with exclusive special features dedicated to our authors and their titles

READING GROUPS Reading guides, special features and all the information you need for your reading group

LISTEN to extracts from the latest audiobook publications

WATCH video clips of interviews and readings with our authors

RANDOM HOUSE INFORMATION including advice for writers, job vacancies and all your general queries answered

Come home to Random House

www.randomhouse.co.uk